# *on my life*

## A SANDPIPER COVE NOVEL

### GENEVIEVE PAUL

Edited by Sara Tallary

Cover Design by Acacia @ Ever After Cover Design

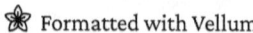 Formatted with Vellum

*dedication*

To my husband—

My favorite person to watch sunsets with.

*content notes*

This book contains adult material including multiple descriptive sex scenes, attempted sexual assault, physical assault/violence, discussion of mental health struggles including anxiety and loss of a parent.

_playlist_

On My Life

1. "Runaway" - Linkin Park
2. "Fire and the Flood" - Vance Joy
3. "Wine into Whiskey" - Tucker Wetmore
4. "I Can Do It With a Broken Heart" - Taylor Swift
5. "I Remember Everything" - Zach Bryan feat. Kasey Musgraves
6. "Risen" - O.A.R.
7. "Notice" - Thomas Rhett
8. "Love You Anyway" - Luke Combs
9. "You and Tequila" - Kenny Chesney feat. Grace Potter
10. "Face Down" - The Red Jumpsuit Apparatus
11. "In My Veins" - Andrew Belle
12. "Worst Way" - Riley Green
13. "God Speed" - Zach Bryan
14. "My Home" - Myles Smith
15. "Banks" - Jordan Davis and NEEDTOBREATHE
16. "Back in Time" - Pitbull

17. "Cover Me Up" - Morgan Wallen
18. "Kokomo" - The Beach Boys
19. "When I Get My Hands on You" -
The New Basement Tapes
20. "Tick Tick Boom" - Sage the Gemini
feat. BygTwo3
21. "The Luckiest" - Ben Folds
22. "She Likes It" - Russell Dickerson
feat. Jake Scott

# *prologue*

Lyla

MY SKIN PRICKLES the minute I walk in the front door of my house. The hair on the back of my neck stands up, and it feels like the blood in my veins has gone cold. Something is off, but I can't put my finger on what it is.

With my hand still on the door knob, I look around, but nothing seems amiss or out of place. There's a smell I don't recognize, and I take a few deep sniffs, trying to pinpoint where it's coming from. Cheap cologne, mixed with sweat is the best description I can come up with. It smells like chemicals combined with something sour. It's overpowering and makes me think of a high school locker room.

The house is eerily silent, and despite the fact that it's not ransacked, I can't shake the feeling that someone was here. Or that someone is still watching. I want to kick my own ass for not turning the alarm on when I went out. I've been so diligent about it, but Quinn was in the driveway. I hate making someone wait on me and I guess hearing her honk to let me know she arrived made me forget the precautions I usually take.

I can't decide if I want to close the door and lock myself in or run out to my car and hightail it back to the bar where I know I'd be surrounded by people.

*Simmer the fuck down, Lyla. There's no one here. I'm just paranoid. I could call Dad, but really, what could he do from Sandpiper?*

No. I shake my head at myself, even though no one is around to see it. That will only add fuel to the fire and, before I know it, he'll insist I move back home for my own safety.

In the end, my pride wins out over my anxiety, and I take a few deep breaths before pulling the door closed and twisting both locks. I toss my keys onto the table near the door, kick off my flip flops, and make my way to the kitchen.

Despite hitting up our favorite place for happy hour, I didn't have anything to drink, so I reach for the bottle of El Tesoro Reposado, my favorite tequila. I throw some ice in a glass and pour a few ounces. I felt off all day—anxious. Like I was waiting for the other shoe to drop. I wish I could say it was a foreign feeling, but lately it's been ever-present.

With my drink in hand, I walk to my bedroom. It's not even seven o'clock yet, but I'm desperate to put on pajamas, fuzzy socks, and zone out in front of the TV with my drink and a pint of ice cream. When I get into my room, I feel a chill, and not one that necessarily has to do with the temperature. Goosebumps pebble on my arms and the hair on the back of my neck stands up. I suck in a breath, and the air feels cold. Way colder than it should this time of year. The curtains billow as a breeze sneaks through my open window. A window I don't recall leaving open.

"Fuck," I say out loud. I mentally retrace my steps, and while I'm certain I wouldn't have left it open, I guess it's possible. *Possible but not probable*, I think to myself as I look around my bedroom and look for anything that might be out of place. Nothing is glaringly obvious. Despite the open window, the smell that hit me when I walked in the front door lingers in here as well. The unfamiliarity of it really doesn't sit well with me and my stomach starts turning. I bite my lip, willing myself to keep my panic from rising.

I walk over to the window and slam it shut, double-checking the lock before I pull the curtains closed. If I was feeling on edge before, I'm a damn bundle of nerves now. My breath is shallow and my hands are clammy. I reach down and wipe them on my pants but they immediately feel damp again. I brush a loose piece of hair from my face, feeling the clamminess there as well. As I reach for my pajamas, I look down and find my hands shaking. I snatch them back and rest them on my hips, taking several deep breaths as I try to calm myself down.

"Get out of your head, Lyla. Hollman is in jail. He can't get to you." I say it out loud in an effort to convince myself that I'm safe. Marcus Hollman is not a man to be trifled with. If my best friend hadn't died from the cocaine she got from one of his people, I wouldn't know his name from Adam.

I quickly change, pull on my socks, grab my glass, and slowly pad back down the hallway to the living room, distracted by my emotions, frayed nerves, and thoughts of ice cream.

As I walk past the bathroom, I vaguely notice the door is almost completely closed, something else I never do. I always leave the shower curtain and doors open so I have a full view. It wasn't until recently that this constant paranoid started following me around like a permanent shadow. Living alone doesn't help. It's always in the back of my mind that someone could be lurking in the corners.

Noting the difference catches me off guard and revs my pulse up another notch. That same feeling that came over me as I walked in the front door comes back with a vengeance. My chest tightens as I pause, listening for any sounds or movements. I'm met with silence. In a moment like this, silence feels even more ominous.

The fear slowly works through my body, starting at my toes and working its way up. My muscles seize as that terror takes over. I'm frozen, at a loss of what to do as my heartbeat thunders in my ears, like a musician going to town on a snare drum. But I know that standing in the hallway, with no access to a quick exit is the last thing I should do. Eventually my mind clears enough that I take a hesitant step forward.

I try breathing deeply, but my panic smothers me. Every instinct inside of me is screaming that something is wrong. I stare at the door and swallow the thickness at the back of my throat. Is it moving? Or is it just my imagination? I swear it moved ever so slightly as I stared at it, my eyes narrowed suspiciously. I blink my eyes a few times, trying to get rid of the fuzziness that has taken over my vision from staring so intently. This is a mistake on my part.

The door flies open. It's so fast that it thumps loudly into the wall. The noise startles me, but my focus is on the man dressed in dark clothes who lunges for me. My feet root to the ground. As a kid I always used to wonder what quicksand felt like. Now I know. This man, this stranger dressed in black, reaches out and grabs me. His hand is around my throat before I can move a muscle.

I try to catalog everything I can about this man's appearance before he yanks me to him. Tall, broad, dark hair, no facial hair, dark eyes. Strong as hell.

I'm overwhelmed by the oppressive smell of that damn

cheap cologne, and a wave of nausea rolls over me. I already know that I'll never be able to forget it.

As he starts to drag me down the hallway toward my bedroom, I realize his hands are covered in black leather gloves. The material is cool against my skin, but it also means he's not leaving fingerprints behind. I don't need to watch Dateline or be a cop's daughter to know that, but I do and I am.

He towers over me, but no matter how wildly I thrash, I'm no match for his strength. The closer we get to my bedroom, the more my panic bubbles to the surface. There's no phone back there, no door to escape through. An overwhelming sense of hopelessness pinches at the back of my eyes, and tears well, blinding me. I try to blink them away to get my vision back as he quite literally drags me with him.

My screams get muffled by the hand covering my mouth. The pressure in my chest is reminiscent of a panic attack— something I haven't experienced in a long time. The heat starts in my chest, like it always used to, before spreading to the rest of my body and my throat starts to constrict. A hot flash rips through me and I can feel the sweat start to collect at the base of my neck. I know if I don't somehow pull myself out of this downward spiral, I'll be as useless as a rag doll.

"Cut the crying, bitch," he snaps at me, his breath hot on the side of my face as he pulls me down the hall. "I can't wait to tell Hollman how easy you made this for me. Thanks for leaving the window unlocked."

I *knew* I shut that fucking window earlier.

The mention of Hollman's name sends a chill throughout my entire body. Fuck. That man doesn't kill those who cross him quickly. Or cleanly. I knew something like this could happen when I stirred shit up with my article, but I'd hoped that since Marcus Hollman was sitting in jail, I'd be okay.

We're at the threshold of my room when I realize I'm still holding my glass. In a move of sheer desperation, I slam it against his head once, twice, three times before the heavy crystal shatters, sending shards of glass and amber liquid everywhere. I'm wearing thick socks, but I cringe as I step on the remnants, fighting like hell to stay on my feet despite the fact that my knees are weak.

"Fucking bitch," he swears as he takes a hand off of my mouth. With both of my hands now free, I claw at his arms and scream again. It's not as impactful as I was hoping since he's wearing a long-sleeved shirt. I'm met with thick cotton fabric, and between that and the fact that my nails are cut short, I don't do any damage.

My eyes dart around in alarm. I'm not going to say I get a second wind—I'm still scared shitless—but the panic in my chest alleviates a minuscule amount.The fight side of 'fight or flight' awakens within me. I look down for the spot of bare skin between where his glove stops and his shirt starts and bite down as hard as I can.

"Arghhh!" he yells, trying to pull his arm back. I stay latched on, like a literal dog with a bone. He howls in pain as my teeth cut deeper into his flesh. I pray I don't break a tooth. "Bitch!" he yells as he jabs me in the ribs with his free hand. *This guy needs to expand his vocabulary.*

Without realizing his mistake, he covers his wound with the other hand, giving me enough time to pivot and run. My heart pounds like a fucking jackhammer as I bolt out of my room and down the hallway of my small one story home. The bedrooms are on one side of the living room, and the kitchen, where my phone is currently sitting, is on the other. It feels like a million miles away. I'm not confident I can get to it in time.

I take a split second to weigh my options, praying my legs don't freeze up. My eyes zero in on the alarm pad on the wall next to the front door. I don't dare look behind me as I race for it. With trembling hands, it takes me two tries to enter my code and hit the panic button. I cry with relief when the shrill beeping starts blasting through the house.

The man comes for me, running into my living room. There's something frantic in his eyes, as if the night didn't go as planned. But it's the anger that flares in his eyes that washes over me in a wave of terror.

*Where the fuck is the alarm company?*

Blood trickles down from where I smashed the glass against his forehead. We stare at each other for a few more seconds, the tension and my fear overwhelming every part of me. The air feels heavy with the scent he's wearing, and bile rises in my throat. I swallow it back down, hoping I don't vomit. He smirks at me. It's a look that'll haunt my dreams.

"Hollman wants you gone. So I'll see you soon, Lyla," he says in a sickeningly sweet voice before he runs through the family room and out the back door.

*Fuck. This is bad.*

I lean back against the front door and slide down until I'm sitting on my heels, the alarm still screaming. Breathing heavily with my hand on my chest, I hear my cell phone ring. I know it's the home security company so I rush to answer it, confirming there's an emergency. I'm told the police have been dispatched and will arrive shortly. I hang up the phone but don't dare turn the alarm off. I don't want that asshole coming back in.

It's ten minutes later when flashing lights pull up to my house. I finally turn the alarm off and open the front door to greet the officer.

"Ma'am, are you okay?" he asks.

Somehow, I find my voice, but it's thin and quivering and I don't even recognize it when I answer. "Yes. There was a man hiding in my bathroom. He attacked me, tried to drag me into my bedroom to hurt me." Saying it out loud makes it seem so much more real, and this time, I don't even attempt to stop the tears that spring to my eyes.

The next few hours are a blur. I sit on my porch and watch the organized chaos unfold. While I wait for the detectives to interview me, my focus wavers, and I find myself lost in thoughts about how I got myself into this mess. Biting my lip, I think about the driving force behind my obsession with learning and exposing everything I could about Marcus Hollman and his nefarious ways—not wanting someone else to lose someone they love because of him. If I could help prevent even one person, it would all be worth it.

I hug my knees to my chest and think back to the last time I saw her. It was the perfect beach day and, despite tourist season being in full swing, we were still able to get a great spot at Swamprose Beach, my favorite beach in all of Cape Cod.

*"Tell me you're not serious about this guy, Liv," I say to her. She's been spending a lot of time with this Dylan person, but something feels off about it. He's definitely not her usual type, giving off the bad boy vibe. The fact his name isn't unknown to my brother and Theo —who are cops—only makes him all the more suspicious in my book.*

*"Nah. It's not serious. You don't marry the bad boy, Ly. You just have fun with him until it's time to get your shit together."*

*"Yeah, good point. It would probably just be easier if you married one of my brothers, though," I joke, but Liv just gives a forced chuckle.*

* * *

A fresh batch of tears come like a faucet that's just been turned on. If I knew it was going to be the last time I'd see her, I never would have let Olivia leave the beach that day. I've been wracked with guilt since the night she died, wondering why I didn't call her out for partying more than normal. To this day, I still don't know if that night was the first time she tried cocaine or not. What I do know is that the cocaine was laced with fentanyl, and she was dead within minutes of that first hit. It came out later that she got the cocaine from that shitbag boy toy, Dylan. It didn't take me long, once I did a little online searching, to find out he had ties to Marcus Hollman.

I worked for years to dig up everything I could on Hollman. I've been told I can hold a grudge like no other, and this project was indicative of that. Locked in like a damn heat-seeking missile, I didn't quit. What started with hours and hours of internet sleuthing eventually led to driving back and forth to Boston to go to house parties and seedy bars, flirting with scumbag guys and holding back a lot of college girls' hair while they puked.

It was all worth it, though. The miles on my car, the money spent on alcohol, the secrets I kept from my family. Once I was able to get the right people talking, I finally put names to the faces of low-level dealers who were selling drugs to college kids. I also worked my way up to the top of the food chain and linked them all back to Hollman. And not just drugs, but women, too.

Marcus' facade of being a pillar of the community in Boston shattered when I published a lengthy exposé that tied him to millions of dollars in drug sales, trafficking, and pimping out women.

It was just a few weeks ago that my article went live, blowing my quiet little existence to smithereens. I had the domain name ready and uploaded the files to what I thought was a private server, waiting for me to pull the trigger. When I finally hit publish, I'm certain I looked just like Ariel did in *The Little Mermaid* when she signed her deal with Ursula.

I had also drafted emails to send to a bunch of different news stations in Boston. My last step was to hop on my social media account and share the story there as well. I have a decent enough following of local news sites just from all the freelance I've done over the years, so I didn't doubt this would spread like wildfire. And spread, it did. In just a few days time, Marcus Hollman was front-page news throughout all of New England.

Now here I am, sitting on my front porch being interviewed by detectives. I give the officers a description of the man and answer what feels like a million questions.

"You said you didn't recognize him, but do you have any idea who might want to hurt you?" the officer asks.

I stare straight ahead as I answer his question with one of my own. "Do you know who Marcus Hollman is?"

"I think everyone in New England knows who he is. We're not that far from Boston."

"Well, I'd venture to guess he's less than thrilled with me right now considering I'm the main reason he's sitting in jail without bail," I say. When I finally meet the officer's eyes, I see the moment he makes the connection. If Hollman had a voodoo doll, I don't doubt I'd be in a tremendous amount of pain right now.

"Lyla Sullivan. Shit, I didn't even put two and two together when you gave your name earlier." I nod my head. "Okay, well this changes things significantly. Gives us a jumping off point. Do you have anywhere else you can stay tonight? Can I call anyone for you?"

"No, thanks."

No way am I going to bring this drama to Quinn's door.

And calling my parents would result in them immediately driving to Vermont, with my brothers in tow, and all but dragging me back to Sandpiper Cove. They're already sour as hell I never told them anything about Hollman.

The officers canvas the neighborhood, knocking on doors to ask if anyone saw anything suspicious. A CSI team arrives to look for fingerprints, but because the man was wearing gloves, it feels hopeless. A few hours later, the police pack up and leave. They tell me they're going to send a patrol unit throughout the night, and that they'll call as soon as they have any information for me.

I turn on my alarm the second I close the door. *Do not cry again, Lyla,* I tell myself as I sit on my couch, head in my hands, trying to figure out my next move. The adrenaline I felt all night finally wears off and exhaustion hits me like a freight train, but I know damn well I won't sleep a wink tonight.

# ONE

## *Lyla*

SEPTEMBER

COME ON, *Lyla. Get your ass moving and chase those endorphins*, I think to myself as I walk out the door.

I hate running. I think people who like it and do it for fun are actual psychopaths. I don't care how beautiful the scenery is or how perfect the weather—I dread the idea of putting on sneakers and leaving the house. The only good thing about it is feeling clear headed and fanfuckingtastic when I'm done.

Running is my second form of therapy. It also allows me to eat as much ice cream, gummy bears, and nachos as I want without my pants getting tighter. It's still sheer misery from start to finish, though.

I get to the end of my parents' street and snake my way through Sandpiper Cove. While I have mixed feelings about moving back to my hometown, I can't deny that I love the charming, sleepy seaside town whose name comes from the cute little birds that pepper our beaches—beaches I've spent half my life on.

After I was attacked in Vermont, my parents insisted I move back home. To be fair, they were pressuring me to do so since I released my exposé on Marcus Hollman. But having someone break in upped the ante and was enough for them to beg.

As much as I wanted to be defiant, the reality is that I was scared shitless. Living alone after what happened wasn't something I was exactly jumping for joy over. I wasn't sleeping well, had permanent dark circles under my eyes, and felt like I was constantly on the verge of having a panic attack.

I was also wracked with guilt for causing them so much worry. That guilt clung to me the way smoke clings to your hair after you've sat around a campfire. So, I packed up my things, hugged my best friend goodbye, and have been living in my childhood bedroom ever since.

The sun isn't fully up yet, and there's not a soul around. That tranquility is part of why I drag my ass out of bed so early. The other reason for the early wake up is that I can avoid crossing paths with anyone I know all while praying I don't get hit by a car or a rogue deer. Or get murdered by a drug dealer who's out for revenge.

Five miles and forty-ish minutes later, I'm about to walk up my parents' driveway when a sudden chill rushes over me, and I get goosebumps all over. I immediately look every which way but see nothing suspicious. It brings me back to that night in Vermont, and I bite my lip, panic building in my chest. I didn't listen to my gut then, so I take another look around, bracing for something terrible to happen.

I remind myself that I'm safe and living with people in law enforcement. I try my best to shrug off the nerves. I continue my way into the garage, knowing that both of my parents will be awake. I'll have to deal with their wrath for venturing out on my own despite their explicit request not to. I can feel their stares on me before I even get my sneakers off.

"Well, well, well. I remember a time when we had to worry

about you sneaking out at night to go to parties with your friends," my mom, Lori, says while filling a mug for me. "My how things have changed, haven't they Chris?" she asks my dad with a smile.

My dad says nothing. I don't even need to look at him to know he's unhappy with me. I blatantly ignored one of the only requests he's made since I moved back in. His frustration emanates from him. He's usually very stoic and calm, so when he's not, the energy around him shifts, sucking all the air out of the room.

"You probably never thought your thirty-one-year-old daughter would be living in your house again either but here we are. I figured most drug dealers and other shitbags are still sleeping, so it seemed like the safest time to go out for a run."

Under the weight of my dad's glare, my stomach starts to turn and I'm hit with a wave of remorse for being the cause of his worry. I'm not trying to be difficult on purpose—more so because I just want control of my life. As terrified as I was in Vermont, moving home was something I likely wouldn't have done if not for my parents pushing. Ultimately it was my decision, but I'm not naive enough to think my parents didn't influence that choice. Heavily. I know that when my dad lays down the law he's only thinking about my safety. I make a mental note to try and be more conscious and appreciative of that because while he can be protective and strict, it always comes from the right place.

My mom hands me a plate of eggs, and while I was originally planning to scurry away and avoid my dad's wrath, I suck it up and sit down next to him. When he sighs loudly, I know I'm about to get a lecture. Before he can open his mouth, my mom talks.

"We saw Olivia's parents last night," she says as she sits down at the table with us.

I swallow a bite of my eggs and try to keep my composure. I've been extra emotional lately when it comes to Liv. Anytime her name comes up, or I spend too much time dwelling on the past, I usually end up in a puddle of tears or lost in the thought of wondering what life would be like today if she was still alive. I close my eyes and bite my lip, willing the prick of tears away. I take a deep breath and look at my mom.

"How are they?" I carefully ask.

"They're okay. Proud of you, but also worried, too—like the rest of us."

"You really kicked the hornet's nest here, kiddo. And completely behind our backs," my dad says, frustration lacing his otherwise calm voice. This has been his main point of contention since I moved back home a couple of weeks ago. The fact that I put myself in danger and kept it from them until the rest of society found out. I immediately get defensive, pushing my shoulders back and straightening my spine.

"You make it seem like I did all of this just to spite you, Dad, and that's not the case at all. It had nothing to do with you. I didn't think my digging would lead to all of this—"

"Exactly. You didn't *think*. You are so damn headstrong and stubborn that you didn't stop and think about the risks you were taking. You didn't think to reach out to me, or your brothers, to get insight on how much danger you were putting yourself in. And I'm also willing to guess that the only reason you agreed to move back is because someone broke into your place with what were most certainly ill intentions." His voice is slightly raised now, his frustration morphing into anger.

"Hollman was responsible for my best friend dying, Dad. I couldn't ignore that and just pretend I never figured out just how big of a piece of garbage the guy is." It's all I can do to keep myself from jumping out of my chair. It's not that I'm defensive about the work I put into the article I wrote. It's that

I don't understand how he can't see that the ending justified the means.

"But you didn't need to pull at the string yourself, Lyla. You could have gone to law enforcement much sooner. You could have exposed him without putting yourself in the damn crossfire." He slams his fist down on the table. I flinch at the noise.

"As a cop yourself, I'd have thought you would be happy to have someone like him off the streets," I challenge. Judging by the flush that creeps up his neck, I might have pushed him a little too far.

"Of course I'm happy in that sense. I just wish it wasn't *my* daughter who was on the chopping block now. Jesus, Lyla. A man broke into your home and attacked you. He was directly connected to Hollman. Do you have any idea how close we came to losing you? Do you even care?" he spits, arms wild as he waves his hands to make his point. His eyes blaze, and I'm damn near certain his irises turn the same shade as the red on his neck.

"Of course I care! Don't insult me with a question like that!" I exclaim. Having lost my appetite, I set my fork down and rub my hands through my hair in frustration.

"Enough you two," my mom finally says. "What's done is done. Could it have been handled differently? Probably. But we can't Monday morning quarterback this, Chris. All we can do is move forward and be vigilant when it comes to safety."

My dad leans back in his chair, his frustrated glare still on me.

Mom swings her gaze back to me. "Olivia would be really proud of you, sweetie. But she would rip you a new one if she was here and witnessing you be nonchalant when it comes to your well-being."

At the mention of Olivia's name, my dad's anger fades. A

flicker of sadness passes through his eyes, and he takes a deep breath.

"She really would be," my dad adds, his voice softening slightly.

"I miss her so much," I whisper, trying to fight back the tears that threaten to spill over from the sadness of losing her and the frustration that she's no longer here. My mom gets up and moves to the chair next to me, pulling me into her arms.

"I know, Lyla. It never gets easier when you lose someone you love. You just have to adapt to that new normal. Some days are going to be harder than others, no matter how much time goes by."

I wipe away the wetness on my cheeks. "Everything went to shit after she died. We were attached at the hip since we were little kids and in an instant, she was gone. I'd never felt so alone, but I had you guys and Theo to keep me from completely falling apart. And then Theo left and I really was alone. Both of my people–gone. I basically ran away from home to avoid memories of either of them. I got myself in deeper than I ever imagined when I was researching Hollman —and yes, I can admit that it was risky and careless. I'm constantly looking over my shoulder. And let's go ahead and add the fact that I'm living in my childhood bedroom with no job and no life."

"You're selling yourself short, honey," my dad says, his voice a complete one-eighty from what it was a minute ago. "You went through an incredibly difficult time in your life and came out the other side. Your resiliency and ability to over-come loss is something you should be proud of. You put in the work to get back to a better place. You are a spectacular writer. I'm equal parts horrified and impressed by your investigative skills." I can't help but laugh at that.

"Thanks, Dad. I'm sorry I've been so terrible when it comes

to following your rules. I guess I just feel like so much is out of my own control right now, and I need to assert my independence wherever I can. I'll do better. I promise." I give him a small smile, but he just looks at me, his hazel eyes identical to mine. He bites his bottom lip, another habit I inherited from him, and one that tells me he's trying to make some sort of decision. He lets out a loud sigh, and I just know I'm not going to like what he says next.

"I appreciate that, Lyla, but I'm taking matters into my own hands."

"Why do I feel like I'm going to hate this?"

"While you're living here, and until Hollman is in jail permanently, I'm going to have officers watching over you."

"I know you're the chief of police, Dad, but that sort of feels like you're abusing your position."

"Lucky for us, I only have myself to answer to. I'll make it easy on you. To start, it'll just be Colin and Theo." He holds up his hand to stop me from responding. "Just when you're out and about. I'll leave a police car in the driveway or out front and make sure units are patrolling the neighborhood. I'm sure Colin's work friends, Drew and Clayton, wouldn't mind helping out as needed."

His broad shoulders that were up to his ears just a minute ago, sink down, telling me he's completely at peace with this idea. Meanwhile, I'm about to bounce out of my seat in frustration. "Dad! *No.* I won't run alone. Hell, I'll get a treadmill. I don't care if Colin looks after me, or even Clayton or Drew, but not Theo. Please." I can tell by the stony look on his face that my pleading doesn't work, so I try a different route. "I'm an adult. I moved home because you all but insisted I do so, but I can make my own decisions about who I spend time with."

"I beg to differ. The fact you're out running in the dark every morning, even when you know better, shows that you can't handle making your own decisions right now. At least not when it comes to your safety." My dad looks at me, sympathy in his eyes, but doesn't back down. "Every time we see Olivia's parents, my heart breaks all over for them. I can't imagine waking up every day and trying to function after losing a child. Despite everything you and Theo have been through, there's not a doubt in my mind he would stop at nothing to keep you safe. That's worth the trade-off of you being pissed at me."

"How about Derek? He can help out instead," I say referring to my other brother. He's not a cop like Colin—he owns his own construction company—but he's a black belt in jiu jitsu and scary as fuck.

"Oh, I know he'll help out when he can, but I don't have control over his schedule like I do the rest of them."

I stand up, my legs shaky, and grip the edge of the table. My voice trembles when I say, "That man is a coward who broke my heart, Dad. I can't believe you're going to put me in a position where I'm forced to spend time with him. It's cruel and unnecessary."

I put my dish in the sink and leave the kitchen without saying another word.

Theo Morgan didn't just break my heart; he ripped it out of my chest, stuck it in a blender, and proceeded to pour it down the drain. Then he turned on the garbage disposal for good measure. Even now, six years later, those cracks are still present.

Up until Dad's news, I've successfully avoided him since I've been back in town. The idea of being face-to-face with him again makes me want to crawl under the covers and hide from the world.

My dad and brothers are beyond protective of me—they always have been. I know my dad and Colin went through their own shit with Theo when he first left me, but over the years, they've rebuilt their relationships with him. Derek still holds a grudge, so I consider him a Team Lyla ally. My mom, however, is a fair weather fan who just wants everyone to get along.

I sit on my bed, my eyes wandering around before landing on a collection of pictures of Theo and me. Photos that capture all sorts of little moments from a time when everything was perfect—or, rather,perfectly imperfect. When we'd laugh until we were crying, spend hours wrapped up in each other, and watch countless sunsets. I don't know why the pictures are still up, haunting me. I don't know why I let them.

There's a knock at my door a few minutes later. My mom pokes her head in. "You okay, honey? That was...a lot." Her eyes follow mine, taking in the pictures that almost have me in a trance. "We can always redecorate and repaint if you want, Lyla. I never wanted to do anything while you were gone, but if you need to change up the scenery in here, take them down," she says.

"I can't bring myself to do that. Apparently, I'm a glutton for punishment." She sits down next to me on the bed, and I can tell she has something to say because she's twisting her hands in her lap.

"Don't write him off, Lyla. Not before having a real conversation with him. If for nothing else, maybe it will give you some closure to really move on if that's what you want." I sit up and look at her.

"Move on?" I scoff. "It's been six years since he left me. I've spent countless hours in therapy, and I still don't think I've fully moved on from him. And now Dad is throwing me to the wolves, forcing me to spend time with the one person I don't want to see or speak to."

"Maybe this will encourage you to confront those feelings

head-on. Say all the things you've kept bottled up for those six years. It could be cathartic," she says optimistically.

"I'm not sure I'm ready for that, Mom. Or if I ever will be. Maybe I'll just be stuck in this soul-sucking middle ground forever." I sigh and stand up, effectively ending the conversation as I head into my bathroom.

She calls out to me. "I'm going to run some errands shortly if you want to come. We can stop at the bookstore!" She's trying to smooth things over by offering a trip to One More Chapter. I tell her I'll join her once I'm done getting ready for the day. But as I shower, my mind wanders to Theo.

The heat of the water seeps into my bones, helping to alleviate some of my tension. I stare down at the water circling the drain and will my sadness and frustrations to go with it. I rub my hand along the tattoo on my ribs. I always catch myself doing so when I think about him for too long.

Sometimes I kick myself for getting a permanent reminder of him inked on my body, but most of the time, I'm glad it's there. It reminds me that, for at least a few years, everything was perfect.

All that fades once I step out of the shower. I skip washing my hair so Mom doesn't have to wait more than necessary. I'm sitting on my bed mentally mapping out my day when my phone dings, alerting me I have a new message. I roll onto my stomach and grab it from the nightstand, my heart stopping like it always does when I see his name pop up. It's like he has a sixth sense, always knowing when I'm thinking about him.

**Theo: Swamprose this morning.**

The picture comes through and, sure enough, it's a breathtaking sunrise at my favorite beach in all of Cape Cod. The sky is a medley of orange, red, and yellow, and the reflection of the colors on the water is nothing short of stunning.

This is what he does. What he's done for years. He's never

overly intrusive, doesn't ask questions or try to engage in conversation, but he sends me random texts with links to books, songs I need to listen to, and pictures like this one. Books, music, and the sky; they're the three things he knows I love endlessly.

And yet, I still do what I've always done over the years—ignore him and leave the message on read.

*theo*

"MORGAN! SULLIVAN! MY OFFICE!"

When Chief bellows from his cave, I give Colin a look wondering what we could have done to get into trouble so early in the day. Colin, as clueless as I am, shrugs his shoulders and rolls his eyes.

Although I'm comfortable with my position, and my competence at my job, I still get antsy when I'm called into the boss's office. Even if the man on the other side of the desk happens to be my best friend's dad. If anything, that makes it worse.

We file into his office, me taking a seat in front of his desk while Colin fiddles around with the pictures on his father's wall.

"What's up, Chief?" Colin asks, finally flopping down into the chair next to me.

"Your sister is driving me up the wall, that's what's up. She snuck out again for a run this morning before we woke up." He pinches the bridge of his nose in exasperation.

"That's like the third time this week, and it's only Wednesday. You guys are terrible babysitters, yet you complain about not having grandkids. I don't know how you raised children without losing one. It's truly a miracle I survived my childhood and turned into such a well-adjusted adult," Colin replies with a straight face. I stifle a laugh and cough into my hand to cover it up. Chief gives him a hard stare, but Colin doesn't crack.

I break the silence by finally saying, "Okay, sir, what can we do to help? I'm assuming she knows she's not supposed to do that. She can call the station to find someone to run with her when she wants to. Everyone is happy to help."

"Her mom and I have reminded her repeatedly of the risks that are out there right now. We have no idea if Marcus Hollman has someone watching her, waiting for the chance to grab her or hurt her. She kicked a hornet's nest and pissed off a really bad guy. Despite the fact that a man broke into her home and attempted to assault her, she's still insisting that because the feds haven't offered her protection, it's not that serious. It's like she doesn't even care about her safety, so here's what we're going to do. You guys are going to keep an eye on her. If she wants to go for a run, one of you will go with her. If she wants to go for a hike, one of you will go with her. If she wants to spend hours at the bookstore, one of you will go with her. If she wants to go to the beach—"

"One of us will go with her," Colin fills in. "We get it, Dad."

"When she's at the house, I'm not concerned. The alarm is on. The neighbors look out for each other. I'll leave a patrol car there twenty-four-seven and arrange for officers to drive by throughout the day. But when she's on her own... Well, that won't be happening anymore. We start tomorrow morning."

"No can do, Dad. It's guy's night, and I'm hoping to get laid after. I'll do Friday," Colin volunteers.

"She will be beyond pissed if she walks out the door and sees me waiting for her. I'm happy to help out, but she's already grumpy as hell in the morning. Now you want to poke that bear by sending me to run with her?" I ask.

"Oh, please, don't act like you're not dying to get back into her good graces," Colin says, his face serious. "This is the perfect way. She always talks about how she hates running, but that it's good therapy, and she has to do it every day to get those endorphins and shit. This might be the only way she'll tolerate spending any time with you. For the record, you upset her again, and I'll kick your ass." He looks back at his dad and his tone turns more playful. "Dad, are you sure you're not doing this just to get them back together?" Chief stares him down, not breaking a smile.

I think about what Colin said. I am dying to get back into Lyla's good graces. The amount of time I spend thinking about her and the ways I can worm my way back into her life would probably qualify as a part time job, at a minimum. She's as stubborn as ever. She's ignored and avoided me the few times I've seen her since she's been back in Sandpiper. She doesn't respond to any of my texts, but I guess I should just be grateful she hasn't blocked me. Maybe this forced time together is my way back into her life. So, I tell Chief Sullivan that I'll be there and try to keep my eagerness in check as I do.

"It's settled. Tomorrow morning at five. Coffee and breakfast will be waiting for you when you guys get back. We can figure out a schedule for the rest of the week then, and Colin? Get a haircut," Chief orders, turning his attention to a stack of files on his desk and effectively dismissing us. Colin and I walk out of his office and over to the pool of desks in the center of the room. It's my turn to flop into my chair dramatically.

"In all seriousness, Lyla's going to be *livid* about this, but her safety comes first, and my dad's right—she is being somewhat cavalier about her own well-being," Colin says.

Thinking about Lyla being attacked has me burning up on

the inside. The fact she's so lackadaisical about her safety has me grinding my teeth. To think of her alone in her home, with some man's hands all over her, trying to hurt her, has me seeing red.

"Do you think this will get me back on her good side?" I already know the answer, but it's still a kick in the nuts when Colin says it out loud.

"Fuck no. I don't want to sound like a girl here, but you broke her heart. That girl can hold a grudge like nobody's business. She's still pissed at Derek for blowing her birthday candles out when she turned ten. I know you had your reasons, Theo. I'm not sure I'll ever understand it, but I know it made sense to you. She thinks you bailed on her when she needed you the most. I think the only thing that will get her back into your life in any real capacity is if you tell her the truth. And before you interrupt, I don't want to hear that it isn't an option. The truth is the only option, even if she blows a gasket when you tell her."

"Damn, I hate when you sound like the smart one," I say, digging a Nerf football out of my desk drawer and tossing it at him. Usually we save this for when we're talking about work, but the idea of spending one-on-one time with Lyla, even if it results in being ignored the entire time, has me practically bouncing out of my chair with anticipation.

Lyla and I have barely spent any time together since I left for the Army. She pretty much boxed me out of her life, and it kills me. It keeps me up at night. I have wracked my brain trying to think of ways to get back into her life, but she hasn't given me an inch.

When she pops into town, she avoids me. And if she can't, she ignores me. There was only ever one time over the past six years she let her walls down.

* * *

It's her last night at home and I've decided to grow some balls and find her. I took a guess that she'd be at Swamprose Beach and, sure enough, I was right. She's lying on a blanket, staring at the sky. I can hear Vance Joy playing softly from her phone. The beach is empty except for her. I can't stop the smile that spreads across my face when I'm close enough to recognize that familiar perfume. The scent of roses and oranges mixed with jasmine hits me, bringing along a flash of memories with it. It's the only fragrance I've ever known her to wear, and I'm shocked it's still her go-to choice.

"Hey, Sunshine," I say, using the nickname I've had for her since we were teenagers. I cringe at the way she jumps into a sitting position, clearly startled. Her shoulders relax when she sees that it's me, but the look in her hazel eyes almost brings me to my knees. There is so much sadness there, and I'm a major contributor to that. I join her on the blanket without asking for permission. Something I know pisses her off, but I can't risk asking her and being rejected. I lie down and, after a few seconds, she joins me, reclining back in her original position.

It's the first time we've been alone together in years, and the air between us crackles. It's wild to me that even after so much time apart, I still want her so badly. My body is on fire from being so close to her, and for the first time since I walked away from her, a sense of peace washes over me.

Sitting here with her is like coming home after a long time away. All I want to do is pull her on top of me and kiss her until the sun comes up. As I try to think of a conversation starter, it dawns on me that I have absolutely no fucking clue what to say to this woman. I'm sorry, or I've missed you, just don't seem like the way to go.

"Beautiful night, huh?" is what I finally come up with.

"It's been years since we've had a conversation, and that's what you're going to start with?" Lyla snaps.

28

"Not my best work. I acknowledge that," I say with a chuckle. "You look good, Lyla. How have you been?"

"Fine. I've been fine."

If there's anything I've learned about women it's that the word fine is just about the worst thing they can say. So I decide to go right for the jugular.

"You thinking about staying in Vermont for good, or do you think you might end up back here? I miss you. Your family misses you. I'm sure you're missing being this close to the water. Those Vermont sunrises and sunsets must pale in comparison to the ones we get here." I know it's risky to say, but if I don't say it now, I don't know when I'll get the chance. Lyla and I planned a future together. Hell, we had our kids' names picked out, knew what neighborhood we wanted to buy a house, and had our careers mapped out. I know my departure is part of the reason she moved.

Lyla shoots back up to the sitting position and looks at me, venom in her eyes. "You have a lot of fucking nerve, Theo. You left me. You knew I was absolutely gutted over losing Liv, and what did you do? Did you stay around and help me pick up the pieces?" I stay silent because I'm smart enough to know her question is rhetorical. "No. You fucking left me. Yeah, you joined the Army, and yeah, that's obviously super honorable, but that doesn't negate the fact that when the chips were down, when life got hard, you bailed. So you don't get to say that you miss me. You don't get to pull that shit and try and guilt me into moving back here on the pretense that my family misses me, too. I know they do because I talk to them all the fucking time. They didn't ghost me like you did. If you didn't love me anymore, you could have just said so. If you didn't want that life we had planned, you could have been a fucking man and just told me. You wanted to get away from me so badly that you went and fought a war in a shithole desert. So, no, Theo, you don't get to say that you miss me because us not being together is entirely your doing."

We stare at each other. She's breathing heavily from the verbal ass-kicking she just gave me. Her eyes are wet like she's trying to hold back tears. Fuck. She's more upset than I realized. Everything she said is true, but it crushes me that she thinks I left because I fell out of love with her. But then again, she doesn't know why I left, so why would she think anything else?

"I broke both of our hearts when I walked away from you, Lyla."

She scoffs at me and rolls her eyes.

"I'm serious. I don't deserve your trust, but I'm going to prove to you that I'll never walk away again."

"And I'm supposed to just believe that? Why?"

"Because I have never stopped loving you. There's been no one else, Lyla. And there never will be because you're it for me. And I know I owe you so much more than that—"

"Ah, yeah, Theo, but it's a little too late for that now. If you're looking for someone to assuage your guilt, you're barking up the wrong fucking tree." She takes a deep breath before she continues. "I don't begrudge the relationships you've maintained with my family over the years. I know they're the closest thing to a real family you have at this point, but that doesn't mean I'm ready to open myself up to having one with you."

I nod because she's right. She doesn't owe me a damn thing, and I don't deserve it, but just because I don't deserve it doesn't mean I don't wish for it with every fiber of my fucking being. I would do almost anything to get back into her good graces.

I want to pull her onto my lap. I want to wrap my arms around her, hold her close to me while we listen to the waves lightly crash on the beach. I want to hold on to her and never let her go. But I don't. Because I have no right to do that. I have no right to put her in that position, to make her feel uncomfortable. It's the last thing I would ever want to do.

Instead, I turn my body toward her. She looks at me, the combination of sadness and anger still shining in her eyes as a few tears slowly roll down her cheeks. She shrugs her shoulders as if she doesn't *know what to say. I can tell her I love her until I'm blue in the face, which is the truth, but it would only push her farther away from me. And I owe her more than that. Like an explanation regarding the real reason I left.*

*I gently wipe her tears away with my thumb, my body lighting up at the touch. Her skin is warm, probably from being so worked up. The urge to pull her into my arms and tell her everything is going to be okay is so strong. Until I remind myself that I'm the reason for the tears she's shedding. Because of my own cowardice, I've hurt the person I love most in this world.*

*"I'm not going anywhere, and I'm going to work my ass off proving that to you." I don't want to let her go, not when it's been so long since I've had her in my arms, but I pull back and give her space. She lays back down on the blanket, staring up at the starry sky that I know she loves.*

*I weigh out my options. I can say goodbye and walk away, keep an eye on her from my truck until she heads home, or I can take a chance, push my luck, and try for a little more time in her orbit. I go with the second option and lay down next to her, keeping a respectable distance. Even though our bodies aren't touching, I can feel her tense up. She sucks in a deep breath and folds her hands over her stomach. When I look over, I find her chewing on her bottom lip.*

*Goddamn, I just want to kiss her.*

*"It was this or I sit in my truck and wait for you to leave to make sure you get home safely," I tell her. She sighs before turning up the music on her phone. So we lay there, the space between us like a chasm that I have no idea how to navigate. Despite that, it's the best night I've had in years.*

\* \* \*

I bail on going out. We have long standing plans on Wednesday nights. Colin, sometimes Derek, and a few of our other friends and I always go to the Dusty Bird Pub, our favorite local place for wings and darts. I know Colin wanted a wingman, but I can't stop thinking about Lyla. I know he'd call me out on it the second he saw me. I truly don't think many people would be happier if Lyla and I got back together than him, but I also know he's serious about kicking my ass if I make her cry again.

Instead, I hang out at home, nursing a beer while my cat, Diego, mills around demanding attention. I think about my relationship with the Sullivans and how lucky I am that Lyla's parents have been so good to me all these years, even when I didn't deserve it. Yeah, Derek still hates me, and he makes that very clear every time we're around each other. We've had a few moments over the years when I thought I was making progress. We've spent time together, even worked on projects together, without killing each other, but that guy is as stubborn as his sister.

I think back to the choices I made all those years ago. At the time, it felt like it was the only thing I could do to avoid the suffocating fear of loss. The reality is that I *was* a coward. I watched how my dad completely shut down after my mom died. I might have been a little kid, but it was plain as day to see. He went from being the kind of father who coached my t-ball team and read bedtime stories every night to someone who barely had the bandwidth to do more than make sure I had clothes that fit and food on the table.

I didn't think much of it as I got older, maybe because I was just used to it by that point. It certainly didn't scare me away from getting into a relationship with Lyla and being a damn good boyfriend. Until I wasn't. Until I left.

I always had the fear of something happening to her in the back of my head, especially once I became a cop. Life can change in an instant and you can lose everything. A car accident, a random act of violence. No one is safe. But I didn't let those worries overpower the love and absolute devotion I had for the woman.

But then Olivia died. The loss hit Lyla the hardest, but we all walked away from it with scars. It's impossible not to when you lose someone who's like a sister. In an instant I was reminded of my mom's death and that soul-crushing grief that always follows as you try and navigate the world after a loss.

I spiraled. All I could think about was—what if I lost Lyla? What if something took her from me? The woman was the air that I breathed. I couldn't survive without her. I loved her so fucking much that I scared myself right out of the relationship. If I had stayed, I would have suffocated her with my worry. Stealing away her free-spirited mindset was something I couldn't do.

Over the course of the year that followed Olivia's death, I watched myself become someone I didn't recognize. Someone so paralyzed by my fears. I was possessive and paranoid—not because I thought she'd cheat on me, but because I was so afraid something catastrophic would happen to her. I wanted to be by her side constantly to ensure her safety. I was over-bearing and hyper-vigilant, and my intensity spoiled our good times more often than not.

After I broke up with her, when I was home on leave before my first deployment, I opened up to Lori. Did my best to explain to her what snapped in me and why I needed to leave in the first place. I asked them not to tell Lyla. She was beyond pissed at me, and by that point, she had already moved out of Sandpiper and was making a nice life for herself.

Her parents were far more understanding than I deserved, and I think that's because, over the years, they had really become like parents to me.

At first I thought maybe they knew what Lyla had been up

to, but just hadn't filled me in. I wasn't a part of her life anymore, so I figured they were respecting her privacy. Turns out none of us had any idea Lyla was conducting her own investigation into Marcus Hollman. My heart races a mile a minute just thinking about the danger she put herself in by outing this long-standing community man as a drug dealer and a trafficker.

Later that night when I climb into bed, I toss and turn for hours, before eventually drifting off to sleep. I drive to Chief's house the following morning on autopilot, thinking about what I'm going to say to her.

# THREE

## Lyla

"FUCK, it's early. What the hell was I thinking?" I utter as my alarm goes off at 4:45. I rub the sleep out of my eyes before I dramatically roll out of bed. I act like I'm not the one who set the damn thing. I strip out of my pajamas and throw on the leggings and cropped tank top I set out last night. I grab a thin long-sleeved shirt in case it's a chilly morning and my earbuds. I snag a mini bag of gummy bears from my stash in the kitchen as a pseudo pre-workout snack and do a half-assed stretch in the garage.

I am fully aware that I'm breaking Dad's number one rule, but I've got so much anxious energy running through my body, despite the shitty night's sleep, and I need to burn it off. I set my alarm for earlier than usual so that in case my dad really does follow through with having someone run with me, I'm gone before they get here.

I don't want to wake my parents, so I exit the garage through the door on the side of the house as opposed to clicking the button to open the large doors. As I walk outside, I can see that the motion sensor lights on the front of the house are already on. Despite the warm temperature, a chill runs through me. My head snaps from side to side, but I don't see any animals that would have triggered the sensor.

I take a deep breath and stealthily make my way to the end of the house, staying as close to the siding as possible as I move. I lean back against the side of the garage, trying to muster up the courage to turn the corner. *Jackass,* I say to myself when I realize I walked out the door without my pepper spray. I wait another minute, not making a sound while my eyes dart back and forth, looking for anything out of the ordinary.

The lights still haven't turned off, which means whatever tripped them must still be nearby. Since I haven't heard a single sound, I figure it must be a spider or some flying bug that keeps tripping the sensor. *Just a bug. Definitely just a bug.* I nod my head in satisfaction as I peek my head around the corner. I immediately spot a large figure in a dark hoodie halfway up my driveway. As if I'm on a roller coaster, my stomach drops, and I gasp.

Time stands still, and I want to kick my own ass. I should have listened to my parents. This shitbag could be here to murder me in my driveway. That gasp that escaped got his attention, and when the figure turns, I realize it's the only person that could actually make me wish it was Marcus Hollman. "What are you doing here?" I snap, scowling at the man in my driveway.

"Don't freak out," Theo replies, holding his hands up.

"It's a little late for that, Theo. I thought you were one of Hollman's dudes here to whack me." My hands are on my hips as I take a few deep breaths, trying to calm myself down. My heart is thumping so quickly I'm shocked my watch hasn't alerted me or asked me if I was already working out. I could deny it's because of the man standing in front of me—the man who shredded my heart, my confidence, and every single vision I had for my future—but I'd be lying through my damn teeth.

"Well, that actually brings us to the reason why I'm here. This is your dad's way of making sure you stay safe."

I stare at him, saying nothing while he rambles. "I know you're not happy to see me, and I'm not trying to give you a hard time. You're obviously on edge if you thought I was someone else here to hurt you, which, by the way, I would never do. Please don't freak out and don't make me go home. Your dad will be pissed, and I'll never hear the end of it. Plus, it's dark as hell out, Lyla. There's no way you should be running on your own. Let's just get going. It might be the only thing that shuts me up at this point."

Theo is right. I'm not happy to see him. I'd like to say it's because he scared the living hell out of me, but I know that's not the real reason. In reality, the idea of having company this early is kind of reassuring. I don't know if my dad has gotten into my head or what, but there have definitely been a few times when I felt a weird vibe; like someone was following or watching me. I haven't said anything to anyone because I don't want to egg them on. I'm convinced I'm just being paranoid.

I quickly put on my long-sleeved shirt, not wanting him to get a glimpse at the tattoo I have on my ribs. I'll sweat to death before I give him the opportunity of knowing it's there. I give him an exasperated look while putting my earbuds in, turn on a Dateline podcast, and take off down the driveway.

It takes me longer to find my stride knowing that Theo is so close. My pace starts out way quicker than I planned, so I take a few deep breaths and force myself to slow down so that I'm not sucking wind after two miles. Thankfully, he doesn't try to make conversation during the first ten minutes. It gives me time to think about how to handle being stuck with a body-guard for the next chunk of time.

I wanted to do my eight-mile route today, so I have my work cut out for me. I'm petty enough to ignore him the entire time, but there's a tiny part of me that doesn't want to do that. I tell myself if he really wanted to be here and talk to me, he could break the ice himself.

Theo is in great shape and has zero problems keeping up. He's always been active, and from the glances I've stolen of him over the years, especially lately, it's clear his body hasn't gotten soft. He's fit and strong, and his muscular legs and forearms confirm that. He could blow my pace out of the water if he really wanted to, but he stays close and falls in place behind me when the path narrows. I push aside the fact that I definitely feel more relaxed having him with me.

He doesn't have headphones on, and I spend a solid mile wondering how the hell he can stand running like that. Doesn't he get bored without music or a podcast to listen to? What does he think about the entire time? My watch dings that we've hit the three-mile mark, and I congratulate myself for not folding. I'll be damned if I'm the one who talks first, no matter how much nervous energy oozes out of my pores.

We continue to trudge along as dawn begins to break. I realize that I'm so distracted I haven't heard a damn thing Keith Morrison has talked about in this week's podcast. I slow my pace to a near walk without warning, and Theo pretty much plows right into me. I can't get mad at him—it's my fault —but cursing is my visceral reaction as I stumble forward. "Fuck!"

I'm about to faceplant when Theo's strong hands grab my arms, and he hauls me back up, his grip lingering on my arms as I straighten. It feels like I've been struck by lightning. I can't stop the gasp that escapes my lips. He lets go of me, and I turn to face him. I immediately feel the loss of his touch, one that still takes my breath away no matter how much I want to deny it.My skin burns from his touch, and I rub my arms as if I'm putting out the flames. I take out an earbud and say, "Sorry about that. I should have warned you I was stopping."

"It's fine. You good?" Theo asks, glancing around to take stock of his surroundings.

"Yup. I was just changing from a podcast to a playlist." He stares at me so intently, that for a second, I think about how easy it would be to get lost in those blue eyes again. Hell, I could drown in them from a single look alone, and there's not a life preserver on the planet that would be able to bring me back to the surface.

I break eye contact before it has the chance of happening. I've already been reminded of how good it feels to have his hands on me, even if it was just to save me from eating concrete, but I can't risk his touch lingering longer than it should. I put my earbud back in, turn, and start running again, settling into my pace.

I think about our relationship as we run. About the future we planned. About the fact that while he is a stranger to me now, for a huge chunk of my life he knew me better than anyone else. With a single look, he could read me. It was like he knew me better than I knew myself. He had the ability to sense my emotions, to know exactly what I needed. I think about how, despite the broken heart he left me with, no man has ever made me feel the way he did. I wonder if he realizes I would have waited for him if he'd asked. One time, he told me there's been no one else, but can I believe that?

*Fuck, no. Look at him. There's no way he's not getting laid.*

The thought of him dating around and sharing intimate moments with someone else churns my stomach. My mind conjures up a beautiful woman who's just his type. His hands on her, kissing her delicate collarbone, his rough hands grazing her tits as he says all sorts of dirty things in her ear while he fucks her. I hate her with the fire of a thousand suns.

I briefly close my eyes and shake the thoughts out of my head. I have no business thinking of Theo in any capacity, let alone with another woman. That serves no purpose except to crack my already fragile heart a little bit more.

Unfortunately for me, no man has ever compared to him. No man has ever made me feel as safe and adored. No one has ever made me laugh as hard. If we're being honest, no man has ever fucked me as good as him, either. Sex with Theo was always mindblowing. He would move with reckless abandon, as if he couldn't get enough and wanted to make sure I knew just how much he desired me. He knew how to be tender and gentle, as if trying to prove to me how much he cherished my heart, mind, and body.

I think about all the things I wish we had more of: more nights of laying in the back of his truck and looking for shooting stars, more sunsets, more puzzles, more rainy days being snuggled on the couch drinking copious cups of coffee and reading, more concerts and bonfires, more nights of heart pounding sex.

I remind myself that no other man has broken me the way Theo Morgan has. It's the perfect remedy and helps me put my walls back up. I know that I can't, under any circumstances, handle another piece of my heart being taken by him.

Theo lets me set the pace for the rest of our run. There are a few moments where he looks like he's about to say something, opening his mouth but then quickly closing it to stay quiet. I slow down to a walk when I get a few doors down from my parents' house. It's the closest I get to doing any sort of a cooldown.

When we reach my driveway, I pause my music and look over at Theo to say goodbye. "Thanks for the protection, which, for the record, I don't need." With that, I open the garage door and walk inside. Theo follows, then gently grabs my arm, forcing me to turn back to face him. This simple touch buzzes through me, as if jolting my body to life again. I want to pull back but can't bring myself to do it.

"Happy to do it, Sunshine." His blue eyes are so dark they're like a midnight sky with no stars. As mesmerizing as they are, it doesn't stop the twinge in my heart at hearing him call me that nickname.

He lets go and walks through the garage, kicking his shoes off before opening the door to the house, reminding me how often he must come over since he knows my mom has a strict no shoes inside rule. I've only been home for a few weeks, but Theo hasn't been here very often. Mainly he just comes by with Colin during the day. He hasn't been at Sunday dinners, either. I feel a slight tinge of guilt at the fact that my presence here has impacted his relationship with my family. *Fuck that. This is your house.*

My parents are in the kitchen when we walk inside. Dad is making my favorite chocolate chip pancakes, which means he's anticipating me being grumpy, despite my endorphin-boosting run. He's not wrong.

Mom's eyes light up when she sees Theo, and she immediately grabs another mug for him. I watch him immediately scoop an ungodly amount of sugar into his mug before he adds milk and coffee. I feel a pang of something—sadness, or maybe nostalgia—when I see that he still drinks his coffee the same way.

The sweet smell wafts through the kitchen, causing my stomach to grumble. Vanilla, cinnamon, and maple all meld together and my mouth starts watering. If one could bottle this scent combination, it would be the perfect representation of a pancake breakfast.

I'm starving, but I know I need to put distance between Theo and me. I grab a mug, fill it with coffee and walk out of the kitchen and toward my bedroom on the other side of the house. I'm too sweaty to flop onto my bed, so I opt to hop in the shower. I bring my phone with me and put on an upbeat playlist.

I love music for a myriad of reasons, but its ability to completely change my mood has to be the top one. Once I'm done in the shower, I wrap myself in a big fluffy towel before using a second one to dry my hair. My *Fresh Start: For Real This Time* playlist has helped put a smile back on my face. I'm back in my room, jamming out to Taylor's "I Can Do It With a Broken Heart" in my bra and panties, contemplating an outfit when I hear a knock. I pause the song.

"Same time tomorrow?" I hear Theo say through the door. I roll my eyes in frustration.

*Dear god, please just leave before I lose my mind being around you.*

"Fine. Whatever," I reply before turning my music back on. I flop onto my bed with a sigh, singing along to the chorus as I turn my music back on. I roll onto my back and look around the room. On the walls are various framed photos of sunsets, sunrises, and night skies that I've taken over the years.

I've always been obsessed with the sky. Something about how vast it is, the different colors, and the moodiness of it has always fascinated me. These prints are mixed in with a few collages from high school, college, and vacations. I don't fancy myself a skilled photographer, but I have always loved capturing the moments and places that are special to me.

My eyes land on ones of Theo and me. He and my brothers became best friends the minute Theo and his dad moved to Sandpiper when we were all in elementary school. It was in high school when I finally realized I actually enjoyed spending time with him. It was also around that time that I noticed how hot he was. That coupled with the fact that he was interesting, altruistic, and we had a lot of shared interests paved the way to us getting together.

Our relationship was solid in college. He began his career at Sandpiper Cove Police Department, and I finished grad school. We had our entire life planned out. But the funny thing about that is you can have it all mapped out in your head, and in a second, it can change.

As I lie in bed, thinking back to the day he told me he was leaving, my stomach gurgles, and my mouth starts to sweat. I'm tempted to sit up and lean against the wall, thinking that it'll help the nausea pass, but my memory of the day he left keep me frozen in place.

*I'm sitting on the patio reading when Theo joins me. My eyes light up when I see him, reminding me that I always feel better when he's around. He looks tired, but I still take a second to acknowledge how handsome he is. He's well over six feet tall with broad muscular shoulders. His dark hair is a little longer than what I'm used to and in need of a trim. The scruff on his face is the same. I put my book down when he sits on the couch next to me. The fact he doesn't offer any type of physical contact immediately puts me on edge, raising my hackles because we're always affectionate with each other.*

*"What's wrong, babe?" I ask. He looks down at his hands, which I notice he's wringing together, and hesitates before answering, as if he doesn't know where to start.*

*"I'm leaving, Sunshine," he says before meeting my eyes. His usually cheerful features are dull, those clear blue eyes darkening to the color of slate. I've always called his eyes 'mood eyes' and this grey blue color immediately says sadness to me.*

"*Where are we going?*" *I ask.*

"*Not we. Just me.*"

"*What do you mean? Where are you going?*" *My voice trembles, emotion climbing my throat.*

"*I joined the military. The Army,*" *he tells me almost robotically, and my entire world starts spinning.*

"*I'm going to need a second to absorb what it is that you just said because I can't possibly have heard you right. How can you walk away from your job? It's all you've ever wanted? And what about us?*"

"*This past year has changed everything, Lyla.*"

"*Yeah, I'd say that's an understatement. Losing my best friend has been nothing short of traumatic, but what does that have to do with us?*"

"*I need some space, some distance from Sandpiper.*"

"*Space? Where is this coming from?*" *I ask, my eyes blinking hard as I try to make sense of his words.*

"*It's just something I have to do, Lyla. Navigating this loss with you, seeing how it's broken you... It's brought up some shit for me that I haven't dealt with in a long time. I don't think I can deal with it here. I just... I just need to go.*"

*I can't stop the tears that run down my face. The couch shifts as he stands up and for a second I think he's just going to walk out on me. Instead he kneels down in front of me. His hands squeeze my thighs before he moves them to my face. He cups my chin in his hands, using his fingers to wipe my tears away. "I love you, Sunshine. I always will, but I need to do this. I don't want you to sit around and wait for me." He leans forward and kisses me hard. When he pulls back, I look at his face. He's not crying, but the expression on his face is one of utter devastation. There's a broken-ness in his eyes. Something I don't quite understand since he's the one ending things. He runs a trembling hand through his hair and leans forward to kiss me again. When he leans back on his heels, he studies my face, as if he's taking a mental picture of it, before he stands up.*

*I want to beg him to stay, but I can't even formulate the words to do so. I've never begged for anything in my life, and I'm not about to start now. My eyes narrow as I stare him down. I feel my nostrils flare in anger. I'm fucking livid that he's pulling the rug out from under me, under us. I love this man with every fiber of my being. I have for almost ten years, and now, he's leaving.*

My heart slams in my chest as I think about how hurt I was when he left. After serving four years, he came back to our hometown and picked up where he left off as a police officer.

Liv dying changed me, but Theo leaving broke me, and it took years to piece myself back together. Even now, there are days I feel like I'm hanging on by a thread.

Frustrated at my seemingly out-of-control emotions, I give myself one more song to sulk before getting up. I throw on a pair of jean shorts with a fitted tank and grab a light button down to wear over it. After I finish getting ready, I head into the kitchen.

My mom is still in the kitchen when I walk in and refill my coffee mug. She grabs a plate of pancakes out of the warming drawer by the stove. "Your dad saved you some," she says as she places my pancakes on the table where I usually sit. My stomach growls the second I get a whiff of the food. "How was your run?" she asks.

I sit down and start eating. "It was fine. Nothing eventful. If you're hoping that forcing Theo to run with me every morning will make me hate him a little less, I'm sorry to disappoint you, but it's not happening."

"You and I both know you don't hate that man. I know he

hurt you, but you two share a connection that is a rarity. He owes you a hell of an explanation and an apology for leaving you. And if that's not enough for you, if it doesn't make up for the hurt, that's okay. Maybe you'll finally gain closure and be able to move on, *truly* move on. But even after all this time, that man still looks at you like you hung the moon. It reminds me of the way your father looked at me when we were young and still does," my mom says, her voice full of compassion.

I look up, and immediately feel at ease when I catch the tender expression on her face. With her natural tan and light brown hair pulled into a low ponytail, my mom is stunning. Her cheeks are a dusty pink, the color of the blush she's worn since I was a little girl. It's the same blush I've worn since the day I was allowed to start wearing makeup. Faint wrinkles have started to make an appearance around her eyes when she smiles. Those blue eyes that Derek and Colin both have are what really showcase her compassion. One look alone can make someone feel included and accepted. Seen. It's her unyielding compassion that always made her a great nurse. It's part of what makes her an amazing mother.

"Mom, stop. He's only going with me because Dad has him convinced I'm in some sort of danger. He's doing his boss and best friend a favor." I say the words but after the way he looked at me today, like he could see into the depths of my soul, I'm not sure I buy them. "Enough about Theo."

"What's that about Theo?" Dad asks as he comes back into the kitchen dressed in his uniform of a SCPD polo shirt and work pants, gun and badge at his hip.

"Nothing, Dad. I was just letting Mom know that it was an uneventful morning, and there is really no need for me to have an escort."

"Lyla, I can't tell you how nice it was to wake up and enjoy my coffee without worrying about you. Besides, Theo doesn't mind." He kisses me on the head before saying goodbye to my mom. "Bye, love. Have a great day," he says as he wraps his arms around her. He whispers something in her ear that makes her laugh and gives her a long kiss on the lips. I'm pretty sure he squeezes her ass, too. I nearly throw up all the pancakes I just ate.

"I need to move out. I can't handle this lovey-dovey shit at this hour."

Mom completely ignores my complaint. "What's your plan for the day? I was thinking of taking a pilates class at ten." My mom works at the hospital but recently scaled her hours back to more of a part-time schedule.

"You could have told me that before I showered."

"If you would have sat down for breakfast with us instead of rushing off to your room like the cowardly lion I would have," she shoots back at me.

"Fair enough," I mutter, pushing my plate away. "I have to make a dent in an article I'm working on and respond to a few emails but maybe we can go to Morning Current for a coffee later?" I'm positively addicted to their coconut cold brew.

"It's a date," she says with a smile. I finish eating, clean up after myself, and head back to my room to grab my laptop. My parents have a kick-ass screened-in porch that is my favorite room to work in, so I head out there and prepare to dig into my assignment, but my mind keeps wandering to my new running partner.

I think about throwing in the towel with running altogether and just sticking to working out at the house—and yoga and pilates with my mom—but nothing clears my head quite like hitting the pavement and getting lost in my stride.

Seeing him everyday is going to be a problem. I have to shut this shit down quickly before I do something I'll regret. This might require bribing Colin to run with me. Better yet,

Derek is a morning person and he hates Theo, so he might be easier to guilt trip. I reach for my phone to send a quick text, but instead of texting either of my brothers, I send a message to Theo. Apparently, I like playing Russian roulette with my emotions.

**Me: The only reason I run at five is so I can avoid human contact, but since I'm stuck with you, we might as well push it back an hour.**

**Theo: Six it is, Sunshine.**

## FOUR

*theo*

WALKING INTO MY HOUSE, I let out a sigh and throw my keys on the counter with my phone. I sat in my car in front of Lyla's house trying to collect myself for longer than I should have, and I need to get my ass moving. I strip as I walk down the hallway to the bathroom and turn on the water. I'm keyed up for a lot of reasons, and they all have to do with her.

Getting to touch her today, even if only for a second and to keep her from falling on her face, has me more worked up than anticipated. Her skin was warm and flawless. That small touch alone ignited something deep inside of me. It was like a fuse was lit inside of me and it had my body humming. It damn near killed me to let go.

A cold shower is an absolute necessity at this point, so I quickly jump in, resisting the urge to fuck my hand even though her body in those workout clothes is the first thing that comes to mind when I close my eyes under the water.

I'm also frustrated as hell. Not with her—I don't blame her for keeping me at arm's length. More so at myself for giving her enough reason to keep me there. I don't think she said more than twenty words to me this morning, but I knew she wasn't going to greet me with open arms and let me waltz back into her life. I wanted to break the ice and get the conversation going, but I was afraid she'd ignore me. So, here I am, once again being the coward.

I need to take this slow. Spending time with her, in any capacity, is an improvement from where we've been, even if she was less than thrilled about it. I need to let her warm up to being around me again before I try to initiate more conversation. I owe it to her to respect her space.

I'm glad I was with her, though. Knowing she's been doing it solo the past couple of weeks has me grinding my teeth. That old, jittery tension that I felt when I was on a deployment is back and it has my body tight, on alert. That feeling of impending doom, like you know shit's about to go off but you have no idea when or why. My fear of losing her, the way my dad lost my mom, has never faded from my mind. Even when I was overseas, I was more worried about her than I was myself.

After I finish up in the bathroom, I throw on plain clothes, grab my gun and badge, and head back into the kitchen. Diego peels his lazy feline ass off my bed and follows me, meowing for attention. I reach down to scoop him up, and he purrs for approximately seven seconds before he starts swatting and biting at my hands. "Don't be such an asshole. I promise I had a good reason for leaving you this morning."

I set him down and give him a few treats from the jar. To say this cat is food motivated would be an understatement. When I pick up my phone, I see a few messages, but the one from Lyla is the only one I'm interested in. Even though there's nothing overly friendly about it, I still can't help but smile. I miss the natural banter we always had, but this is the first time my phone has lit up with a message from her in years. I quickly reply, give Diego one more scratch behind the ears, and head back out the door.

I get into my unmarked police car and shoot Colin a text that I'm on my way. Since I'm fairly certain he brought a woman home last night, I probably should have given him more of a warning that I was en route, but considering he's allergic to commitment, he probably asked her to leave an hour ago.

As predicted, his SUV is alone in the driveway when I pull up, and he's coming out the front door within seconds.

He climbs into the car, gives me a once over as he puts on his seat belt and says, "You're alive. No claw marks down your face. I assume your balls are still attached to your body, too. Glad to see my sister didn't do any damage this morning."

"I wouldn't say she was happy to see me, but she didn't rip my head off, either, so I'm calling it a win. I told her I'd be there again tomorrow, so you're off the hook for at least another day."

"Yeah, I bet you're really upset about having to see her again."

"After this morning, I'm surprised it's taken your dad this long to get someone to escort her."

"I didn't realize she was doing it so often, otherwise I would have joined her. She conveniently leaves that information out when we talk during our hikes," Colin says. Unlike his brother and sister, Colin is not a beach lover. He's not opposed to spending a few hours there, but he has to be doing something the entire time. He prefers walking and hiking trails. Despite being surrounded by water on three sides, the Cape still manages to offer plenty of those. I know he and Lyla try to get out at least once or twice a week for some quality sibling time.

"I know she hikes with you, but what else has she been up to since she's been home?" I nervously ask, running a hand through my hair as if smoothing my wet head will sooth my nerves.

"She lays pretty low. Hangs with my mom. She and Derek will go fishing or to the beach. She's been doing some writing, and her nose is always in a book. Her closest friend is Quinn, but she's in Vermont so it's not like she's around to force Lyla to be social. On the rare occasion she goes out, she doesn't take anyone up on their offers for drinks or dancing, and dudes have asked. Derek would probably know better than me. I'm sure he would love to sit down and chat with you," he says with a smirk.

There's not a snowball's chance in hell Derek will talk to me. I actually have a better shot at getting Lyla to sit down with me. He might have helped me work on a huge home project, but I think that has more to do with his inability to turn down a good renovation for his portfolio than helping me out of the goodness of his own heart. The dude could power a small country with the hate he has for me. When he finds out I'm running with his sister, he'll make it a point to get to her house before I do just to spite me.

"I think it's good your dad is locking things down a little bit. In the minimal words she said to me this morning, she claimed everyone was overreacting, but she definitely looked over her shoulder a few times during our run and nearly jumped out of her skin before she recognized it was me in the driveway. I know Hollman is bad news because we've busted guys that are attached to him before."

My stomach twists into knots. It does this every time I think of Lyla being in danger. When I read through her exposé for the first time, I felt a tremendous amount of pride in her.

She might not be mine on paper or in any real capacity, but she's still the love of my life.

The fact that she wrote such an impressive investigative piece was damn inspiring, but that pride turned to terror really fucking quickly when I absorbed the depth of her investigation and just how much she exposed Marcus Hollman and his entire enterprise. Because he made himself out to be a good guy, it was really only those in law enforcement who knew what a bad motherfucker he is.

I think the attack on her in Vermont took a solid ten years off of my life, and I didn't get a good night's sleep until she moved back to her parents' house. Being that close to actually losing her, despite the fact that she isn't mine anymore, had me breaking down. I won't say that I was sobbing into my pillow, but there were definitely a few tears of frustration and fear shed when I was alone dealing with my own thoughts. Her being in true danger has brought those fears that had me running in the first place back to the forefront of my mind, which only adds to the coiled tension that has been constantly running through my muscles. I shake my head a few times to center myself and listen intently when Colin responds.

The playfulness that was in his tone just a few seconds ago dissipates when he responds. His tone is serious, which has me cracking my knuckles. "I wish the feds took it more seriously. They seem to think that since she's not a witness to the case, and therefore not testifying at his upcoming trial, she's not in harm's way. But anyone in law enforcement knows how these guys work. She's the reason he got pinched in the first place. They've assured my dad that they haven't heard any chatter about her, but there is definitely room for concern."

"You or Derek think about staying at their house for a while? Just for an added layer of security and extra piece of mind?"

"I brought it up, but Derek pointed out that it would probably piss Lyla off and make her feel all sorts of guilty. The last thing we want is for her to start talking about moving out. That's part of the reason my dad is so set on someone running with her instead of trying to tell her she can't do it at all. I think he's having a hard time balancing wanting to make sure she's safe but still letting her do her own thing. Until the trial is over, and Hollman is presumably found guilty, he doesn't want to do anything that will push her too far," he replies.

"That's a good point. Well, I'm happy to run with her every morning if I need to." For more than just her safety. I'll take any opportunity I can to breathe the same air as her.

"Yeah, I bet you are," Colin says with a smirk.

As we get to the station, I know I have to get my shit together for the day. I park and walk in with Colin. I dump my gym bag under my desk, grab my mug, and go into the kitchen to fill it with coffee. I notice Chief's door is open, so I pop my head in to say good morning. "All good, sir? Oh, and thanks for the pancakes."

"No problem, Theo. I know she doesn't make it easy on you. Breakfast was the least I could do."

A small laugh escapes me. "There's not one part of me that thought she would."

"Well, you know what they say—anything worth having isn't easily gotten. Or some shit like that." His phone rings, and he gives me a nod, casually dismissing me.

I head back to my desk and soak in the energy. The space is buzzing with gossip and updates of anything that happened overnight. Sandpiper is a decent-sized town with just enough action to keep us busy. Mostly, it's small-town crime, but it gets busier in the summer with the influx of tourists. We're close enough to some of the bigger towns on the Cape that their drugs and crime slip through. We stay busy even in the shoulder season, and I fucking love it. I've wanted to be a cop since I was seven-years-old. Graduating from the police academy was one of the best days of my life.

I worked for three years before enlisting in the Army, then came back to work as a detective. Our schedule is pretty flexible. We work a loose day-shift schedule but are pretty much always on call depending on where we are in the rotation. Having Colin as my partner is just the icing on the cake. Most people wouldn't be able to spend this much time with their best friend without wanting to kill each other—that's not saying we aren't at each other's throats now and again—but it's always fun, and I know no one on this planet has my back more than him.

After spending a couple of hours at our desks getting caught up on reports, I get antsy. "I can't sit here for another minute. Let's go lift," I say to Colin. His attention span is way shorter than mine, and he can't jump out of his chair fast enough. I grab my gym bag and head into the locker room to change. One thing that Chief Sullivan did when he stepped into the role was secure the funding to upgrade the gym we have in the basement of our building.

It's so well-equipped there's no need to go anywhere else to work out. Colin has been badgering him to figure out a way to get a sauna, too. He's constantly sending him research about the benefits it has on the mind and body. It wouldn't surprise me if one shows up soon.

We're about halfway through when Colin says, "You're quiet today. What's up? My sister in your head already?"

"Your sister is always in my head. I know it's fucked up of me to say that to you, but I can't help it. All I've wanted for years was an in. A way to get back into her life, and now that I finally have one, and I don't know what to do. The reason I'm getting to spend time with her at all is shit, and she's so closed off. I know it's my own fault, but fuck bro, I just want to fix things." Colin stares at me, and I have no idea what to expect when he opens his mouth.

"She doesn't trust you, Theo. You need to earn that trust back, but I have no idea how you do that. I've never fucked up as badly as you have when it comes to a woman." This elicits a laugh from me. He looks at me with a straight face and his voice drops to a lower tone when he says, "But in the words of the great Dominic Toretto from the OG *Fast and Furious* movie, 'You break her heart, I'll break your neck.' And if it's not me, it sure as shit will be Derek. Unless you're 110 percent sure you want to be with her again, and it's not just an itch to scratch, back the fuck off. She won't survive another broken heart from you. And you won't survive it, either."

"I've never not been in love with her, Colin. Why do you think I've never dated or been with anyone else?"

"Well then, figure your shit out. Fix it. And with Derek, too. You guys have bad energy when you're together, and it's a real pain in the ass."

"Don't look at me. I've tried to bury the hatchet with him dozens of times over the years. Everytime I think we make progress, he gets pissed at me all over again. I thought working on the cottage together would help, but that was just temporary."

"Well, try harder. I can't even entertain the idea of being in a serious relationship. What if she wants to get married? I can't get married because I have two best men and they hate each other. So, really, now that I think about it, my inability to commit is your fault. Wow. Who needs a therapist to figure shit out? I'm a genius."

I shake my head and laugh. "Your parents have arguably one of the best marriages on the planet. They're like something out of a family sitcom. How are you not influenced by that even a little bit? Especially at our age?"

"You talk like we're pushing fifty or something. We're thirty-two. I still have plenty of one-night stands ahead of me before I have to think about really settling down. We're not all like you, bro. We don't all meet our soulmates as kids. Some of us have to wait a bit longer."

"Wait, you mean to tell me that you, Mr. One Night Stand, Mr. Allergic to Commitment, believes in soulmates?" I ask incredulously. I definitely didn't see this coming.

He gets serious again. "Yeah. You can't be raised by my parents and not believe in soulmates. Just because I don't want to be tied down by one woman right now doesn't mean I don't want it in the future. I'm aware of how lucky I am to have parents who are so rock solid. I want that someday— a woman to worship and take care of. A family. Anyway, are you going to add a few more plates to the bar for bench press, or are you going to pussy out again?"

We settle into our usual ball busting for a bit. He tells me of his plans to hit up one of his favorite trails in nearby Wellfleet this weekend, and we brainstorm about a case that's been hanging over our heads for a few weeks now while we finish working out.

The rest of the day passes fairly quickly. We have a few cases, small petty crimes, we wrap up.

It's around four thirty when we get ready to bounce for the day. Colin comes out of his dad's office as I'm returning from the bathroom. "I'm going to go to my parents for dinner and a few beers. You want to come?"

"Hell yes, I want to come. You think Lyla will throw a plate at my head if she sees me sitting at the table?"

"She and my mom won't be home. Girl's dinner or something like that, so my mom left us with steaks to dull the pain of my dad having to fend for himself."

"I'm in." I love going to the Sullivan house. When Lyla and I first ended, my relationship with her parents was strained—understandably so. Opening up to Lori before that first deployment was a huge step in mending my relationship with them, but it wasn't until Lyla got her spunk back that they warmed back up to me fully.

Years ago, Lori figured out how to perfectly blend being a maternal figure for me while trying not to take the place of my mom. When I was a kid, she was nurturing, would cheer for me just as loud as she would for her own boys at games. She included my dad and me in their holiday plans. Hell, I still put her down as my emergency contact when I fill out any kind of form.

I'm grateful that I was able to rebuild my relationships with most of the Sullivans, but I won't give up until I've figured out a way to mend the most important one.

I drop Colin off at his house and then stop home to shower and feed Diego. After stopping at the store to pick up a few six-packs of beer I make my way to the Sullivan house.

Dinner's uneventful. Derek isn't exactly happy to see me, but we manage to get through the night without any fists flying and with just a few snide remarks from him along the way. I know better than to think he's finally getting over his issues with me, but it's always a nicer meal when he refrains from shooting me dirty looks.

I'm far from a pushover and have no problem dealing with conflict head-on, but for some reason, I always give Derek a pass. I know damn well the reason is Lyla. Getting into a fight with Derek is not something that'll help me get back into her good graces. There's a small part of me that appreciates what an asshole he is when it comes to Lyla. All the men in the Sullivan family are protective of her, but Derek especially so.

We stay outside after dinner and Colin gets a fire going. We have a few beers while we wait for the Red Sox game to start. We're all lounging comfortably in the chairs that surround the firepit.

"Dad, what's going on with Lyla? She was pissing and moaning about you giving her a hard time when it comes to running," Derek says, effectively killing the relaxed vibe that was present just a few seconds ago.

"What's going on is she's being her usual stubborn self and refusing to acknowledge the danger she's put herself in. I've wrangled Theo and your brother into going with her and keeping her company any time she wants to venture out. I figured you could jump in, too."

Derek immediately stiffens. "Why the hell didn't you come to me first? Just because I'm not a cop doesn't mean I can't help keep her safe."

"Chill, bro. No one is keeping anything from you," Colin interrupts. "Dad literally just talked to us about this yesterday. Theo pounced at the opportunity to be her escort this morning. He jumped out of his seat to volunteer before Dad even finished asking. Didn't even give me a chance to say I would," Colin finishes with a smirk. Derek snaps his head over to look at me, no doubt ready to rip me a new one, but before he can say anything, their dad steps in.

"Jesus, Colin. Can you ever resist stirring shit up between them?" He turns his attention to Derek and says, slightly exasperated, "Derek, I'm not saying you can't keep her safe. Stop that shit. I figured I'd bring you into the loop when you came for dinner tonight and here we are. And for the record, Theo did not push your brother out of the way to volunteer first. You guys are grown men. It's been years since they broke up. Move on. I don't care who it is, but someone needs to be with her each morning with their eyes open, head on a swivel."

"I'll be here tomorrow. What time does she run?" Derek asks.

"I've got her tomorrow. We already agreed on a time," I say, finally entering the conversation.

Derek rolls his eyes. "Of course you do. If you let anything happen to her, I'll kill you. I don't care how much the rest of my family loves you."

Now it's my turn to get defensive. "Screw you for thinking I'd let her get hurt on my watch."

He glares at me. "Just because my parents and Colin forgave you for hurting Lyla, doesn't mean I have to. Take your reasons for leaving and shove them. I made a promise to my sister a long time ago not to kick your ass, but I'd welcome rolling at the gym any time you want to man up."

He takes a long pull from his beer. I contemplate my response. I'm certain I could take Derek in a fistfight, but he would wipe the mats with my ass if we ever rolled jiu-jitsu. I've done it a few times with him and always regret it.

"Enough, you two. This doesn't help the situation at all," Chief says. "Colin, stop egging them on. Derek and Theo, let this shit go. Derek, you seem more pissed off than Lyla, and lord knows your sister can hold a grudge."

My blood starts to boil. I'm not one to bite my tongue or stand down—far from it—but when it comes to Derek, I'm constantly having to keep my thoughts to myself. He knows how much his family means to me and that I would never react in a way that would jeopardize my relationship with them. It would devastate Lori, and Lyla, if things got physical between us.

He knows this and pushes my buttons, anyway. It's a constant battle of wills when we're in the same room. It's only because of Colin that Derek and I hang out. It's almost as if he keeps throwing us together, hoping that we'll just be close again one day.

I may keep myself composed physically, but I'm annoyed enough that it doesn't stop me from finishing my beer, standing, and saying, "Thanks for dinner, Chief. I'm gonna hit the road since I'll be up for another early morning tomorrow with our girl."

I give everyone a nod as they send me a wave. Except for Derek. When I look at him on my way out the door, I wink.

*theo*

I GET to Lyla's house a few minutes before six and am stretching in her driveway when she walks out of the garage door. "Morning, Sunshine," I say with a smile. She rolls her eyes and mutters some semblance of a greeting back at me. "For someone who has never been a morning person, you sure do like to get these runs out of the way early."

"You don't know anything about me anymore, Theo. For all you know, I could love being up before the sun. It might be my most favorite thing ever. Anyway," she huffs, "are you good with five miles today?" she asks as she puts in an earbud.

"You're the boss."

She gives me a nod as we walk to the bottom of the driveway. I don't miss her glancing around and focusing on an empty car in front of a house a few doors down. "You good?" I fight the urge not to come across as overprotective, but I do step in front of her and shield her body with mine.

"Yeah. I just don't recognize that car. Guess I need to improve my neighborhood watch skills." The fact that she even notices the vehicle tells me she's on edge. Most people wouldn't give it a second glance. Then again, most people didn't help expose one of the biggest drug dealers in Massachusetts. I pull out my phone to take a quick picture of the plates. I'll run them at work just to make sure it's nothing to worry about.

It's only the second time we've done this, but we settle into a comfortable pace quickly. I stay a couple of steps behind her so she can lead the way without me cramping her personal space. It also gives me the opportunity to stare at her ass without getting caught. She's wearing bike shorts today, so the view is pretty sweet.

Her ass is firm and muscular, and I have to adjust my shorts a few times to calm my cock down. Her long dark blonde hair is in a high pony tale that swings back and forth as she moves, mesmerizing me. I picture it wrapped around my hand as I gently tug, forcing her to look up at me right before I devour her mouth with mine. I shake the thoughts from my head before they wander off into a territory I can't come back from.

I spent the last twenty-four hours thinking about how I can use this forced proximity situation to my advantage. I know I can't come on too strong with her because she'll turtle into herself, but I miss hearing her snarky comments and her infectious laugh. I miss hearing her voice in general. I have to figure out a way to get her talking more.

So, I fall back on one of her most treasured topics: music. "Favorite Zach Bryan song?" I ask. "I know you've gotta be a fan." When her pace slows down slightly, I know I've peaked her interest.

"'Tourniquet,'" she replies with zero hesitation. "Or 'God Speed.'" She doesn't ask for mine, but I give them anyway.

"'Sun to Me" is my all-time favorite, but 'I Remember Everything' hits me hard." When I first heard 'Sun to Me,' I couldn't screenshot it and send it to her fast enough. She didn't respond, of course, but that song will forever make me think of her.

Lyla scoffs at my answer. "Really? 'I Remember Everything?' You make it seem like you're not the one who walked away," she says cooly as she picks her pace back up. It's her attempt to end the conversation. I grasp at straws to keep it going.

"That's not fair. I'm not the only one who left."

She scoffs. "You left first, but you're right, Theo. I left too because aside from my family, who I love more than anything in this world, there was literally nothing left for me here. My best friend died. The man I was sure I was going to marry left. And my family was walking on eggshells around me. Misery loves company, and I didn't want to keep dragging them down. I left to survive. You leaving was a cowardly way to break up, so with all due respect, get fucked." My lips turn up into a small smile before I can stop myself. She does a double take and her hands ball into fists. "Are you smiling at me? What about this is funny? Why the fuck are you smiling right now?" She stops, hands on her hips while she reams me out, her eyes wild.

"There it is. The spunk I've missed so much. I was wondering when I'd see it again. I almost forgot that you curse like a sailor."

This is the most she's talked to me since she's been back in town for good, and while her words aren't exactly friendly, I'll still take it as a step in the right direction. I push my luck and take a step closer. "I have tickets to his Boston show. Wanna go?" I do not, in fact, have tickets to his concert, but I'm not opposed to selling a kidney to get them if she says yes.

"That's not how this works, Theo. You don't get to waltz back into my life like this. Just because you're appeasing your boss by running with me doesn't mean we're friends." She blows a piece of loose hair out of her face and, for a second, I'm at a loss for words. She's sweaty, her face lit up with irritation, and I can't help but think how beautiful she is.

"Wait a second. I'm not doing this to appease my boss. My boss, *your* father, is worried about you. When he shared his safety concerns with me, it was a no-brainer. I don't care how pissed you are at me. I don't care how much attitude you throw at me or how many f-bombs you drop. Making sure you're safe is the priority, and I will always, *always*, step up in making sure that happens."

She looks at me, her hazel eyes looking like they're on fire. She's biting her lip which means she's nervous or she's weighing what she wants to say. Just when I think she's going to rip into me again she rolls her eyes, turns away, and starts jogging again.

The rest of our run is awkward because we're both pissed off. Lyla increases her pace, probably in an effort to get away from me, and her footfalls are harder than they usually are. Her body is ramrod straight as she runs, her shoulders up by her ears with tension. Meanwhile, I'm a few steps behind, grinding my teeth in frustration, my hands balled into fists.

She's pissed at me for a million justifiable reasons, and I'm annoyed that she'd ever think my concerns are disingenuous. I don't want to stay for breakfast, but I know Lori is anticipating I do. When we finally make our way back to her house, the first thing I notice is the car we saw earlier is gone. As we walk up the driveway, both breathing heavily, Lyla grabs my arm. The fiery look in her eyes is gone. In fact, it looks like all the life in her eyes has been put out. It damn near breaks my heart.

"I don't know how to do this, Theo. I don't know how to be around you. It has taken me years— and a shit ton of therapy —to find myself again. I've worked my ass off to put myself back together. When I'm around you, I feel fragile. There was never an in-between for us. It was always going to be us together forever or one of us heartbroken beyond repair. You chose the latter. You can't undo that now just because it's convenient for you."

My heart beats so fast I can feel it in my throat. "Let me try, Lyla. Just give me a chance to prove it to you. I fucked up. I should have been more open with you back then. I shouldn't have just left the way I did, but I promise I had my reasons. I always thought we'd end up back together. You're the woman I'm supposed to grow old with. The most important person in the world. I will never hurt you again. I promise. Let me back in and give me a chance to prove myself to you. I won't let you down again."

"That's the problem. You keep those reasons so close to the vest that they don't exist to anyone other than you. Years ago, you promised on your life you'd never hurt me. Every note, every email, every card... You signed them all with *on my life.* You held my heart in your hands and swore we'd be together forever. You promised we'd get married on the beach and dance to Ben Folds. We'd grow old here, in our hometown, and watch our grandkids play on Swamprose Beach. You broke those promises, Theo. You broke me, and there's no coming back from that. How can I ever trust you again? How can I trust that you won't walk out on me again?"

I close my eyes for a second, my heart in my throat, and think of all of the plans she just mentioned. She's not yelling at me or talking with her hands. She wears a look of utter defeat. Tears fall silently down her cheeks, and I can't stop myself from wiping them away with my thumbs. I'm honestly surprised she lets me.

I try to gather my thoughts as I hang on to her for dear life. "You aren't fragile. You've never been fragile. You are the love of my life, Lyla. It's always been you. It always will be you, and I intend to prove that to you. I'm not going anywhere. If it takes me the rest of my life, then that's what it takes. On my life." I wipe the last of her tears away and kiss her forehead. "I know you probably want to be alone but not coming in for breakfast is going to raise questions. You tell me what you want me to do here."

As she thinks, a pick-up truck comes down the street and parks in front of her house. I roll my eyes when I see it's Derek.

"I heard Mom was making French toast," he says as he gets out and trails up the lawn. His eyes dart from Lyla to me and then back to Lyla. He spots her watery eyes. "What the fuck, dude?" His voice overflows with venom.

In an attempt to defuse the tension, Lyla says, "Chill, Derek. You want to go inside for breakfast or do you want to go to Hot Bagels and get sandwiches? They should be open by now."

Eyeing me one last time, he says, "I'll drive," before reluctantly turning and heading for his truck. If looks could kill, I would definitely be struck down because, based on his scowl and the stiffness in his shoulders, he's pissed.

I give her shoulder a squeeze and softly say, "Let me know about the concert," before walking into her garage.

## SIX

*Lyla*

DEREK DOESN'T SAY a word to me as we drive. He simply hands me his phone so I can put on whatever song I want. This is typical of him—always silently offering his support but never pushing. I throw on an O.A.R. song and let out a dramatic sigh.

"You good, Ly? Want me to finally kick his ass?" he asks.

"You helped put an end to an intense conversation I'm not even remotely ready for, so thanks for the good timing."

There is so much shit swirling around my head, I can't think straight. Everything Theo just said—him still being in love with me, wanting me back, and wanting a future together has me spinning. But one thing he didn't tell me is why he left in the first place. Until that's a conversation we have, I'm not sure I can even consider a friendship with him.

"Do you want to talk about it?" he asks. His knuckles are white from gripping his steering wheel so tightly. I know he's bothered that I'm upset.

Derek may come across as a tough guy, and he is, but he has the added trait of being a complete empath. Seeing someone else upset or in pain hits him harder than the average person. But while he's actually a teddy bear underneath that broody exterior, he doesn't hesitate using his fists to protect someone he cares about.

"Nope. At least not right now. I need to get my thoughts together. Sorry you're missing out on Mom's French toast. Also, I don't have my wallet so breakfast is on you." He laughs but I continue. "Believe me, I'm not complaining that you're here, but don't you have a job site that requires your presence?" Derek owns his own construction company, and he's made quite the name for himself around the Cape.

"I do, but the boys can handle it until I get there. At dinner last night, Dad updated me on what's going on. You shouldn't be so nonchalant about Hollman, Lyla. He's a serious shitbag, and you really screwed him. Theo mentioned he took on the task of running with you, and I just wanted to check and make sure you were good with that. I should have come ten minutes earlier. I could have clipped him with my truck."

It's my turn to laugh, and it feels really good to be doing it.

"I know you're around him more than you'd like to be. You guys take your boys' nights very seriously. But...what's Theo's deal? Has he dated a lot over the years?" The second I ask the question, I immediately regret it. Derek all but slams on his brakes. "Damn, I didn't think your knuckles could get any whiter, but you really have a death grip on that wheel."

Despite having boyfriends and fuck buddies over the past six years, I know that seeing Theo with another woman would cause me to unravel. Even with years of therapy to work through the bitterness, hurt, and anger, I'm not completely there yet.

Mainly because I'm afraid I'm still hopelessly in love with him. My heart jumps when I see his name pop up on my phone. Without fail, hearing our song stops me in my tracks. Every sunrise and sunset makes me think of him. I close my eyes and try to shut out the thoughts of a future that'll never happen.

"Don't tell me you're going to get back together with him, Ly. I will withhold your bagel sandwich if you tell me that you are."

"First of all, that's not a real threat. I forget my wallet all the time, and they know I'm good for it. Second of all, I'm absolutely *not* getting back together with him. I wouldn't even consider him a friend at this point. I'm just curious to see if his behavior tracks with what he said to me."

"I have the unfortunate luck of being out with him often since our brother refuses to accept the fact that we don't like each other, but no, definitely no girlfriends. He's essentially a monk from what I know. The only constant in his life, besides annoying me by simply existing, is his cat."

My knee jerk reaction is to let out a sigh of relief. Not just because he hasn't had any girlfriends, but more so because it means he was telling the truth. The news settles my heart in a way I don't expect.

"Well, I guess that's good to know. I mean, I haven't exactly been celibate."

"Jesus fucking Christ, Lyla, that is so much more information than I want to know about you. It's bad enough watching guys hit on you when we're out, but that is a visual I do not need to think about when it comes to my sister."

"No one asked you to create that visual in your head, you freak. That's your fault, not mine. Anyway, I have to accept he's still a part of our family's life. To know he's at least been somewhat honest with me about something makes me feel a tiny bit less bitter toward him. Also, he has a cat?"

"Fortunately for you, I'll take the bitterness you no longer feel about him and add it to the ever-growing mountain of dislike that has his name on it." And people say I hold a mean grudge. "But yeah, some stray that was hanging around the station. The cat, Diego, apparently took a liking to him. Didn't get the memo that he's a prick. Theo brought him home a while ago. I'm more of a dog person, but he's a pretty cool cat."

Okay, I'm going to be honest... The idea of Theo having a cat kind of tugs at my heartstrings a little bit. I say nothing about that to Derek. Obviously.

We get to Hot Bagels and order our sandwiches, chatting with the employees while we wait. This is one of the things I love about small towns. We get a lot of seasonal people that come through, but the locals stick together and know each other pretty well, especially those who have lived here for a long time. The amount of joy I get from being a regular at these small shops is almost embarrassing. I didn't realize how much I missed the quirkiness of our beach town until I came back home.

When our sandwiches are ready, we go back to Derek's truck and eat in the parking lot. He tells me about the current project they're working on—a custom build right on the beach a few towns over—and we enjoy our breakfast.

While we eat, Derek tells me all about his latest project. He puts his bagel down and pulls out his phone, swiping from picture to picture so quickly in his excitement, I need to grab the phone and scroll back to see them. While I'm holding the phone, he tells me about some of the features he's included, his hands flailing all over the place as he goes. "You'll have to come check it out. The stonework turned out so well, and the clients are super pumped that we're ahead of schedule."

His enthusiasm is so contagious I can't help but smile, my heart bursting with pride at the work he's done. "I'm so proud of you, Derek. I hope when there are no drug dealers trying to kill me, I can move out of our parents' house and you can renovate the little bungalow I hope to one day own."

"Aww, that's cute, Lyla. But you'll never be able to afford me," he says with a laugh. "Just kidding. I'll give you the family discount."

I reach over to knock his baseball hat off and mess up his hair before we go back to our sandwiches.

We finish our coffees, and Derek dumps our trash before we head home. "I'm going to come in and say hi to Mom and Dad," he says as he parks his truck back in front of their house. Theo's truck is already gone. We walk through the garage and into the kitchen. My mom is at the sink doing dishes while my dad pours a cup of coffee into a travel mug.

"Theo looked a little shell-shocked when he came in here earlier. You must have really done a number on him today," my dad says. He gives me a big smile and pinches my cheek affectionately.

"Chris! We agreed not to say anything to her literally five minutes ago." Mom snaps him with the dish towel. "You just can't help yourself, can you? This is where Colin gets it from."

I roll my eyes but bite my lip to keep from smiling. When I'm not stressing him out, my dad is laid back and playful. He's who Colin gets those traits from. Derek, on the other hand, gets most of my dad's physical features. Tall with dark hair, broad shoulders, and eyelashes I would kill for, my younger brother is a carbon copy of our dad.

"Sorry. You're right. Lyla, forget I said anything. Theo was his normal self and didn't seem at all distracted by whatever conversation you two were having in the driveway before your brother pulled up." When Dad sees Derek behind me he gives him a smile and reaches for another travel mug. "Take some coffee to go and walk out with me, Derek. I want to hear how the project is going. Lyla, thanks for appeasing me with your running buddy. I'm getting much better sleep knowing you're not alone."

Thank god, I didn't actually set Theo up and run before he got here this morning. My dad would have had a coronary. Derek pours his coffee, gives Mom a quick hug, and gets even with me by messing up my hair before walking out the door with my dad.

"Since your dad brought it up," my mom starts. "Theo did look a bit frazzled when he came in. Something happen on that run?"

"We're not friends, Mom. A few mornings of forced proximity isn't going to erase broken promises and dreams."

"You guys were so young when you got together. You had to know there would be growing pains along the way."

I'm about to snap. Being left behind out of the blue is a bit more than growing pains, but she keeps talking before I can interrupt.

"I'm not trying to minimize the heartbreak, Lyla. You're both older now. With age comes wisdom, and the realization that life is short. If you don't have feelings for him anymore, then tell him and allow yourself to move on. Allow yourself to be open to someone new because you deserve that love and you've been holding yourself back from getting into another serious relationship for years. But if you think there's still something there with Theo, maybe think about letting the walls down a little bit, Lyla. My biggest fear, other than that drug dealer wanting you dead is that you're going to let your stubbornness and fears get in the way of your happiness."

I want to make some sort of witty, sarcastic comment, but I literally can't think of one to respond with. My mother always gives the best advice. Liv used to refer to her as her personal therapist and life coach.

"I'll think about it, Mom. I promise, but don't think I don't see what you're doing here."

"What do you mean?" she asks with feigned innocence.

"You bring Theo up every chance you get and give me all sorts of words of wisdom about relationships and true love and second chances. You're like a walking Hallmark Christmas movie," I say, and she laughs.

"I know you have a million things going through your mind, but when you're ready, I'm here. Talk to me. Or talk to Quinn. Let someone in, Lyla."

I wipe my eyes for the second time today, and it's not even 9 a.m.

"I'm off to the hospital for the morning. You're on your own for lunch. Don't burn down the house."

"Don't worry about me. I'll find something to entertain myself. Love you."

She says goodbye, and I head back to my room to grab my laptop and notebook, firing off a text to Quinn as I go.

**Me: Hey, QB! Desperate need of a Facetime date tonight. You free?**

**Quinn: I'll clear my schedule. What time and what are we drinking?**

**Me: 8? And it feels like a whiskey kind of night.**

**Quinn: Shit, girl, this must be serious. Gotta run! Class is coming in. TTYL**

I get myself settled on the porch, fire up a playlist that I know will help me focus, and attempt to put the finishing touches on my work. I stare at the screen with my mind a million miles away for I don't even know how long. I snap back to reality when I hear the beginning of a Zach Bryan song start. Without even thinking about it, I pick up my phone to text Theo.

**Me: If the offer still stands, I'm in for the concert.**

# SEVEN

*Lyla*

"HEY, GIRL, HEY!" Quinn says, and I can't help but smile as her face pops up on my screen. I miss her like crazy but because I don't want to bring any possible danger to her, Facetime has been our way of getting together. She has a goblet filled with ice cubes and whiskey and holds it up to cheers me through our screens.

Petite with long chestnut hair and dark brown eyes, she's absolutely gorgeous. She's also one of the kindest, most sincere people I've ever met. Without even trying she commands the attention of every room she's in and can make me laugh until I cry. Today though, my eyes immediately zero in on a bruise on her forearm.

"What's that?" I ask her, pointing to my arm before I take a sip of my Knob Creek.

"Oh, it's nothing," Quinn says as she pulls her shirt sleeve down. "I was working in my classroom and banged it into a cabinet."

I don't like the way she avoids eye contact when she says it and I eat a handful of gummy bears from the bag I just opened to buy me some time to decide what I want to say next.

"Is everything good, QB? Everything okay with Justin?" They've been dating for about a year now, but I've always felt like he dulls her light and tries to control too much of her life. He used to give her a hard time about happy hours if he couldn't make them and expected her to show up at every single game when he was coaching.

"Yeah, everything's fine. Besides, we're here to talk about you and that sexy ex of yours." She's obviously trying to change the subject, and I won't press her right now, but I file this in the back of my mind to keep an eye on. If Justin is putting his hands on her, I will drive my ass to Vermont and deal with him myself. "So what's up? You've spent the last two mornings with him. How's that going? How does he look? Any more tattoos? Is the spark still there? Do you talk on these runs? Don't tell me you just put an episode of Dateline on and ignore him."

I'm fairly certain she'll keep firing off questions if I don't interrupt her. "QB, that's a lot of questions you just ran through. Take a sip and calm yourself down. It's actually unfair how well he's aged. More ink than the last time I saw him and that only adds to his appeal. He has one on his quad now that I can't get a good look at and my curiosity is killing me. Of course I went with Dateline. There's nothing as soothing as Keith Morrison's voice. You know that. Switched halfway through, though."

"Okay, okay. What's it like being around him again after all this time?" She seems infinitely more relaxed now that the conversation isn't about her.

I take another sip of my whiskey to buy myself time, because when I think about it, I don't really know how to answer. "It's...a lot. I feel like I'm juggling a lot of emotions being around him. I'm annoyed at his presence. I'm pissed off that he can be so seemingly normal around me after everything that's happened. Mostly, I'm sad. Sad over everything we had and everything we lost." Quinn nods her head in understanding, compassion in her eyes. "And then I get mad again and the cycle continues. My runs don't feel quite so relaxing right now. It also doesn't help that I'm wildly attracted to him."

"What happened this morning that has us drinking whiskey in our jammies at 8 p.m. on a Friday night?"

"I told him I don't know how to act around him. That I can't trust him. Next thing I know, he's confessing that he's still in love with. He told me he'd do anything to earn my trust back. Then he wiped my tears away like we were in some kind of a fucking romance novel."

Quinn's jaw drops.

"Wow. Okay, well, I can see why you picked whiskey, then. What happened after that?"

"Nothing. Derek pulled up. Thank God, because I still don't know what I would have said."

She taps her nails on her glass, which she always does when she's deep in thought. "Do you still have feelings for him?"

"I don't think I ever stopped, QB. But I'm not ready to admit that to anyone else yet." I take a sip while I wait for her to respond. Quinn is sensible and methodical in everything she does.

"Well, then this is a safe way to explore those feelings. To dip your toes in the water. It's limited contact on your terms. You don't want to see him, then don't go for a run that day. He has the opportunity to grovel, and when you're ready—*if* you're ready—to have a conversation, you can turn off the music and talk. Either way, the ball is in your court. And the bonus is that you have someone to look out for you when you're out there," she says.

"That's some pretty solid advice," I say, nodding my head, because the more I think about what she just said, the more I like her outlook.

"You ever think about telling him how you wrote to him when he was overseas?"

"Nope," I say, with a pop on the P. Quinn is the only person I've ever told about the letters.

"Maybe one day you'll feel ready."

I grab another handful of gummy bears and shrug my shoulders.

"Doubtful. They're too raw. Too personal. The early ones are too mean."

She laughs in response. "Oh, based on how much of a magician you are with words, I can only imagine how you torched his ass in those letters." She sips her drink. "So, tell me what else is going on? You keeping busy?"

"I'm trying. I have a handful of freelance articles I'm finishing up in the next few weeks. I think I need a break from it. I need more direction and stability."

"How about subbing at a school out there? Or getting back into teaching in general?"

I shake my head, nixing both of those ideas.

"Teaching isn't my path anymore. I'm okay with that, but I just need to figure out what this new path is. This Hollman shit hanging over my head has me feeling like I'm in purgatory. I fear it won't go away until he goes to trial and gets convicted. Then we'll know he's in prison for life."

"When is the trial supposed to start?"

"I'm actually not entirely sure. Later this winter is the last I heard," I reply. "I'll figure my shit out eventually. Until then, I'll just be squatting at my parents' house."

"Your brothers keeping you entertained?" she asks.

"You know it. Colin's taking me to Wellfleet tomorrow to

go for a hike. We try and get out once a week. Derek has been swamped with work, but we do our *Love is Blind* nights. I'm working on convincing Kristin, the owner of the local bookshop, to let me start a book club that would meet weekly at the shop after-hours."

"Look at you!"

"Your school year is off to a good start?" I ask as I drain the rest of my drink. "Wait, hold your thought. I'm going to grab more." I rush out to the kitchen and am back in front of my computer less than a minute later. I nod at her to continue.

"Yup. I have some great kids. A few who are already tugging at my heartstrings."

"Which is exactly why you got into teaching. To reach those kids. They're lucky to have you, QB. How are things at the outreach center?" Quinn's job might be teaching, but volunteering at the local outreach center for at-risk youth is her passion.

"Busy. Never enough money to go around for all of the initiatives I want to get up and running, but we're adding a few new ones this fall."

"Proud of you, QB. You give so much of yourself to that center."

She smiles and a blush creeps up her neck. She's not one to enjoy being the center of attention or getting complimented. It's almost like she doesn't know how to accept them so it's no surprise she changes the subject.

"I miss your margaritas, Lyla. Haven't had a good one since you left me."

"Hah. Well, come visit me as soon as the dust settles and I'll make you as many as you'd like." Her eyes perk up at the idea.

"Deal."

We chat for a few more minutes before saying goodbye. I

miss our girls nights, but these video calls do a great job of keeping us connected.

I bring my glass into the kitchen and join my parents in the family room for a little before finally making my way to my room. Theo was right this morning when he said I was never a morning person. These early runs definitely make for early bedtimes.

*  *  *

It's after ten in the morning by the time Colin shows up at my parents' house. He sits at the table for a cup of coffee before we head out. It's a perfect September day in Sandpiper. Warm, but not muggy, with blue skies and sunshine.

We hit some traffic so the drive to Wellfleet takes a good thirty minutes, but the trail is worth the drive. It's a five-mile hike that offers a mix of shady, wooded areas and open spots that show off the picturesque water views.

We fall into easy conversation as we walk. I ask him about his dating life, to which he playfully responds, "Lyla, I'm far too young to be settling down already. Give me another ten years before you ask me to get wifed up."

I roll my eyes and laugh in response.

"You happy to be back in Sandpiper?" he asks.

"Overall, yes. I'm glad to be around you, Derek, and Mom and Dad. I love being close to the water again. There's something so comforting about being back in this town where everyone looks out for each other. It's not without its downsides, though."

"Do you think you would have moved back here if it wasn't for the shitstorm you started?" he asks, and I'm shocked he opts not to bring up Theo.

"I do. The Hollman thing might have given me the kick in

the ass a little sooner than I had planned, but I think it would have happened within the next year, anyway."

"Were you getting bored?"

"Not bored, just stagnant. I'm ready to move on from freelance and subbing. Find something that feels more productive and consistent. Between us, Vermont is just a little too granola-y for me. Too much hippie stuff. Lots of tie dye, crystals, and talk about Mercury being in retrograde."

He laughs. "Mercury in what?" He puts his hand up as if to wave off the question. "I don't even want to know. Well, as much as I'd prefer your safety wasn't at risk, it's damn nice to have you back. Just promise you won't move out on your own until after Hollman is in prison for good."

"Okay, Dad," I say in a mocking tone.

An hour later, we're back at his truck, debating what we want to do next.

"Let's go visit Derek. He's at that job site he's been talking nonstop about today. Let's get smoothies and surprise him," I suggest. Colin is all in, so that's exactly what we do.

When we pull up to the site, smoothies in hand, a huge smile spreads across Derek's face when he spots us. He takes his hat off, wipes the sweat from his brow, and puts it back on. "What are you clowns doing here?"

"Figured it was time we cramped your style and saw what you've been doing with all your time these days." I hand him his smoothie and look around. The house is, well, it's fucking beautiful. "Damn, Derek. This is gorgeous!" It's huge, with cedar siding and a beautiful wood and stained glass front door.

"Come on, I'll show you guys around." Derek spends the next half hour walking us through the property. We *ooh* and *ahh* the entire time.

"I gotta say, bro, this is really impressive. Too bad it's out of my budget," Colin says, slapping Derek on the back.

"Hah. Mine, too," Derek says, pride written all over his face.

Eventually, we say our goodbyes, and Colin and I head back home. He drops me off, but not before informing me that he's going out tonight and will, under no circumstances, be waking up early to hit up any trails tomorrow.

The rest of my weekend passes quickly, though it's not like weekends are much different than weekdays in my world right now. Theo sends me a text on Sunday night, confirming a 6 a.m. run time. I give him a simple thumbs-up in response.

I get into bed, thinking sleep will come easy after helping my dad with yard work all day, but I toss and turn for an hour. I try a bedtime meditation with zero success and eventually sit up and let out an exasperated sigh. I stare at my closet, trying to decide if I want to play Russian roulette with my emotions or not.

Since sleep feels a million miles away, I get out of bed and walk over to the door. On the top shelf, tucked underneath my sweatshirts, is a sneaker box I reach for and pull down. I don't climb back into bed. Instead, I sink down to the floor, my back against the wall as I hold the box in my lap.

When Theo was overseas, he wrote me emails. Much like the texts he continued to send when he returned to Sandpiper. They were proof-of-life messages, pictures of the sky, and song lyrics. Despite my conflicted feelings toward him, they always meant the world to me.

I needed a hard copy of them, in case something happened to him when he was deployed. The pages are all worn, showing that I've been through the contents of the box a time or two, and they're numbered based on the order he sent them. I pull one out randomly and see that it's number thirty-three—from his first deployment.

. . .

Sunshine,

Read *The Terminal List.* It's a political thriller you'd love. Heard they're turning it into a show. More stars than you could imagine out here.

OML,

Theo

Attached is a photo of an endless sea of stars. Tears stain the page. His way of saying he was okay and keeping some sort of a tether between us, even if I never wrote back or acknowledged them. Every email was signed "OML" as if writing out *On My Life* was too painful.

I return the paper to the box, resisting the urge to take another one out, and lean my head back against the wall. I knew what would happen when I moved back to Sandpiper. I knew it would open the door to seeing Theo again but hearing his words today still threw me off-kilter.

Eventually, I reach back in and pull out another piece of paper, this one pink. It's an email I wrote but never sent, something my therapist suggested I do. They're numbered as well, and I leaf through until I find number one.

Theo,

They say that love and hate are different sides of the same coin. They also say that hatred is not the absence of love, but the destruction of it. But me? I say that I love you *and* hate you. I'm constantly bouncing between the two. I want to throw you off a cliff and then run down and catch you. Today, I'm leaning more toward hate. I hate that you ruined us—ruined me. I hate that you ruined me for every other man. I hate that you wanted to get away from me so badly you put yourself in danger. I hate doing life without you. But most of all right now, I just really hate *you*.

    Lyla


I cringe, knowing that all my letters in the beginning were laced with so much fury. I put it back in the box and glance at the clock. It's after midnight now. I put the box away, burying it back under my clothes as if they'll serve as some sort of forcefield to keep me from thinking about them and crawl back into bed.

*theo*

A NIGHTMARE WAKES ME UP, and when I look at my clock, it's just a few minutes before my alarm is set to go off. I rub the sleep out of my eyes, trying to forget about the dream that just woke me up.

You'd think it would be the horrors of war, or even some of the dark shit I've seen at work, that has me waking in terror, but it's not. It's about Lyla. About having her back and then losing her.

They're the straw that broke the camel's back all those years ago. These dreams that paralyzed me with the terror of losing her. I remind myself that she's still here, in the flesh, and that I need to get moving so I can keep her safe.

I leave my lazy cat sleeping in bed, get dressed, and hit the bathroom before making my way into the kitchen. After eating a banana, I grab my keys and head out to my car. The drive is short, and I'm there before I know it. Lyla must have been watching for me because she comes out as soon as I pull up to the curb. "Morning, Sunshine," I greet.

"Morning," she says, looking me in the eyes. I have to keep

my knees from buckling in surprise because it's the first time she's spoken to me without looking sad or spitting venom.

I give her a smile as I do a quick stretch.

"I'm going to yoga with my mom later, so I'm thinking we do five again today."

"I'm at your service, Lyla. If you wanna do five, five it is."

She gives me a small smile and puts her earbuds in. I let her set the pace and lead the way like usual, and we cruise down the desolate streets. Eventually, we end up by the water, and a quick glance at my watch—and the sky—confirms the sun will be rising in just a few minutes.

"Hey," I call, loud enough so she can hear me. She stops and pulls an earbud out, looking around with panic in her eyes. A wave of guilt passes through me that I startled her. I resist the urge to pull her close and rub her arms in comfort.

"Hey," I say again, softly this time. "I didn't mean to startle you. Just wanted to see if you wanted to take a break so we could watch the sunrise. Should be in just a couple minutes." Her shoulders tense as she quickly scans her surroundings before settling her eyes on mine. "You good, Sunshine?"

She nods her head a few times, as if she's trying to convince the both of us. "Yeah, let's sit down and watch the sunrise. Sky is clear so it should be good."

I follow her over to one of the benches, and we sit down. I kick my legs out, crossing one ankle over the other, and lean back, stretching my arms out over the back of the bench.

I'm careful not to make contact. Even though I'm crawling out of my skin with the need to touch her, I wouldn't dare do that intentionally at this point.

"You comfy?" she asks pointedly.

I look over, immediately distracted by her hazel eyes. She always used to talk about mine and how the color changed with my mood but would never believe me when I said the same about hers. They're more of a green today with honeyed flecks. When she's angry, that golden hue looks like it's on fire. They're the eyes I've seen the most from her as of late. On that beach last year. And when she ripped me a new one the other day. Today, though, they're earthy and calm.

"Yup," I say with a grin.

The left side of her mouth tips up into the smallest smile. It's so quick I almost miss it, and my heart skips a beat. Together, we watch the sun come up over the horizon, the sky going from a deep blue to a golden orange reflecting on the ocean. There's a stillness that envelopes us, as if the rest of the world, the rest of Sandpiper, is still asleep.

Neither of us says anything while we watch. While Lyla seems perfectly content in the silence, I'm chomping at the bit to talk to her. But I don't want to scare her off. This right here is more than I expected her to give me, and I don't want to push my luck.

Eventually, Lyla stands up, puts her earbud back in, and gives me a nod. It's as we're heading back down the street to her parents house that she slows to a walk and looks down at her phone. She grins as she responds to a text, and my heart immediately drops down into my stomach.

Is it a guy? Has she met someone? *Fuck me.* I knew this was always a possibility, but my mind spins at the possible reality of the situation where I'm not the guy she's smiling at. Have I lost her for good? Before I've even started trying to win her back? I'm as panicked as Lyla looked earlier when we stopped to watch the sunrise.

It's as we walk into the house, the smell of coffee greeting us, that she says to her mom, "Derek's going to stop by to get me. We're going to hit the beach for an hour before he has to head to work. Should give me enough time to get home for yoga with you at ten." A sigh of relief escapes my lips, and I swear I have more pep in my step now that I know it was him she was messaging.

Lori looks at me and asks if I want to stay. "Just coffee, please." She hands me a mug filled with the nectar of the gods and I doctor it up with some milk and far too much sugar. My overly sweet coffee is a habit I just can't break, no matter how much the guys at work make fun of me. I sit down and suck back what will surely be the first of many cups I consume today.

"Seems like you're making progress," Lori says as she sits next to me.

I nod my head in agreement. "I'm not going to say the ice is thawed, but there were a few slushy spots today."

"You know, Theo, being vulnerable doesn't make you weak. Telling her the truth about why you left might be the only thing that puts you back in her orbit," she says matter-of-factly before taking a sip of her coffee.

"Lori, leaving her was the most cowardly thing I could have possibly done. I was so consumed by the idea of losing her, and turning into a shell of a man like my father, that I ran away. Literally. It doesn't get much weaker than that. It was the biggest mistake of my life."

I look behind me to make sure Lyla isn't in the room. I can't help but raise my voice when we talk about it. I'm so angry over my actions. My shoulders sag, as if I'm ashamed of myself, and the truth is, I am. I am so fucking ashamed for walking away from the best thing that ever happened to me.

I close my eyes and blow out a breath to try and expel some of the self-loathing that consumes me.

She gives me a sympathetic nod and pats my hand. "Your biggest mistake was not explaining it to her before you left, Theo. That open dialogue would have changed things. Because she wouldn't have begged or guilted you into staying. She would have understood the sudden urge to leave. Maybe even given you the space and support to do so."

"Well, I guess I'll never know." I sink back in my chair and slowly rub my temples, feeling completely defeated. Defeated at the idea that I might never get her back. That I might have to live the rest of my life without her. A life that would be empty. Kind of like what my dad had after Mom passed. The irony doesn't escape me.

"But you could tell her now," she says in an encouraging voice. Like it wouldn't be somewhat embarrassing for me to admit that the shit swirling around in my head had me running away. Before the conversation can go anywhere else, the door opens, and Derek walks in. He leans down to give his mom a hug, offers me a nod, and says good morning. I finish my cup and stand.

"Thanks for the coffee. I'm going to check with Lyla to see if we're running tomorrow before I head out." I look at Derek. "Have fun at the beach." He gives me a quick thanks, and I head down the hallway.

I'm so distracted from my conversation with Lori, and the true realization that I might never be able to win Lyla back, that I don't knock before I open the door to her room.

# NINE

## *Lyla*

I'M STANDING in my bikini when Theo barges into my room.

"Jesus! Can you knock?"

Theo stares at me like I'm his dinner. His eyes get darker as they move from my toes all the way up to my eyes, lingering on my chest and then my lips. The way he's looking at me, like it's the first time he's seen a woman, has me pressing my feet into the carpet to stay grounded.

"I'm sorry," he offers in a husky voice. That same tone I've heard a million times in the past when we'd be in bed together. Heat pools between my legs just remembering those moments.

We stare at each other for what feels like minutes but is probably only twenty seconds. He runs his hand through his dark hair, frustrated. "Fuck, you look good, Lyla. I should have knocked but I don't actually feel sorry."

"Can you at least throw me my cover-up?" I say, pointing to my desk chair. As much as I liked the way he was looking at me, putting some more clothes on might help alleviate the sexual tension that crackles between us.

He begrudgingly breaks eye contact while he reaches for

the dress. Instead of tossing it to me like I anticipated him doing, he walks a few steps over and holds it up with both of his hands. I raise my eyebrows at him, unsure of what he wants. He tilts his chin at me and motions for me to raise my arms. As if I've lost control over my own body, I do as he silently asks.

He slips the gauzy dress over my head and guides it down over me. His hands softly graze my body, leaving a trail of heat behind. He takes his time, his knuckles grazing my shoulders. The dress falls slowly down my body, his fingers pulling the sleeves down my arms. His touch is gentle and possessive; slow and methodical, as if he has all the time in the world.

Our eyes have been locked on each other the entire time and I don't realize that I've been holding my breath. My body lights up at his touch. Like it's been in hibernation for the past six years and all of sudden woke up. I can't stop the sigh that escapes and Theo's eyes turn darker with lust.

"Thanks," I finally manage to mumble, breaking us from the trance we were both lost in.

"I just wanted to say bye, and that I'll see you tomorrow morning. Same time?"

"Yup."

He pauses before he turns to walk out, and for a second, I think he's going to say something else but he doesn't. I stare down at the floor, a pang of disappointment ringing in my chest. I don't know what that moment just was, but it reminds me that I cannot trust myself around that man. Whatever we had all those years ago, is still there. Maybe it never went away. I don't know what I wanted him to say, but I do know that I wish he said *something*.

Because I wasn't ready for him to walk out yet.

* * *

The rest of the week passes quickly. Theo runs with me every morning, and while I haven't let the floodgates down, I did open up and offer more conversation than normal. I know he wanted to talk more—I could tell by the way he constantly glanced at me. But I appreciate how he doesn't push.

It's on our Friday run, when we're sitting on that same bench watching the sunrise again, that he musters up the nerve to break the ice a bit more.

"Can you tell me about Hollman? How did you get started with investigating him?" he asks.

I'm pleasantly surprised by his question because it's a safe topic I can handle. It has nothing to do with my conflicted feelings. I won't have to talk about how my heart races whenever I'm near him or how I find myself thinking about him throughout the day.

I don't have to consider the hurt and the pain and the resentment I felt when he walked away from me. How he absolutely crushed me and ruined me. Nope. I don't have to think about any of those things at all.

"I started going to off-campus parties in and around Boston. College girls are always chatty when you're willing to hold back their hair while they puke." I cringe over how many times I did just that.

"Really? That's how it all started?" I can't tell if he's impressed or horrified. Probably a little bit of both.

"Yup. Then social media made it really easy to get linked into the social scene. So I just kept going to these parties and observing everything, like who was buying, who was selling, who was afraid of who, what names were being whispered."

"And then what?"

"I followed the names. Followed the people. You know how investigations work."

"Yeah, I do. Which means I know how dangerous they can

be. Did you know you were playing with fire while you were doing it?" he pushes, and I give him a look like he might have gone too far. He throws his hands up as an apology and raises his eyebrows at me, waiting for me to continue.

"Of course I did. But once I started I couldn't stop, especially when I realized he was pimping out women. Boston PD kept brushing me off, seeing me as a scorned woman with a vendetta, so I knew I needed foolproof evidence. I didn't stop until I had just that. I did the best I could to be safe. All's well that ends well." I shrug my shoulders. I'm not trying to minimize the risks I took, especially because it might bite me in the ass in the long run, but what's done is done.

Theo takes a few deep breaths. "I'm not going to lecture you."

"That's good because I wouldn't listen to you even if you did."

"I'll just say that what you did was dangerous and reckless as hell, but I admire the shit out of you for doing it. You did some impressive work, Lyla. You found and followed leads that took down someone who had an entire community fooled. And it all started with holding back the hair of puking girls in the seedy basement of an off-campus party."

We both laugh.

I stand and nod my chin toward the road, indicating I'm ready to get back to running. Before I know it, we're back on my street. I don't want to give him the opportunity to ask any more questions about my pseudo-undercover work. He doesn't need to know about the skimpy outfits I wore or the guys I had to flirt with to worm my way into their world.

We're nearing my driveway when he says, "I have to get to the station early today so tell your mom I'm sorry I'm missing breakfast. See you Monday?"

"Yup." I start walking into the garage and then turn back to him, seeing that he was watching me walk up the driveway. "Thanks, Theo. I do feel safer having company, even if it's just to make sure I don't get hit by a car or something."

"Anytime, Sunshine."

He gives me a big smile, one that reaches his eyes, and winks. I turn back and head into the house.

I make a cup of coffee and take it onto the patio, turning on some music while I watch the hummingbirds buzz around. I take a second to do a mental rundown of the freelance articles I need to finish and realize I'm in pretty good shape. I open my computer and go to my social media so I can look up some of the authors I'm debating between for the book club. It's been a productive week, which is a good confidence boost.

The only eventful thing that happens this week is something I don't whisper a word to anyone about. Dad would blow a gasket if he knew, but things are finally more relaxed at home since I'm no longer running alone. I don't want to throw a wrench into that. I get a little queasy as I think about what happened the other day, but try to push those thoughts aside.

*On Wednesday, I ride my bike over to Main Street and spend a few hours popping in and out of my favorite shops, casually chatting with anyone I know. When I go into One More Chapter, I feel a chill run down my spine. It came from out of nowhere and has me stopping in my tracks. My eyes dart back and forth as I walk past the register that's at the front of the shop, giving the owner a small wave while she helps a customer. I make my way to the tables that house recent releases. Instead of getting lost in the titles like I usually do, I find myself unable to concentrate on anything I read. It feels like there are eyes on me. The doors chime half a dozen times, while I*

wait to talk to the owner about a book club. My nerves are getting the best of me as I jump each time they ring.

When the goosebumps pop up on my arms, I scan the store. Not seeing anyone, I go back to browsing, but I can't shake the feeling. My hands are trembling as I mindlessly pick up books and place them back down. Since the incident in Vermont, I've tried to pay more attention when my body reacts like this. I look up again as I get to the end of the aisle and find a man maybe ten feet away, looking directly at me.

I've kept my eyes peeled for the intruder who broke into my home in Vermont, but this man... I don't recognize him at all. I also don't pick up on that cologne scent that lingers in the back of my mind. Even if he's not right next to me, I'm so sensitive to that smell that I think I would notice it. He's wearing a beat up baseball hat that is pulled down low over his face, but I can still see the mustache and shaggy blond hair

Kristin, the owner who is a good friend of my mom's, has made her way from the register at the front of the store back to the rows where we are. "Can I help you find something, sir?" she asks in a friendly, chipper voice. Her question forces him to break his eye contact with me.

He looks away, then glances at me one more time before mumbling under his breath and stomps his way to the door. He pushes it open with more force than necessary. My thoughts spin and I blink my eyes rapidly, as if trying to wash the moment away. I look down and see that my hands are still trembling and I shake them out, hoping Kristin doesn't notice how shaken up I am.

"Okay, have a great day, asshole." Kristin mutters so softly I barely catch it. She turns her attention to me. "Okay, Miss Lyla, I know you sent me a few emails and brought it up the last time you were in the shop with your mom. I apologize for not getting back to you sooner. I was just trying to think of the logistics and how we can make this book club work. Then I decided that you can just have free run and plan it however you'd like."

I'm so excited I completely forget about the creepy guy and squeal with excitement. I have been hoping that Kristen would give me the green light.

"You won me over when you mentioned focusing on indie writers. You can have the back sitting area on Wednesday nights until 9. Post some signs around town, post it on Facebook, or whatever you young kids do. I would love it if you could convince everyone to buy the book from me, but it's not a deal-breaker."

I rush up to her and give her a big hug. "Thank you! Thank you! Thank you! I'm even more thrilled than I thought I would be. I'm going to work on getting word out about it." I give her one more hug before I skip out the door, already brainstorming ideas for our first book, snacks to bring, and themed drinks. Basically, the whole nine yards.

I decide to celebrate my win with a stop at The Morning Current. I figure I'll get a latte and let the baristas know about the book club so they can start spreading the word. It's when I walk out, paying more attention to the slice of lemon loaf I bought than where I'm going, that I bump into someone on the sidewalk.

When I look up to apologize, I realize it's the same man who was in the bookstore. My spidey senses, and my tingling skin, tell me there's something nefarious about this man. He turns and walks away before I can pull myself together to say anything.

Fuck. Am I being paranoid? Main Street is not a very long road, so it's not unusual to run into the same people more than once while you're out shopping. Maybe he's just a local I haven't met yet. It's the only way to rationalize it and settle my nerves.

I try my best to shake it off, making my way to my car while I repeatedly glance over my shoulder to make sure no one is following me. I debate telling my dad or my brothers about what just *happened but decide not to. It would only send them into overdrive, and it probably doesn't have anything to do with Marcus Hollman, anyway. I'll just be extra vigilant when I'm on my own.*

# TEN

## *Lyla*

IT'S another rager of a Friday night in the life of Lyla Sullivan. I'm in cozy clothes, drinking a glass of pinot noir with my laptop open while I wait for Quinn to Facetime me. Right on time, her name pops up on my screen, and I quickly accept the call.

"Hey, QB!" I exclaim. I'm always happy to see or talk to Quinn but especially tonight. I'm in desperate need of some girl talk.

"Hey, girl! I decided I'm joining your book club from afar so let me know what book you pick, and I'll order it."

"Okay! How's school? What's new?" She fills me in on what's been going on at work, the headway she's made with one student who's been giving her a hard time since day one, and the volunteering she's doing with a local outreach program that advocates for homeless kids. Her eyes light up when she talks about the new activity she got approved since the last time we spoke.

"I was able to secure a recurring donation from a wealthy family that's very involved in the equestrian world. We're going to be able to take a dozen kids twice a week to one of the local riding facilities. The kids will learn all about how to take care of horses, how to ride, and go on trail rides. I'm hoping to get equine therapy as part of the program soon." Her smile spreads across her entire face.

"QB, that's incredible! I've read a lot about equine therapy and how beneficial it can be. What a fantastic opportunity." My heart feels so full with pride in everything Quinn has done for the outreach center. Having grown up in the foster care system, and essentially raising herself, she knows exactly how these kids feel.

"I'm thrilled about it. These donations are the only perk to going to those stupid fundraisers with Justin"

"And how is Justin?" I ask, trying to be as polite as possible.

"He's fine. You know, busy busy. We do the same job, but he's obviously a million times busier than me," she says with an eye roll. It's been awhile since she's said anything positive about him. I try to think of a response before she can change the subject.

"Guess it's not easy being the mayor's son and all," I reply with a small laugh.

"Don't get me started. I have a list of events I'm expected to be at that I need to buy clothes for. Like I have all this money just sitting in my bank account, waiting to be spent on clothes I'll never wear again." She says it calmly, but I don't miss the hint of frustration that's there.

I tread lightly with what I say next. The last thing I want to do is let Justin cause a wedge between us. I've already lost one best friend, and I'll be damned if I'm going to lose another.

"You don't have to go to those events, QB. You know that, right? Justin might be your boyfriend, but you're not some trophy wife who has to drop everything to be at her partner's beck and call."

She lets out a sigh, and it's then that I really see how sad and exhausted she looks. Her shoulders are slumped, as if in defeat. She has dark circles under her eyes, and her attempts at smiling feel forced. I wish I could reach through the screen and hug her.

She responds slowly, as if it takes effort. "I know. It's just easier to be agreeable. And the events aren't that bad. It gives me a chance to network with people who have deep pockets and can spare money to donate to the outreach center."

"I know the outreach center means the world to you, Quinn, but you shouldn't have to sacrifice your own happiness to help the cause."

"I know. They don't expect me to drum up donations. I just figure if I'm mingling with wealthy people who are always up to donate to a good cause and score themselves a tax write-off, I might as well take advantage of it."

"Are you sure you're okay, QB?" I ask, imploring her to talk more. I know from past conversations that she's itching to change the subject, but I want to give it one more shot.

She wraps her arms around herself before she finally says, "I'm sure. Really, Lyla." She gives me a tight smile and reaches for her drink, taking a long sip. "How are things with Theo?"

I don't press her any further because I know it won't do me any good. I don't want her to get pissed off and hang up the phone, so I take a sip of my own wine before answering. "They're...slightly less frosty. We've had some brief conversations throughout the week. He's careful not to try too hard or ask too many questions, which I appreciate."

"Okay, that's a step in the right direction! Have you thought about seeing him outside of your morning workout? Like meeting him out at the bar or something with other people around?" It's like she does a complete one-eighty now that we're no longer talking about her. She throws her hair up in a messy bun and then clasps her hands together, as if she's coming up with an evil plan. Her eyes sparkle with mischief.

"I don't know. It probably wouldn't hurt to be social, so it's not a terrible idea," I say, contemplating the suggestion.

"Hear me out. I'm not saying you should go get sloppy drunk and profess all your feelings to him. Especially since we don't even know what those feelings are. But, maybe being out somewhere, with a drink or two to relax, will allow you to feel like you can let your hair down just a little bit. I'm not trying to push you into anything, Ly. I'm just putting it out there as a way to let him in a tiny bit more, if that's what you want. To explore your own feelings. And proceed from there. If the night ends with a kiss, then who am I to judge?" she says with a laugh.

"Nooooo. There will be no kissing. The way that man can kiss... If I let that happen, it'll be over for me." She gives me a conspiratorial smile. "Why do you have that look? I don't like that look, QB."

"I'm not saying you need to kiss him! Buuuut, and just listen, what if a kiss helps you sort out your feelings? What if you kiss him and you're completely grossed out? Might be helpful information to know," she says matter-of-factly.

"I'm not sure where my head is at right now, but I don't know if I could handle the idea of him moving on with someone else if he kisses me and realizes he's not in love with me anymore." The idea of that, of us being truly finished and him moving on without me takes my breath away.

"Damn, you are in a tizzy. I'm surprised, though. Trying to get you to open up is usually like trying to open a book that's been gorilla-glued shut. Even now, knowing you the way I do, I know there are pages still stuck together. You have to open yourself up, even if just a little bit. Because you could be missing out on something magical—either with Theo or someone else," Quinn says. "Exploring your feelings for Theo a bit, doesn't mean you need to jump into a relationship with him. You can take shit as slow as you want."

"I guess you're right."

"Of course I'm right," she casually says, as if it's the most obvious thing in the world. "Letting him in a little bit is not saying everything is fine and you're back together. It's you figuring out for yourself if you want to go down that road with him again in the future, near or far."

I take a sip of my wine, slowly swallowing it before I start chewing on my lip, pondering everything she just said.

"It's Friday, and there's no time like the present. Your brothers and Theo are probably out for a couple of beers, watching the game somewhere. I'm proud of you for starting that book club. It's a great first step to putting yourself out there, but getting more social and going out on a Friday night for a drink will be good for you. Put your makeup on, fix your hair up pretty, and go meet him tonight somewhere in your tiny city."

"You did not just quote Bruce Springsteen to me," I say with a giggle.

"I sure did. Bruce knows best. Now, finish that drink and text Colin to see where they are or I'll do it for you." She's practically bouncing off the walls and a big smile lights up her eyes in a way they weren't earlier. If this was her vibe when we first got on the call, I never would have suspected something was wrong.

If I know my brother at all, they're probably at the Dusty Bird Pub, a local spot we all love. I swallow my pride, and nerves, and send Colin a text. We go back and forth for a few messages before I say, "Colin is going to pick me up, and we're meeting Theo and some of their friends at the Dusty Bird. I caught him just in time, but I need to get ready since he's on his way."

Quinn squeals with delight, and I can't help but smile through the anxiety that's ripping through me. "Great. I'll keep you company while you get dressed. Pants that show off your ass are a must."

I throw on my favorite pair of jeans and a lightweight sweater that slouches off one shoulder. "Put on a cuter bra with that sweater. Something lacey since the straps show."

"Yes, Boss," I deadpan, though there's a tiny smile on my face.

I make the instructed adjustments, put on some mascara, and let my hair down, giving it a few shakes before posing for approval.

"Two thumbs-up. Relaxed and effortlessly sexy. I don't know how you do it. It's a look only you can pull off. Now go have fun!"

"Thanks, Quinn. You're the best. It feels good to be going out so thanks for the push. I'll text you later!"

"So, anything you want to tell me?" Colin asks from next to me as he makes a turn. He's never been one for silence. It makes him antsy, which is evident by the fact that he's tapping his hands on the wheel as he drives.

"Nope. Just decided I needed to get out. Seeing as though my only friend lives in a different state, you're the next best thing. Plus, I figured Derek was home watching HGTV."

"Hah, he's not coming tonight so he probably is. But if I remember correctly, you can't stand my usual plus one. So while I'm thrilled to see you joining the human race at the bar on a Friday night, I can't pretend I'm not at least a little surprised that you want to come out knowing Theo will be there. Nevermind the fact that you have makeup on."

"I have *mascara* on," I say with an eye roll.

"Yeah, yeah. I guess this night just got a little more interesting. I didn't give him a heads-up you were joining, FYI."

"That's fine. It's not like I'm going out to see him." I mean, not entirely. Because I am actually hyped to be going out.

I've gone out a handful of times since I've been back in Sandpiper Cove, and even though it usually took one of my brothers dragging me out kicking and screaming, it always ended up being a good time. It's nice catching up with the locals I see out and the Dusty Bird usually has live music on weekends.

We wrestle over music for the ten minutes it takes to get to the bar. Everytime I pick a song, he skips to the next one. He turns the volume up and sings at the top of his lungs. I'm laughing at his antics as he parks. This is something I love about Colin—he never fails lightening my mood and makes me laugh with his playful spirit.

Colin spots his friends before I do and gently puts his hands on my shoulders to steer me in the direction to find them. They're in the back corner of the bar, near the restrooms, giving them a good view of the entire place.

Theo has his back to us as we walk up, and I can't help but stare at his ass. The broken-in denim jeans he has on hug his thighs and ass in all the right places.

He's mid-conversation with Clayton and Drew—who are also officers—so he doesn't notice us until we reach them. Colin says his hellos, reminds Clayton and Drew to keep their paws off of me, and then leans over the bar to order. I tell him I'll take a whiskey.

Colin flirts with the bartender while ordering and, before I know it, a Knob Creek on the rocks is passed over to me. "You can just add them to his tab," he says pointing to Theo who rolls his eyes. "It's the cycle bro. I'll get the tab next time. You know it always evens out."

I'm a little nervous and find myself chewing on my bottom lip before I loosen up and join the conversation.

Theo crowds my space, leaning down to my ear to softly say, "Good to see you out, Sunshine." He taps my glass with his before knocking his back. I look into his eyes and lose all train of thought. When I told him earlier that I didn't know how to act around him, I wasn't joking. So, I just smile and try to avoid getting lost in his blue eyes.

It's striking how handsome he is. He has this chiseled jaw covered with a light scruff. A dimple that shows itself when he smiles. His dark hair is long enough to need a trim, but not bad enough that my dad would be on him for a cut. Perfect length to run my hands through, to hold his head to me.

*Do not go there, Lyla. Do not start picturing yourself touching this man no matter how hot he looks.*

He has a glass of what I'm assuming is whiskey in his hand, and I can't stop staring at his thick forearms, the naturally tanned skin, the way the muscles flex when he moves. The tattoo of grey and black trees, mostly pine, runs from his wrist up towards his elbow. The shading of ink makes it look like a haunted forest. When I look back at his eyes, he's smirking at me.

"Just felt like I needed to get out of the house tonight," I reply, trying to distract him from the fact that he just caught me checking him out. His smile reaches his eyes, telling me that he's genuinely happy to see me.

He takes another sip of his drink before jumping back into the conversation with the guys. I listen and laugh at their antics, trying to ignore the uneasiness that has started to spread through me.

It's that tingling feeling that has the hairs on the back of my neck and arms standing. And it's not because of my proximity to Theo. These aren't the kind of tingles that come when I'm turned on. These take me back to my house in Vermont. Someone has eyes on me and I don't like it.

I subtly look around the bar to see if there's anything amiss, if anyone jumps out at me, but the reality is that if someone is here to shut me up, he's not going to be holding up a sign with his intentions written on it for me. Nothing, and no one, jumps out at me. It's a seemingly normal night at the Dusty Bird. The musician, Ned Ryerson, is setting up his equipment. People are milling around, laughing and talking. At first glance, there's no reason for my skin to be feeling so prickly.

As I scan the room a second time, I notice a man at the other end of the bar who gives off an immediate creeper vibe. He's sitting by himself, nursing a bottle of beer, not making conversation with anyone near him, and the place is pretty crowded. His ball cap is pulled down low, but I can tell he's looking directly at me.

I quickly realize it's the same man I saw earlier this week in town and a chill runs down my spine. I quickly avert my eyes and try to keep a lid on the growing panic in my stomach.

The metallic taste of blood tinges my tongue when I bite too hard into my cheek. A second later, Colin pulls me out of my thoughts and says, "You're going to chew a hole through that lip, Lyla. You good?"

I debate mentioning something to my brother but ultimately decide against it. No one else seems to be looking at him with suspicion. Maybe he's a townie and I don't even know it. I've been gone for a long time, so it's not unreasonable to think there are locals I don't recognize. Besides, I'm in a public place. It's not like the guy can do anything to me when we're at a pub.

"I'm fine," I finally reply, turning my attention back to the conversation that the guys are having about the Red Sox and their chances in the playoffs. I laugh as they bust each other's balls about who bested who during their workout today. I've been around Clayton and Drew a few times since being back in Sandpiper.

Drew grew up a few towns over, is the more outgoing of the two, and fits in perfectly with my brother. They're both good humored and love to laugh, even when it's at their own expense.

Clayton is the quietest of the bunch. He's from a Boston suburb, and while he's polite and courteous, he seems to have this chip on his shoulder here and there. He's a little rough around the edges but maybe that comes from growing up closer to the city.

My glass is empty, so I lean toward Colin and ask him to grab me another drink next time he flirts with the bartender and excuse myself to use the restroom. I'm in desperate need of some lip gloss to keep me from biting my bottom lip, and I need a minute to breathe.

The hallway leading to the bathrooms is narrow and shaded, but I don't give my safety a second thought since I'm still inside the Dusty Bird. I lean against the door and take a few deep breaths before moving over to the sink. I grab the lip gloss out of my purse and apply a layer before giving myself a once over in the mirror.

As I exit the ladies room, I collide with a body.

"Oof...sorry!" I take a step back and look up and into the eyes of the creepy guy from the other side of the bar. My heart drops into my stomach and I'm overwhelmed by the pungent odor that always lingers around smokers. I recoil at the stench of beer on his breath.

He's got at least six inches on me and his imposing frame blocks my view when I try to glance around, hoping to find a way around him to get back to the guy. His eyes narrow as he looks down at me and walks closer, effectively forcing me further away from the bar until my back hits the wall.

"Hey! What are you doing?! Get away from me!"

I spot an emergency exit at the end of the hallway. I've listened to enough true crime podcasts to know I can't let this asshole get me out that door. I slam my fists against his chest in an effort to get him to back up. I just need a little space and I can knee him in the balls, but my effort is fruitless.

"What the hell... What do you want??" My eyes dart past him, and I realize I'm getting farther away from the doorway that leads out to everyone else. I open my mouth to scream but nothing comes out. I can feel the heat spreading throughout my chest and my hands turn clammy, panic overtaking me like a dark, misty shadow.

His hands grip my biceps so tightly I'm sure it's going to leave marks. I can't get away from him fast enough. After all the worrying about me running on my own before dawn, I can't believe this is going to happen at a crowded bar with my brother and his friends yards away.

Before he can respond, a voice from the end of the hallway closer to the bar catches my attention. "Yo! Get your fucking hands off her!" I recognize that voice and when I look over the stranger's shoulder, I see that it's Clayton. At the sight of a friendly face, I gasp with relief. I sag with relief, and am damn near close to sinking to my knees, but this shithead's hands are still on me.

"Did you hear me, asshole? Let go of her." Clayton stomps

toward us. "There's a bar full of cops out there, so if you know what's good for you—"

Before Clayton can finish his sentence, the stranger grunts and lets me go. He pushes me aside and storms for the emergency exit and out the door.

I lean back against the wall, breathing heavily, and look at Clayton. His eyes are wide with concern as he looks me over.

"Thank you," I manage to get out. I bring a hand to my chest and try to slow my breathing while praying my eyes don't start watering. The last thing I need is my mascara running and drawing attention to myself.

"Do you know that man?" he asks.

I shake my head to say no.

"Maybe we should get your brother over here."

"No." It comes out a little louder than I mean it to. I take a deep breath and try to compose myself, lowering my voice. "Please don't, Clayton. I'm sure it was just some drunk guy who decided to get handsy. I'm okay now. Let's go back to the bar."

"Fuck. Fine," he finally says, his hands on his hips. "But if you see this guy again, you better tell me."

"I promise I will. Thank you." My brother and Theo would go absolutely bananas if I told them what just happened. And my dad—forget it—I'd never be able to leave the house again. Clayton nods and says he's going to hit the bathroom, but he watches that I make it back to the rest of the guys okay first.

I hear Colin ordering shots, and I jump back into the conversation, hoping the shake in my voice is gone. "I leave for three minutes, and you're resorting to shots, Colin? Aren't we a little old for that?"

"Blasphemy, little sister. One is never too old for shots. And you're welcome for sticking with whiskey," he says as he passes out the miniature glasses. Theo skips his so Colin takes two. Colin will be leaving his truck in the parking lot and going home with a woman for sure.

We clink our glasses and throw them back. I signal the bartender for water because if I don't drink some of that between all of this booze, I'm going to be hurting tomorrow.

I loosen up more as the night goes on. My breath hitches every time I catch Theo staring at me. When he hands me a drink, I feel a jolt through my core. As the bar gets more crowded and we're pushed closer together, I relish in the contact. When he guides me closer to the bar, a hand on my lower back, I feel like I could combust.

Quinn was right. Being in a social setting definitely has me more relaxed and receptive to conversation with Theo. I find myself enjoying the casual banter with him–talking about books we've read lately, concerts we've seen, and hearing stories about his cat.

"So you have a cat?" I ask, taking a sip of my drink.

I swear the man's eyes light up at the question. "I do! Want to see him?" Before I can even respond, he's got his phone in his hands. He shows me a picture of a large, tabby cat sprawled out on a couch.

Colin leans over and points to the phone. "Look at my nephew. Isn't he adorable?"

"He really is," I say with a laugh.

"He's a judgmental little prick, but I love him. He's gotten me through some hard times," Theo says, passing his phone over to me and motioning for me to swipe.

I scroll through his pictures and see the entire camera roll is composed of photos of the sky, the beach, home projects, and his cat. I try not to melt at the selfies, his face smushed up against the enormous feline. I relish at the window I currently have into this man's personal life. I know so little about him these days and that realization hurts my heart in a way I don't quite understand.

"I have a folder that's all books I've read or want to read. And one of songs I've screenshotted along the way. In case you want to check those out." These are comfortable topics for him and I and I move over to the scroll through the album that has pictures of book covers.

"I'm hooked on that James Reece series by Jack Carr," I say, my eyes meeting his.

"Told you! Those books are intense but fun." I nod my head in agreement. "Reading anything good now?"

"Nothing you'd be interested in." I feel myself blushing. The books I read are the best distraction from thinking about the man in front of me that I've been able to come up with and they still don't do the job.

"What about that question has you turning red, Sunshine?" When I look at him, he's smirking.

"Unless you're into romance, mainly cowboys or cops, you probably wouldn't want me to rattle off the last few books I've read."

He takes a sip of his drink before leaning closer, and when I look into his eyes, they're crystal blue. "Trust me, Lyla. The way you're blushing, I'm more than interested in knowing what books you've been reading."

The air between us crackles and if I looked down, I'm pretty sure I'd see literal sparks. When our eyes meet, the rest of the world ceases to exist. The silence between us isn't awkward like it was the first few times we ran together. It's electric. Maybe it's the whiskey, or maybe it's the fact that this man has me under his spell once again, but I don't shy away from answering.

"Well, I'd be happy to text you the titles when I get home later."

"Please do. Let me know which one you're currently reading, too." He winks.

*Fuck me, I'm in trouble.*

For my own sanity, and the fact that the heat is pooling between my legs, I steer the conversation back to a safe topic. "Have you been to Red Rocks yet?" Seeing a concert together at Red Rocks is something that was on both of our bucket lists.

The smile drains from his face and he solemnly shakes his head. "That was always in *our* plans. Could never bring myself to do it without you."

His words hit me like a ton of bricks and suck the air right out of me. Because when our relationship ended I swore I'd never see a show there, either.

"Tequila and Red Rocks. Two things I wrote off a long time ago, Sunshine," he says. My eyes widen.

"But you love tequila." We both do. Once we were of age, we loved nothing more than researching and trying new tequilas. I ended up with an extensive collection of bottles that I've slowly drowned my sorrows in over the years.

"I do love it." He shakes his head, as if trying to gather his thoughts. "Too many memories, Lyla. The smell of it alone is enough to send me into a tailspin. I'd end up crying at the bottom of the bottle and that doesn't do me any good."

"So you're telling me that you haven't had tequila in years because it brings up too many bad memories?" My back is up and I'm feeling defensive as hell at those hurtful words.

He brings his lips to my ear and says softly, but firmly, "No. I'm telling you I haven't had it because it brings up the thing that haunts me. Reminds me of the biggest mistake I've ever made. It's bad enough that I have to live with the regret of walking away from you every single day. That I wake up without you because of my stupid decision. I don't need to drown myself in tequila to remind me of that, Sunshine. It would only make me hate myself more."

My jaw drops. I have no idea what to say so I take a sip of my drink to buy myself some time. A few sips later and I still can't formulate words.

He lets me off the hook. "Happy to take you to Red Rocks any day of the week. Pick a show and we're there." I give him a small smile and he reaches over and gently squeezes my forearm. I look down when he releases me, sure there will be a burn mark from the heat of his touch, but of course there isn't.

The guys pull him into a debate about firearm preferences before I can respond to his offer and I'm happy for the reprieve.

I don't mind that he's standing so close I can smell his cologne—a blend of warm spice and sea minerals. It's masculine and combines the saltiness of the ocean with the freshness of nature.

The scent has me feeling nostalgic for the past. For all of the memories we made together. It also brings a sense of comfort. Being in such close proximity to him, while dangerous for my heart, gives me a sense of safety I haven't had in a long time.

It's nearing midnight, and exhaustion slithers its way in. Theo puts his hand on the small of my back and leans in so his mouth is right by my ear. "These guys can hang until last call and grab Ubers. If you want to get out of here, I can give you a ride home."

I'm a 4th of July sparkler that's just been lit. Warmth spreads from my core down between my legs at the thought of being alone with him. It probably doesn't help that I'm buzzed. I've had a great night—laughing with the guys and catching up with a few people who stopped to say hi when I saw them. This is only me getting a ride home from someone who I know will get me there safely.

"That would be great, thanks."

We say our goodbyes. Colin gives me a hug and makes sure I'm okay with him staying while Theo drives me home. "It's fine, Colin. You've been flirting with the bartender all night, so I kind of figured you were in it for the long haul. Have fun but don't forget to wrap it up."

Theo says bye to the guys and puts his hand on my lower back to guide me out. I resist the urge to lean into his touch. *It's just the booze talking, Lyla. That, and the fact that you need to get laid. Rein it in, girl.*

He opens the passenger's door for me, and I hop up into his Ford pickup truck. He walks around the front and gets in, starting the engine while fumbling with his phone to put on music. Vance Joy starts playing through the speakers. To say that music is a huge common interest of ours would be an understatement. The song gets me thinking about the past.

"I'm sorry I always ignored your messages. I always listened to the songs. I even read most of the books," I blurt out before I can stop myself. *Fucking whiskey courage.* I cover my eyes with my hands, horrified by my word vomit and the way I'm suddenly exposing my vulnerabilities.

"I didn't send them in hopes of hearing back from you. Sure it would have been nice, but I never expected anything. I know you, Lyla." He shrugs his shoulders before he continues. "I knew your stubborn ass wouldn't acknowledge them. I sent them to you because every single one of those songs made me think of you, and it was the only way I could let you know that you were always on my mind."

"Always? Like all of the time over the last six years?" I ask.

"*Always.* On my life, Lyla. It didn't matter where I was, who I was with, what I was doing. You were there. First thing I thought of in the morning. Last thing I thought of before bed. When something good happened, I so badly wanted to call you. When things went to shit, I was desperate for you, because your voice alone is the only thing that steadies me. I've spent hours out of each of my days wondering how I could make things right with you."

"Quinn told me that I should kiss you."

*Fucking word vomit.* He glances over at me from behind the wheel. My skin is on fire from his quick look alone, but I don't have the balls to turn and meet his eyes.

"Is that right?" he asks, a mischievous tone to his voice.

"Yup. To see if there's still a spark there. Aside from me just thinking you're hot."

"You think I'm hot."

When I look over at him, he's smiling. "That's not the point."

"So what do you think about Quinn's idea? By the way, I think she's my new favorite."

"I asked you first, Theo."

"No, you didn't ask. You made a statement, not a question," he points out, the corners of his mouth turning up into a smile.

I roll my eyes. "Semantics."

He pulls up to my house and puts the truck in park. He takes my chin in his hand and gently turns it toward him so I can't avoid his gaze. His eyes are no longer the light crystal blue they were earlier; they're a dusky black. And they're filled with so much desire I'm mesmerized looking into them. "Sunshine, I would take whatever you're willing to give me. And I'll wait for as long as I need to. I'm not going anywhere. I will *never* walk away from you again."

I nod and force myself to put some space between us. My skin cools from the loss of his touch. He gets out of the truck and comes around to open my door.

"Want to hit the beach tomorrow? Weather's supposed to be perfect. Gotta capitalize on the summer while we can." Now that the tourist season is over, the beaches will be less packed. I mull over the invitation.

"Don't think that hard over it, Lyla. It's just the beach. We can invite your brothers if that'll make you feel more comfortable."

"I'll think about it," I finally say.

"Fair enough." He gives my shoulder a squeeze, and I feel a current rip through my body. I'm flabbergasted that his touch still has so much of an effect on me. He makes sure I get into the house before getting back into his truck.

After a quick rinse off, I get into bed and text Quinn.

**Me: Back home. Thanks for the push. Felt good to be out again.**

**Quinn: Yay! Glad to hear it. And how was Theo?**

**Me: Perfect gentleman. But it was definitely nice to be more relaxed around him. He asked if I wanted to go to the beach tomo.**

**Quinn: And...?**

**Me: I told him I'd let him know.**

**Quinn: Well, whatever you're comfortable with, I support. Let me know what you decide.**

**Me: Will do. Thanks for the advice, QB. Talk soon. Xo.**

I bring up Theo's message thread as I wage an internal debate about the beach. . It'd be nice to have company there, especially after that run-in with the guy at the bar. Eventually, I start typing.

**Me: I'm in for the beach.**

**Theo: I'll pick you up at ten.**

**Theo: Want me to invite your brothers?**

I internally think for a few minutes before finally answering.

**Me: No**

I put my phone on my night table and think about what

happened at the bar. A queasiness overcomes me just thinking about it. Regret about not telling Colin seeps in. I quickly push the altercation aside, convincing myself it was purely coincidental. Just some drunk at the bar who thought he could put his hands on me. Despite the drinks I had, I toss and turn for a while until my thoughts drift to Theo. Not long after, I fall into a fitful sleep.

# ELEVEN

*theo*

I'M RUNNING around like a chicken with my head cut off, getting ready for the beach. I pack the cooler full of sandwiches, snacks, and drinks. Am I packing like we're going to be stranded on a deserted island? Yes. Am I making sure to include all of Lyla's favorite seltzer flavors and Haribo gummy bears? Also, yes. Once I'm satisfied, I fill my backpack with a towel, extra sunscreen, and a small speaker.

Diego weaves in and out of my legs as I mill around the kitchen. I bend down to scoop him up. "What's up buddy? Is there a reason you've been up since 5 a.m. meowing at the top of your lungs?" He headbutts me a few times and then swats at my face, so I put him back down.

He's such an ornery bastard, but I love him. He was a stray outside the station that Chief Sullivan convinced me to adopt. Over the years, he's provided—mostly—unconditional love and company, as well as a healthy dose of judgmental looks.

I look around the house I grew up in to make sure I'm not forgetting anything. My dad was happy to sell it to me when he moved off the Cape. I love the location—it's closer to the beach than to work or Main Street, but that means it's much quieter in the offseason. It's dated and needs some love, but I've been spending any extra money and time I have on another project that means way more.

I climb into my truck and start the engine, heading to Lyla's right on schedule. I stop at Hot Bagels along the way for food and coffees before going to her house.

Chief is outside doing yardwork, so I give him a wave and then head into the garage, knocking three times before I go into the house. Lyla and her mom are both in the kitchen. Lori drops what she's doing and immediately comes over to give me a hug. "It's going to be a perfect day at the beach today. Which one are you going to?"

"I was thinking of hitting Swamprose. Figured now that it's September, it'll finally be more relaxing and quieter. That sound good to you, Lyla?" She smiles and nods as she fills up her water bottle.

"Oh, Swamprose is my favorite. Especially this time of year," Lori says, smiling as she looks back and forth between Lyla and me.

"Let me hit the bathroom, and I'll meet you outside. My beach chair is in my trunk," Lyla says.

"I'll grab it and see you out there." She turns to walk to the bathroom, giving me a view of her from behind as she goes. She has on a long-sleeved crochet coverup over a black bikini that only leaves so much up to the imagination.

She's heartstoppingly stunning and my mind goes wild thinking about all the things I'd like to do to her. If I don't stop thinking about my hands running up and down her body, my mouth all over her, and how sexy she'd be withering under me as I kiss her breathless, my cock is going to be hard as a rock.

I take a deep breath and grab her bag and water bottle. By

the time she comes outside, I've already thrown her chair in the bed of my truck and am talking to her dad. She comes over to say goodbye to him.

"Bye, guys. Have fun. Theo, take care of my girl."

"Always, Chief," I say as we walk toward my truck. I open the door for her to get in and then go around the front to get into the driver's seat. "Coffee and bagels for the ride there. I didn't know if you'd want to grab lunch at some point, but I made some sandwiches just so we have them and plenty of snacks." I pass a bagel and coffee over to her. She takes a sip of it and covers her mouth, gagging.

"Jesus, Theo... I can't believe you still drink your coffee like this! It's disgusting." She passes it right back to me, a look of disgust on her face, and grabs the other cup to take a sip. "Much better. Seriously, your teeth are going to fall out with all the sugar in that cup."

I look over at her and smile before taking a sip of my *appalling* coffee. "Ahhh, just the way I like it."

Her dark blonde hair is up in a messy bun, and she doesn't have a stitch of makeup on. Since she's been in the sun more lately, the freckles on her face are more noticeable. She has on a pair of old-school Ray-Ban wayfarers. She's so fucking beautiful it takes my breath away. And she smells amazing. Citrus with a hint of rose and some other underlying notes I can't quite pinpoint.

"Cat got your tongue?" she asks.

"No, I just... You still wear that same perfume." It's always made my knees weak and my dick twitch.

She gives me the biggest, most radiant smile I've gotten since we started running together and I swear my heart stops.

"Chanel never goes out of style. I can't believe you still remember the perfume I used to wear."

"I remember everything about you, Lyla. How many bottles

of it did I buy you over the years? Had to be at least half a dozen. I'm not ashamed to say that I still have the one you left at my house years ago."

She turns to me in surprise. "That has to be seven or eight years old. I bet it doesn't even smell pretty after all this time."

"Doesn't matter. The only way it smells good is when it's on you."

I start driving toward Swamprose Beach. Despite multiple other beaches within the same distance, this one has always been our go to. There's a marsh not too far from the sandy shore that's always overgrown with swamp roses, which are some of Lyla's favorite flowers.

We find parking pretty quickly. There are some people on the beach but everyone is spread out. We get our chairs and umbrella set up. I lay out a large towel while Lyla takes it upon herself to link her phone to my portable speaker. I glance her way when I'm done setting up, just as she's taking off her cover up and stuffing it into her bag.

If I thought she looked good in tight-fitting workout clothes, seeing her in a bathing suit is going to ruin me. It's a simple black bikini with triangle tops and a small, racy bottom. Not a thong, but enough ass showing to make me grind my teeth and say a silent prayer that my cock behaves itself. Lyla has always been in great shape, but her body is on fucking fire now.

She's about five-seven, and slender but curvy. She has toned muscles on those long legs and trim arms. She's got a flat stomach, a tight ass, and perfect tits. Her hazel eyes rarely look the same—the green and gold constantly battling for dominance. I have to remind myself not to stare at her lips— pouty, full, and begging to be kissed. She oozes femininity and sexiness without even trying. My cock stands at attention, and we haven't even been here for ten minutes.

It's when Lyla reclines her chair all the way back and puts her hands underneath her head that I notice the tattoo on her ribs. And when I look at it, I can't stop staring. My sunglasses aren't within reach, so I'm not being subtle, and I don't give a fuck.

Because looking at that ink, those swirls of black on her skin, I feel like I'm looking at the female version of the one I have on my shoulder and arm. The one I got years ago, when we were both broken in our own ways, and I decided to run away instead of dealing with my issues head-on.

The focal point of her tattoo is a sun with a cluster of flowers, swamp roses and hydrangeas, covering the very top and running down the side of the sun. Sticking out from the top of those flowers is a crescent moon.

I know without her even opening her mouth what this tattoo represents. It's us, with the sun and the moon symbolizing one of our favorite pastimes—watching the sunrise, the sunset, and the night sky.

Hell, my nickname for Lyla has always been Sunshine. The flowers... I've given her enough bouquets to fill a football field. It's a stunning piece of art, with the elements melting into each other.

She finally turns her head toward me and sees that I'm staring right at her ribs. She murmurs, "You were never supposed to see it." She bites her lip, which is clearly a habit she still hasn't broken.

I'm still staring at the ink, completely enamored by it. She's looking at me like I've lost my mind. It's then that I stand back up and take off my shirt to allow her a second to look at the tattoo on my upper body. It starts on my bicep and hooks up over my shoulder.

While it's not dainty and feminine like hers, it includes all the same elements—the sun, the moon, the flowers. There are also some waves in the background to connect it all, to represent my love of the ocean. There's no escaping the similarities. It's clear as fucking day that these tattoos represent *us*.

"Well, shit," she mutters. "You'd have thought we got them together."

# TWELVE

*Lyla*

LOOKING at the tattoo on Theo's arm renders me speechless. If I'm being completely honest with myself, the parallels between our tattoos unsettles something deep inside of me. It connects me to him in a completely different way.

We weren't together when we got them. Hell, we weren't even talking—he was holding strong in the number one position on my shitlist. Yet, here we are with strikingly similar art on our bodies. Art that pulls so many of the elements that were special to us together.

My feelings toward Theo, the way my body reacts to being near him, and now the ink, it's all turning into a complete mindfuck. My feelings are already so conflicted and all of this is making me question everything—why I left, why he left, why he always messaged me, why I never responded, why he came back, why I refused to come back for so long when I could have done my digging from the Cape more easily than Vermont, why my brothers never told me about Theo's tattoo when they've both seen mine. Did the war change him, what did he see, who did he lose, why I never sent those letters, why he didn't try harder when he finally did come back.

These thoughts run me over like a freight train, but everything comes back to wondering why the fuck he left me in the first place. Being back here with him, on this beach, feeling these feelings, spending this time together... It's why I avoided coming home so much. Because as angry as I was, and still am, spending time with him the past few weeks has confirmed I'm still, on some level, hopelessly in love with him.

It's an all-encompassing love I feel deep in my bones. My body hums to life when I'm near him. It scares the ever-loving shit out of me. I need to stop this train of feelings barreling through me before it runs off the tracks.

We look at each other, as if daring the other to talk. One of us finally needs to break the silence so I step up to the plate. "It's just a crazy coincidence, Theo," I say, turning my gaze out to the water in my attempt to distract myself from the myriad of feelings running wild in my head.

"Don't do this, Lyla. I can see you shutting down right in front of me. You know I don't believe in coincidences. I can't ask you to forget the past. Hell, I can't forget the past, either. I wouldn't want to, anyway. Pretend we never saw the tattoos. I'll put my shirt back on if you want. Be here with me, today. On this beach. Just spend the day with me like we planned." His pleas sound so genuine that they chisel away at the walls I'm desperately trying to keep around my heart.

I'm quiet for a while, staring at the water. Theo doesn't push me for a response, but I know he's dying for one. "Let's just exist together today. I'm not ready to call you a friend. Theo. There's too many skeletons in your closet." I look at him and force a smile. "You said something about a kickass snack bag. Share the goods."

He passes the bag over to me and says, "You'll never be just a friend to me, Lyla. Besides, I don't picture any of my other friends naked." His words have me curling my toes and that

125

sexual tension I felt between us last night comes back in full force. The way he stares at me, with so much affection and desire, would make me weak in the knees if I wasn't already sitting down. I bite my lip as I look at him, desperately trying not to think about this man naked.

The day passes quickly, which is a definite sign that it's going well. I wouldn't say that we pick up where we left off, because it's been too many years and too much has happened for it to be like that, but we drift into effortless conversation about anything and everything. We read. I laugh at the stories he tells me about my brother, and the trouble they get into, and I secretly swoon when he talks about his cat.

Being around Theo like this, when we're just trying to have fun and push all of the heavy stuff to the side, reminds me why I fell in love with him all those years ago. Because I always have fun with him. No matter what we're doing, being around him is always easy. Natural.

We go in the water for a quick dip a few different times. We people watch and pet the dogs that come running up to us on their way to the water or back to their owner's blanket. It's not until my "Beaching It" playlist is over that I realize hours have passed. It's been the best day I've had in a long time.

Theo jumps up out of his chair and reaches for my hand. "Come on, Sunshine. It's been hours since we've been in the water." I've sneaked a lot of looks at him today and I have to say: the man has aged like a fine wine. His skin is still bronzed, hanging on to that summer tan. My eyes move to his chest and work their way down to his abs. I stop the moan that's worked its way up my throat before it escapes my lips.

Theo looks good. Simple as that. He's well built, broad and athletic looking. His body proves that he's active and that he watches what he puts into it, but his diet doesn't rule his life. He reminds me of Theo James, but with ink which automatically makes him ten times as sexy. The sweat glistening over those tattoos draws me in more, and I feel flutters in my stomach and a wetness between my legs that has me stifling another moan.

Along with the one he has on his forearm, he has another on his upper arm and shoulder that I'm pretending doesn't exist, and a third on his muscular quad. His body is solid, sexy as fuck, and I can't help but imagine how he would feel on top of me.

It's not until I hear him say, "Hello? Earth to Lyla," that I realize I am staring at him like he's a piece of meat. I throw caution to the wind and take his hand, letting him pull me out of my chair and hold my hand as we walk down to the water. The beach is nearly empty now, peaceful beyond belief.

We slowly wade into the ocean, near each other but not touching. We're about knee deep when he splashes me. He doesn't soak me, but it's wet enough to get my attention, that's for damn sure. I gasp and turn to him. "Oh, you're gonna pay for that!"

He gives me a wicked smile in return.

I splash him back. Before long, we're laughing like kids, splashing like crazy, and both soaked to the bone. "I look like a drowned rat, Theo. Thanks for that," I say, still laughing as I push my wet hair out of my face.

"Nah, you're gorgeous as always, Sunshine."

I head back toward our set up, Theo a few steps behind me. Before I can do it myself, Theo reaches down and grabs my towel from my chair. We're standing face-to-face as he gently wraps it around me, tucking a stray hair behind my ear. A spark races through me at his light touch. He looks into my eyes, but then his gaze drops to my lips, like he's considering if he should kiss me or not.

I'm torn between being absolutely desperate for it and

wanting to run back into the water to avoid the possibility of it happening—and the heartbreak that could come if I go down that road again. I've never felt so conflicted in my life as my heart and my mind battle for control.

Theo leans forward then, and his lips brush against mine, softly, tentatively. Just that soft brush of his lips awakens something inside me that's been asleep for the last six years . He pulls back and looks into my eyes again, as if asking for permission to go further. I give him a nod, and he takes my face in his hands before slamming his lips to mine.

It's a searing kiss that turns into something deeper in a split second. We're ravenous for each other. It's everything I've missed for the last six years. It's raw. It's carnal. It's desperate. There's nothing gentle about it as his tongue roams my mouth, dancing with mine.

His hands move from my face and down my body, gripping my hips as he pulls me closer to him. I can feel his hard length through his bathing suit. A desperate moan sneaks out of my mouth. Our kiss feels like a collision of want and need and everything in between. He kisses me like it's a promise, and I surrender to whatever that promise is.

"Fuck, Lyla, I've missed this," Theo says when he breaks away for a breath before claiming my mouth again. He nips at my bottom lip before his tongue is back in my mouth. I wrap my arms around his neck, but there's no possible way for us to get any closer than we already are.

We consume each other as our kiss goes on and on. I never want it to end. He breaks away from my mouth and drags his lips down the side of my throat to my collarbone. He bites it gently before licking his way back to my mouth and claiming it again. It's like we've forgotten we're on a public, albeit empty, beach as we devour each other like we're making up for lost time.

This kiss doesn't just make me weak in the knees. This kiss knocks my world off its axis. The second his lips touched mine, the world tilted, and I'm certain it will never right itself again.

I wonder if this moment was inevitable. If it was fate, and on some level, I knew that when I agreed to come with him today. Because when I think about it, we're inevitable. Like the sun coming up every morning and then letting the moon take center stage every night. Like the promise of stars in the sky every night. Like the tide coming in and out every single day..

I buried these feelings for years, but now they're bubbling to the surface, threatening to consume me. And that thought shakes me to my core.

Theo leaving me flashes through my mind, and I wonder if that's inevitable, too. I wouldn't survive losing him again. So as much as this kiss is everything, my body on fire from the heat of it, I pull back.

"I can't do this," I say. I'm breathing heavily, partially from kissing and partially from what feels like sheer panic at the idea of loving and losing him again. I wipe my hair out of my face and bring my hands in front of my mouth. Anything to keep them from reaching for him again. Theo must see the panic that's in my eyes because he immediately takes a step back, giving me the space he can see I'm desperate for.

"I'm sorry, Lyla. If I pushed you... If you felt pressured... I'm so sorry," he apologizes, looking broken as he holds his hands up in surrender. I nod my head, trying to calm my thoughts.

"It's okay. You didn't push. I don't..." I take a deep breath. "I just don't think I'm ready for this. I can't go down this road again. I won't make it out alive. I'm petrified to trust you again, Theo," I admit, pressing my palms to my eyes. When I finally look at him again, I don't just see sadness in his eyes. I see utter devastation. A look that is probably reflected in my own eyes at the realization that we might never get back what we once had.

"I'm sorry. I can't say it enough, Lyla, but I'm so sorry. I can't take back hurting you. I wish I could so fucking badly. All I can do is work to prove to you, to show you every day, that I will never hurt you again. You own me, Sunshine. My heart is tethered to yours in a way I can't put into words except to say that I am so fucking in love with you. You're the air I breathe. And for as long as it takes, I'll keep trying to show you that. I'll show up everyday, trying to prove that to you, trying to make you understand that you are my life. And without you, my life is incomplete. You are everything to me, Lyla."

His mood eyes change. They're now dark blue, almost midnight in color. They're filled with lust and desperation, and I feel like he's looking into the depths of my soul when he stares at me. As if he can't stop himself from touching me, he reaches out, taking my face in both of his hands.

"I just need time, Theo. I'm not trying to be wishy-washy, but I need space to figure things out. To figure out if my feelings for you outweigh my fear of being hurt by you again."

"You can have all the time you want, Lyla. All the time you need. When I tell you I'm not going anywhere, I mean it. Til the wheels fall off. Til the end of time. Til the apocalypse comes. Whatever. You are everything to me, Sunshine, and I'll be here waiting for you. Working every day to prove that devotion to you. On my life."

I nod my head at him, still keeping my distance.

"Okay. No promises, Theo. There's still so much you haven't told me."

*Like why you left me in the first place.*

"My promises stand no matter what you decide. I can only hope and pray that you give me another chance. I swear to

God, you won't regret it. Now come on, let's watch the rest of this sunset and then I'll take you home."

So that's what we do. We sit in comfortable silence, listening to the gentle waves lap the shore and watch as the sun dips below the horizon.

# THIRTEEN

*theo*

THE DAY SPENT at the beach is like a few huge steps forward with Lyla. It was carefree, relaxing, and just plain old fun. We talked for hours and shared endless laughs. And that kiss? That kiss is something I've thought about for years. Something I'll think about every time I fuck my hand in the shower.

It's like it brought me back to life after years of being dormant and empty inside. Feeling her breath, tasting her, holding her body up against mine, seeing her be just as lost in the moment as I was lit me up in more ways than I ever could have imagined. If I never get to touch her again, that kiss will be what I think about during my last seconds on Earth.

But she pulled away. Told me she couldn't do it. It feels like a dozen steps backward in my quest to get her back. She was quiet the rest of the night, closing herself off from me. It was like some of the warmth that was there all day was gone. Faded, like the sun.

It's a scary reminder of how quickly things can change. One minute, I'm thinking we're on our way to getting back together because there's no way to ignore the chemistry that's between us. The next, I'm throwing my hands up to show her I'd never push her to do something she wasn't ready for or didn't want.

I know it won't be easy. I've caused her so much hurt, done so much damage, I don't deserve it to be. I guess, in a way, I let my guard down, too, thinking I'd be able to waltz back into her world and break down her walls in a matter of weeks. But I can be a persistent motherfucker when I need to be, so I'll give her the space she wants for now. There's no way in hell I'm giving up on her, on us.

As I lie in bed, mentally making a Sunday to-do list, my phone dings with a text. I'm irrationally hopeful it's Lyla, but when I pick up my phone I see it's Colin. I try to ignore the pang of disappointment.

**Colin: Call me.**

My mind immediately goes to the worst case scenario as I dial his number. He answers on the second ring. "Hey, bro, I know I told you I'd be there by nine, but I'm running a little late."

"We didn't make plans for today, Colin."

"Yeah, yeah. I'll pick up bagels. See you in half an hour." It dawns on me what's going on.

"You had company last night, didn't you? And now you can't get her to leave," I say with a laugh. This is classic Colin.

"Yup." His voice gets louder as he continues. "And I definitely need to sweat out the alcohol, so I'm glad we have these workout plans. I have to pick Derek up on the way, so I'll head out soon... Oh, good morning, Kayla!"

"It's Kaitlyn, asshole," I hear in the background, and I shake my head.

"Fuck. See you soon, Theo."

I laugh as he hangs up the phone. My mouth waters thinking about a fresh bagel. I know Colin will see this entire charade through and actually go to Hot Bagels just so he doesn't feel like such a dick. He probably called Derek before texting me.

It's not quite an hour later when the guys roll up, bagels in hand. Colin is yammering on about god knows what, and Derek has a scowl on his face that can be seen from a mile away. The guy could give Grumpy from Snow White a run for his money.

He's never happy to see me but we coexist well. He gives me a chin nod and a clipped, "Hey," as he walks in the door. Diego immediately comes over, flops on his belly, and meows like he's been starving for attention all morning. As if he wasn't glued to me since I got home from the beach yesterday.

"What's up, you furry little bastard?" Derek asks as he squats down to pet him. Diego lets him for longer than most people, and Derek gets a solid minute in before he swipes at him. "Cats are such assholes."

"Hey! Don't talk about Theo's son like that. It might be the only nephew we get out of him." Colin scoops Diego into his arms and says something about how Uncle Colin is glad to see him. "Unless he and Lyla kissed and made up at the beach yesterday."

Derek's head snaps to look over at me.

"You are such a shit starter, Colin. We had a great day. That's it."

"And nothing happened between you guys?" Colin scratches Diego behind the ears while he waits for my answer. The cat absolutely hams it up, purring so loudly I can hear him from where I stand.

Because things with Lyla are so touch and go, I don't want to talk about anything that happens between us until I know with more certainty we're on the path to getting back together. Plus, when it comes to stuff we do, it's no one's business but our own. So, instead of giving him a real answer, I just say, "If she wants to tell you what's going on between us, she can. I'm going to leave it up to your sister."

Surprisingly, Colin drops the subject and gives me a nod before heading off to the kitchen with the bagels in one hand and my cat in the other. Derek and I follow and start unpacking the food.

"I'm just going to get this off my chest, and I don't care if I sound like an asshole," Derek says.

"Here we go," Colin mutters under his breath. Derek shoots him an impatient glare.

"You pulled the rug out from under her, man. Leaving was a real dick move, Theo. Lyla worked her ass off to move on from you. She's more like herself than she has been in years, and I swear to God, if you break her heart again, I will kill you. I will kill you and bury the body on a jobsite and no one would ever find it. And then I'll take Diego and be his new dad and tell him everyday what an abhorrent piece of shit you are."

"Jesus, Derek, that's some dark shit. But I'll help," Colin says, a mouthful of food in his mouth.

I look them both in the eyes and say, "I don't know what's going to happen in the future. Do I want to be with her? Of fucking course. With every fiber of my being. But the ball's in her court, and I'm following her lead. But I promise you, I will never hurt her again. On my life."

Derek nods at me.

"Okay. Let's eat and work out," Colin says. "I really do need to sweat out the booze."

"So this wasn't just an act to get Kayla out of your house?" I ask.

"Seriously, Colin? Her name was Kaitlyn," Derek says with exasperation.

"That was just a bonus, shithead."

· · ·

After we eat, we make our way to my garage where I have a decent home gym set up. We debate the workout for a few minutes before coming to an agreement on a plan and writing it on the white board.

"Derek, is this the week Mom and Dad are going away?" Colin asks as we get started.

"Yeah. They leave on Tuesday. Don't you pay attention to anything?"

"Why do I have to when I have you and Ly to keep me in line?" He gives his brother a smile, and Derek rolls his eyes and laughs.

"I'm surprised your dad is okay going out of town right now. With how worried he's been, I'm impressed they're still going," I say.

"It took a lot of convincing on Lyla's part. Promising them she won't leave the house by herself." Derek glances at me before he continues. "I know you'll be there to run with her every morning, so I'm sure that pacified him as well."

"To be fair, she's home alone a lot during the day with Dad at work and Mom buzzing around here, there, and everywhere. She can just keep doing what she's been doing—keep the doors locked and the alarm armed," Colin says after he finishes the last reps in his set.

"It's only for four nights. I'll stay over one night for a Love Is Blind marathon. If she wants company the other nights, she'll let us know. We can't smother her," Derek says.

As much as I'd like to invite myself for a four-day sleepover with Lyla at the Sullivan house, I don't breathe a word about it. Derek is right. If she wants company the other nights, she'll ask, and I'll be happy to swoop in and stay with her. Their couch is comfortable as hell, so it's not like I'd be hard-pressed for a good night's sleep. Hell, I'd sleep in far worse conditions if it meant getting extra time with her.

# FOURTEEN

## *Lyla*

I WAKE up on Sunday feeling the weight of yesterday's heaviness on my heart like a damn elephant sitting on my chest. It was a day that was reminiscent of hundreds of days Theo and I spent together. It was easy, almost like all the pieces fell back into place.

And that kiss was beautiful chaos. The world could have burned down around us and we wouldn't have noticed the flames. He kissed me like he was making up for all of the lost years while also being afraid he might never get to do it again.

It was all of the things I remember about the physical side of our relationship—intense, carnal, feverish.

He was honest about his feelings for me. I could see it in his eyes, hear it in his voice. I know he meant what he said about loving me, wanting to be with me, and being willing to wait. I want so badly to trust him, but I can't help but be apprehensive. It's why I had to pull back. Another heartbreak from him would be the end of me. Not just a bruise, but my demise. It would bury me..

When you shatter something, it's never the same again, no matter how carefully you put it back together. I've slowly and painstakingly repaired my heart over the years, but it's still fragile. I wonder if I'll always be waiting for the other shoe to drop. Waiting for him to up and leave for one reason or another. As much as I want to give him another chance, I don't know if that risk is worth it.

* * *

After rolling out of bed and drinking a couple cups of coffee, I spend a huge chunk of the day hanging out with Dad. We hit the farmers market in town and go to the garden center to pick up shrubs for a bed of dirt we cleared last weekend. After lunch we tackle planting our new purchases.

We work side by side in the flower bed digging the necessary holes for the plants we bought. It's methodical and relaxing.

"Thanks for not giving me a hard time about Theo running with you, kiddo," he says as we work.

"I'm sorry for being a pain in the ass about it at first, Dad. I get my stubbornness from you, so really you have no one to blame but yourself." He laughs as I continue. "I promise I'll be on my best behavior while you're gone."

I know he's stressed about leaving me. And if I'm being honest with myself, after my run-ins with that creepy man in town and then at the bar, I'm a little uneasy myself. But this is the one trip my parents are religious about taking every year. They go to Nantucket for their anniversary and have been doing it since my brothers and I were kids.

"No running alone. Keep the alarm armed when you're home. If you go out at all, make sure one of the guys is with you. And for the love of all that is holy, please don't use the grill," my dad rattles off, as if going down a mental checklist of reminders for me.

"I almost set the house on fire *one* time and you guys act like I'm a liability," I reply. He raises an eyebrow at me. I throw my hands up in surrender. "Fine, I promise I won't touch it."

"And if you get nervous just call your brothers. Or Theo. I'm sure any of them would be happy to keep you company. Speaking of Theo, you seem to be getting along better as the weeks go by."

Now it's my turn to roll my eyes.

"Smooth, Dad, real smooth. Mom put you up to asking that?"

"She's dying for an inside scoop," he says with a sheepish smile.

"I don't know. I'm letting myself enjoy spending time with him again. I've missed him. Being around him again makes it feel like he's the puzzle piece I've been missing all these years. But I don't trust him, and I don't know if I'll ever be able to give him 100 percent of myself because of that."

"That's understandable. Don't rush things. Just keep following your heart, Lyla, and see where it leads you. If it's not him, then it's not him." He reaches over and squeezes my shoulder. "If I haven't told you lately, I'm so proud of you, kiddo."

"Thanks, Dad."

"I mean it. I don't think you give yourself enough credit for what you've overcome and all of your hard work. As much as it scares the shit out of me, I'm damn proud of those investigative skills. Like a dog with a bone when it came to sniffing out Hollman and his crew. And your writing... I find it painful to even proofread officer reports, and here you are, writing *pages* without batting an eye. But please don't put yourself in danger again."

"Not making any promises, Dad. But I'll try my best to stay

out of trouble." He nudges me gently with his elbow and when I look at him, he gives me a warm smile.

We spend a few more hours working in the yard, talking about their Nantucket plans, and the possibility of them finally getting a dog. Eventually, we call it a day, and I spend the rest of the afternoon relaxing on the back patio. My brothers come over for Sunday dinner—a weekly tradition that always ends with sundaes.

Theo gives me space outside of sending me a picture of the book he just finished and a quick message confirming our meetup time for tomorrow. After a crappy night of sleep and a day of being outside, I hit the hay early, and thankfully, sleep like a log.

\* \* \*

Theo is already waiting for me when I walk out. Even in the dark morning, I can see his face light up when our eyes connect. His messy bed head hair and the way his shirt clings to his broad shoulders has me reminding myself not to drool.

"Hey, Sunshine." He meets me halfway up the driveway with his arms somewhat extended, as if he's going to hug me, then stops himself. I reach forward and squeeze his forearm in greeting. He looks over at the yard and comments, "Shrubs look great. You guys put in some work yesterday."

"We did and I'm feeling it today. I was thinking of a longer run this morning, just in case work gets in the way this week and we have to skip a few days," I say as I put my earbud in.

"Works for me. Can we make our way to Main Street? I've been jonesing for a donut for days, and if we plan it right, Glazed Gull will be open by the time we pass by." My mouth waters at the thought of a donut, so I eagerly nod my head in agreement.

Like we have the past few runs, we make our way past the beach just as the sun comes up. We stop at what I've subconsciously dubbed "our" bench and sit down to soak it in. He sits closer than he has on past mornings and I can feel the heat radiating off of his skin.

Watching the sunrise is something I'll never get tired of, and I find some solace in watching the sky light up as the ball of fire rises. I've been quiet these first few miles, my guard back up without me even realizing it. But when Theo leans down to tie his shoe and his chain falls out of his shirt, my silence breaks with a gasp.

"Is that... Is that the necklace I gave you?" I ask, my voice barely above a whisper.

He pulls the chain and pendant all the way out until I'm able to see the small silver compass. "Of course it is. Aside from when I know I'm going to swim, I never take it off."

I can't stop myself from leaning toward him and gently skimming my fingers over the charm. His breath hitches at our close proximity. It was my birthday gift to him when he turned twenty-one. "I can't believe you still have it," I say softly. I look at the backside of it and brush my thumb over the words I had engraved on it—*The Luckiest*. The name of our song by Ben Folds.

"It's been around the world with me, Lyla. This compass has seen me through some dark times but led me back here. It's the most important thing I own."

I can't explain how much it means to me that he still has it. I just nod my head and try to keep my eyes from watering. When he puts his arms on the bench behind us, he pulls me closer to him. Because I find myself craving his touch, his warmth, I don't move away.

Eventually, we get back to our run and find ourselves walking into The Glazed Gull where we find Clayton at the counter, already in his uniform. Theo goes to use the restroom but says hello to him along the way. Clayton turns and his gaze lands on me. Once Theo has gone into the bathroom he makes his way over to where I'm standing.

"I don't like keeping secrets from your brother or your dad, Lyla. Have you seen that guy around since the other night?"

I shake my head and lean forward when I speak. "Nope. I promise. Please, Clayton, just keep it between us. I'm sure it was nothing. I'll let you know if I have another run-in with him." My eyes are locked on his and when I say the words they're laced with desperation.

"Fuck." He runs his hand through his hair in frustration. "I hope this doesn't bite me in the ass."

Theo comes back out and tells Clayton he'll see him at the station shortly. We order our donuts and devour them at the counter before heading back outside. We take it slow the rest of the way and Theo says goodbye to me in the driveway.

"I'll text you later, Sunshine."

I don't reach out to hug him, and he respects my space, giving me a smile before I head inside.

\* \* \*

My parents leave for Nantucket on Tuesday morning. I offer to drop them off at the ferry, but they insist on driving themselves. I once again promise to be vigilant about my safety and call if there are any issues. I give them both hugs and send them on their way.

Theo and Colin go into work early to deal with a case so Derek runs with me. He absolutely smokes me, and I know I'm going to be hurting from it later. I spend the rest of the day finishing the last freelance article that's been hanging over my head and sending it off to the editor.

While it feels good to be done with all of the work I've taken on, it's strange having nothing on my plate. I need to do some serious soul-searching about what my next steps are with my career, but I decide to be irresponsible and shove those worries aside.

Colin, Derek, and Theo all check in on me throughout the day and offer to come over for a sleepover if I'm feeling lonely. I turn them down and watch chick flicks in my pajamas while eating ice cream for dinner and a gold bag of gummy bears for dessert.

On Wednesday, Theo is still tied up with their case and Derek needs to get to his job site early, so I skip my run and take the opportunity to sleep in. My lazy morning turns into a lazy day. I check in with my parents. I make plans for a Facetime date with Quinn later, and Derek confirms coming over to watch *Love is Blind* and eat pizza.

Theo sends me a text after lunch asking if he can stop by to say hello on his way home from work. He calls me right on time to let me know he's out front, and I disarm the alarm for him to come in.

"Can I hug you?" he immediately asks, and I let him pull me in his arms, hesitating before wrapping my arms around his waist in response. "I don't even care how desperate I just sounded. It's been a shit couple of days, and I just need to hold you in some capacity," he murmurs into my hair.

It's damn comfortable being in his arms, but eventually, I pull back and walk into the family room. He locks the door and follows behind. I sit on the couch and wait for him to join me before responding. He sits next to me, but not so close that we're touching.

"Rough case?" I ask.

"A frustrating one. An assault and no one wants to talk. It's like pulling teeth dealing with the witnesses, who, of course, aren't locals. It's also been a pain in the ass driving the thirty-forty minutes toward Boston when we need to locate one of them." He lets out a frustrated sigh. "Enough about me. You smell like gummy bears. How are you making out on your own?"

"Everyone can rest easy. I haven't attempted to turn on the grill." He laughs. "But I've been fine. Had ice cream for dinner last night. I think I need to start rationing my gummy bears because I'm crushing a pack a day. Was a lazy sloth today. Derek is skipping guys' night to join me for *Love is Blind* and pizza."

"I can't believe you two watch that shit."

"Watch it and love every single minute of it."

"You want company tomorrow night?" He looks so hopeful when he asks that I almost feel bad for not saying yes. But I'm not ready for that. I need to maintain some level of space while I figure out what I want. While I wait for him to open up to me about why he left.

I'm also not sure I trust myself with him, from a physical standpoint. It's been a long time since I've been fucked properly, been brought to the pinnacle of pleasure in a way that only he can offer.I'm not sure I'd be able to resist him. The attraction between us... It wouldn't take long for hands to wander, and I'm just not ready to do anything that will cloud my judgement.

"Thanks for the offer, but I'll be okay." A few beats of silence pass before either of us talk.

"I'm afraid that kiss, as mind blowing as it was, might have done more harm than good, Sunshine," he murmurs softly. "I can feel you pulling away, feel that distance between us again. Like we're back to the beginning. Don't shut me out, Lyla. Please."

"That kiss was...intense." I take a second to get my

thoughts together and let out a breath before I continue. "It was like being struck by lightning, Theo. It rocked me to the core. Six years have gone by, but that kiss felt like coming home. I've replayed the scene in my head dozens of times, and each time I'm reminded of two things—my feelings for you have never gone away and those feelings scare the shit out of me. I can feel the pull, Theo. That gives you the power to break me and I wouldn't survive it."

Theo shakes his head in disagreement. "I would break myself into a thousand pieces before I ever hurt you again, Lyla."

"You say that now, but—"

"Wait. So you're admitting you still have strong feelings for me?" He gives me the most genuine, adorable smile as he waits for my answer.

"I'm still sorting through them, but yeah, I'd say so. Why are you looking at me like that?"

"Because I can work with that. I'm relentless, baby. The way I feel about you... It's not something I'm going to ignore any longer. The years apart didn't dull that for me. I thought I loved you then, but now? Just being around you again? It's deeper than that. I feel it in the depths of my soul. You're like a lifeline for me, Lyla. In the end, if you told me you didn't want to be with me, I'd back off. Because more than anything, I want you to be happy. It would kill me if you married someone else, if you had his babies, if you grew old with him. But if that's what you want, I'd never stand in the way of it. Knowing that you still care... Sunshine, I'll stop at nothing to win you back. To win *us* back."

It astonishes me—how open he is with his feelings. It shouldn't, because he was always this way. But I assumed his life experiences and the passage of time would have hardened him.

While he still hasn't opened up to me about why he left, the way he speaks so freely about his feelings, never mincing words no matter who's in earshot, has always been something I found incredibly sexy about Theo. That balance of strength and protectiveness coupled with a gentleness and a raw honesty, has always been the most masculine thing about him.

He leans forward and gently cups the sides of my face. "I'm relentless when it comes to you, baby," he says softly before he sits back. His phone rings not a second later. I assume it's Colin based on the way he answers the call. "I'm at your sister's. I'll leave in five and come pick you up."

"Stuck driving again?" I ask.

"I don't mind. It's the only way I can ensure it's not a late night."

"Smart," I say, giving him a nod of approval.

"What time is Derek going to be here?" He looks around, as if he's afraid to leave me.

"He texted right before you got here to say he was leaving work shortly, so I would imagine by 6:30. Which is perfect because I have a Facetime date with Quinn once you're outta here."

He stands up, and I walk him to the door. "Lock it behind me and turn the alarm on."

"Yes, Boss." I give him a playful salute.

He kisses me on top of my head, a gesture that is sweet and innocent but still has my heart pitter-pattering, and is out the door, looking back to make sure I shut it. I lock myself back in, turn the alarm off, and head into the kitchen to pour myself a glass of wine. I settle onto the couch with my laptop and smile when I see Quinn calling.

"It's been days! Fill me in on what's happening!" Quinn says as soon as I answer. She holds her wine glass up and shimmies it. "Leave nothing out or I will kick your ass."

I start by recounting our entire day at the beach on Saturday, drawing out the conversation with the smallest, most minute details just to drive her crazy.

"Okay, get to the part where you talk about your feelings. And the kiss."

As instructed, I leave nothing out and Quinn eats it up. Before we can dive into more, there's a knock at the door.

"Hang on, let me get this. Derek wasn't supposed to be over this early, but I guess he was hungry and moved quicker than he thought he would." As I move to disarm the alarm, the knock grows louder. "Dang, Derek, just give me a second!"

I don't know if it's the glass of wine that dulls my vigilance, or just the fact that I'm so certain it's Derek, but I don't even look out the window before I unlock the door. It swings open, but before I can register what's happening, there's a man in the foyer, crowding my space. .

A man who looks vaguely familiar but I don't know.

A man who shouldn't be here.

# FIFTEEN

## *Lyla*

I SCREAM as I recognize the man from the bar. I'm so loud that Quinn must hear me because she yells out my name, concern and panic evident in her high-pitched voice.

He pushes me against the wall that's in the entryway of the house, knocking a few frames off the wall. The glass shatters as they hit the hardwood floor. His hands are wrapped around my throat as he slams me into the wall so powerfully I can't catch my breath. His tight grip telling me he's strong as hell. *Deja fucking vu* I think to myself as I gasp for air.

I desperately try to claw at his hands but don't do much more than scratch him. I switch strategies and start kicking, trying to aim for his groin but I'll take any contact I can get. It only pisses him off. His hands get tighten, his hot breath fanning over my face when he says, "You think you can fuck with Hollman and live to tell the tale? I'm just getting started here, *Lyla*."

*Shit. He clearly wasn't just a drunk getting handsy the other night.*

I have to calm down and think more methodically. Expending energy by throwing my body around, coupled with my airway cutting off, is making my vision fuzzy. Those tell-tale black spots start dancing in front of my eyes.

*Calm down, Lyla. Dead weight is heavier to move.*

Derek always says staying heavy in jiu jitsu means your body is tougher to bump off.

I stop fighting him and allow my body to go limp, but his arms keep me upright. I can feel tears running down my face, and it's then that I also realize my nose is running. I spit the biggest wad of phlegm I can muster right in his face.

He takes one hand away from my throat to wipe it away. It gives me enough time to take a deep breath. I scratch his face as hard as I can, aiming for his eyes. I take another deep breath, but the air is sharp and sends a shiver down my spine.

Quinn yells from my computer in the background a second time, her voice nearing hysterics. I'm hoping and praying she'll call the police, but even then, it'll take time for her to get connected to the local department. I'm scared out of my mind, but I resist the urge to break down. If I can hang on a few more minutes, Derek is bound to get here.

*Please don't let Derek be too late.*

Unfortunately, the man comes back at me with a vengeance, slapping me so hard stars enter my vision and metallic coats my tongue.

"Please, stop!" There's no hiding the panic in my high-pitched voice. He grabs my biceps and squeezes tight. It reminds me of the way he grabbed me in the hallway at the bar the other night, and I keep screaming. His hands are like iron clamps on my arms as he shoves me farther into the family room. He pushes me so hard, I trip and fall backward. I land on my ass with a thud and wince from the pain that blossoms in my tailbone.

"The more you fight, the more I'm going to like this," he growls at me as he adjusts himself in his pants. *Well, this guy is one sick motherfucker.* I turn onto my hands and knees in an attempt to crawl away. My head pounds, my vision blurry from my tears, and I can feel blood dripping from somewhere on my face. I take a second to quickly wipe my eyes in hopes it'll give me the ability to see better. I've made it into the family room, but he grabs my ankle, yanking me back toward him. *Fuck, this guy is strong.* I tuck myself into the fetal position when he lets go.

"Hollman wants you dead, but he didn't say I couldn't have fun with you first." His tone is menacing, my composure so shot, and I have to choke back the sobs that threaten to escape.

As he punishes me with a few kicks to my back, I think about how my brother is going to walk into this house soon and see my dead body.

I attempt to crawl away again, but he's already too close to me for it to matter. When he flips me onto my back, I lash out, wildly kicking my legs and throwing my arms. No matter what I do, I can't seem to get away from him. He's too fast, too strong, and simply overpowers me. My mind races, but I can't move past the panic that rips through me.

Still on my back, I sweat bullets, writhing and wriggling, trying to get away from him. He plants himself on top of me. He's so heavy that no matter how much I buck my hips, he doesn't move. Quinn is still in the background, reminding me that I'm not alone. She's yelling at me to keep fighting and help will be here soon. *Quinn is going to know what it's like to lose a best friend if I give up.*

The man coils one hand back up around my throat and squeezes just enough to slow me down. I immediately try to loosen his fingers, but again, he's just too strong, his grip too firm. He rips my shirt open next, the buttons scattering to the floor around us. He grabs one of my breasts with his free hand and squeezes hard while rubbing his crotch on me. "You feel that, bitch? I told you, the more you scream, the better it is for me."

Terror envelops my body, wrapping around my throat with a tighter hold than his hand. Every cell in my body tells me this man is going to kill me. I yell as loud as I can, but my voice is already so brittle.

He slams me against the floor with such force it knocks the wind out of me. A throb courses through my skull. I'm getting weaker by the second, and I'm horrified over knowing that every move I make to fight him turns him on more.

I can't hold back my sobs as I cry, and my body shakes as I try to fight him off. "Please!" I plead. "Please don't do this." My voice is broken and low, my breathing ragged as I stare at him. My body freezes, my arms and legs locked in place as terror takes over my body. I turn to stone and, for a second, am disgusted with myself for seemingly surrendering to this man.

My mind screams. *Move! Fight! What are you doing? Do you want to die?* But my body and mind are disconnected. Time seemingly stands still as I lie still, zoning out as tears collect in my eyes. It just adds to his excitement. The room closes in on me, the air thick and heavy, making it harder for me to breathe.

I tell myself that maybe laying here and letting him rape me might be the only way to buy enough time to keep him from killing me. I'm so spent that I have no energy to fight back. But when he leans in closer, his erection poking me through his jeans, his hot, disgusting breath in my face, I decide I'm not going to let him get away with it without a fight. *You just rested, Lyla. Now, fucking move.*

I change my previous strategy of trying to get his hands off of my throat. This time I go right for his eyes, digging my thumbs into the sockets. He doesn't expect it, and it throws him off his game. His grip loosens, and I'm able to buck my hips again.

*Think about what Derek has taught you with jiu jitsu. Keep trying to bump him off.*

The fact that he stumbles a bit and has to work to right himself tells me that he's unstable. I take advantage of his moment of weakness and kick him off me.

I scoot backward on my butt, using my hands for leverage and hoping to put enough space between us that I can get up and run. Before I'm able to do that, he's back on his feet, grabbing for me. His reach is long and he yanks me by the hair, causing my head to snap back. "Fucking cunt!" he swears at me.

A stinging pain spreads throughout my scalp. I yelp from it, and my eyes fill with fresh tears. "Fuck!" I yell.

He shoves me again and I go flying into the coffee table. It sounds like a leg broke off of the table and I reach around blindly hoping to find it. Before I do, he slams me down to the floor with so much force my teeth rattle. He sits on my chest again and holds my hands above my head. His grip is so tight, there's no way I can break free. He slaps me hard, my face whipping to the side. It's enough to stop me from wiggling. I want to give up so badly.

*No! No giving up!*

He uses one hand to undo his belt buckle. The metal clangs together as it falls away from his waist. The sound is worse than nails on a chalkboard and bile rises up my throat. I swallow it down and look around, trying to find something, *anything*, that might help me.

My strength is completely drained. I can barely fight back, but I keep trying to get my hands loose. He grabs the waist-band of my shorts and pulls them down as I scream bloody murder.

## SIXTEEN

*theo*

WHEN I WALK into the Dusty Bird, I find Colin, Drew, and Clayton at a table near the back of the bar, beers and wings in front of them. I say hi to Nate, the owner, and a few other people I know as I make my way over. I sit down and jump into conversation with Colin and Drew. Clayton immediately buries his head in his phone.

I don't get to eat one wing before Colin jumps out of his seat, his phone pressed to his ear. He moves so fast, he sends his chair flying backward. "We gotta go! It's Lyla!" he yells.

I freeze, my hand hovering over the basket of wings. Thoughts of losing my mom leap through my mind, and fear paralyzes me. Sometimes I forget how raw that loss still is for me. Thinking about it sends me into a tailspin, and my thoughts land on Lyla. On the possibility of losing her. I shake myself out of it as Colin books it past me toward the door.

I'm hot on his heels, and since my truck is closer, we hop in. I know Drew and Clayton will be right behind us, but I don't wait for them. They can meet us there. Settling our bill doesn't matter, Nate knows we're good for it. It's not the first time we've had to dine and dash for something work related.

"Quinn, I can't understand what you're saying. I need you to calm down and tell me again," he says into his phone before signaling I give him my phone. He manages Quinn on his and calls the station from mine, all while I'm driving as fast as humanly possible to his parents' house. He tells the station to send units and then focuses on Quinn, putting her on speaker. "What's happening right now, Quinn? What do you see? What do you hear?"

"Someone came into the house. I can't see anything, Colin, but I can hear her screaming, and they're definitely fighting. You have to get there now!" Quinn is breathing heavily, her words are frantic. It's clear that whatever she's witnessing has her terrified.

We're still a solid ten to fifteen minutes out. I can only hope and pray Derek gets there before us. Quinn screams Lyla's name, and the panic in her voice pushes me over the edge. My heart's in my throat, my future slipping between my fingers.

"Fuck, I knew I shouldn't have left her. I should have stayed with her until your brother got there. This is my fault." I say more to myself than to Colin.

"We're not playing the blame game right now, bro. Just concentrate on getting us there without hitting a deer or wrapping us around a tree," Colin replies.

I'm driving as fast as I can, and it still feels like I'm going at a snail's pace.

This is one of those moments when it feels like time stops, and there's something terrible unraveling that I'm powerless to stop. It's a feeling of utter helplessness.

We're quiet for a minute or two, just listening to Quinn who cries while periodically yelling outLyla's name, telling her to hang on. Every time I hear Lyla scream or some other noise that's indicative of a fight, I get closer and closer to losing it. My hands grip the wheel so tight they start to go numb.

Finally, Quinn says, "I think someone else just came in! I still can't see anything, but it sounds like a guy, and he's really pissed off."

"Hopefully, it's Derek. A few units should be pulling up any minute. Quinn, I'm not going to hang up until we get there so tell me if you hear or see something I should know." Colin is eerily calm, the complete opposite of how I feel. I'm so tightly wound that I'm hoping and praying Derek doesn't kill whoever attacked her so I have the opportunity to do it when I get there.

We're about three minutes out when Quinn tells us she can hear sirens in the background. When I finally do pull up to the house, I put the car in park and jump out, gun in hand, darting up the front lawn as fast as I possibly can. Colin tells Quinn he'll call her back and is right behind me as we approach the front door.

To say the scene is chaotic is an understatement. You can cut the tension with a knife, and the tangy smell of blood is in the air. Officers hold Derek back, his hands stained red, as he fights like crazy to get at Lyla's attacker again.

An officer works to get the man cuffed and Clayton and Drew, who were right behind us, appear. My eyes immediately zero in on Lyla, and it's like I've been punched in the gut with an iron fist. "Oh my god," I say to myself as I rush to her side.

She's lying on her side, curled up in the fetal position. Even from a distance, I can tell her face is battered and bruised, her skin marred from the hands of that piece of shit.

## SEVENTEEN

*Lyla*

THE NEXT THING I KNOW, he's no longer on top of me. I keep kicking and shoving, pushing at the empty air, until I realize it's not my eyes playing tricks on me. It's Derek. I can't see him, but I can hear him grunt and swear as he yanks the man off of me. I let out a sob as relief crashes over me.

"Derek!" I cry. "Be careful!" He might not be a cop, but Derek is tough as nails. His solid muscles and black belt in jiujitsu allow him to turn the tables on this guy and perform some sort of takedown before getting on top of him.

All I hear is flesh hitting flesh and grunts coming from both of them as Derek pummels the guy. I look around for something I can use to help, but when I try to stand up, my legs give out on me.

I fall back to the ground as Derek spits, "You piece of shit! I'll fucking kill you." I've never heard my brother so angry, and as I watch him hit this man over and over again, I'm afraid he might actually kill him. I think I hear sirens in the background, and I pray it's not my mind playing tricks on me.

As I sit on the floor bleeding, I watch my brother beat the ever-loving shit out of the guy. I let out a cry of relief when I hear tires screeching to a stop and car doors slamming. Despite the fact that help is here, my heart still pounds with fear. The exhaustion hits me, and I lie back down on my side, curling into myself.

Very quickly, the living room is filled with officers. It takes three of them to pull Derek away. They get handcuffs onto the man who assaulted me and attempt to calm Derek down. This proves to be quite difficult, and the officers still need to hold him back to keep him from finishing what he started. My head, but I can hear them read the guy his rights.

Theo is next in the door with Colin, Drew and Clayton right on his heels. The entire scene feels incredibly chaotic, and there's enough testosterone in the house to light a small city. I close my eyes and, even though I'm in a ton of pain, I just want to go to sleep and avoid the fallout from the night's events. After what just happened, I'm not sure I'll ever be able to close my eyes at night and not feel those hands wrapped around my neck.

One of my eyes is swollen shut, but through the other I slowly look around the room and see Colin take in the entire scene—the bloody criminal in cuffs, the trashed living room, Derek being held back by two officers, and me, his sister curled in a ball on the floor. Theo doesn't give a shit about anything other than the latter and rushes to my side, squatting down next to me.

"Lyla. Lyla, look at me. Are you okay?"

I struggle to focus, but when I finally make eye contact, I see that his are a dark gray blue that hold a myriad of emotions —fear, guilt, anger. I blink a few times but have a hard time focusing.

"Shit. Is there an ambulance on the way?" he calls out to the other officers.

Everything hurts. I tell myself to hold on, to not pass out. I look over at the man in cuffs. *How many more men is Hollman going to send after me?*

Someone confirms there's an ambulance en route. Theo's voice softens, and he looks back at me. "I'm right here, baby. Fuck, I'm so sorry. I shouldn't have left you, but I'm here now. You're safe." I don't think I'll ever feel safe again, but I can't articulate that thought into words.

Theo raises his hand to bring it to my face, but because I'm so out of it, I shrink back. The look of anguish that crosses his face is enough to break my heart.

"Sorry," I murmur.

"Don't you dare apologize." He brings his hand up again and looks at me for permission. I give the slightest nod in an effort to avoid making my headache even worse. He softly brushes my hair out of my face. When he helps me sit up, he notices that my shirt is torn open. His eyes go even darker, something I didn't think was possible. "Hang on, Sunshine. Let's cover you up."

He reaches for the buttons on his flannel shirt and quickly works his way down. He shrugs out of the shirt and wraps it around my shoulders. The soft fabric and the faint scent of his cologne envelope me and bring me immediate comfort. He touches his forehead to mine and asks so quietly I can barely hear him, "Lyla, did he rape you?"

His body trembles."No. Derek got here in time," I manage to say, my throat raw from screaming. He breathes a sigh of relief. "Help me stand, please," I manage to get out, but he doesn't pull me to my feet. Instead, he leans down and gently scoops me into his arms.

From there, he takes a few steps over to the couch and sits me down, claiming the spot next to me. I hug my knees as close to my chest as I can without making my ribs hurt more, hold his shirt tightly around me, and look around to take everything in.

The living room, the scene of so many holidays, birthdays, movie and board game nights, is in total disarray. All of the warmth and joy that this room usually represents has been sucked out of it.

I look at the spot in the corner where our Christmas tree always goes and see broken glass and frames. A glance at the coffee table, usually decorated with a candle and a few books, and I see it tilting down at one end, two legs broken at some point during our struggle. I lean my head back and close my eyes, wondering how I'll ever feel joy in this room again.

Derek finally appears to calm down and makes his way over to us with Colin. Colin is the senior officer at the scene, so even though I imagine it's a conflict of interest for him to take charge, at this moment, it's exactly what he's doing.

I'm so used to him being my goofy, happy-go-lucky brother that the seriousness in his body language is almost unrecognizable. His eyes are hard, his shoulders tense as he barks orders. My mind clears up enough that I start to think about the ramifications Derek could face for the absolute ass kicking he delivered.

"Is Derek going to get in trouble?" I ask quietly.

"Fuck, no," Colin says firmly. "The motherfucker forced his way into this house, attacked you, and had a gun and knife on him. He wasn't here to sell you encyclopedias, Lyla. He was here to hurt you, and the shape you're currently in is evidence of that. Derek acted in defense of you and your life which is justifiable. As much as I would have liked for that piece of shit to be dead, the fact that Derek didn't kill works in his favor, too. Look at me." His voice goes soft, and I bring my eyes to him. "Jesus. You're going to the hospital, and I don't want to hear an argument about it. They're going to examine you and take pictures for evidence. You won't be alone tonight, and I'll make sure there's extra security at the hospital."

I give him a gentle nod and lean back onto the couch cushion.

*Keep your eyes open. If you close them, you're going to relive what you just went through.*

Colin walks back over to the officers who are escorting the man who almost took my life out of the house. I hear him ask who's next on rotation for detectives. He seems satisfied with whatever answer they give him. I startle at the feel of a hand on my leg and look over to find Derek there. "Fuck, Lyla, I'm sorry," he says sadly, pulling his hand away.

The fact that I'm this jumpy around two men who I know would protect me with their lives forces me to acknowledge the status of my current emotional state—anger and sadness are battling it out. One second I want to scream, the next I want to cry as these emotions go to war with each other. I'm sad I'm hurting these two men who love me by recoiling away from them, and I'm beyond pissed that this piece of garbage has made me fearful of being touched by anyone right now. I reach out and squeeze his hand so he knows I'm okay.

"You're bleeding," I say, my voice still scratchy.

"I'm fine. I'll deal with it once we get you squared away."

Colin walks over to us again, this time holding his phone out while it rings. "Someone take this. It's Quinn, and she's probably worried sick waiting for an update."

Before I can say a word, Theo grabs the phone and swipes to answer. I know Quinn is dying to hear my voice, to hear for herself that I'm okay, but my throat feels like I swallowed glass, my head feels like it could split open from the relentless pain, and I'm teetering on the verge of breaking down completely.

Theo quickly updates her and hangs up the phone. "Needless to say, she's relieved you're safe. Thank god she has Colin's number because she called him the minute that guy broke in to alert us."

I didn't think I had any tears left but the idea of Quinn being on Facetime, feeling so helpless while having to listen to everything that was happening is heart-wrenching. If the tables were turned, I think it would scar me for life, and the sounds of the screams would haunt me.

Theo gently puts his arms around me as I cling to the flannel he wrapped around me earlier. "Hang in there, Sunshine. You're okay."

"I hurt everywhere, Theo."

"I know, Lyla. Paramedics are here now. Let's get you checked out and to the hospital."

Derek moves aside so the paramedics can get closer to me, but Theo remains glued to my side. After a quick assessment, they determine I'm likely dealing with a concussion, some bruised, if not broken, ribs, and in need of stitches for the cuts on my face.

I insist on walking to the ambulance. My brother and Theo slowly help me off the sofa. Without saying a word, Theo gets into the ambulance with me and watches me like a hawk while they take my vitals.

I know it'll be a cold day in hell before he leaves my side.

# EIGHTEEN

*theo*

I THOUGHT I knew what fear was. I've faced down the barrel of a gun more times than I'd like to admit. I've fought in war. I've watched insurgents shoot my friends. I've watched people be blown to smithereens. I've had moments where it felt like time stood still as someone's world imploded. I've seen appalling things that have kept me up at night. I don't know a single soldier who fought in war and can say they were never scared.

But tonight, I was confronted by my biggest fear in the world. The one that sent me running to the military to avoid facing the possibility of it, no matter how small of a chance. And confronting the reality of this fear, the one of losing the person I love most, is unlike anything I've ever experienced. My mind goes blank, like leaves scattering around in a windstorm. I fight the urge to go after the man who did this to her, and instead, zero in on Lyla.

She's lying on the floor of the family room. As I get closer, I notice where tears have dried in the blood, leaving splotches on her marred face. I take a deep breath and swallow back the rage that begs to bubble over.

I breathe slowly, deliberately, as I fight to get control of my emotions. I'm one second away from exploding. This absolute ray of light, my sunshine, is on the floor, broken and battered. The idea that I could have lost her, in the most permanent way, literally brings me to my knees in front of her.

When I reach out, she immediately recoils. My chest splits in two. My composure is a fraying rope, and I'm about to snap. I'm careful not to let it show on my face how much it kills me that she just drew back from me because, right now, it's not about me.

I left her, thinking she'd be okay, and this happened. She was attacked again in her own home and is so frightened by the trauma, she can't handle me touching her. I'm so pissed at myself, I want to kick my own ass. To make me feel like an even bigger piece of shit, she has the gall to apologize to me, as if this is all somehow her fault. I vow to myself that I'll never leave this woman vulnerable to being hurt again. I will never run from her, no matter how scared I am.

I hold my hand up to reach for her again, and she gives me a barely noticeable nod. I gently wipe her hair out of her eyes. That curious sparkle that so often lights up her eyes is gone. She moves in an attempt to slowly sit up, so I reach over and help her.

I thought I was at max capacity for anger when I walked in the door, but when I see her shirt torn open, it's grown tenfold. To a level I didn't know existed. Despite my time fighting in a war, I'm not overly prone to violence.

My mother being taken from us because of a violent crime probably has something to do with that, but the rage that runs through me has me wanting to make this guy pay, slowly and painfully, for laying a finger on the woman I love.

I slow my breathing—four counts in, four counts out—and start unbuttoning the flannel shirt I have on. I pull it off and gently wrap it around her shoulders and bring my forehead to hers. It takes me a few more slow breaths to ask the question I'm afraid to hear the answer to. "Lyla, did he rape you?" I whisper.

Her voice is raspy when she says, "No. Derek got here in time."

For a second, the storm inside me quiets, as if I'm in the eye of it.

I feel an immense amount of gratitude toward Derek. Obviously, he would do anything to protect his sister; as evident by the fact that the attacker just got his ass handed to him, but I'm so fucking thankful he got here in time to stop this man from going any further.

When the paramedics arrive, I breathe a sigh of relief that one of them is a woman, because based on her body language with Derek and myself, she's not ready to be touched by a man in any real capacity.

Lyla gets a quick once-over, and we slowly make our way to the ambulance. I toss my keys to Derek in case he needs to move my truck and jump in behind her. Whether she likes it or not, I'm going to be stuck to her side like glue for the foreseeable future. If I have it my way, it'll be forever.

\* \* \*

Even with being rushed through, it still takes forever in the emergency room. The only saving grace is that it's a week night and the summer crowds are gone. I insist on staying in the room while Lyla is examined and wait outside the door when she needs to get some tests done.

Because it's getting late and she still needs a doctor to tend to the various cuts on her face, they decide to admit her for the night for observation. A little while later, her brothers and two other detectives join us in her room to take photos and interview her about the night's events.

I know she's exhausted, but it has to be done while it's fresh in her mind. She was in no shape to be interviewed back at her house. Besides, Colin was adamant that someone else take her statement and photos. Because he's family, and I'm whatever I am to her, in order to protect the integrity of the investigation and avoid any blowback about personal involvement in the case, we stay off to the side.

As suspected, the MRI shows she has a concussion, but she somehow escaped without broken ribs. The nurse assigned to her is a friend of her moms and is not at all happy with all of the visitors. She goes into full-blown mama-bear mode, making sure Lyla is comfortable and not getting more stressed out after the traumatic events of the evening.

"I know you feel like shit, Lyla, but can you hang in there for a little longer so these guys can ask you some questions while it's all fresh in your mind?" Colin asks.

I pinch my nose as I feel a headache coming on from listening to her recount everything. My anger simmers, and I bite down on my cheek to keep myself in check. I'm sitting next to her and desperately want to reach for her hand, but I have no idea if she even wants to be touched or comforted right now.

After about twenty minutes, the nurse can see that Lyla is fading and finally shuts the officers down, reminding them she still needs to have her cuts tended to, and she's dealing with a concussion. Basically, she tells them to get the fuck out and come back tomorrow.

It's well after midnight at this point and as tired as my body is from the crash of the adrenaline rush, my mind is wide awake. Lyla looks pitifully small and vulnerable in the hospital bed. Her eyes look heavy, and she winces when she yawns.

Colin motions for me to join him near the doorway, and I see there's a uniformed officer sitting right outside her door.

"I called my parents. I couldn't put it off any longer, and I haven't heard the end of it for not calling the minute we had him in cuffs. They would have been able to catch the last boat if I had, but it was the last thing on my mind. They'll be on the first boat in the morning, which gets them in before nine."

"I was so wrapped up in Lyla, it didn't even cross my mind to call them earlier. Your dad's right to be pissed."

"I know. Fuck, I can't believe this happened," he says shaking his head in disbelief. "I'm going to head to the station from here. Check on how things are going with the interrogation. I know you won't leave her side tonight, but there's a uniform in the hallway."

I nod my head, relieved that there will be someone else here in the event that I doze off.

"I won't make that mistake again."

"Just crazy that it all happened so fast. What are the odds whoever this guy is knew that she'd be home alone tonight? I'd think the cameras or motion sensor lights would have tripped if he was lurking in the yard."

"Fucking Hollman. This has to be the end of it," I say with more confidence than I feel.

"Well, hopefully I'll find that out tonight. Derek is getting his hands cleaned up, and then I'm sure he'll camp out here with you guys,"

Colin walks back into the room and gently says goodbye to his sister. He waits until she acknowledges him before leaning down to kiss the top of her head. He gives my shoulder a squeeze, and then he's gone.

I use the attached bathroom to take a leak and put on the sweatpants Derek threw in the overnight bag he brought with him. After I wash my hands, I grip the sides of the sink and suck in a few steadying breaths. When I look in the mirror, I see the exhaustion and fear in my eyes.

When I close them I think about what Lyla looked like when we got to the house. I think about the blood and the bruises. About her voice, raw and hoarse. I think about how close I came to her being taken from me. A sound, one I don't even recognize as coming from me, escapes before I can stop it. It's guttural—like the noise a wounded animal would make.

I bring a hand to my mouth to stifle it and squeeze my eyes shut. I cannot break down right now. It's the last thing that Lyla needs. When I'm sure my composure is back I finally open my eyes again and leave the bathroom.

I pop my head in the hallway and let the officer know we're going to get some rest and to knock if there's anything amiss. After closing the door, I slowly walk towards the bed.

I gently rub Lyla's arm. "You want me to get into bed with you, Sunshine?"

"Yes." She says it so quietly I barely hear her.

I climb in gingerly, trying to avoid any quick movements. Her back is to my front, and she settles into me, taking my arm and stretching it over her body, holding my hand tight. We lie like that for a couple of minutes before she starts shaking.

# NINETEEN

## *Lyla*

"SHHHH, LYLA. I'VE GOT YOU," Theo says as he nuzzles my hair. "You're okay. You're safe."

His arm is holding me loosely, as if he's afraid to squeeze too tight, but I have a death grip on his hand. My body trembles from fear and exhaustion. Probably a little shock, too. I don't even realize I'm crying until I taste the tears, and it doesn't take long for sobs to take over.

I don't know how long I cry, how long those tears pour out of me, but eventually they begin to subside, as if my body is completely cried out. The entire time, Theo holds me, brushing my hair out of my face and reassuring me that I'm safe. And as hard as it is for me to admit, I feel secure in his arms. There's a level of comfort, of security, that comes when I'm around him and I know that his protective instincts will keep anything else from happening to me.

The dull ache in my ribs turns into a throbbing pain, like the result of the way I was just bawling. I shift slightly to get more comfortable, and Theo immediately scoots away from me.

"You get comfortable first, and then I'll work around you," he says softly.

"I thought you were backing off to get out of bed," I say, the relief heavy in my voice.

"Hell no, Sunshine. I'm not leaving your side until we figure out what the fuck is going on. And even then, you're stuck with me." There's a finality to his voice that tells me he's not messing around.

"Do you have enough room if I lie on my back?" I ask, as I shift, cringing from the discomfort that rips through my chest.

"Lyla, lie however you feel the most comfortable. I'll squeeze into whatever room is left."

I wiggle to the edge, trying to give him as much room as possible as he rests on his side next to me. He drapes one arm lightly over my waist. He's so careful to keep all of his weight off of me, and I relish in the comfort of his touch. "Close your eyes, baby. Try and get some sleep."

Eventually, exhaustion and the meds they give allow me to drift into a restless sleep. A nurse comes in periodically to check on me. Machines beep. There's nonstop noise in the hallway. It's hard to sleep through all of that. At one point, I wake up and see Derek sleeping in one of the chairs, his feet up on the windowsill.

Mom working in this hospital for years helps us get discharged bright and early the next morning. My parents being on an early ferry back from Nantucket likely put fear in the staff, knowing that my mom would come tearing through here like a tornado if I was still here when they got home.

It's strange walking back into the house. Up until now, this place has only held happy memories for me. Yes, I've obviously gone through dramatic events as a teenager, but I've never felt anything but safe and comfortable here.

After last night, I'm not sure I'll ever be able to look at the family room the same way. Or be able to twist the knob on the front door to open it. Or sit on that couch with a glass of wine. Every bit of safety, security, and sanctuary I've ever felt flies out the window, an overwhelming sadness taking its place.

My shoulders slump as I bite my lip, immediately regretting it since it's so raw and tender. My eyes dart around the room, taking in the broken coffee table and the frames that still lay broken on the floor. I look over at Theo, anxious to get away from the family room.

"I'm desperate for a shower," I say, my voice still raspy and my throat still sore. I try to keep the emotion at bay.

As if sensing my uneasiness, he lightens the mood and says, "Well, Sunshine, I'm happy to help you with that, but we better move quickly because I can't imagine the shitstorm I'll be in if your dad catches me in the shower with you."

I'm not sure if he's serious about the offer, but either way, I take his hand and lead him to my room. Based on the sting of pain that had me gasping when I lifted my arms to get dressed at the hospital, I know there's no way I'll be able to wash my hair. I'm going to need his help.

Theo drops the overnight bag that Derek brought to the hospital onto the floor, and I grab my robe from the back of my chair. He sees me grimace when I try to take off my shirt and walks over to me.

His eyebrows raise in concern. "Do you need help?" I give him a nod and slowly lift my arms, fighting the urge to yelp from the movement that has me wanting to double over in pain. He gently tugs my shirt over my head, doing his best to avoid it from brushing up against my face.

I hear him suck in a breath as he looks over my body and takes in all of the bruises before wrapping my robe around my body. He pushes my sweatpants down, and I'm able to kick them off without any help. We head into the bathroom that's connected to my bedroom, and he leans down to get the shower going. I drop my robe and look in the mirror, seeing the aftermath of the attack for the first time.

My torso is a watercolor canvas, shades of black, blue, and purple spread over my light complexion. My arms are also bruised from where he grabbed me multiple times. My throat is still red, and I can see his handprints from when he choked me. My face looks like I went a few rounds with a prized fighter and lost. My lip is split, the skin around my eye a few shades darker than it should be. There's a cut on my cheek that the doctor applied a butterfly bandage to. I needed stitches to close the one on my temple.

I feel Theo's eyes on me, and I lift my gaze higher in the mirror to see him staring. His hands are clenched in fists as he takes in all of the bruises and marks on my body. His eyes linger on my back, and I assume there are some back there, too.

His face twists into an angry scowl and I can feel the anger emanating from him. He inhales and exhales slowly, intentionally, as if he's counting. When I meet his eyes in the mirror, they're hard and icy, like frozen steel. I'm not sure I've ever seen him look so intense, so hell-bent on revenge.

"I know I need to be careful with the stitches, but I'll feel so much better if I can wash my hair."

"At your service," he says as he strips off his clothes. I give him a questioning look when he helps me step into the shower because he still has his boxer briefs on. "If I had a bathing suit, I'd put it on. The last thing I need is your dad or brothers thinking I'm taking advantage of this situation by getting naked with you in the shower."

A small chuckle escapes me, and it has me wincing in pain.

"But Sunshine, once you're healed and ready, I'll get naked in the shower with you as often as you'd like."

He's a perfect gentleman in the shower. His eyes stay

focused on the task at hand and never wander to my chest. The hot water and steam soothe my body. The water feels cleansing in more ways than one. I know it will stick with me but rinsing the events of last night off of me gives me a small sense of relief.

He turns me so that I'm facing away from him. We share the stream of water, and I tip my head back. Theo runs his fingers through my hair, making sure it's wet enough to put shampoo in. He's extra careful to avoid getting my face wet.

He grabs the shampoo, squirts some into his hands, and works it into a lather. He starts at the top of my scalp and works his way around, gently massaging my scalp as he works the shampoo into my hair.

"Oh god, that feels good." I practically moan at how delicious it feels. His touch is soft but firm as he works his fingers through to the tips and then starts again at a different spot on my head. I don't know how long it goes on for, but it's so relaxing and sensual I don't want it to end.

Despite the fact that I'm exhausted and my legs feel like they could give out at any moment, being in such close proximity to Theo, while wet and naked, brings me back to life in a way I don't expect.

"Cover your face, Sunshine," he instructs before he starts rinsing. He works his fingers through to make sure all of the soap is out while he holds the sprayer with his other hand. When he's sure I'm soap free, he says, "What's next?"

I point to a bottle and say, "Just put the conditioner on the bottom half of my hair, please. And don't rinse it out right away."

"Yes, Boss," he says, his tone playful as he follows my instructions, softly weaving the conditioner through.

While he waits to rinse that out, he squirts a glob of body wash into his hand and works that into a soapy lather. As gently as possible, he washes me. He goes up and down each arm, his eyes narrowing at the bruises peppering them. His touch is tender as he washes my back, his hands glossing over my ass as he goes.

He squats down, his touch unhurried as he works his way up and down my legs. When he gets to the top of each thigh, I hold my breath in anticipation. Because him being that close to the apex of my legs has all the blood in my body rushing there.

When he stands up, I can't help but lean back into him. I could blame it on the exhaustion, but I'd say it's only maybe 10 percent due to that, max. The other 90 percent is because I just feel safe and grounded around him and want to be as close as possible to that feeling of protection.

From behind, he works his soapy hands up my stomach, stopping below my chest. He hesitates before separating his palms and gently working them up the sides of my body. He pulls me closer so that my back is pressed to his front and I sink further into his arms.

Water rains down on us as his hands roam my body. His touch is not timid, but it's like he's treasuring the experience of exploring my body again.

The orange-vanilla scent of my body wash surrounds us. It's one I've used forever as it compliments my perfume and serves as a great base layer. "God, I can't get enough of this smell," he murmurs into my neck, his hands going still. "Every time I smell it, my pulse jumps."

I reach a hand down and gently squeeze his thigh. His hands start moving again, his fingers like feathers tracing my ribs. His length, hard and steely in his boxers, press against my back and it takes every ounce of self control I have to suppress the moan that's desperate to escape.

This is not the first time I've been in the shower with Theo, but with the steam surrounding us and the soft, yet possessive way he's holding me, it's the most intimate one we've ever shared.

His lips press against my ear. "I'm so sorry, baby." His voice is soft, as if he's afraid it might crack.

"It's not your fault, Theo."

"I should have been there. I'm sorry you went through it." I nod in response, not trusting myself to come up with words. He drops a kiss on my cheek before reaching for the sprayer. He rinses the soap from my body before he tackles the conditioner. "Anything else, Sunshine?" he asks, clearing his throat.

"Nope. I feel better already," I reply.

Damn it's hot and steamy in here, and not just from the water. The heat of my skin pales in comparison to the heat I'm feeling between my legs as I watch Theo. He quickly washes his hair and body, the water and suds pouring down him. I'm mesmerized as I watch his muscles flex when he moves, droplets tracking down every muscle and ridge of his hard body.

This shower has been an almost out of body experience. Watching Theo, and having his hands all over my body, have distracted me from the pain and discomfort that rocks mine.

He shuts off the water and steps out before turning to offer his hand. My knees shake from what was surely an out of body experience in that shower, so I grip his hand while I step out. He grabs one of the thick, fluffy towels from the hook on the door and carefully wraps it around me.

My body shivers, not from the cold, but from his touch. Once he's sure I'm sufficiently wrapped in mine, Theo grabs his own towel and wraps it around his waist, slipping his boxers off from underneath the towel.

As he delicately dries my hair with another towel, I look him in the eyes and say, "Thank you, Theo. For staying with me last night and for helping me with this."

"Anytime, Lyla. I'd do anything for you."

I bite my lip, and immediately regret it, as I debate telling him that I recognized the man who attacked me. I need to find a new nervous tick while my lip heals. I buy myself some time by going into my room to get dressed. He helps me throw on some cozy clothes before he puts his sweats back on.

"I think I need to tell you something, but you have to promise to not get mad at me," I finally say.

"I don't like where this is going."

When I look into his eyes, they're laced with concern. "That man, I've seen him before," I tell him, wringing my hands.

He freezes. "What do you mean? Where? Do you know him?"

"I've seen him in town a few times. At the bookstore. At the coffee shop."

"Did you talk to him? Did you recognize him as a local? Or as the man that came after you in Vermont?" He's in cop mode now. His hands go to his hips and he stands up a little taller. His tone is serious, having lost the gentleness it had just minutes earlier.

"Definitely not the Vermont guy. I'll never forget either of their faces, or the way they smelled, and I know 1,000 percent it wasn't the same guy. I didn't talk to him, but it was strange. It felt like he was following me. I've had that feeling of someone watching me the past few weeks."

"Lyla, why didn't you say anything to anyone?" he asks, trying to keep his voice even.

"Well, there's more." I cringe as I say it because I know he's going to lose it when he hears the rest. He looks at me with raised eyebrows, waiting for me to continue. "He was at the Dusty Bird last weekend. I had a little run-in with him near the bathrooms."

"A little run-in? What does that mean, Sunshine?" He pinches the top of his nose and takes a few deep breaths.

"I saw him at the bar, and even with his hat pulled down low, I knew it was the same dude. He approached me as I walked out of the bathroom. Shoved me against the wall. I don't know if he was drunk or what—"

"He put his hands on you?" His voice, low and sharp, slices through the air. He doesn't yell the words, but his hard tone, and the fact that he looks coiled and ready to strike, is even more intimidating. His gaze has me cracking my knuckles to deal with my nerves, having learned the hard way that biting my lip is not an option right now.

His eyes are dark and cold. I know this anger isn't directed at me, but damn if it doesn't scare the hell out of me. The man that was comforting me in the shower, treating my body like a fragile flower, looks like a force to be reckoned with. He looks hell-bent on extracting revenge.

"I don't know if he was drunk or what his goal was. I don't know if he was going to push me out through the emergency exit back there or just cop a feel." My voice turns shaky, and I suddenly can't find the words to continue.

Theo gently rubs his hands up and down my arms. "It's okay. He's sitting in a cell at the station. He can't hurt you." I nod and take a step back. "How did you get him away from you?"

"Clayton happened to walk down the hallway to the bathroom."

A flash of surprise flickers in his eyes. "Clayton knew about this?" he asks, pissed as hell. If it could happen in real life, there would be steam coming out of his ears.

"Don't be mad at him. I made him promise not to say anything."

"Oh, I'm fucking livid, Lyla. He's a cop. He should know

better than to bury something like that. Especially if you had run-ins with him in town and felt like someone was watching you," he says, his arms crossed.

"Well, he didn't know about any of that stuff," I say as if that's obvious. "I should have said something sooner. I'm sorry."

"Don't apologize. Should you have told one of us about this guy sooner? Yes. But it's done now. You're the victim here, Lyla. Don't forget that. You don't have to apologize for shit. But please, just promise me that you'll tell me, or your family, *someone*, if something like this happens again. I'm begging you. Please don't keep this stuff to yourself."

"I promise."

"Sunshine, I feel like I'm stating the obvious here, but this guy is obviously tied in with Hollman. This is the second attack in a month, and I can't stomach the idea of a third. I don't even want to think about how it could end, considering how the second one progressed from the first. If you see anyone suspicious, or get any sort of weird feeling, you have to speak up. I can't stress that enough."

"My dad is going to be pissed."

"Understatement of the year, baby."

# TWENTY

## *Lyla*

I'M EXHAUSTED, physically and mentally. I feel like shit run over twice and a quick glance in the mirror tells me I look even worse. The parts of me that aren't bruised are pale and my eyes look hollow. My shoulders sag, as if they're tired from carrying the weight of the past twelve hours.

Guilt that I never mentioned this man after seeing him at One More Chapter and again at the coffee shop seeps through me. I knew there was something off about him. Maybe if I listened to my instincts, I wouldn't be in this position. My skin wouldn't be crawling and I wouldn't feel like I'm on the verge of vomiting at the thought of spending time in the family room.

All I want to do is take a nap and wake up to find out the last eighteen hours were just a nightmare. Except for that shower with Theo. I don't want to ever forget that. After we get dressed, Theo opens my bedroom door, and the voices of my parents float down the hallway.

"How about I stay here and you go deal with my family?" I stare longingly at my bed as I say it.

"Not a chance. You can try, but if you think your mom

won't come knock this door down to see you, you got another thing coming. Come on. They want to see proof you're in one piece, then you can rest," he says, motioning for me to get moving.

I brace myself for the reaction I know is coming once my parents get their eyes on me. The second we make it to the kitchen, my mom gasps loudly and then quickly covers her mouth with her hands.

She walks over to me and holds her arms up, as if asking if she can hug me. I walk into her arms, and she wraps them around me, her embrace soft and comforting.

"Don't squeeze me," I say softly. When she pulls back, I note the tears welling in her eyes. "Please don't cry."

My mom somehow pulls herself together and immediately goes into nurse mode, asking me a barrage of questions and inspecting the bandage on my face.

"Lori, take a breath. They wouldn't have released her if doing so put her health at risk. Let's just sit down and talk about where we're going from here," my dad says. He walks over to me and gently wraps me in his arms. "I'm so sorry, kiddo. This shouldn't have happened, and it won't happen again."

"Thanks, Dad. I'm going to go make some tea and then we can talk about what happens next." I walk toward the other side of the kitchen only for my mom to stop me.

"Honey, go relax on the couch. I'll bring it over to you." I freeze at the idea of sitting on it, fumbling with my hands and cracking my knuckles.

It's like he can read my mind because Theo pipes up and says, "How about the porch? It's not too hot out today. Might be nice to relax out there instead of inside. Vitamin D is good for recovery."

I give him a small smile and head out the door. I overhear

him quietly say something about helping my brothers clean the family room when they get here.

Not even a minute later, Theo's on the porch, placing a light blanket on me. He knows that even if I'm warm, I like to be snuggled in. "No electronics. No reading. Just relax, okay, Sunshine?" He squats down next to me so we're eye level.

I ask the question that's been rattling around in my head since I woke up this morning. "What happens next, Theo?"

"That's what we're going to figure out now. I have an idea, but I'm not sure how it will go over with the men in your family. I think it might be a good idea for at least the next week or two."

"Care to share with the class?" I ask, squeezing my eyes shut as a wave of nausea rolls over me.

"Until the feds are brought up to speed, and we get this situation under control, I think we should go to Nantucket. Stay at my house out there."

"You still have your grandparents' place?" I ask.

There was a time when Nantucket real estate was slightly more affordable than it is now. Theo's maternal grandparents bought a little cottage there before he was born. They lived there full-time for a number of years before moving to Cape Cod. They kept the house in Madaket to rent out, but we would go there all the time in high school and college. It's one of my favorite places on Earth, and I had no idea he still had it.

"Yup. They left it to me when they passed away. I get out there as much as I can. I spent a few years slowly renovating it, slapped a new name on it." A few beats of silence pass before he continues. "A lot of memories tied to that place, Lyla. Selling it would have been like selling a piece of our story, and I could never bring myself to consider it."

"And now you think I should hole up there until, when?

The dust settles? The trial? Hollman decides it's not worth killing me?"

"Not exactly. I think *we* should hole up there. Together."

My mom walks out with my tea and some Oreos. I got my sweet tooth from my dad, and it's well-known that, for us, sweets can fix anything. "Your brothers should be here soon. We'll get the family room cleaned up in no time." She sits in the chair across from me, placing the cookies on the table between us.

"Thanks, Mom." I look back at Theo. "I want to be involved in decisions, Theo. I'm not some damsel in distress who needs the men in her life to make all the decisions."

"Even if the men in her life are in law enforcement?"

"Even then. I'm not saying you guys don't know best when it comes to this stuff. What I'm saying is that I will be involved in the conversation."

He looks me in the eye and says, "Deal. Drink your tea and relax." He tucks a piece of hair behind my ear before he stands up and goes inside.

"I know you have a million questions about what happened last night, but honestly, Mom, my head is killing me. Am I allowed to take a nap with a concussion?"

"Naps are fine. Your brain can use the rest. How about we drink our tea, eat our Oreos, and then you can get some shut-eye out here? I'll get you something for the headache once you get those cookies in your stomach." We sit quietly together on the porch, listening to the birds and drinking our tea.

"Don't let them talk about anything important without me, Mom," I say to her, my voice heavy with exhaustion.

"I won't. I promise. I'm going to go inside to supervise the clean up. Holler if you need me."

My eyes grow heavy and every muscle and bone in my

body screams, but the warmth of the sunlight wraps itself around me like a warm hug. It doesn't take me long to nod off.

* * *

My mom gently rubs my arm to wake me up, and when I ask her how long I was out for, she tells me it's been close to an hour. She hands me Tylenol and a glass of water before informing me that my dad made pancakes.

"You're probably not too hungry, but you'll feel better if you get something down, and carbs are usually the best bet when you're dealing with nausea." She stands and holds out her hand to help me up. We head inside. My brothers and Theo are both seated at the table, and my dad is doing his thing at the stove.

"Why isn't anyone at work?" I ask as I slowly sit down, gripping the table for support. "And why are you all looking at me like I've lost my mind for asking that question?"

It's Derek who finally responds.

"I don't know, Lyla. Maybe because you were attacked in your own home, spent the night in the hospital, and the feds are doing nothing to help us keep you safe. Oh, and we've spent the last hour arguing with your boyfriend about what we should do moving forward. All of that seemed a bit more important than checking on the job site this morning. And Dumb and Dumber," he nods toward Colin and Theo, "are technically on the clock."

"Please tell me I'm Dumb and Theo's Dumber," Colin says with a mouthful of pancakes. "Also, notice that she didn't deny him being her boyfriend." When I look at Colin, he smirks. I roll my eyes.

"It depends on the day," my dad interjects as he places a plate of pancakes down in front of me. Theo just laughs and passes me the syrup, which has been warmed to perfection. My dad takes his pancakes very seriously.

"So what's the plan?" I'm met with silence as they look at each other as if deciding how much to tell me. Napping has given me energy, and the Tylenol has dulled the pain for the time being, so I keep going. "Don't treat me like I'm some fragile, broken girl. We're not doing that again. I recognize that you're the professionals here, but that doesn't mean I don't have a right to know what you're thinking when it comes to my life and my safety. I get a voice here."

"She's right." It's my dad who speaks up first, which surprises me. "You're right, Lyla. I haven't gotten the feds on the phone yet, but I'm not feeling optimistic about them doing anything to help us."

"Knowing it's linked to Hollman, you'd think they'd be more obliged to do something," Colin says.

"You might have been the one who brought the heat on Hollman, but you're not a witness in the trial, so they're not obligated to provide protection. That means it's up to Sandpiper PD," my dad says.

He says it so matter-of-factly. The reason Hollman wants me dead is bigger than the words in my article. It's because I shattered the picture-perfect image that his community had of him. He donated generously to homeless shelters and food banks. He helped fund youth centers and covered pet adoption fees at the local shelters.

No one would have believed he was a wolf in sheep's clothing until I outed his entire operation of selling drugs and trafficking girls.

My dad comes to sit down with his own plate of pancakes and cup of coffee. "The bottom line is that you need to be under protection twenty-four-seven at this point. At least until we learn more about who sent this guy that attacked you."

"He's based out of Boston, right? That's where he'll be tried?" Colin asks.

"Yep," my dad replies.

"Well, we need to reach out to our sources. Someone's got to have intel when it comes to this. Find out just how committed he is to hurting her. I have a few people I can talk to, and I'll ask around at the station when I go there shortly."

"Colin's right. As much as it pains me to say, " Colin smiles as Theo continues, "I've avoided asking my sources in Hyannis that I've always suspected were linked to him just to keep from drawing attention, but I think that ship has sailed. Did they get anything out of the guy last night?"

"He wasn't too forthcoming when I was there, and I haven't checked in yet to see if he was any chattier after I left," Colin says.

"Hopefully, we'll have a better picture today. I think Lyla and I should go to Nantucket. Get her out of town for a little. It would be easy to lie low out there," Theo suggests.

Derek leans back in his chair, arms crossed and chin lifted, as he asks with conviction, "You don't think it makes Lyla more vulnerable, being stuck on an island? What if someone else comes after her, tracks her down out there, and you're stuck?"

Theo keeps his cool with his reply. "The point of going out there is so that no one knows where she is."

"Well, that's putting all your eggs in one basket. We didn't even know this guy had her in his sights," Derek argues.

"That's not necessarily true," I say softly as I push my pancakes around my plate. When I look up, everyone's eyes are on me, waiting for me to continue. I take a deep breath before I continue. "I've seen this man a few times."

"Where, Vermont?" my dad questions.

"No, not in Vermont. In town. He was at One More Chapter

when I was there, and then I saw him again when I was leaving the coffee shop the same day."

"And you didn't think to mention that to any of us?" Colin asks.

"There's more," Theo says, urging me to continue.

"More?" My dad growls, his voice sharp.

"I saw him at the Dusty Bird last weekend. He accosted me as I came out of the bathroom."

"Why didn't you tell us about this?!" Colin asks in an accusatory tone, looking from me to Theo.

"Don't be mad at Theo. I only told him right before you guys got here."

"Who we can be mad at is Clayton," Theo spits out.

This peaks my dad's interest. "Clayton? What does he have to do with this?"

"He saw the guy with his hands on Lyla," Theo says.

My dad's eyes narrow as he looks at Theo. "He, what?"

"I never liked that guy," mutters Derek.

"Derek you don't like anyone," I say in an effort to relieve some of the tension in the room. "I walked out of the bathroom and that guy grabbed me and pushed me up against the wall. Before he got the chance to do much more, Clayton came into the hallway. He chased the guy off, and I made him promise not to tell anyone."

"He should know better. This is not something he should have let you sweep under the rug," my dad says, his voice harsh. "I'll deal with him at the station later. Lyla, are you sure he wasn't the man who attacked you back in Vermont?"

"No." My voice is firm. "I'll never forget that man's face and cheap cologne."

"Did you know he was at the bar before he went after you?" Colin asks.

"I got the creepy crawly feeling shortly after you and I got there that someone was watching me. Then, I noticed him across the bar. I recognized him from when I saw him at the bookstore." Theo gives me a pointed look as if he wants me to keep going. "I should also probably tell you that I've had that feeling quite a few times over the past couple of weeks. Like someone has been following me."

The men at the table look like they're about to explode, their faces red with fury, their shoulders so tense they're basically up by their ears. My mom fiddles with her napkin.

"Lyla, this is the kind of shit we need to know." Colin grits through his teeth.

"I'm sorry. I just thought it was Dad getting in my head about someone possibly coming after me. And yes, before you say anything, I'm well aware someone already tried that once, but I didn't think it would happen again,"

"I already told you, Sunshine. No apologies. Just going forward, please be more open with us," Theo says.

When I think about it, I have no one to blame for what happened to me last night but myself. I mean, besides the asshole who attacked me. I felt like someone was following me a few times over the past few weeks and never mentioned it.

In the back of my mind, I knew there was something up with that guy. I saw him before he came after me in the hallway, and I didn't make a peep about it, even after he grabbed me.

I can't help but think that last night never would have happened if I had told my dad, my brothers, or Theo sooner. It's hard not to be mad at myself for putting everyone through this ordeal, because it's not just me dealing with the ramifications.

The guilt gnaws at me and I know it will weigh heavily on my conscience no matter how much I will it away. My eyes sting with tears and I want to kick my own ass for how emotional I'm being. I close my eyes hoping to seal them in.

"Lyla, honey, do you want to go lie down?" my mom asks.

"No. Not until I know what the next step here is." I look at my parents, my brothers, and Theo and see the concern in their eyes. "I promise I won't keep things like this from you guys again."

Colin says, "I think Nantucket is a good idea." Derek's eyes shoot daggers at him. "Don't look at me like that, Derek. I understand your point, but Theo's right. If we can get her on the island before Hollman realizes his guy is pinched then she'll be harder to find. If you're up to traveling, Lyla, I say we get you out there tonight. Hunker down at Theo's until we get a better grip on things here."

"I have bruised ribs and a concussion, but I'm not an invalid. I can handle the ferry. Plus, it's a weekday in October... It won't be too crowded."

Nantucket is my happy place. The island has the nickname "The Grey Lady," and her mercurial climate is one of the reasons I love it so much. Living so close to it, we grew up going there for day trips as a family. My mom and I used to do girl's trips there once a year starting from when I was a little girl.

Theo and I have shared so many memories there, too, and it's part of the reason why the island is so special to me. The idea of lying low on that island with Theo stirs feelings I'll have to decipher after I take another nap. "Wait... Theo, how can you come with me if you're working?"

"I'll take leave if I have to. I promised you I wasn't leaving your side, and I won't make that mistake again," Theo says.

"I'll see if I can figure something out, Theo. If I can get it on the books that it's our duty as a department to protect one of our citizens, paying overtime to make sure she has around-the-clock protection isn't a problem. Just might take me a few days to figure out how to put it on paper," my dad replies, clearly supporting this plan as well.

"With all due respect, Chief, I don't give a shit about over-time. I don't care if you have to dock my pay for not coming in for however long this takes," Theo says.

Colin speaks up again and says, "We tell no one where you are. You made your statement last night at the hospital, and if the department needs to speak with you again, they can do it on the phone. No one gets to know this plan or where you're going. They'll assume Theo is with you since he's not at work, and everyone knows he's obsessed with you, but we don't give anyone details. Are we all clear on this?"

Derek scrolls through his phone, finding the ferry schedule. We agree on a time, and he buys the tickets for us. "This will give you enough time to get to Theo's house before it gets dark. I'm going to go do a few things, but I'll be back to take you to the dock later," Derek says as he stands up, bringing his dish over to the sink.

"Colin, head into work and get updated on the case. Don't stick your nose in too much or it'll come back to bite us in the ass since it can be seen as a conflict of interest. I'm going to reach out to the Chief in Nantucket. He's a good friend of mine, and I trust him. I'll give him a brief summary of what's going on, so he can keep his eyes and ears open. Theo, go home and pack whatever you need."

Theo's head shoots up like he has no intention of leaving me, but my dad presses on. "No arguments. I'll be here the entire time. Stop at one of those corner stores in town on the way back and grab a few burner phones to have just in case you end up needing them. Use cash when you can while you're out there because anyone who knows you or asks around will assume you're with her."

Colin gets up to put his dishes in the sink. I slowly stand so that I can say goodbye to my brother. He waits for me to make the first move, but once I go in for the hug, he reciprocates in the most gentle way.

"Be careful, Lyla. We're going to end this shit. And call Quinn because she's probably anxious to hear your voice. Love you," he says, and after he hugs me, he and Theo do the classic bro hug to say goodbye. Colin whispers something into his ear, but I can't quite hear it.

"Eventually, we're going to circle back to why Quinn has your number in the first place," I say, giving him a pointed look before he walks out the garage door.

Theo gives me a long hug before he takes a hesitant step back. "This will be the last time I leave you until we know, without a doubt, that you're safe. I promise."

That conversation took a lot out of me, and with nothing better to do anyway, I make my way to my room to lie down. My mom comes to wake me up an hour later and lets me know that Theo and Derek will be back soon.. I slowly get out of bed and pack my weekender bag, throwing in comfy clothes, some workout outfits, a few bathing suits, and a couple of light dresses. I add my toiletries and a pair of flip-flops, along with a couple of hats.

Being alone with Theo for who knows how long? This will be a battle of willpower and discipline and I'm not sure which will win. I'm hopeful that we'll have the chance to talk, and that I'll be able to really sort through my feelings for him while I'm out there.

The reality is that being forced to be together will stoke the flames between us and we'll surrender to the desire we have for each other, or it'll cause a complete implosion of whatever it is we're trying to salvage.

## TWENTY-ONE

*theo*

I START to feel relief the minute the ferry pulls away from the dock. I won't say the tension leaves my body completely, but I don't feel quite as tightly wound. I breathe a little easier.

I know there's not some protective bubble around the island but putting space between Lyla and all of those associated with Marcus Hollman offers me comfort.

The boat is mostly empty, which is ideal because the less attention Lyla draws with her bruises and cuts, the better. Carrying around a cat in a backpack also doesn't help with flying under the radar. I knew Diego would be fine if I left him with Chief and Lori, but he loves Nantucket almost as much as I do, and he's an easy travel buddy.

We make our way into the main cabin and have our pick of tables to sit at. Holding her hand, I lead Lyla to the opposite end of the boat, letting her slide in first so she has the window to lean on if she wants.

I sit next to her, and place Diego's carrier on the seat next to me. Lyla pulls her hat down lower and tries to get comfortable, wincing slightly as she moves around. I put one arm behind her so she knows she can use me as a cushion and, after some fidgeting, she finally settles in and falls asleep. Thankfully, the Nantucket Sound is calm so the ride is smooth.

I stay awake the entire ride, thinking about what's transpired over the last twenty-four hours. I can't stop my mind from branching out to all the other ways last night could have ended. If she wasn't on Facetime with Quinn, we wouldn't have known what was happening. If Derek got there five minutes later, would she have been raped? Was the attacker's plan to kill her or just assault her?

I left Sandpiper Cove all those years ago because the death of our friend triggered so many memories of my mother dying and how that grief broke my father. I had buried those memories for so long and I went into a tailspin, thinking it wouldn't be possible to make it through another loss.

I wouldn't survive another bout of that kind of heartache. I walked away from Lyla because I was so petrified that something would happen to her, and I'd have to grapple with her absence. Because it wouldn't just be an absence, it would be a hole in my heart. I would never come back from it.

I pull at the collar of my shirt, feeling like it's too tight, like I'm being suffocated by the memories and fears. I'm desperate for fresh air, but with Lyla sleeping against me, there's no way I'm moving another inch. I close my eyes and slow my breathing, eventually getting my heart rate to slow to a normal level.

Lyla wakes up as we're docking, and we gather our stuff. Diego stays quiet the entire trip, but the way he's fussing and his demanding little meows tell me he's anxious to get out and explore. We disembark and head to Madaket five minutes later.

Before we left Sandpiper, I made a quick phone call to my favorite people on Nantucket—my neighbors, Lou and Holly. They're year-rounders who have lived next door for as long as I can remember. They serve as my de facto property managers and keep an eye on the place when I'm not around.

I told Lou I'd be coming in later today, would be staying indefinitely, and flying under the radar. Because he's awesome, he assured me he'd drop my old truck off at the parking lot right by the ferry and insisted he'd pick up groceries so that the house would be stocked for us.

"We'll be able to make the sunset if we go right to the beach before we head home," I say as I look over at Lyla. Her eyes light up at the suggestion. Seeing that glimmer of happiness has me smiling in return.

Nantucket is pretty small, but the traffic can be so brutal it rivals Boston during the high season. This time of year, we're able to cruise out of town quickly and pull up to the beach.

I pull an oversized beach towel out from under the seat, take Diego out of the carrier and clip a leash to him before scooping him up, and help Lyla down from the truck. We're just in time to catch the sun dipping under the horizon. And from the best place on the island, too.

"Sit however is most comfortable for you and tell me where you want me," I say to Lyla as she moves very carefully. I offer my hand for assistance as she slowly sits down. When she takes my hand it feels like the world stops. It's more than just a touch, it's like a current runs through my body, pulling me closer to her.

Anytime our bodies come in contact, skin to skin, it feels like an electric surge racing through my body. And that shower? Fuck, it was all I could do to keep my cock behaving. The sight of her body so bruised and battered had my blood pressure through the roof, but my hands on her as I soaped her up had me momentarily forgetting.

"Can I sit between your legs so I can lean back?" she asks, looking up at me.

*Fuck yes, you can* is what I want to say.

"Of course, Sunshine," is what actually comes out of my

mouth. I put Diego down. With my legs on either side of her, she rests her arms on my knees and leans back on my chest. Diego eventually worms his way onto her lap as we watch the sun sink lower.

"I can't believe I gave this cat a home, and he drops me like a hot potato for you," I grumble.

I actually can believe it, because that's the effect Lyla has on anyone she's around. She's magnetic without even trying. She's genuine and kind-hearted. When she talks to you, she makes you feel like you're the most important person in the room in the most genuine way.

Her laugh is a beautiful melody, rich and full of life. She has a warmth to her that makes everyone she comes in contact with feel like they belong. I saw the light in her when we were kids, and it's only gotten brighter. It went out after Olivia died, but she relit it on her own, and it means everything to see it again.

It's vulnerable sitting out in the open like this, but I needed to give this to Lyla. The beach during sunset or a clear night sky was always her refuge, especially when she was stressed or anxious.

"I needed this, Theo. Thank you," she says, her voice still raspy from the manhandling she got last night.

"The circumstances are absolute shit, but there's nowhere else I'd rather be right now," I say softly into her ear. We sit in comfortable silence, Lyla watching the sunset while I watch her. Once the sun disappears, I lean forward and whisper in her ear, "Time to get going."

We get back to my cottage, and I'm suddenly nervous for her to see the place. When I inherited it from my grandparents, I envisioned it as a safe haven we'd be able to come to when we wanted to get away from it all.

I pictured us making remodeling decisions together, but

instead, I had to do that all on my own. More than anything, I want her to feel at home here.

Like every property on Nantucket, the siding is traditional cedar. Since the siding is only a couple of years old, it's still honey-colored but will eventually patina to a light gray.

The door is navy blue and I chose the color because it reminded me of the ocean at dusk. I renamed the house once I took ownership, and the light yellow sign hanging above the door identifies it as *Sunshine.* I unlock the door and step back, waving for her to go in ahead of Diego and me.

The house isn't huge and originally there were so many walls closing off the rooms, but I did my best to open it up and maximize the space. The front door opens into the great room with the kitchen along the back of the large space, and Lyla stops to look around.

"A bit different from the last time you saw it, huh?" I ask. I put Diego down and unclip his leash before running out to grab our bags from my truck.

When I walk back in, she's over by the built-ins that surround the wood-burning fireplace, looking at the framed pictures that are propped between books and other treasures.

"Theo," she whispers. "It's beautiful. I can't believe you still have some of these pictures," she says as she picks up one of the frames.

She hasn't even noticed the prints that are hanging around the room. My stomach does a little flip while I wait for her to look around. Photographs of the sunset, Madaket Beach, and various other spots around the island hang on the walls, and they're all pictures she's taken.

"Come on, I'll give you the grand tour."

I take her through the house, starting in the kitchen and opening the cabinets to show her where the most important stuff is located, like coffee and Diego's food. She looks at me and smiles when she sees the glass jar of gummy bears I keep on the counter.

"You did all of this yourself?" she asks.

"Lou, your dad, and I did about seventy-five percent of it."

"Who did the rest?"

"Derek," I reply, and her jaw drops.

"He's never once mentioned it to me."

"Yeah, well, we don't ever mention the times he's not a total asshole to me. Will ruin the facade he puts out."

She laughs. "How did you convince him to do the work?" she asks.

"He came out once with your dad, and I think once he saw the project in the works, he couldn't help himself. When he walked around, he started brainstorming a few other ideas, and at that point, there was no stopping him. He probably just pretended it was for someone else."

"That man can't say no to a project once he starts envisioning it."

"That was probably your dad's plan to begin with. Your brother is a gifted contractor. I'm lucky he took pity on me."

"It's amazing, Theo. I can't believe it's the same place. You guys did an incredible job. The kitchen is gorgeous. You know I don't cook, but I can't wait to watch you cook in it."

"Wait until you see the tub in the bathroom."

"Ahh, now you're talking my language. You know I'd give up a kidney for a good soaking tub," she says.

*Yeah, and I can't wait for her to be naked, soaking in it, prefer-ably with me and a bottle of tequila.* My mind wanders even further before I can stop it. I think about our naked bodies in that hot, soapy water. Lyla leans back into me, her elbows resting on my knees as she turns her head to the side. I kiss my way down her neck as my hands start to wander over her wet

195

thighs, up her stomach, landing on her breasts. Her nipples harden as my fingers start to play with them.

I look up at the ceiling and bite my lip, begging my cock not to betray where my mind just went. I clear my throat. "Speaking of dinner, let's see what I can scrounge together. Take a load off and relax."

She sits at one of the stools at the island, and Diego pops up on the stool next to her, looking at her longingly until she scratches his head.

I open the fridge to see it filled with everything I asked Lou to pick up and more. There's also a covered Tupperware dish with a note on it indicating it's for dinner tonight. "Lou and Holly don't mess around. She makes the best baked ziti."

"Wait, Lou and Holly, as in your old neighbors? They still live here?"

"Yup. They keep an eye on the place when I'm not here. I texted him earlier, asking him to drop off my truck downtown and grab groceries so we can stay under the radar." I turn on the oven and get plates and glasses out for water. I also grab a bottle of Tylenol from the cabinet and pass two to Lyla.

"Thanks. The day is catching up with me. I need these. Any word from my dad or Colin about how things went at the station today?" Lyla asks.

"I'm going to give Colin a call as soon as I get this in the oven."

"Promise me you won't keep anything from me, Theo. Even if the news is scary or nerve-wracking."

I walk over to where she's sitting and lean forward, looking her in the eyes. "I promise, Lyla." Once dinner is in the oven, I join her at the counter, and we call her brother. I put him on speaker, which I know he hates. I'm sure I'll regret it later. The man has no filter.

He answers on the third ring. "What's up, Susie Homemaker? Let me guess... You've already prepared a three-course meal for my sister? Trying to impress her with your cooking skills since you're probably boring as hell in bed."

Lyla nearly chokes on her water.

"You're on speakerphone, and you never disappoint, dude," I say, shaking my head.

"You know better than to put me on for everyone to hear. You guys tucked in for the night? Uneventful trip out there, I assume?" he asks.

"Yup. Update me on what you learned today."

Ignoring my request, Colin keeps talking. "Lyla, what do you think of 'Sunshine?' Paint colors and flooring up to your standards? How do you like the bathroom? You don't even want to know how much Theo hemmed and hawed over every single choice when he was redoing that place. 'Would Lyla like this? Would she like that?'" He changes his voice to mock mine.

"I love it all, Colin. Weird that when Theo mentioned who helped him with the renovations, he didn't mention your name at all."

"I thought it was understood that he can't do anything without me, so it should just be assumed that I was there to hold his hand."

"Alright, alright. Let's get serious for a minute here or I'll call your dad instead. What did we learn from interviewing that shithead?" I ask, trying to get this conversation under control.

"That asshole started out like a steel trap. Wouldn't say anything at all. But once we started digging into his background and ties, we were able to nab some leverage and then he sang like a canary."

"And what did he sing about? Don't leave us in the dark here," Lyla says.

"His name is Scottie McDavid. As we expected, sent by

Hollman to eliminate, 'the bitch who ruined everyone's lives with her stupid article.' His words, not mine. A mid-level guy in Hollman's crew, but someone Hollman saw as competent and capable enough of killing you."

Chills run down my spine from what Colin tells us.

"Well, I guess I should be thankful he was such an underachiever with this assignment," Lyla says with a forced laugh. Out of the corner of my eye, I see her wrap her arms around her body. I yank the leg of her stool to bring her closer to me.

"Yeah, I'm sure his boss is less than happy with him. He's got a rap sheet filled with simple assaults, a robbery, and minor drug distribution with intent to sell. A few domestics that were mysteriously dropped when the victim backed out. Guess he's trying to graduate to the next level in terms of jobs within Hollman's organization, and you were a good test run," Colin says.

"What do you mean? How is this a test run?" Lyla asks.

I jump in and answer. "Well, the damage is already done. Lyla, you exposed Hollman for who he really is. You blew up his entire operation and got him on the radar of local and federal authorities. You're the reason he's sitting in jail right now. But you aren't going to be a witness at his trial. He doesn't need you gone by a certain date. It's more so that he wants you eliminated for putting him in this position in the first place."

She slowly nods her head as she tries to wrap her head around what we're saying.

"So, now what?" she asks.

"He's being booked and charged with attempted rape and murder because it was premeditated. He came with the intention of ending your life. The feds want to come talk to him and see if they can get him to flip on anything useful for their case..." Colin says, his voice calm but filled with disgust at the idea.

Lyla's jaw drops and I turn my head toward the phone and try to keep my composure.

"No fucking way is this guy getting a deal after what he did," I snap.

Colin lets out a breath before he replies. "I know, Theo. I'm as pissed as you. They're not going to let him walk. The idea of them lessening his charges makes me want to throw shit. They're so desperate to make sure Hollman goes to prison for life, I can see them cutting a deal to get this guy slightly less of a sentence."

"Did he say if Hollman is going to send someone else since he didn't get the job done?" It's a question I'm petrified to hear the answer to, but I know it needs to be asked. It's why we're hiding out.

"As of now, he's not giving that away. I don't know if it's because he truly doesn't know or if he's fucking with us because he can. That might be something the feds can get out of him tomorrow." We all sit in silence as we absorb Colin's news.

I look over at Lyla and reassure her that she's safe, that we won't let anything happen to her. I can see she's trying to hold back tears. She grips her thighs so tightly her knuckles turn white.

"Take me off speaker for a second, Theo."

"No!" Lyla says, her voice firm. She sits up taller, as if she's getting a second wind. "You guys are not doing this to me. I want full disclosure."

"I'm giving you full disclosure here, Lyla. I promise. You know all the pertinent details of what we learned today. I won't hide shit from you, but that doesn't mean you need to know every single minute detail," Colin says.

Patience is not always Colin's strong suit, and I can tell it's taking a lot for him to stay calm.

"I'll let Theo take you off speaker if you tell me why Quinn had your number," Lyla barters with a smirk.

"Man, Theo, she's already running the show. She'll *let* you take me off speaker. Already lost your balls," he says with a tsk. "Quinn got my number a few years ago. She wanted to know your favorite kind of cake, and when she snuck a look at your phone, mine was the first she saw. I guess she's kept it ever since. I am irresistible after all."

"She has a boyfriend, Colin. I don't like him, but he exists. Thanks for making sure she knew I loved carrot cake."

"Yeah, yeah, yeah. I know she does. You still feeling shitty?" His voice softens, letting the worry he has for his sister show through.

"Yeah. Exhausted. My body is throbbing from head to toe but I just took some Tylenol. Hopefully that'll take the edge off."

"Okay. Stay ahead of the pain. Make sure Theo takes good care of you. Love you and take me off speaker now."

I do as he says, holding the phone up to my ear. Lyla doesn't leave my side, but she's quiet the entire time. When I look over I see that her eyes are closed. I give her leg a squeeze and let Colin speak, uninterrupted, for the next few minutes.

"Hollman wanted her dead but also told McDavid he could play with his food before he killed it." I don't think I'll ever forget those words. The anger is radiating off of my body, my jaw clenched so tight that my back teeth grind together. I knew how serious it was when I walked into the house last night, but hearing confirmation that this piece of human garbage went with the goal of raping and murdering Lyla has me ready to erupt. I have to stand up and concentrate on my breathing as I pace the room, listening to him. "Listen, Theo. I know how you feel right now—"

"We could have lost her, Colin. *I* could have lost her. For good, this time. This asshole needs to rot in a cell next to Hollman. He should be dead."

"Agreed. I don't have much more to report. Obviously, the most important detail we were hoping

to get was if and when Hollman would send another guy after her, but he's being tight-lipped. We'll work on that again tomorrow before the feds get here. I'll let you know how that goes. In the meantime, keep the house locked up and take good care of her."

He hangs up after promising to call me in the morning.

Lyla and I sit down for dinner, but it seems like both of us have lost our appetite. She picks at her ziti, and I move mine around on the plate taking a bite here and there.

I would put my fork down but keeping my hands busy is the only thing that stops me from reaching out and touching her. The desire to hold her, feel her body against mine, reassure myself that she's in one piece, is so intense I can hardly keep it contained.

"You changed the name of this house," she says quietly.

"Sure did, Sunshine," I reply with a smile.

"Why? Until recently we hadn't talked in years."

"Doesn't matter. This was always meant to be our happy place. I'd never bring anyone else here, anyway. If it wasn't going to be you, it would have just been me," I say.

She nods her head as she takes my words in.

"I'm exhausted and just want to sleep. Can you text Quinn from my phone and let her know I'll try and call her tomorrow?" she asks.

"Of course." I leave the dishes on the counter and lead her back to my bedroom. I put her bag on the chair in the corner, and she sorts through it, grabbing pajamas and her toiletries before heading into the bathroom.

There's no en suite, but when I redid the house I expanded the main bathroom so that we were able to give it more of a spa feel with a huge soaking tub and walk-in shower with dual heads.

I hear her gasp as she walks in. "You good, Lyla?" I ask.

"Yeah. This bathroom is amazing. I wish I had the energy to get in that tub."

"When you're up for it, I'll set you up with the bubbles. Now, get ready for bed."

Lyla comes back into the bedroom, her hair in a messy bun and dressed in a pair of sleep shorts and a long-sleeved shirt that falls off her shoulder. Beautiful, even when her face is marred with cuts and bruises.

I pull down the blanket and help her climb into bed. Diego immediately jumps in after her and walks around the mattress a few times before curling up next to her head.

"I'm going to go do the dishes, and then I'll be back to check on you. I'll bring back a bottle of water to put on the nightstand. Call if you need me before I come back in, okay, Sunshine?"

Her eyelids are getting heavy, and I can see she's fading fast. She reaches out and grabs my arm. "Thank you, Theo, for bringing me here. I don't think I can handle sleeping at my parents' house right now."

She says it so softly I can barely hear her. It hurts my heart knowing she's uncomfortable and feels unsafe in her own home, though I can completely see why.

"Anything for you, baby. Now rest." I lean down and brush my lips against her forehead, giving her a soft kiss before reaching over to pet Diego, who purrs so loud he sounds like a noise machine.

I clean up in the kitchen, text Quinn, double-check the doors are locked and the alarm is on, and then make my way back to my bedroom.

Lyla sleeps peacefully with her arm around the cat. I put the water on the table next to her. I walk around to the other side of the bed to grab my pillows before pulling the throw blanket on the foot off.

While I would love nothing more than to lie down next to her and wrap my arms around her like I did last night in the hospital, it's not something I would do without asking if she's okay with it. But there's also no way I'm going to sleep on the couch or in the other bedroom. I want to be close if she needs something or wakes up not feeling well, and quite frankly, I don't want to let her out of my sight.

Thankfully, the area rug in my bedroom is a comfortable one. *Don't be a pussy, you've slept in far worse places than this,* I remind myself. It takes me awhile to fall asleep, because anytime Lyla moves, I jump up to see if she's okay.

At some point my exhaustion overtakes me and I doze off.

## TWENTY-TWO

*Lyla*

I WAKE up to the sound of rain, and when I glance at the clock, it's just after six. I slowly stretch my arms above my head and grit my teeth. My torso is so sore and tender, like someone took a bat to it.

I hear Diego purring, but I don't feel him next to me. It takes me a minute to realize that the other side of the bed's completely undisturbed. I start to sit up, but bite back a yelp from the pain.

"Let me help you get up, Sunshine." My mind must be playing tricks on me because while I hear Theo, I don't see him. I prop myself up on my elbows and peek over the edge of the bed.

He's stretched out on the floor, a few pillows propped under his head. The blanket that was on the foot of the bed last night haphazardly kicked off of him. Diego is sitting on his chest. He moves the cat off him so he can stand and helps me slowly sit up, giving me time to swing my legs over the side of the bed and then helping me get to my feet.

Once I'm up, I make my way to the bathroom, cringing

when I get a good glance at myself in the mirror. The bruises on my face, neck, and arms are darker, the swelling around my eye and cheek the same. I brush my teeth before heading back to the bed.

"I don't know how I'm still this tired," I say in frustration.

"Your body and brain need rest to recover. You want me to bring you some tea?" Theo asks as he helps me back into bed.

"Yes, please. And some Tylenol." Once I'm situated in bed, he fluffs my pillows a few times, then turns to walk out, pausing at the door to look back at me.

"I'm fine, Theo. You'll just be in the kitchen."

The worry doesn't leave his eyes. "I know, baby. It's just hard seeing you like this. It kills me."

"They're just bruises. They'll go away. I'm going to be okay." I say it with more conviction than I feel, but that's okay. It was more for him anyway.

He clutches the doorframe, his knuckles turning white from his hard grip. He nods at me, as if trying to convince himself to believe the words I just said. He looks...just like the man I remember from years ago. From the time when we were perfect, when our life together seemed like a guarantee.

Which means he looks...dangerous. Because it would be so easy to let my carefully constructed walls fall down. I can already see them slipping.

"That's good, Sunshine. Because I wouldn't survive if something happened to you." He turns and walks toward the kitchen, Diego hot on his trail.

A few minutes later, he's back with my pain medicine, a fresh glass of water, and a cup of tea that, by the smell alone, I can tell is my favorite; cinnamon spice.

"You sleep okay?" he asks as he hands me the teacup and sits on the edge of the bed. I take a sip, careful not to spill it and feel his gaze on me. Concern outlines the blue-gray of his eyes. There's something else, too, guilt maybe.

"Better than you," I respond, nodding my chin toward his stuff on the floor. "You could have slept in bed, Theo."

"It just wasn't something I was going to do without talking to you first, and you fell asleep so quickly. I wasn't going to disturb you. Besides, I've slept in way worse places, Sunshine."

"Well, going forward you can sleep in bed with me. Just stick to your side of the mattress," I say, half joking, half serious. More like thirty-seventy.

"Yes, ma'am. You want anything to eat?"

"No thanks. I think I'm going to lie back down after I drink this. You don't have to sit in here and babysit me all day, you know."

"Wild horses couldn't drag me away, Lyla. I'm going to call your brother shortly and have a few things to do around the house, but I'll always be in earshot." He keeps me company while I drink the rest of my tea.

"This is still my favorite. Thanks for remembering," I murmur as I hand him my cup.

"I remember everything," he says with a wink before helping me get comfortable. "There's rain in the forecast for the rest of the week. Perfect for rest and recovery. I'm going to grab a book, and then I'll be back."

I fall asleep before he returns.

* * *

The next couple of days go by quickly. I sleep a lot, more than I ever have in my life. Theo touches base with my mom and Quinn via text. I know they're both anxious to talk to me, but the idea of being on Facetime or even just a regular phone call feels as appealing as running a marathon.

One night after we eat, Theo asks, "How about I set you up in the bath for a soak? I know you've been eyeing that tub up every time you go in the bathroom."

"That sounds amazing."

"Let me clear these plates, and I'll get you set up. You relax until then." He puts our plates in the sink and disappears down the hallway. I make my way over to the couch, noticing that I'm moving quicker and having less discomfort. Ten minutes later, Theo calls out that he's ready for me.

My jaw drops when I walk into the bathroom. The lights are dimmed, and he has music playing softly from the speakers that are built into the walls. I smile when I recognize it's a Zach Bryan song.

The water is still on as the tub fills, and he clearly poured copious amounts of bubble bath in. There are a few candles lit and placed around the vanity and the ledge shelves near the tub itself. I turn toward Theo, who smiles shyly at me by the door.

"Theo, this is... Well, this is really thoughtful. Thank you." I've always loved baths, a fact that Theo is well aware of. This setup is another way to prove he really does remember everything.

"I'm going to step out so you can do what you need to do before you get in. Please wait for me. Let me help you get situated. I promise I won't have wandering eyes, but I don't want you more hurt than you already are."

I agree, and he steps out and closes the door.

When I call him back in, I have a towel wrapped around me. He walks to where I'm standing next to the tub and reaches out to take my hand. As promised, his eyes don't stray from mine, not even when I drop my towel and take my time sinking down into the hot water.

"Oh my gosh, this is perfect," I say as I lie back, checking to make sure the bubbles have me covered. Theo tells me he'll be right back, and when he returns, he has two drinks. He passes me a club soda with lime, and I can't help but smile at him when he clinks his glass, filled with what looks like whiskey, against mine.

"Keep me company," I say before he leaves again.

"I was just going to sit in the hallway until you said you were done. In case you needed something." Instead, he sits down with his back against the wall, stretching his sweat-pants-clad legs out in front of him. He looks over, studying me and soaking in every feature.

"You're fucking gorgeous, Lyla. That smile still takes my breath away."

"Hah, you must have downed a few shots while you were out there. I look like a punching bag."

"I'm just being honest, baby. You've always been the most beautiful woman in the world."

I hear the lyrics to "God Speed," and smile. I find this to be one of Zach Bryan's most beautiful songs, and I adore it.

"Did you already have the concert tickets when you asked me to go with you?" I ask.

"Nope," he says with a sheepish smile.

I raise my eyebrows at him. "I was wondering who you were going to have to ditch when I said I'd go."

He chuckles. "I went online right after your text and bought the best seats I could find."

I laugh and close my eyes, giving myself a quick pep talk before I bring up what's been on my mind for the past six years. *Rip off the bandaid, Lyla. Just say it.*

"I need to know why, Theo. I need to know why you left. I feel safe with you. It's something I've never felt with anyone else. Playing house like this with you is too easy. It feels too natural. Like something I could get used to but I don't want to.

Not yet. Not until I know the truth." I open my eyes and turn my head toward him, pleading at him with my eyes to talk to me.

He takes a sip of his drink and looks away, his shoulders sagging as if in defeat. I'm not sure if he's trying to avoid answering or trying to put together a response.

I'm beginning to give up hope, to think this is where it all ends because I can't even think about moving forward without the truth. But then he takes a deep breath. His voice is low and laced with sadness and shame when he speaks.

"Olivia dying triggered something in me. She was like a little sister and losing her, watching you deal with the grief of saying goodbye to your best friend, took me back to my childhood. I felt like I was reliving my mom dying all over again. It fucked with my head in ways I never saw coming, Lyla."

I wait for him to continue. I'm frozen in the tub and don't dare move a muscle. I'm almost in shock that he's finally opening up to me, and I don't want to do anything that might distract him.

"I'm not proud of the way I acted. It will forever be my biggest regret. I was so fucking scared, Sunshine. All I could do was think about what if it was you? What if you were with her that night? What if you died? What if I lost you? I couldn't stop the thoughts. They consumed me. Every waking minute and every night when I fell asleep and had nightmares. It was like every possible scenario that ended with you dying was running through my head. I spiraled. Losing you was—*is*—my biggest fear. There's no scenario in this lifetime or the next that has me surviving that, that has me living without you."

"And you thought leaving me was the best solution?" I ask, perhaps a bit more sharply than I intend.

"I thought it was the only way I could protect myself. I'm not saying it wasn't the worst decision of my life, but it was straight self-preservation, Lyla. If I took you out of the equation, I wouldn't spend every waking minute worrying about losing you. Worrying about turning into my dad. That year after Liv died, I was holding on so tight, so scared to let you out of my sight, that I knew I was smothering you. That's no way to maintain a relationship. If I had stayed, I knew I would ruin us and go insane with fear in the process."

"Oh, Theo," I say softly, thinking about how his dad fell apart and checked out after losing his wife. Theo didn't just lose his mom.

Her death caused him to lose both of his parents because his dad was a shell of a man, there in body but never emotionally supportive. I knew it upset Theo, but I never knew how much it downright haunted him.

"You are a part of me, Lyla. Even when we weren't together. Every heartbeat, every breath I take, every moment of my life is inexplicably tied to you. I don't just love you, I *need* you. Like the fucking air I breathe. Take that away, take you away in a permanent manner, and I wouldn't survive. I couldn't exist in this world without you. I would turn into the exact same zombie my dad did if something ever happened to you."

"So you left," I say quietly.

"So I left," he repeats. "It was rotten. It was shitty. It was the coward's way out. But it was the only thing I could think of to stop the fear. Stop the pain. If I stopped it before it became real, I thought maybe I would be able to survive."

I nod my head in sympathy. I may not agree with what he did, but this explanation... I understand now. I understand him.

"I've spent years wondering what I did wrong," I tell him, my voice cracking.

"Nothing. You did *nothing* wrong, Lyla."

I take a breath before I ask my next question. Since starting to let him back in, and letting the walls around my heart that I built fall a bit, this has been on my mind almost as much as the reason for him leaving.

"How do I know it won't happen again, Theo? How do I know that when things get scary or messy, you won't cut and run on me again?"

"I'm here now, aren't I?" he responds.

"You make it sound like it's an obligation," I say defensively. He shakes his head from side to side as if trying to collect his thoughts.

"Shit, that didn't come out the right way. What I meant was that I'm here now, with you. Facing my biggest fear. And this time around, there's actual merit behind it. It almost became a reality, Lyla, on more than one occasion. I almost lost you that night. I can't unsee you on the floor or hooked up to those machines in that hospital bed, looking fragile and broken. In that moment, and every one since, I haven't thought about running. If anything, it's had the exact opposite effect. Since the minute I found out you were in danger, I haven't wanted to leave your side."

He stands up and places his glass on the vanity before walking over to the tub. He squats down before he continues, staring right into my eyes, his voice strong and confident now.

"I ran away once, Lyla, and it is the single biggest mistake of my life. But when I tell you it won't happen again, I mean it. I *swear* it. On my life, Lyla. I'm never walking away from you. No matter what life throws at us, no matter what challenges we have to deal with, I'm yours for as long as you'll have me. And I hope to god that one day you'll say I can be yours again."

The way he's looking at me, his eyes a crystal blue, is so genuine and heartfelt. Like he's telling me that he's mine and every part of him belongs to me. I believe what he's saying, but that doesn't resolve the trepidation I feel.

"Thank you for telling me the truth," I finally say.

"It was long overdue. I've just been too scared to tell you, to let myself be that vulnerable."

"I think I just need some time, Theo. To take all of this in. Figure out where we go from here."

"Take all the time you need but know that I'm not leaving your side. I've loved you since the day I met you, and that's never going to change." He stands up and kisses me on my head. "I'm going to give you some privacy, but I'm not going far. Let me know when you're ready to get out, so I can help you."

I nod my head in response and lean back, closing my eyes and soaking in the warmth of the water. I think about everything he just told me. I don't know why this explanation never dawned on me. I've always known the death of his mother had a huge impact on him. It's part of why he always wanted to be a cop. And I know he struggles with his feelings regarding his dad, bouncing between resentment and compassion.

I always just assumed I was the catalyst for him leaving. I think about all of the years we lost, all of the time we could have been together, if we had just talked and communicated better.

I want to move forward with him so badly, but I'm fucking terrified, too. Despite his promise, and the fact that he hasn't left yet when I'm in the most danger I've ever been in, I'm still afraid that something could shift his perspective. I worry I'll spend the rest of our life together waiting for something to send him running. And I'm afraid that concern will suffocate any chance we have of a future together.

\* \* \*

It's the day after Theo's confession when I decide to call my mom. I have the sneaking suspicion that she already knows everything Theo told me last night, and I need a sounding board.

"Hi, sweetie! How are you?" she says when she picks up, and I swear I can hear the smile in her voice.

"I'm okay. Slowly but surely feeling better. I don't think I've ever slept so much."

"That's what your body needs right now. Theo has been keeping in touch with updates, but it's great to finally hear your voice."

"Speaking of Theo, we had a pretty deep conversation last night..." I trail off.

"Did you now? You going to leave me hanging or fill me in?" she asks.

"In my heart of hearts, I think you already know what he finally opened up to me about." I wait for her reply.

"I do." She speaks softly, as if full of remorse. "If you see it as a violation of our trust in each other, our relationship, I understand. But I hope you can see it from my perspective."

"Maybe you could explain it to me, Mom. Because I understand he probably told you in confidence, but you watched me mourn the end of our relationship and deal with the fallout for years."

"I have always thought of him as another son, you know that. When he came to me and spoke about his fears and how much they were eating away at him... Lyla, he seemed just as broken as you. The idea of losing you was too much for him. And he was so afraid that if he stayed with you, he'd stifle you and ruin your relationship, your life, by smothering you."

It makes my heart ache, thinking of the anguish he felt making that decision to leave. The fact that he was so burdened by his own fears and emotions that he made that decision cuts me to the core. I can't even imagine how lonely and isolated he felt.

I don't say anything, waiting for my mom to continue.

"I didn't want to tell you while he was overseas because I didn't know how you would take it or if you'd contact him. The last thing I wanted was for him to be distracted while he was deployed."

"And after the Army? You didn't think to tell me then?"

"I hoped and prayed he'd come to that decision on his own, honey. I didn't feel it was in my place to disclose his struggles. It wouldn't fix anything coming from me, anyway. "

On that point, she's right. My mother telling me his truth wouldn't have had the same impact. It certainly wouldn't have me considering a future with him like I am now.

"What if I spend the rest of my life walking on eggshells, Mom? Waiting for his fears to take over again and convince him to bolt?" Losing him again would be the end for me. It would be like the world lost its sun. There's no way I'd be able to recover from that loss a second time.

"Well, I guess you just need to decide if you have enough faith in him to take the chance." I'm quiet as I think about that. "Lyla, are you still there?"

"I'm nodding." Literally, I'm nodding my head as I think about what she just said. "Thanks, Mom. I admit that it did hurt that you never told me, but hearing it from your perspective, I understand more. I'm glad he had you to talk to."

"Love you, honey. Just follow your heart. It's never steered you wrong. Go get some more rest."

"Love you, too," I say before hanging up.

I fall asleep minutes later, wondering if my heart is going to lead me to happiness or my demise.

\* \* \*

Theo continues to dote on me, making me tea, helping me in and out of bed even after I'm able to do it myself, keeping me fed, and changing the bandage on my face when needed. He sleeps in bed with me every night but stays on his side of the mattress.

I know he would hold me if I asked him to—he did it in the hospital. But it already feels like we're playing house in a lot of ways, and I can't let those lines get any blurrier until I figure out if I can move past my doubts.

I know he's getting updates from my dad and brother on what's going on with Scotty McDavid. Based on the huffing, puffing, and edginess to his voice when he's on the phone, I can tell he's not happy.

By Sunday night, our fifth night on the island, I'm finally starting to feel better. My bruises have started to fade and turn yellow. My headaches are fewer and further between, and the throbbing around my ribs dulls to an ache. The discomfort is still there, but it doesn't take my breath away anymore.

We're sitting at the counter eating dinner when I ask him for an update.

His voice is strained and full of doubt when he responds. "Not too much to say. Scotty McDavid isn't saying anything else. He's being wishy-washy about his involvement with Hollman now."

"That's bullshit. He told me that Hollman sent him. I said that in my statement."

"I know. He admitted to being associated with Hollman in his first interrogation. Their ties are clear. I think he's getting cold feet that Hollman will have him taken out if he talks too much."

"Okay, so what happens next?" I ask.

"The feds head back to Boston and continue to prepare for

Hollman's trial. McDavid sits in jail until *his* trial. He wasn't granted bail."

A trial.

Somehow I forgot that this would end up there eventually. As someone who lives for Dateline and has probably seen every *Law and Order: SUV* episode, I should have known better. The idea of facing this man in person, of having to relive that night chills me to the bone. I push my plate away and feel my body start to tremble. Theo puts his fork down and turns toward me.

"Look at me, Sunshine. Breathe." I bring my eyes to his, not even realizing I'm holding my breath. "A trial is months away. This isn't TV. It doesn't happen overnight. You will be prepped and ready to face him, if it even comes down to that. He could take a plea."

I nod, slowly breathing in and out.

"I see his face when I close my eyes, Theo. I don't want to see him again in person," I whisper. Theo gently uses his fingers to tip my chin up so that I'm looking into his eyes. They're full of compassion.

"I swear to God that man isn't going to hurt you again. We won't let him. Do you hear me?" It takes me a second, but I eventually whisper that I do. "We'll cross that bridge if and when we get there, okay? You done eating?"

"Yeah, I lost my appetite."

"Go relax on the couch. I'll join you in a second."

I head over and plop down, getting comfortable under a blanket when Diego hops up to cuddle with me. I absentmindedly pet him, my thoughts drifting to facing Scotty McDavid at trial. Of having to testify against him, feeling his eyes stare at me while I recount the scariest moments of my life. Of having to repeat the things he said to me, the way he grabbed my throat and ripped my shirt open.

I'm on the verge of breaking down again when Theo walks in and joins me on the couch. "Lyla, look at me."

I do.

"I know you're scared but let's not borrow tomorrow's troubles. That man won't get the chance to hurt you, or anyone else, ever again. You might not be ready to trust me with your heart yet, but you can trust me with your safety."

## TWENTY-THREE
*theo*

I WAKE up to the sunshine coming in through the blinds for the first time since we've been on the island. But more importantly I wake up to Lyla's body pressed against mine, her back to me. I resist the urge to wrap my arms around her, even though the temptation is strong. Her breathing is still slow, so I can tell she's sleeping.

I think back to our conversation when she was in the bathtub. Without opening up to her, we didn't stand a chance. But to actually do it was exhausting and scary and exhilarating.

While the fear of losing her still runs rampant, going back to what I felt like at that time took a lot out of me from a mental standpoint. It's also a bit of an ego check to be that vulnerable with someone else. She makes it easy, though. Seeing the compassion in her eyes had me wishing I did it years ago.

The pain I feel when I think about Lyla saying she thought she did something to push me away has me massaging my chest to get some relief from the sharp burst of pain I feel.

I would never want her to shoulder that weight. Knowing that she did, that she blamed herself for all those years, brings my own guilt to a whole new level. I caused her even more pain than I realized.

As draining as the conversation was, it also feels like an enormous weight has been lifted off my shoulders. If I opened up to her sooner, would that have changed things? Maybe we would have gotten back together sooner. Maybe if she knew my truth, she would have washed her hands of me.

Or maybe this is when and where it's all meant to fall back into place—or fall apart for good. I guess it could have gone a hundred different ways but none of that matters now. We are where we are, and all we can do is move forward in one way or another.

My phone vibrates on my dresser, so I sneak out of the bed, careful not to disturb her or Diego, who she has an arm wrapped around. *Lucky bastard.* I can't believe I'm jealous of a cat. When I get into the kitchen, I find a text from Derek.

**Derek: How's my sister?**

**Me: I think she finally turned a corner yesterday. Moving around a lot better.**

Bubbles appear and disappear a few times before he responds.

**Derek: Has she had any nightmares?**

**Me: Is this a test to see if I'm sharing a bed with her? Because, full disclosure, I am. But we stay on our own sides.**

**Derek: Just answer the question, asshole.**

**Me: No nightmares that she's mentioned or that I've noticed.**

**Derek: Good. Wouldn't wish that shit on anyone.**

I'd be lying if I said his last message didn't have me wanting to call him. Wanting to check in. I consider the possibility of him dealing with his own trauma from walking in on his sister being attacked.

I decide to hit the call button after all. It rings a few times before he finally answers. "You sat there with your phone in your hand debating if you should answer."

"I don't know if I'm up for a heart-to-heart with a guy I hate seventy-five percent of the time," he says, sounding exhausted.

"Wow, only seventy-five percent? That's an improvement."

"So Lyla seems to be doing okay?" he asks.

"Like I said, definite improvement in how she's feeling. More of an appetite. Her head hasn't been bothering her nearly as much. No nightmares, but she did have a moment of panic when she realized she'd have to face that asshole during a trial."

"Maybe he'll take a plea. I'm relieved she's doing better."

"How are you doing, man? Walking into the attack couldn't have been easy."

This could go either way. He could hang up on me, or he could engage in conversation. Colin hasn't mentioned Derek at all to me over the past few days, so I really have no idea the headspace he's in.

Derek typically keeps all of his feelings close to the vest. Always has. I have no idea if Colin even thought to ask how he was doing because Derek gives off the facade that he's always fine.

He lets out a breath of air. "It wasn't. I close my eyes and see it happening. I could hear her screaming when I got out of my truck. I don't think I'll ever get that sound out of my head."

"Fuck. I'm sorry you can't turn it off. But you saved her life, Derek. She's still here with us because you got there in time. Don't you ever forget that."

He changes the topic. It's not surprising, considering he doesn't like me much. "What'd she think of the cottage? Did you tell her how you poured over every single decision with her in mind?" he asks.

"No, I had your brother on speakerphone, so he took care of that for me. But she loves it."

"That was your own stupidity," he laughs. "I'm anxious to hear what she thinks of the little details, but this is about enough of a conversation with you for the day. Tell her to call me later if she's up for it. And take good care of her, Theo. That seventy-five can go back to one hundred real quick."

"Noted. I'll talk to you later."

I sit with a cup of coffee until I hear Lyla get out of bed. "Coffee or tea?" I call out to her before she goes into the bathroom.

"Coffee, please." I fix her morning caffeine, just a splash of milk, no sugar, and sit the mug on the counter for when she comes out. "Do I dare ask who you were already on the phone with?" she asks as she sits next to me.

"Derek." She looks up at me in surprise and I continue. "I know. Part of me thought he'd send me to voicemail. But he texted checking in on you, and I figured he could benefit from someone checking in on him, too."

"I'm sure that went over well. He's not one to let anyone in."

"He's struggling," I admit to her, and she nods in understanding.

"Now that I'm finally feeling better, I'll make sure to check in on him daily."

"I think that'll help." I take a sip of my coffee. "The weather is finally beautiful. We should get outside today. Come on, let's start with the backyard." I tip my head to the glass door that leads to the yard. Diego follows us out, ready to chase any bug or bird he comes across.

Between the rain and how crappy she's felt, Lyla hasn't

been in the backyard yet. She stands in awe, spinning in a slow circle to see it all.

"This is like a private little oasis back here. It's gorgeous," she says. There's a huge paver patio that's roomy enough for a dining table and two couches. A fire pit is on the corner with four more chairs circling it. But it's the landscaping that really makes it feel like paradise. The rest of the yard is grass, emerald and vibrant, and there are hydrangea, rose, and swamp rose bushes everywhere. They aren't as full and colorful as they are in the summer, but there are still plenty of blooms hanging on. "I bet it's heavenly back here in July and August."

"It is. Come sit." She joins me on the couch. "Want to hit up the beach?"

Lyla looks at me, and her eyes literally light up. "Yes! Which one?"

"Let me check the forecasts and see which looks best." We enjoy the sunshine and our coffee while I debate which beach to go to. It's sunny without a cloud in the sky, but some beaches on the island will be windy. Eventually, I settle on a winner.

"It looks like 40th Pole will be our best bet today. Do you want to go after breakfast?"

She shrugs her shoulders and says, "I've got no other plans."

* * *

An hour later, we're in my truck heading to the beach. 40th Pole is on the Nantucket Sound opposed to the ocean, so it's usually calm and the water pretty warm, even this time of year. We drive onto the almost empty beach, and I set up our chairs, an umbrella, and the beach blanket.

Lyla links in to the speaker I brought and gets some music

going. She pulls the coverup she's wearing over her head and tosses it onto the blanket.

She's an absolute smoke show in the bathing suit she has on. It's a white one-piece with a low cut front and back. Her bruises have continued to fade and are more yellow now, but my blood pressure still spikes anytime I get a view of them.

In an effort to draw my attention away from the bruises, I find myself staring at her long, lean legs before my eyes wander up to her tits. Perky and mouthwatering in that suit. Her hair is piled on top of her head, and she has oversized sunglasses on. She's a knockout.

The beach is pretty empty, save for some fishermen and a few people walking dogs. Small waves gently break on the shore, the sound rhythmic and relaxing. I take a look around at our surroundings, relief settling in my gut when I see that everything looks copacetic.

As if we're on the same page, Lyla says, "I don't think I've felt this at peace in awhile. I forgot how much I loved this beach." When I turn back towards her, I catch her eyeing up the tattoo I have on my quad. "What's the quote?" she asks.

I pull my swim trunks up a little to make the tattoo more visible. It's a quote with the wings of an eagle and clouds behind it, black and white but with a very patriotic vibe.

"'So it goes,'" she reads aloud. "From your favorite book." My lips turn up into a smile, glad that she still remembers.

"Yup. I got it after I left the Army. A reminder to keep moving forward, and a way to remember the guys we lost. Had to beg Derek's guy to pull an all-nighter for me."

"And the one on your forearm?" she asks, pointing to the one on my arm. The trees start at my wrists and go up towards my elbow. They're different heights and the varied shading gives it a misty forest feel.

"I got that one when I was on leave after my first tour. I

was so fucking tired of the desert and wanted something earthy to keep me grounded. What better than pine trees, you know?"

"They're all beautiful. And meaningful. Exactly what a tattoo should be."

\* \* \*

We spend the next few hours relaxing, napping, wading in the water, and talking about anything we can think of. These carefree moments, when neither of us are wrapped up in worry or anxiety, remind me that she's not just the love of my life.

She's my best friend, and I fucking love spending time with her. I'm lying on my stomach on the beach blanket, facing Lyla while she sits in her chair. She's biting her bottom lip, which is almost healed, so I know something must be on her mind.

"You're going to open up that cut again if you keep chewing on your lip, Sunshine."

"How many women have there been over the years?" she asks out of the blue. Didn't see this coming but I welcome the question.

"None. I already told you that." I look right into her eyes when I say it.

"Really? None?" she asks in disbelief. "But you look like that." she says, waving her hand up and down my body.

"I've never wanted anyone else."

"You've never needed someone to take the edge off?"

I hold up my hand and wave it. "Nah, I have this." That elicits a laugh from her, but then I turn serious. "There's never been anyone else. It never even crossed my mind. It's always been you, Lyla."

She leans forward as I prop myself up on my forearms and take my watch off to show her the oldest, most weathered tattoo I have. I keep it hidden most of the time, but it's the one that means the most to me. On the underside of my wrist, scripted in an old-fashioned typewriter font is her name. She covers her mouth with her hand and pushes her sunglasses up with the other.

"How long have you had this, Theo?" she asks with a shaky voice.

"I went from the recruiting office to the tattoo shop the day I enlisted."

"But you enlisted before you broke up with me. So you got it even though you knew you were going to leave me?"

"There was never going to be anyone else for me. I've known that since we were kids. There hasn't been a day that's gone by that I haven't loved you, that I haven't been *in love* with you."

She sits back in her chair, trying to digest what I've just told her. If being open with her last night was challenging, telling her that I've always loved her is the complete opposite. Truer words have never been spoken, and they easily roll off my tongue.

"I'm pretty sure I've always been in love with you, too, Theo."

# TWENTY-FOUR

## *Lyla*

"TAKE ME HOME, THEO."

He looks up at me, his face a mix of desire, surprise, and something else that takes me a minute to identify. I glance down at the tattoo on his wrist, the one I never knew existed before looking back into his eyes when it finally dawns on me.

Devotion. It's spilling out of his eyes. Seeping out of every pore. Even when we weren't together, this man has been utterly, infinitely devoted to me and I had no idea. "Take me home and make love to me. Unless you don't want to."

"Unless I don't want to?" He scoffs. "Jesus, Lyla, I want to do more than just make love to you. I've had six years to think about what I would do to you. I want to worship you. I want to devour you. I want to suck on those tits while my hands wander all over your body. I want to run my tongue down your spine, slowly. I want you writhing underneath me, rubbing yourself all over my dick. I want my mouth on that pussy, on that clit. I want to hear that sweet moan you make right before you come on my tongue. Then, I want to bury my cock so deep inside of you that we both see stars. I want to sprinkle kisses over that collar bone while we make love. And I want to do it again and again."

I squeeze my legs together to stop the need pulsing there. I can't even string any words together so I don't try. I just nod my head. I'm sure my own desire is written all over my face.

Theo jumps up and immediately starts gathering our stuff. I don't think I've ever had such a quick beach exit, and I can't help but giggle as we hop into his truck and head home.

"I was going to ask if we could get Juice Bar on the way," I say, giving him an innocent smile. The Juice Bar is a Nantucket staple offering up the best homemade ice cream and waffle cones on the planet.

"Tomorrow. I'll get you as much as you want tomorrow," he says with a gruff voice. We make it home in record time, and he's opening his door before the truck is in park.

Leaving everything in the car, he all but sprints around to open my door. He takes my hand and leads me to the front door before stopping and turning to face me.

He takes my face into his hands and brushes his lips against mine. "I can't wait to get my hands on you, Sunshine." Just when I think he's going to kiss me again, he turns back to the door and unlocks it before taking my hand and tugging me inside.

Diego rushes over and sniffs us, no doubt smelling the beach on us. The look he gives Theo is one of utter disgust before he turns and walks away.

"Is he pissed at you?" I ask, almost in disbelief over what I just witnessed.

"Oh, yeah. Super pissed that he didn't get to come with us. We'll take him tomorrow." He locks the door and turns on the alarm before giving me his full attention. "Are you sure about this, Lyla?"

"I am." It's all the confirmation he needs.

"I'll be gentle, but tell me if anything hurts you. If it's too much. If you want me to stop."

I assure him I will, and then he gently scoops me into his arms, one arm under my knees, the other around my back. I relish in being this close to him and kiss his neck as he walks us to the bedroom.

"I want this, Theo. All of you. I promise I'll tell you if I need you to stop," I tell him, still in his arms.

"I want it all with you. Every sunset. Every night sky. I want lazy Sunday mornings reading. I want rainy days and coffee in bed. I want date nights and puzzles on the dining room table. I want dancing in the kitchen and s'mores on the beach. I want you telling me about your day while I cook us dinner. I want the good times and the scary times and everything in between. I want nights of slow love making, when we take our time and savor every touch, every taste. I want the hard fucking, when we can't get naked fast enough and I have to take you wherever we are. I want to eat that pussy every night while you drip all over my face. I want deep belly laughs and tears. I want the morning runs and Sunday dinners with your family. I want to hold your hand while you chase your dreams. I want to worship your body every day." His voice is raspy as he says all of this. He kisses me between each of his wants, as if those kisses serve as the punctuation.

I don't even care that tears escape the corners of my eye and roll down my cheeks. Everything he just said is everything I've missed over the years.

He's painted a picture of a life, a future, I didn't think would ever exist. I lean forward and kiss him. He takes control of it and runs his tongue across my lips as if asking me to open them. I do, and he groans as his tongue meets mine.

I don't know who deepens the kiss, mainly because I don't know where he starts and I begin. What I do know is that this is the kind of kiss I've been missing for half a dozen years. It's passionate, it lights my body on fire, it makes the world disappear around me.

We don't battle for control, instead our tongues dance, taking turns with leading. If the kiss on the beach the other day knocked my world off its axis, this kiss kicks my world into another galaxy entirely.

He puts me down and I lean back for a second as he pulls my coverup over my head. He yanks me closer to him, his arms going around my waist, one hand gripping my ass. When I feel his hard length against my stomach, I'm reminded of just how big he is, and for a second, I'm nervous he won't fit.

His lips leave mine, and he kisses his way down my neck, leaving a trail of heat in his wake. He wraps my hair around his hand and gently tugs, forcing my head back and giving him better access.

My hands hang over his shoulders as he sucks on the sensitive spot of my collarbone. A moan escapes, and I feel him smile against me. "This spot still gets you, huh? I told you, I remember everything."

He brings his lips back up my neck and starts to slowly kiss away the tears that fell earlier before making his way back to my mouth. This time he takes control, and he's hungry for me. He moves his hands up my body, being careful of my ribs, until his hands are at my shoulders, his fingers slipping under the straps of my bathing suit.

I give him an almost imperceptible nod, and he lowers them, pushing my suit down to the ground. "While I'd love to pick you up and toss you onto the bed, I think I should probably wait a few weeks on that," he says between kisses. His hands move to my breasts, and I suck in a breath at how good it feels to have him touch me.

"We're going to get your sheets all sandy," I manage to say.

"Fuck the sheets, Sunshine. Get into bed," he replies gruffly.

I lie down in bed and prop my elbows up so I can watch him tear his shirt over his head and push down his own bathing suit. Between his solid frame and the tattoos, his body is like a work of art. His cock is hard, standing at attention, and I can't take my eyes off of it.

He climbs into bed after me but stops at the bottom. He takes my foot in his hand and brings it to his mouth, kissing his way from my ankle, up my calf, and to my thigh. He does the same thing to my other leg, stopping just short of the apex of my thighs. There's no doubt my pussy is soaking wet. Every touch of his hands is like a spark, and I can't wait for us to burn together.

"Fuck, you're gorgeous. Spread those legs, baby. Show me that perfect pussy that I've missed all these years." I do as he says and let my legs fall open. He licks his lips as he looks at me. "I'm going to eat this pussy, Lyla, like it's my own personal feast, and you're going to come all over my face. I want you to make a mess of me, baby."

"God, yes, Theo," I breathe heavily, desperate for him to touch me more.

"But first, these tits need some attention," he says, smirking at me.

"Tease," I hiss.

"I'll make it worthwhile," he says as moves up my body, careful not to let any of his own

weight fall on me as he takes a nipple into his mouth. I immediately arch up into him. He circles his tongue around me as he gently squeezes my other breast.

I'm in sensory overload. I could come from nipple play alone. He alternates between licking and sucking on one side and twisting and tugging the other.

It's the most delicious balance of pleasure and pain, and there's no doubt he can't feel how wet my pussy is as I try to get closer to him. I'm going to combust any second.

"You're going to make me come just from what you're doing with your tongue and hands, babe."

He pauses and looks up at me, his hand still kneading my breast. "Say that again," he says.

"You're going to make me come, babe?" I say in question.

"I didn't think I'd ever hear you call me babe again." I smile at him in response. "And I'll happily take the challenge of making you come just from playing with these tits. But on another night. Tonight, I want you on my tongue and cock."

He dives back into my chest and for the next few minutes, he tortures me in the most delicious way. He licks and sucks, twists and pulls as I squirm underneath him.

He comes up for air and then works his way down my stomach with sloppy kisses. My body hovers close to the edge. I shake in anticipation, wishing for Theo to push me over that cliff when he puts his mouth on my pussy.

Sure enough, the minute he runs his tongue along my seam, I moan his name.

"Baby, you're already dripping." It's like fucking Niagara Falls down there, so he's not wrong. Before I know it, he buries his face in me. He runs his tongue up and down my sex. His groans only turn me on more. "There's nothing in this world that tastes as good as your tight, hot pussy," he says in between licking me and nibbling on my clit. When he gets to that bundle of nerves, I moan even louder, which has him backing off a little.

"Please don't stop," I plead, my hands tangling in his hair. He grips the globes of my ass to keep me close to his mouth. When my breathing slows down a bit, he goes back to my clit, showering it with attention. He eats my pussy like a starved man, and I love every fucking single second of it.

"Stop? God, baby I could do this all fucking day. Eat this pussy. Squeeze this ass. Watch you wriggle under me and hear you moan my name." My breathing is labored. I can't string together enough words to form a sentence, my body almost overflowing with pleasure. "You want to come yet, Lyla, or should I keep you on the edge a little longer?" I groan in response. "I'll take that as you saying I should tease you more. That's fine with me. I'm a very happy man with my mouth on your cunt."

He goes back to running his tongue up and down me, staying away from my clit to give me time to come down. He kisses me all over, moving to my thigh where he starts sucking.

"I forgot what a dirty mouth you have, Theo," I say when I catch my breath.

"You fucking love it, though," he says before kissing his way back to my pussy. I whimper something that sounds a lot like a yes as he ravishes me.

He brings his mouth back to my clit and slips a finger inside me. Then a second. He alternates between flicking and sucking, holding my thigh down as I reach the ledge.

I sail over that cliff to the most explosive, mind blowing orgasm I've had in years. He doesn't let up, milking every last drop and moan out of me as I grind against his face.

I have one hand on my chest, the other still in his hair as I attempt to catch my breath. He gently works his way up and down my pussy and groans with pleasure as he licks me clean.

Once he's satisfied, he kisses his way back up my body until he reaches my mouth. I pull him closer, wrapping my legs around him as we kiss. I taste myself on his tongue, and it lights the fire in me again. I rub my pussy on his cock, making it slick with my arousal.

Theo pulls back and says, "Fuck, I don't have a condom."

"I have an IUD. I don't want anything between us. If you're okay with that," I say as I kiss his neck.

"Being inside you bare? There's nothing I want more, Sunshine." He sits back and lines his cock up to my entrance. He looks up at me before he pushes in. I give him a small nod.

He enters me slowly so I can feel every inch of him. Every ridge of his cock. That thick vein that runs down the side of it. The way it pulses when it's inside of me.

Once he's all the way in, I freeze and look him in the eyes. His dick is huge, and it takes a second for my body to adjust to his size. When I exhale the breath I was holding, he leans back down.

I grab hold of the chain around his neck, bringing him so close to me I can feel his breath on my face.

"Holy shit, Lyla. This is heaven. This is like coming home, baby," he says, his forehead touching mine. There are no words to express the overwhelming pleasure I feel having him inside of me, my pussy still sensitive from the first orgasm he gave me.

I tip my head back in sheer ecstasy as he starts to move slowly, methodically. He sucks on my collarbone, the spot he knows is most sensitive as he pumps his hips. There's something undeniable in the way we fit together. Like we were made for each other.

Our bodies move like we're rediscovering something we both lost, but clearly never forgot. While we don't rush, there's an underlying feeling of raw need between us. It's like we're breathing life back into each other after all of these years.

He touches me as if he's the only man who's ever understood me, understood what my body likes and craves. When my breath starts to get heavy, he says, "I want you on top of me." He slowly pulls out of me and lies down, holding his hand out to help me straddle him. I guide his cock into me, feeling him even deeper in this position. He groans in pleasure. "You still love being on top, don't you, baby? I can feel how wet this pussy is." His voice is so low, so gravely, I can feel it vibrate through my body. I shiver in anticipation.

I move my hips slowly, and he gently pulls my face down to his, his hand holding the back of my head. "Answer me, baby. You still like riding my cock this way? Feeling me deep inside of you?"

I whimper from the pleasure of being impaled by him. "I love it, Theo," I finally manage to say. He lets go of my head, and his hands wander down to my hips. I settle my palms on his chest for balance as I start to move my hips. He groans with desire. "Answer me, babe. Do you still like it when I do this?"

I move my hips in leisurely circles on top of him, the way he always used to love, and his eyes close. "Goddamn, I've missed this, Sunshine." He grips my hips as I move my body. He thrusts his hips up slightly, letting me feel him even more. I have to bite my lip to keep from screaming his name.

His one hand moves up my body to my breast, kneading and squeezing before he starts tugging my nipple. My orgasm builds, and I start to pick up speed, moaning in pleasure as I do.

This is more than just lust, though there's no shortage of that. This is a deep, primal need for each other, for what we've had to go without for the last six years. There's a desperation between us as we connect, and we risk starvation for each other.

"Eyes on me, baby. I want to be looking into them when you come." Based on the way he grunts, I know he's close. I also know he won't let himself come before I do, so I'm not surprised when the hand that was on my hip moves down to my pussy.

With one hand tugging on my nipple, and the other working my clit, it doesn't take long before I come, a powerful orgasm rocking my entire body, down to my toes.

It's all I can do to keep my eyes open as I scream his name, coming hard on his cock. I keep moving my hips in fast circles as my orgasm wracks my body. I'm still in pleasure heaven when I feel Theo reach his own climax, feel him come inside of me as he groans my name.

"Lyla, fuck, baby," he manages to get out before he pulls me down to him, his arms wrapping around me as he kisses me passionately. Eventually, I pull back to catch my breath and roll gently off of him and onto my back.

"Holy crap, Theo. That was amazing. I think I saw stars," I say, my voice raspy.

Theo just nods his head in response, pulling me close to him. "That was an out of body experience, baby." I laugh. "I'm serious. I don't know how I lived without that all these years, Sunshine. Lived without you."

I drape my arm over his body and quietly say, "After what just happened, I can say with certainty that I haven't really been living these past six years." He holds me closer, and I burrow into his chest, his heart beating wildly.

## TWENTY-FIVE

*theo*

IF HEAVEN IS REAL, this is what it would consist of. Lyla lying next to me, our sweaty, naked bodies tangled together, our hearts beating wildly but tethered together, completely in sync with one another.

My hand wanders down her back to her ass, and I pull her closer to me, touching her as if I need to prove to myself that she's really here, that *this* is real. I lift one of her legs across my body and feel the warmth of her pussy against me.

Neither of us want to let the other go because being together again is like remembering what it felt like to come home. We're not just reconnecting here, we're rewriting every memory we lost in our years apart.

Our physical connection has always been like a match being thrown on gasoline. Time would stand still in those moments of intensity. So consumed with each other, the world could burn down around us and we wouldn't even notice. Every touch, every kiss, was filled with scorching heat. Never a gentle connection, even in those moments of sweetness, but explosive like a power surge.

Anytime we were together, it deepened a connection that

was already fierce and all-consuming. I remember times when I was at a loss for words after we'd been together because I didn't think we could get any closer, know each other's bodies any better, and then we did.

I never, not for one second, thought that connection would ever fade. After being together again, it's clear it hasn't. Now, after having her in my arms, hearing her moans, burying my cock in her, sucking on her collarbone, looking into her eyes when I came, I'm certain that, if anything, our connection can be stronger than ever if we let it.

Eventually, we peel ourselves out of bed—mainly due to the sandy mess we made of it, and the fact that both of our stomachs are growling.

"Let's get a shower. I'll change the sheets after. We can scrounge around in the fridge for dinner then," I say as I take her hand, helping her out of bed. I wrap my arms around her, holding her close to me. I can already feel my dick hardening again.

Before we can make our way to the bathroom, my cell rings. I glance between the phone and Lyla, noting Colin's name on the screen.

"Just answer it, Theo. You and I both know you're chomping at the bit for any sort of news."

I hit answer and rest it against my ear as I murmur "I'll change the sheets while I talk and then hop in the shower."

"I don't even want to know why you need to change the sheets," Colin says.

"Then don't ask. Anything worthwhile to fill me in on?"

"Nope. I've got nothing. McDavid is still sitting in jail. Hollman is still sitting in jail."

Talk about taking the wind out of my sails. I let out a sigh and run my hand down the side of my face. "Fuck me. I wasn't expecting this guy to tell us any deep Hollman-related secrets, but I was at least hoping he'd know if someone else was going to come after Lyla to finish the job."

"My gut tells me he's being honest when he says he doesn't have a clue."

"So he's essentially useless to us," I say.

"Yup. At least he'll rot in jail until his trial. There's no way he'll be out anytime soon. Hopefully, that'll give Lyla some peace."

"Anything else going on in Sandpiper that we need to know about?" I ask as I strip the sheets off the bed, careful to keep the sand contained as I roll it up.

"The living room at my parents house looks good as new. Mom got a new coffee table and frames. We rearranged the furniture a bit, thought maybe it would help if it looked different. My mom is driving all of us crazy. She calls for updates more than you."

"Hah, I bet. But I'm glad you guys got that done. Hopefully that'll make Lyla feel more comfortable when she gets home. One more thing..."

"Yeah?" Colin asks.

"Keep an eye on your brother."

"Derek? Why? What's wrong?" he asks, concern in his voice.

"I talked to him this morning. I think the trauma of walking in on Lyla being attacked is hitting him."

"Shit. I can't believe I didn't think of that sooner. This is not the kind of shit he sees in his line of work, and with it being our sister, I should have been more cognizant of that. Thanks." There's a short pause, then Colin continues. "Wait, he opened up to you?"

"Not a ton, but yeah. Shocked the hell out of me, too. I don't want to say too much. Let him talk to you about it."

"I'm on it. Tell my sister I said hi. I'll be in touch."

"Later," I say and end the call.

I hear the shower turn off, and I'm filled with disappointment that I didn't get to enjoy time in there with Lyla, our bodies wet and soapy, but there will be plenty of time for that. I feel around to make sure there's no sand on the bed before I grab fresh sheets.

Lyla comes in, a towel around her body, and quickly dries off before throwing on some lounge clothes. She runs her fingers through her wet hair and then sets about dealing with the small bandages on her face.

"Do we need to do something about those stitches? I know enough from EMS training that I could take them out, but you need to talk to the doctor about that," I say as I make the bed.

"The doctor at the hospital said they'd need five to seven days, and I'm right in that range. I'll call him first thing in the morning to see what I should do. It feels like a tomorrow-problem." When I turn toward her, she's leaning against the dresser watching me, her eyes roaming my still-naked body.

"See something you like, Sunshine?" I ask, and she brings her eyes to mine, a blush creeping up her neck.

"Yeah. You could bounce a quarter of that ass of yours, babe." I laugh out loud.

She holds her arms out, motioning for me to put the dirty sheets in them. I pass them over to her before leaning down and kissing her. "I'm going to hop in the shower, and then I'll make dinner."

\* \* \*

By the time I get to the kitchen, Lyla has fed Diego, poured me a couple of fingers of whiskey, and has a club soda with lime in front of her. I root through the fridge to see what our options are.

"Slim pickings here. This is the last of the enchiladas that Lou and Holly dropped off. We may have to venture out to the food store tomorrow," I say as I pull out the food and preheat the oven.

"We can do that on the way home from Juice Bar. And maybe we can get Millie's for dinner tomorrow," she says. My mouth starts watering just thinking about their guacamole and street corn. The restaurant's not too far from my house, and the food never disappoints.

"I like that plan. Let's relax outside while this heats up." I reach for my drink, and her hand, and walk to the glass doors that lead to the patio.

The temperature drops with the sun, so I start a fire in the pit while Lyla gets comfortable on the couch. I join her once I get it burning, using my phone to turn on some music.

She snuggles up next to me, and I wrap an arm around her. "Colin have anything good to report?"

"Nope," I say, unable to mask my disappointment.

"Well, tomorrow's another day. It's not like we expected anything else out of him."

"I was hopeful." Even though her words are optimistic, her body tenses and her grip on my thigh gets tighter. I hold her closer to me and reassure her. "The most important thing is he's sitting in jail and will be for a long time, okay?"

The next song that comes up on the playlist gives me the perfect opportunity to distract her. I stand up and hold my hand out to her. She looks at me with questioning eyes.

"This is one of my favorites. Dance with me?" I ask her. She lets me pull her off the couch. I wrap one arm around her and hold her hand to my chest with the other. The fire crackles while Jordan Davis's "BANKS" plays on the speaker.

Lyla's free hand is around my neck, and she holds herself as close to me as she can, her head resting on my chest. I look down at her and tip her chin up so that she's looking at me.

"I love you, Sunshine. I don't need you to say it back, but I just needed you to know it. You're the love of my life."

She doesn't say it back, but she does bring her lips to mine. I let her take control and she deepens the kiss as we sway to the music. The song bleeds into the next as we dance, unable to pull ourselves apart.

Eventually, the timer on my phone goes off, reminding me that dinner should be ready, and I'm forced to let her go. After refilling our drinks and grabbing plates, we park it at the table on the patio.

"What do you think you're going to do, career-wise?" I ask as we dig in.

"Honestly, I have no idea. I've avoided thinking about the long-term plan because it just stresses me out. I love writing, and freelance lets me take on the work that interests me, or write about what I want and then shop it around, but it lacks stability."

"What about teaching? You ever think about going back down that path?"

"I've thought about it, but I almost feel like that door is closed."

"Just because it's closed, doesn't mean you can't reopen it, Lyla."

"I know, but I feel like I lost the passion I had for it. I think that's because it was always meant to be something Liv and I did together," she says.

"Liv would want you to be happy, Sunshine. And if that's teaching, she'd want that for you. Just because she's not at your side to do it with you doesn't mean she's not with you. Let me ask you this—when you were substitute teaching in Vermont, did you miss it? Did you feel like you wanted your own classroom and your own kids?" I wait patiently while she contemplates her answer.

"No. I didn't miss it at all. I don't know if it's because my year of teaching was such a terrible experience, which was my own fault, or if it's because I've changed so much over the years. Whatever it is, I just don't see myself doing it anymore. I haven't for a while, but I've never said it out loud. Don't get me wrong. I enjoyed working at that high school. I met Quinn there, so I'll be forever grateful I walked through those doors. I had fun, most days, with the kids. But I don't feel that pull anymore. Which is scary because I'm in my thirties and living in my old bedroom at my parents' house. I need to grow up and figure this shit out."

"I'd say you're figuring it out just fine, Lyla. You've supported yourself entirely on your own for years. You and I both know you're not living at home because you're some deadbeat. You moved back home because you were dying to win me back." This elicits a laugh out of her, which was my goal. "Seriously, though, Lyla. Why did you move back home? Be honest with me."

"Honestly? I was feeling vulnerable once the article came out, constantly looking over my shoulder. Being so far from home, I felt like I was on my own island. Once that guy attacked me in my house, I knew I'd never feel safe there again. Never get a good night's sleep there again, and I didn't. Couldn't even bring myself to turn the lights out at night. The electric bill was through the roof in those few weeks. My parents were putting the pressure on, and I felt so guilty with how stressed and worried they were. I could say that I came home just to shut them up, but I was petrified of being attacked again. So, I ran back to my parents like a freaking coward.'

"You think that makes you weak?" I ask, angry that she has such a negative opinion about herself.

"A grown woman afraid of the dark, afraid of being home alone. So afraid of what happened that she ran back home to her daddy. Yeah, I'd say that was cowardly."

"No. You came back home to the place you feel safest. You know that you're a badass right?" She scoffs at that. "No, I'm being serious. You suffered a tremendous loss, baby."

"Yeah, and I sunk into a pit of depression I didn't think I'd ever get out of."

"But you did, completely on your own. You pulled yourself out of it and created a beautiful life for yourself. You spent who knows how long meticulously investigating a man who hid his secrets and his crimes so well the Boston Police could never nab him for anything serious. I don't like to think too much about it because I'll have a heart attack thinking about all the dangerous situations you put yourself in, but Lyla, you did it. Your investigative work and your writing will put that man away for the rest of his life. Don't you see how monumental that is?"

"It doesn't bring Liv back, though."

"And what, you think that makes you a failure or something? Think about how many lives it'll save putting that piece of shit in prison, Lyla. How many girls you're saving from a life of being forced to sleep with strangers. Liv is looking down at you, and she's so fucking proud. You have to know that." I gently grab her chin and force her to meet my eyes. "*I'm* so fucking proud of you. Your family is so proud of you."

She blinks back tears and slowly nods her head, as if she's accepting what I'm saying. When I'm satisfied that I've made my point, I lean back in my chair and take a bite of dinner.

"You love to write, you're extraordinary at it. We know you love to read, too. So write a book."

She laughs loudly and then looks at me. I raise an eyebrow at her as if questioning what she finds so comical. "Oh, you're being serious? Yes, Theo because it's that easy to just become an accomplished author."

"Baby, you are the most headstrong, driven human being I've ever known. If there's anyone who can accomplish whatever they put their mind to, it's you."

"What kind of book would I even write?" She asks, seemingly thinking out loud.

"Whatever you want. A romance with lots of hot sex? Would be happy to give you some ideas there. A thriller with a fucked-up ending? You watch enough true crime that you could come up with something disturbing yet interesting. A story about a woman finding herself after suffering a great loss? The world is your oyster, baby."

She puts her fork down and leans back in her chair. "The world is my oyster," she repeats to herself. "I do love writing. It's been the one constant in my life since I learned how to read. It would be a dream come true to make a career out of it. Lofty and ambitious but," she looks at me and smiles, "I love a good challenge."

That smile of hers makes me weak in the knees. I can't wait to get her back into bed. I can't wait to have her again. "Come on, baby. Let's finish eating and then I can give some inspiration in case you want to include spicy scenes in this future bestseller."

## TWENTY-SIX

*Lyla*

I BOLT AWAKE WITH A GASP, my heart beating so quickly it feels like it's going to come out of my chest. Theo sits up and rubs my back. With a hand to my chest, I take slow breaths, willing myself to calm down.

*It was just a dream, Lyla. You're okay. Just breathe,* I say to myself.

"What's wrong, baby?" Theo asks softly. My body shakes, and I'm freezing despite the fact I'm sweating like crazy.

"Nightmare," I get out, once I finally catch my breath.

"Do you want to talk about it?" he asks, a worried edge to his voice.

I shake my head in response. "Tomorrow."

He doesn't push for more or pepper me with questions. He just continues to rub my back.

"Do you want some water?" he finally asks once the tremors stop. I nod, and he gets out of bed. By the time he gets back, I feel a lot more normal compared to when I first woke up.

"Thanks," I whisper as he passes me the glass. I take a sip before putting it on the night table.

Theo slides back into bed, pulling me close. "Can I do anything?" he asks.

."No. Just hold me."

He kisses the top of my head. "Like I'd ever let you go.

"Go back to sleep, babe. I'm okay now. I promise."

"I'll fall asleep when you do."

I try closing my eyes, but my mind immediately goes back to the nightmare that woke me up. I'm back in the hallway at Dusty Bird Pub, but this time Scotty McDavid is able to shove me out the door and into a parked white van with blacked-out windows. It's always the same vehicle. He ties me up and sticks his hands under my shirt to feel me up. It's when he pulls out a knife that I wake up.

"You're shaking again, Lyla."

My eyes fly open. "It feels so real, Theo. I can't close my eyes without seeing it again."

His grip on me tightens. "You're safe, baby. I've got you."

I nuzzle in closer to his chest, relishing in the comfort of his arms, his steady heartbeat. Theo was always the water to my fire, and tonight is no different. He calms me in a way I'd never be able to do on my own.

Diego sidles up to me, curling next to my shoulder. His purrs soothe me, too. Eventually, I drift back to sleep. The last thing I hear is a soft, "You're safe, Sunshine. On my life."

Waking up tangled in the sheets with Theo isn't a bad way to start the day. But when I turn to face him, his eyes are heavy with fatigue. He looks utterly drained—he probably stayed up all night watching over me.

"Theo, you look exhausted. Go back to sleep."

"Nah, I'm good." He gives me a lazy smile before kissing my neck.

"Please tell me you weren't up the rest of the night, waiting to see if I had another bad dream."

*Tell me you weren't protecting me, even from myself.*

"Nothing a pot of coffee can't fix, Sunshine. While I wouldn't mind ravishing you in bed all morning, you need to figure out what needs to be done for your stitches before the day gets away from us."

I nod in response and slowly stretch out, satisfied that there isn't as much achiness in my ribs. It's my bladder that gets me out of bed, because otherwise, I'd be content lying here for another hour. By the time I make it to the kitchen, Theo has the coffee going and is working on making breakfast.

"I like seeing you in my clothes," he says, nodding at his shirt that I'm wearing.

"I like seeing you in gray sweatpants," I say with a wink as I sit down at the counter with my phone.

Because the doctor who did my stitches knows my mother well, he gave me his number in case I had any issues. I send Dr. Katz a text. With Theo's help, I also include a few pictures of the wound. He determines the stitches are ready to come out.

"Alright. I'm comfortable doing it myself, but you make the call. It's your face—I don't want to do anything you aren't comfortable with."

"I trust you." And I do. In every realm.

"I have a first aid kit that has what I'd need. Let's facetime your mom so I can go over the procedure with her, just to refresh my memory."

My eyes go wide. "Refresh your memory! That doesn't exactly instill confidence."

"I'm confident! I swear. As if I'd do anything to mess with that beautiful face. I've always been

taught to measure twice, cut once. Think of doing a run down with your mom as the equivalent to that."

"Did you just compare taking my stitches out to a house project?" I ask incredulously.

His head shakes with laughter. "I guess I did."

Theo goes to grab his first aid kit while I call my mom. She answers after the first ring, her smiling face filling my screen.

"Hi, Sweetie! How are you feeling?"

"Better every day."

"You look happy. Refreshed and relaxed. You're glowing." I have no doubt that I'm also blushing now when I think about what has me feeling so relaxed.

"Dr. Katz says my stitches need to come out. Theo feels moderately confident..."

Theo cuts me off as he joins me at the counter. "I feel *very* confident."

I roll my eyes. "Okay. Theo feels very confident that he can do it himself, but he just wants to go over a few things with you first."

"It's quite simple. I can definitely talk him through it."

I sip my coffee while Theo and my mom go over the procedure. The thought of needles and stitches makes me slightly nauseous so I do my best to tune them out.

"Thanks, Lori. This will be easier than I thought. I'll send you pictures when I'm done."

"Sounds good. Love you, kids."

"Bye! Love you!" I reply and then she's gone.

Theo goes to the sink to wash his hands. "You ready, Sunshine?"

"Ready as I'll ever be. Just be gentle."

"Well this might be a first. You actually requesting me to be gentle." The mischievous look in his eyes as he puts on a pair of rubber gloves gives me a flutter in my stomach.

"Stay focused, babe."

"I've got this, baby." He motions for me to get up and moves the stool closer to the glass doors. "Better light over here."

He leans in for a kiss as I sit back down. He peels the bandage off and then walks over to the sink. When he comes back, he uses a warm, damp cloth to clean the area. My shoulders raise up to my ears as I get more nervous.

His breath is warm against my skin as he whispers, "Relax, Sunshine." When he's satisfied with cleaning the wound, he puts the washcloth down and grabs the tweezers and scissors. I suck in a breath and close my eyes.

With steady fingers and zero hesitation, he snips each of the stitches, careful not to tug or rush. Once he's done cutting, he gently pulls each thread out, whispering reassuring words as he goes.

"You're doing great, Lyla. One more to go."

My shoulders sag in relief as I feel that last thread being removed. I let out a big sigh. "Oh thank God you're done."

"Easy peasy. Let me just clean it again. Your mom said to only put a bandaid on if it's bleeding but you're good there." He cleans it with a fresh damp cloth, dries it and then puts some ointment on top. When he's done he leans down so that we're eye level, one hand resting on each arm of the chair. "You good?"

"Better than good. Thank you for taking care of me."

"Always, Sunshine." He kisses me so deeply he has my toes curling. We're both breathless when that kiss ends. "I'm going to clean this up and then we'll figure out the rest of our day."

My next order of business is to catch up with Quinn, but when I look at the clock I realize that her school day has already started. I try my luck, anyway.

**Me: Facetime date? Soon?**

**Quinn:My prep is next period. I'll call you!**

**Me: I'll be waiting!**

I fish my laptop out of my tote and set it up on the counter before helping clean up the mess from breakfast, then I sit down to text Derek. I know he's probably knee-deep in work by now, but maybe I'll catch him on a break.

**Me: You better not have watched any *Love is Blind* without me.**

**Derek: Fucked up that you would even think that. How are you feeling?**

**Me: I can finally say that I'm feeling a lot better. Sorry for not checking in on you sooner.**

**Derek:Don't apologize. I'm fine. Just glad you're okay.**

**Me: Thanks for kicking that guys ass, Der. I don't want to think about what would have happened if you hadn't shown up when you did.**

**Derek:Then let's not think about it.**

The bubbles appear and disappear before he starts typing again.

**Derek:Never been so scared, Ly. Don't know what I'd do if we lost you.**

**Me: Well, you'd have to find someone new to watch *LIB* with, to start.**

**Me: Too soon to joke?**

**Derek: Very much so. Don't mean to cut you off but need to focus on what I'm doing so I don't lose a finger. Be careful. Love you.**

**Me: Love you, too. Send pics of the progress you've made since I last saw the site!**

I head off to the bedroom to get dressed before Quinn calls and Theo comes in behind me.

"I want to say hi to Quinn when she calls, then I'll give you some privacy. There's yard work I need to do, and I'll check in with your brother."

I nod in agreement as he walks over to me, boxing me in against the dresser and kissing me. I moan into his mouth just as my computer alerts me of an incoming Facetime call.

"We'll revisit this later," I say as I scurry into the kitchen to answer.

When I accept the call and the video pops up, Quinn appears, holding a cup of coffee. Theo, now dressed in shorts that hug his muscular thighs just right and a worn t-shirt, isn't far behind me. He leans into the frame so he can be on screen, too.

"Can't wait to meet you in person, Quinn. I've heard so many good things about you."

"Me too! I've heard *some* good things about you." Her eyes twinkle with mischief. "And some not so great things, but you do appear to be redeeming yourself."

He laughs in response. "I deserve that."

"Thanks for keeping me updated with how our girl has been doing. I'm not used to going this long without talking to her."

"Of course. Your quick thinking that night, Quinn... It got the cops there so much quicker. And probably saved Derek from killing the guy, not that it would have been much of a loss." Theo's voice is a mixture of emotions—relief on the edges, gratitude seeping through the middle, and anger bubbling at the surface.

"She's our girl, Theo. I'm just so glad we were already on the phone when it happened." Theo gives her a stoic nod and says goodbye, gives my ass a squeeze, and then heads out the back door.

Quinn squeals with delight. "Lyla! You guys are endgame. I knew it! And you're glowing. You totally had sex! Don't even try to deny it!" She clasps her hands in front of her face, her eyes lit up in excitement.

"A lot of cards were put on the table, and I think we're finally moving forward."

"Do you feel like you picked up right where you left off?"

she asks.

I think about it for a second. "No. Where we left off was broken. This... QB, this is something completely different."

"Different, how?" she asks.

"More vulnerability this time around. Realizing how incomplete we both have been without the other. Realizing that loss can happen at any moment, and you need to grab onto the things you love when you can."

"This makes me so happy. You've kept yourself closed off for so long. Even when you went on dates or hung out with guys, I could tell you were never really interested in getting involved in something deep with any of them. I knew it was because of Theo. You were afraid to move on because you were still in love with him. That, or because you were so hurt by him you never wanted to put yourself through that heartbreak again."

"Probably a combo of both."

"Yeah. I know you were scared to open yourself back up, but I'm so proud of you for putting yourself out there with him. But if he hurts you again, I'll kick his ass."

"All five-feet-nothing of you?" I ask with a laugh. Quinn is tiny but tough as hell. "You'd have to fight Derek for the honor. I think we'll be okay this time, though. That's not me being naive. It's just that all the cards are on the table now. I have faith in our future."

She smiles in response. "Your bruises are looking so much better. I can barely see most of them."

"Thanks. Theo took the stitches out earlier and I feel so much better. But enough about me. What's new with you? How are your students? And just how often do you and Colin text?" I take a sip of coffee while I wait for her response.

"Don't get your panties in a twist. We don't talk that often. That boy is trouble with a capital T, Lyla."

"Don't I know it, but he's got the biggest heart," I reply.

"I lifted his number from your phone ages ago. I wanted to know your favorite cake for your birthday, and his name was the first one I could find in your contact's list.I did it when you were in the bathroom."

"Ahhh. Stealthy," I laugh. "I much appreciate the effort because that carrot cake you got me was top notch. Anyway, how's Justin?"

She hesitates before answering. "He's fine, I guess."

"QB, what's going on?"

"He's just gotten so intense lately, so critical and possessive. I feel like I can't do anything right, and it's just wearing on me." I have so many questions I want to ask, but I don't want to push. I've found that the less I ask, the more she'll say. She's always been somewhat private about her relationship with him, and I've always had to bite my tongue because I've never liked him. "I love him, I do. But it's just...exhausting."

"What can I do to help?" I ask.

"Nothing. This is my problem."

"Yes, but your problems are my problems. That's the way it works with best friends."

She gives me a small smile. "I appreciate that, but this is something I need to figure out on my own. Maybe I'll put my foot down a little more with him. Or think about throwing in the towel and walking away."

I try not to get excited at the idea of her breaking up with him. Instead, I offer my support again. "I know you're used to handling all of your shit on your own, but I'm here for you. Anytime, anything."

"Thanks, boo. I love you for it. Thanks for not dying the other night," she says with a laugh, trying to lighten the mood again.

"I miss you. Maybe you can come out for a weekend here.

Clear your head a bit. This island is really good at helping with that."

"And be stuck in that house with you and lover boy? God, no. That man is so wrapped around your finger and so scared about your safety, I'd be surprised if he lets you pee by yourself. Plus, it's an older house, which means the walls are probably thin. I don't need to hear that kind of stuff." I laugh in response. "Once the dust settles, maybe we can do a girl's weekend."

"Yes! Absolutely! As soon as we confirm that no psycho pieces of shit are trying to whack me, we're having a girl's weekend here. It would be perfect." The school bell rings out in the background of her video. "I'll talk to you soon! Love you, QB."

"Love you, too," she says before ending the call.

*theo*

BY THE TIME we get home from running errands, Lyla looks worn out. I tell her to relax while I put away groceries. By the time I'm done, she's asleep on the couch so I head outside. I can't stop the nagging feeling that I'm missing something obvious.

While I work on digging up the tree stump in the backyard, I turn the night of Lyla's attack over in my mind again and again, replaying every detail and looking at it from different angles.

It weighs heavily on me that we have no clue what's coming down the pipeline when it comes to Marcus Hollman. I'm on edge in a way I haven't been in years, and the only time I'm not thinking about it is when I'm buried inside Lyla.

I know that everyone in the department has been working their asses off trying to find out if he'll come after Lyla again. I've even reached out to a few guys I know in Boston to see if they have any confidential informants who might be able to help us. Thus far, I've come up empty-handed, and I know it's adding to my anxiety.

I remember being uneasy as I pulled away from Lyla's

house, but I can't pinpoint why. I didn't see anything suspicious on the street. No unknown cars. No random people on the sidewalk. The alarm was on, and I knew Derek was on his way.

Maybe I'm thinking too much into it but something is giving me pause. I wipe the sweat from my brow and take my phone out of my pocket to text Colin.

**Me: No one at the station knows where we are besides you and your dad, right?**

**Colin: Correct, dipshit. That's what we agreed on. No one outside of the family and Quinn know where you guys are.**

**Me: Just checking.**

**Colin: What's up?**

**Me: I've been replaying the night of the attack in my head, looking for anything out of the ordinary. There's something that popped into my head, but I'm not ready to say it out loud yet. Let me stew over it a little longer.**

It takes about three seconds for Colin to call me.

"Fuck texting. Where's your head at, Theo? I don't care how off the wall it is, tell me what you're thinking."

I take a deep breath. "You got to Dusty Bird before me and had enough time to order beers and wings. I didn't even sit down before we were rushing out. How was Clayton acting?"

"Clayton? Really? I mean, I didn't notice anything off with him but..."

"Hear me out. I got there and the minute he saw me, he was buried in his phone. I didn't think anything of it at the time, but that's not like him. He's never on his phone. He doesn't even have social media."

"This could be completely coincidental, though. Maybe he was texting a chick?"

"Right. But then I got to thinking of that night at the bar. The first night McDavid accosted Lyla."

Colin's quiet for a moment before he says, "He was on his phone a lot that night, too. Even Drew made a comment about it. Joked that he must have been swiping right on Tinder or something. *Fuck.* But if he's tied to this, why would he help her get away from the guy that night?"

"Because we were twenty feet away from her. If she had screamed, the entire bar would have been on him. What if he didn't step in to help her, but to help McDavid? And then the night of the attack, he was giving McDavid the all-clear because we were at the bar with him."

My voice gets louder, more urgent in excitement, as these pieces start clicking together. My pulse quickens as I speak, feeling more confident in my train of thought as I go.

I walk through the front door as we continue our conversation. Because the house is so open, I can see that Lyla is awake, sitting up on the couch with Diego in her lap.

"I don't know, Theo. This feels like it could be a big reach. We know Clayton." He says it hesitantly, as if he's afraid to accuse someone who's been our friend and a fellow officer for quite some time.

"But do we really? Think about it, Colin. How much do you really know about him?" I ask. "You're right. It could be nothing. It could be me just reaching for straws because I feel so out of control here. Or it could be something. It could be everything. We need to dig into Clayton." I say it sternly, as if there's no convincing me otherwise. And there's not.

"I'm heading to my parents' house now. I'll loop my dad in, but this needs to stay between us for now. We dig quietly so he doesn't know we're doing it."

"Agreed. Maybe your dad can talk to the feds on the Hollman case. I know they went back to Boston, but maybe they'd be open to doing some investigating, especially since we're suggesting another tie to Hollman."

"That's not a bad idea." He's quiet for a minute. "If Clayton is somehow linked to Hollman—"

"I'll kill him my fucking self," I snarl.

Lyla's head snaps up, and she looks at me, her eyes wide with panic.

"I'll call you later," Colin says before hanging up. I clench my jaw in frustration before running a hand through my hair.

"You think Clayton is involved?" Lyla blurts out, as if taken aback by the idea.

"I think it's a possibility. We're missing something, a possible connection. My gut is telling me that he has some sort of involvement." I join her on the couch, lifting her feet onto my lap. "I just hope your dad takes me seriously." I shake my head a few times. "Let's eat dinner and you can tell me what you've been writing about in that notebook."

"I was going to suggest taking dinner to the beach for the sunset, but clouds rolled in," she says as she looks out the window.

We end up at the counter, our dinner in front of us. I pull her stool closer to me so that our bodies are touching. "You come up with any good ideas in that notebook of yours?" I ask.

"I did! I just started brainstorming, making lists of ideas for different plots and characters. Next thing I knew, I had a decent framework for a series and a couple of character webs going. I don't even know where it all came from. I just know that I'm really excited about writing again for the first time in a long time."

She talks quickly, a wide grin on her face, her hands moving as quickly as her words spill out of her. There's an energy to her voice that I haven't heard in a long time.

I lean forward and kiss her, my tongue running along her

lips in question. When she responds, I slip my tongue in her mouth and moan at how eagerly she kisses me back. She drops her fork and turns toward me, wrapping her arms around my neck.

"I love hearing that happiness and fire in your voice, Sunshine," I say when I finally pull away. "Let's eat and take a soak in that tub. Give you some ideas for that book."

We're just finishing dinner when my phone vibrates against the table. I reach for it, swiping to accept the call before putting it up to my ear.

"Hey, I'm here with my dad, and you're on speaker," Colin says.

"Theo, I trust your gut, but I need you to run through this with me. You boys hang out with him socially, don't you? Wouldn't that give you some insight into his personal life?" Chief Sullivan asks.

"The reality is that I don't know him that well. I don't think I've ever been inside his house. I have no idea what he does when he's not working or getting beers with us at the pub. He doesn't talk about himself much, but he's mentioned his mom on more than one occasion. Colin, you've known him longer than me." I let out a frustrated breath.

"Nothing pinged on a background check, obviously, and his record as an officer is spotless," Chief says.

"We've got to be missing something," I answer. "I don't know. This is a guy with no digital footprint as far as we know, but the last two times we were out, he was on his phone constantly. And both of those nights involved Lyla. It's not sitting well with me."

Colin speaks next. "Maybe we're too close to this, and it's affecting our objectivity." He's not wrong, but I'm a man who has always—and I mean *always*—trusted my gut instinct.

"Please let's just look into him more. See if he has any old ties from when he lived in Boston. If for no other reason than to shut me up."

Chief Sullivan answers. "You've always been the level-headed one, Theo. I know you wouldn't be making a big deal out of this unless you really had a bad feeling. I'll call the fed who was just here. See if they can do some digging."

I breathe a sigh of relief. "What are you telling people when they ask where I am? Guys at work know that I have a house here." It's been on my mind since I talked to Colin earlier. I know we aren't telling anyone where Lyla is, but it's an easy assumption."

"I've just said you're taking some time off to help her recover at home. Didn't specify whose home, but I'll casually mention in conversation tomorrow that you have a renter in the Nantucket cottage so they won't think you're there," Chief says. "How's Lyla doing?"

"Better every day. You want to talk to her?" I pass the phone over to her and listen as she updates her dad on how she's recovering and what we've been doing before hanging up the phone.

"He said he'll call you tomorrow after breakfast. Do you feel better knowing that my dad is going to look into this?" she asks.

I nod. "Yeah, I do. Like I said, even if it's just to shut me up. There's just something about it, Lyla. I was apprehensive when I left your house that night and couldn't put my finger on why. I walked into that bar and Clayton immediately buried his head in his phone. He heard me tell Colin that you were locked in tight waiting for Derek," I explain.

"Right, but if he was on the phone when you walked in, he wouldn't know that Derek wasn't there yet," she says, thinking out loud.

"True, but if someone was casing the house and saw me

leave,, they would think you're alone, possibly for the rest of the night."

"You really think Clayton could be involved, though? I don't know him well, but obviously he's never been in trouble, or he wouldn't have gotten the job at the department a few years ago," Lyla says, methodically stuffing gummy bears into her mouth. I didn't even realize she had a pack in her hands and I'm certain she doesn't even realize she's eating them.

"A lot can change in a couple of years, Sunshine. Maybe he just got involved recently. Maybe it's something from his past that we know nothing about. He's just not a guy who's attached to his phone like a normal twenty something year old. All I know is that Scotty McDavid had his hands on you twice, and both times Clayton was around and on his phone in a way he never usually is."

She's silent for a minute. "My dad will go ballistic if Clayton is dirty in any way."

"Lyla, if this guy has his hands in any of this, there will be a line of people waiting to kick his ass. He'll be lucky if he makes it out alive."

## *theo*

MY DICK IS HARD JUST THINKING about soaking in the tub with Lyla. She makes use of the bathroom while I make sure the house is locked up and the alarm is on.

"Grab drinks while I get the tub going," I tell her. I light candles, put music on, and dump in a hearty dose of bubble bath while the water line gets higher and higher.

When she comes back in, she has a whiskey for me and a club soda for herself. She sets the drinks on the vanity and pushes her shorts down, her eyes never leaving mine. My dick immediately hardens. Her hands go to the hem of her shirt just as my phone rings. I tear my eyes away from Lyla and see that it's Derek. I mull over whether or not to answer.

"Let me make sure he's good. Be careful getting in the tub. I'll join you in a second," I say as I accept the call.

"I'm going to have to bleach my ears now, asshole," Derek spits at me, and I cringe.

"Sorry, bro. I thought I was quiet enough that you wouldn't hear. Everything okay?"

"Yeah. I just wanted to remind you that I never liked Clayton."

"Okay, well let me remind you that you don't like anyone."

"Not true. Just because I spent the last six years not liking you doesn't mean I hate everyone. I'm just a good judge of character."

"Ouch. And here I thought we were mending fences."

"Oh, don't be such a pussy. Just because I didn't like you doesn't mean you weren't still a part of our family." This statement takes me aback, but I don't say anything as he goes back to ranting. "There's always been something about Clayton that I didn't trust. And I don't like that we don't know anyone who knows him. He's a total wildcard who isn't forthcoming about shit."

He's not wrong.

"I'm sorry, Derek... I'm not used to you being on my side about anything, so I'm not sure I know how to handle this."

"Don't get used to it. If Clayton is tied to this at all, I'll fucking kill him."

"You'll have to take a number."

"What else can we do? Should I follow him around or something? See if he does anything suspicious?" Derek asks.

"Relax, Detective Stabler. While I love your enthusiasm, just sit tight and let's see what your dad can get from the feds. Colin will keep an eye on him at work and will do the usual nights out so as not to raise suspicion. Let's just keep everything status quo for now," I say.

"Fine. Bye," Derek grumbles.

* * *

Lyla is about to get into the tub when I walk back into the bathroom. I whistle at the sight of her naked body. "Fuck, baby. Let me get a look at you before I help you in." I take my shirt off and drop it on the floor as I walk over to her, eyeing her up like she's my next meal. "Pretty sure I have a bet to win tonight," I say into her ear, referring to yesterday when I told her I could get her off just from playing with her tits. She shivers in anticipation.

I can't keep my hands off of her, so I grab her by the globes of her perfect ass and pull her to me, her naked body pressed against me. I squeeze her ass and nip at her ear before I kiss my way down her neck.

Her hands go to the waistband of my shorts, and she pushes them down. When they get to my ankles, I kick them aside before helping her into the tub. She scoots to one end so I can get in behind her, and once I'm in, she settles herself between my legs.

"God, I love this tub. I could stay in here all night," she says as she leans back against my chest.

"Don't threaten me with a good time, Sunshine," I say as I reach for my whiskey, taking a sip before putting the glass back down.

My arms gently encircle her body as I kiss my way down her neck to her shoulder. When my hands reach her tits, I moan into her shoulder before sucking on her skin. I'm sure to leave a mark, but I don't care. The idea of making her mine only turns me on even more.

"I've dreamt about having my hands on these tits for years, Lyla. Fucked my hands to thoughts of them hundreds of times," I murmur.

I'm already hard as a fucking rock, and once I start playing with her nipples, my dick turns into a lead pipe. When I start to twist and gently tug at them, Lyla reaches an arm back and wraps it around my neck.

I suck on her shoulder again before saying, "Jesus, baby. This is going to be even easier than I thought. The way you're squirming like you already can't take it. I bet that pussy is so wet right now."

"Why don't you find out?" she asks, her breath ragged.

"Uh uh," I say as I kiss the back of her neck. "That's cheating. Your pussy, as delectable as I know it is, will get plenty of attention during the victory lap I'll be taking after I win this bet. For now, it's off-limits."

"Fuck the limits," she says, and I smile against her skin. Slowly, as if trying to torture her, I pinch and pull at her nipples with more pressure. Her response is instantaneous— her breath catches and she arches her back.

"So fucking sexy. I want my mouth on you, Lyla. Turn around and sit on my lap." I help her readjust, and her hand grazes my dick as she settles on my lap. "There'll be plenty of time for that, baby. Make sure you tell me to stop if anything hurts or if I'm too rough," I say.

"You don't need to be gentle with me, Theo." I give her a look of disbelief, thinking of everything she's been through in the past week. "I promise I'll speak up if I'm not okay, but I trust you. You know how far to push it."

I lean over and take another sip of my whiskey, keeping an ice cube in my mouth and then lean back. Her tits are the perfect level for me to bury my face in them as Riley Green's "Worst Way" plays on the speakers. "This is fucking heaven, baby."

My lips wrapped tightly around her nipple. The ice in my mouth only adds to the stimulation. She must be enjoying herself because she tries to move her hand to her pussy.

"No touching," I say gruffly as I snatch her hand and put it around my neck before returning my hand to her hip. She arches her body into me as I suck harder on her nipple before letting it go with a pop and switching to the other one.

She tries to grind her hips into me, but I hold her steady,

leaning away from her to say, "That's cheating, Sunshine. I can't say I got you off just from playing with these glorious tits if you're rubbing your pussy all over me."

"Well, we're in a very precarious position then, Theo," she says as she grabs the chain around my neck and pulls me back to her tits. I circle my tongue around her nipple while I twist the other one between my fingers.

I can tell she's getting close because her breathing turns heavy. I'm so fucking turned on, having her wet body on mine, her breasts in my hands. It takes everything in me not to come on myself.

"Oh god. Yes, babe. Yesssssss," she murmurs as I flick my tongue and twist the other one the way I know she likes, with just a bite of pain. This sends her over the edge, and she moans in pleasure as her orgasm hits her.

I don't stop playing as she groans, making sure to give both tits equal attention. "The sounds you make when you come are like a fucking drug. So fucking sexy."

It's only now that I let her rub her pussy on me. "You feel how hard you make me? My dick is aching for you." I kiss her feverishly as she rocks her hips over my length.

Her clit must still be sensitive from her orgasm because she moans loudly, her head tipping back. "Oh god, Theo." She claims my mouth, biting down on my lip before her tongue meets mine.

"I can still feel how wet you are, baby. And not just from the water. You want this cock, don't you?"

"Yes," she breathes between kisses, our mouths urgent and feverish as they come together in desperate intensity.

She lifts her hips and slowly sinks down onto my cock an inch at a time. "Take it all, baby," I grunt. She drops all the way down, both of us groaning in sheer pleasure. "Christ, Sunshine, you feel so good. This pussy is fucking perfect. So warm. So tight."

There's no need for more words. We let our bodies move together, our breath hot and heavy. I have one arm wrapped around her waist, the other holding the back of her head as I devour her mouth.

My body is engulfed in pleasure as she moves her hips, her hot pussy choking my dick in the most euphoric way I've ever imagined.

I move my other hand down to her hip, trying to slow her pace down. I'm close to coming, and I don't want this to be over yet. She grinds against me, working her hips in slow, deliberate circles.

I grip her ass possessively then let my hand forward until my fingers find her clit. I want to get her off again before it's too late.

I slowly rub my fingers over that sweet bundle of nerves, still sensitive and swollen. She tilts her head back as she reaches for bliss one more time.

She moans my name as I pick up speed, working her clit until she tumbles into another orgasm. I suck on her shoulder, and she rides my cock even harder as she comes, screaming my name. I grunt as I come inside of her, her pussy milking every last drop of me.

We both take a second to catch our breath and look each other in the eyes. The air around us crackles with electricity. I pull her face back to mine and kiss her with so much ferocity I surprise even myself. "God, you're spectacular. I can't get enough of you, Lyla," I say as I ravish her mouth. "I can't wait to do that again."

She laughs softly.

We take a quick shower to rinse off and fall into bed.

Because my dick is like a moth to the flame that is her pussy, we make love one more time before she falls asleep in my arms.

* * *

It's the middle of the night when Lyla wakes up with a jump and a gasp. Since it soothed her the night before, I immediately start rubbing her back, not saying anything while she works to slow her breathing.

Once she's calmed down enough to sit back against the headboard, I get out of bed and grab her water. Diego quickly curls himself up in her lap, looking around for danger while he purrs loudly. She absentmindedly starts petting him. I climb back into bed with her drink and let her take a sip before asking her if she's okay.

"I'm sorry, Theo," she says quietly.

"Lyla, don't ever apologize for something like this again," I say. "Same nightmare as last night?" She nods to say yes. "You think it might be worth talking to someone? A therapist or someone? Just to work through what happened to you?" I ask as she lies back down and snuggles up next to me, flinging her arm across my chest. I hold her close to my side and kiss her head.

"It's probably a good idea. I'll reach out to my therapist tomorrow. See if I can set something up virtually. It's not like I don't have the time."

"I wish I could do more, Lyla."

"You just being here calms me down, Theo. And holding me as I fall back asleep... It reminds me that I'm safe."

"I'd burn down the world to keep you safe, Sunshine. Try and go back to sleep." It doesn't take long until her eyes flutter shut and her breathing evens out. Once I'm sure she's out, I let myself follow behind.

\* \* \*

I wake up the next morning to Diego's telltale sign of being hungry—sitting on my chest and his stare burning into me. "Alright, alright, come on," I whisper to him, carefully getting out of bed. I grab my phone off the night table and close the door behind him as he scurries between my feet and darts for the kitchen.

My phone rings just as I'm putting his bowl down.

"Morning, sir," I say to Lyla's dad.

"Good morning. I just spoke with one of the feds. He thinks you're being an alarmist but said he'd ask one of his analysts to dig into Clayton, off the books."

"Oh, thank god." I breathe a huge sigh of relief.

"There's just one caveat. That analyst is out of office the rest of the week, but he assures me he'll have him look into it once he returns."

"Damn. Well, beggars can't be choosers, I guess. Thank you, Chief, for not blowing me off about this or telling me I'm barking up the wrong tree."

"When it comes to my daughter, I'll bark up any tree. Besides, I trust your gut more than I trust most people, kid."

I smile to myself, flattered at the compliment. Because I trust my gut over most people, too. It's saved my ass more than once. We say our goodbyes and hang up.

While I hate the idea of having to wait until next week to get any information, I'm grateful we have someone who will look deeper into Clayton than we can. No one else knows we're on Nantucket, so I'm confident in Lyla's safety.

I'd cut down anyone who came after her, anyway.

## TWENTY-NINE

*Lyla*

THE DOOR CREAKING OPEN STIRRED me from sleep. The aroma of roasted coffee and cinnamon pushes into the room and wraps around me. When I finally open my eyes, I'm graced by the image of Theo in his gray sweats.

He's shirtless, barefooted, and gives me a lazy smile as he walks closer. I sit up as he says, "Morning, Sunshine." He passes me a mug and slowly settles in next to me.

"Coffee in bed. Always making me dinner. You're spoiling me, Theo Morgan," I say as I take a sip.

"Any day I get to spoil you is my favorite day," he says with a wink. "Besides, rainy days were made for lazy mornings."

I'm one of those weird people who loves the rain and could listen to it all day long. Don't get me wrong; I live for the feel of sunshine on my skin, but I can vibe with stormy weather, too.

Especially when I'm holed up in an adorable cottage, on an island that is arguably my favorite place on the planet, with a man I love more deeply than I ever thought possible.

I vaguely hear Theo say something about a conversation with my dad, but I'm consumed by the thought I just had. I love him. I don't think I ever stopped, even when I hated him. Because I didn't hate *him*, I hated the fact that he left me. I love him so fucking much, I feel it in my bones. It's not even a choice, it's like breathing. Completely natural and organic.

Spending time with him has reminded me of what my life has been missing for the past six years. I've been on autopilot, going about my day to day business but not really living. Not really happy.

The first couple of years I kept my nose to the ground, working on my research to sniff out Marcus Hollman. I thought nailing his ass to the wall would give me the satisfaction and closure I needed, and I'd be able to move on. Wrong.

Since then I've just been searching for something that would have me excited to wake up in the morning and tackle the day. When I first opened up to Quinn about everything that happened, she said it sounded like I had destination addiction —the mindset that you'll find happiness once you reach a certain goal. Whether it's a personal achievement or a material purchase, it's the idea that once you get it, you'll finally be happy.

At first I thought she was joking, but some research taught me that it was an actual thing, and she really hit the nail on the head. I kept running farther away from home, trying to find something to make me happy.

It didn't matter what successes I had. I always felt unfulfilled. Empty. I mourned Liv, but I never moved on from Theo. I never fell out of love with him. While I knew I would be successful on my own, being with him, having him as my partner, makes me feel complete again. It's in every beat of my heart, a heart that he owns every piece of. The world makes sense again now that he's back in my life. I could never go back to a life without him.

"Earth to Lyla..." I hear Theo say, cutting through the fog in my mind. I look over at him, his eyes searching mine. "Where'd you just go?"

"I love you, Theo," I blurt out. "I am so hopelessly and deeply in love with you. I've spent so many years being angry at you and being afraid to ever be vulnerable again. To risk my heart again. But I want to move forward with you. No more running unless we're running together. I love you. I never stopped. It's always been you, Theo. Every part of me belongs to you, and I wouldn't have it any other way. You make me feel alive. I am so fucking in love with you, babe." I'm so full of emotion that by the time I'm done unloading on him, I'm out of breath.

Theo looks at me, his eyes a crystal blue, and I swear they're misty. "You have always been mine, Lyla. I'm the luckiest fucking man on the planet that I get to be yours again."

He grabs my coffee cup and puts it on the bedside table with his before climbing on top of me, always mindful of holding himself up so that his weight doesn't fall on me. "You're my whole world, baby. You own me, heart and soul, every piece of me. It's been yours since the day I met you. You're woven into my bones, my blood. I've never wanted anything the way I want you, and I'll never get tired of proving myself to you. I love you so much." His mouth crashes into mine, as if claiming me as his. And I am, in every sense of the word.

He makes love to me slowly, savoring every kiss, lick and moan. I feel every inch of him inside of me as his hands roam my body. He's in no rush, as if we have all the time in the world. His eyes never leave mine as the rain and thunder play in the background.

\* \* \*

Later that day, when we're snuggled on the couch eating ice cream straight from the pint containers, I ask Theo about his time in the Army.

"You don't have to talk about it if you don't want to. I don't know if it opens old wounds for you or not, but it's a part of your life that I know nothing about," I say, explaining my curiosity.

My knowledge of those four years of his life is minimal. Thanks to his emails, I knew when he was deployed and when he got home. I also know that my family would have told me if he was seriously injured or worse. But that's all I was privy to.

I'm sure he would have elaborated more in his emails if I ever responded, but I was still so bitter and broken that I never did. His necklace rests near the collar of his shirt, and I grab the compass charm, absentmindedly rubbing the engraving on the back while I rest my head on his shoulder. I still can't believe he's worn it all these years. I can't imagine the things this necklace has seen.

"Tell me about the scars you have," I say softly, thinking about the angry marks I saw on his back and chest.

"War is ugly, Lyla. Things happen so quickly. For most of them, I didn't even notice the injuries until well after the fact. I'm not even sure I could say when I got each one. Some are from shrapnel. Some are from knives. There's one that came from a bullet graze."

"Was it scary?" I ask.

He bites his own lip as if trying to decide how to answer. "Yeah. Scary as fuck. A lot of the time, I didn't realize how volatile the situation was until we were out of it. Me and other soldiers would be talking after the fact and, all of a sudden, it would dawn on me that everything could have gone real bad, real quick.'"

"Do you still talk to any of the guys you served with?" I ask.

He's never mentioned any Army buddies, nor have I heard Colin mention hanging out with any of them.

"Yeah, a few. We're spread out around the country, so it's not easy getting together, but we keep in touch through text. Losing guys..." He exhales before he continues. "Losing guys was the hardest part. Fucking awful. I don't regret my time in the Army, but seeing guys killed in action, that's the only thing I wish I could forget."

"I'm sorry. For all of the losses. For all of the scary moments. For never responding to your emails."

"I already told you I never expected you to respond. Those messages I sent, they were more for me than you. Something to keep me attached to home and to remind me to never let my guard down because I had someone to come home to."

"Eventually, I started to write you back," I say softly, unable to look him in the eyes.

"What?" he asks incredulously. "I never got anything from you. How did you send them?"

"I never did," I say it so quietly I can barely hear my own voice. "I wrote them, printed them out, and deleted the drafts in an effort to forget about it. Writing to you was cathartic. If I'm being honest with myself, it probably helped me more than I ever realized, but you were fighting in a war. The last thing you needed was to be distracted by my nasty emails. So while I would have loved to rip you a new one from half a world away, sending you those angry words would have been selfish as hell."

"So you never did." He's quiet for a minute and I can't help the silent cheers that drip down my cheeks.

I take a deep breath and softly say, "I still have them."

"Will you share them with me now?" He has so much hope in his eyes I could never say no.

"They're at my parents' house, but when we get back

home, yes. But be warned, they don't start off very kind. I was a grade A bitch in those early ones."

"We can't change the past, Sunshine. We'll always have those missing years, but that doesn't mean we can't know exactly who the other person was during that time in our lives. Either way, we're moving forward, and that's all that matters," he says.

We sit in comfortable silence for a few minutes, each of us absorbing what the other said. My head rests on his shoulder. He plays with a strand of my hair as our ice cream sits neglected, melting in the containers.

\* \* \*

The weather clears around dinner time, and we decide to have a couple of drinks out on the patio. Theo heads outside to get a fire going.

Since I've been headache free for a few days, I decided I'm going to indulge in a couple of cocktails and set about making spicy margaritas in the kitchen.

It's not dark out yet, but the fire is definitely coming in clutch while we relax outside. Diego joins us and is romping around the yard while we snuggle on the couch, sipping our drinks. "Do you worry he'll wander off?" I ask Theo as we watch the cat chase after a fly.

"Nah. He's lived on the streets. He knows a good thing when he has it. He'd miss his next meal too much, and he's a stage-five clinger."

I hum in response. "So, do you have any intel on how long Colin and Quinn have been secretly chatting?" I ask. "Damn, this is a good drink."

"They are? That's news to me."

"Well, I might be slightly exaggerating. She called him

during the attack, and when I brought up her having his number, she said it was because she swiped it from my phone to find out my favorite kind of cake forever ago."

"That seems plausible," he replies.

"Totally. But now I'm just curious about if they've been talking here and there or anything. She kind of played it off like it was nothing but did make a joke that he was trouble with a capital T."

"Didn't take her long to figure that out," Theo says with a laugh. "Full disclosure—the only thing he mentioned to me was that she was smoking hot, which he only disclosed when I was peppering him with questions trying to get dirt on you."

I drape my legs across his lap, and he rubs my feet. "Ohhhh, tell me more," I say, smiling at him over my cocktail glass.

"Not much to tell. I was desperate for any information I could get on you, but rest assured, Colin never divulged much to me. Just reminded me that I fucked up and wished me luck trying to fix it. She's got a boyfriend, right?"

"Ugh. Yes. And I hate him," I say defiantly.

"Harsh, Sunshine. What's your beef with him?" he asks.

"At the risk of sounding like Derek, I've never liked him. He works at the high school with her. He acts like he's some kind of prize. Like she's the one who should be thanking her lucky stars to be with him. If I had a dollar for every time he mentioned his dad was the mayor, I could take the next few years off entirely. Like, relax dude, you're a high school lacrosse coach who can't even get past the first round of state playoffs. Take a seat." He looks at me like I've lost my mind. "In all seriousness, he's possessive as hell, controlling, and dulls her sparkle. I don't trust him as far as I can throw him."

"What do you mean?" he asks.

"I've seen a bruise here and there, but she always has an

excuse. I can't say for sure they were from him, but it wouldn't surprise me. He minimizes her accomplishments and would *always* have some sort of crisis anytime we tried to have a girl's night. It's like he didn't trust her with me or something."

"You really think he hurts her" Theo asks, his voice hard.

"I think it's a strong possibility. I've never flat out asked her if he does, but I always make sure to ask where they came from," I say. "I wish she would break up with him. As much as a disaster Colin is with women, I'd much prefer Quinn dating him rather than that shithead."

"Colin told me he believes in soulmates," Theo blurts out.

"*What?* Colin said that? My brother?" Theo nods. "But he has a different woman in his bed every week, or at least every month."

"I swear it. Don't tell him I told you that, though, or he'll lose his shit." Theo laughs because we both know I'm going to bust Colin's balls about this the minute I talk to him.

When I finally finish my drink, I ask if he wants another round. He smiles and nods, so I stand up, take his glass, and head inside.

I'm at the counter slicing some jalapeños when Theo walks in holding Diego. His eyes are smoldering and full of passion. He says nothing as he puts the cat down and comes up behind me, caging me in while I work on our drinks. I lean back into him while I work and ask, "You hungry?"

"I'm starving, baby," he says roughly as he kisses my neck before licking his way down my neck.

"Okay, what should we have? I guess the more accurate question would be, what do you feel like making?"

He shakes his head behind me, brings his hands up to my tits and murmurs, "Uh-uh. I'm *famished* and can't wait another minute."

When I feel his hard length digging into my back, I finally

understand what he means. He turns me in his arms, and when our eyes meet, I note the seriousness in them. He looks like he's starving. For me. Like I'm his prey, and he's going to slowly devour me and enjoy every second of it.

The energy between us sizzles, and without another word, he pulls my T-shirt over my head, tossing it to the side. He hooks his thumbs into my shorts and slowly lowers them, his hands going to my ass.

He growls with desire when he feels that I'm not wearing any panties. I have never in my life felt as wanted as I do at this moment. He looks downright feral for me.

He grips below my ass and lifts me up, using one of his big hands to wrap my leg around his waist. He moves down the counter a little to where it's clear and sets me down, keeping my legs wrapped around him. He tugs on my hair, forcing me to look at him and claims my mouth. I wrap my arms around his neck and pull him as close as I can.

Our tongues and bodies intertwine. The only noise is our heavy breathing. He pulls back, leaving me breathless, and his hands go to my chest. He fondles my tits, squeezing them and playing with my nipples in a way that has me arching my body toward him for more.

His hands gently push me down so that I'm lying on the countertop, the stone cold against my heated skin.

He's still fully dressed when he drops down to his knees in front of me, his mouth perfectly lined up with my pussy, but he doesn't just dive right in. In a gruff voice, he says, "Spread those legs, baby. Let me get a look at what's mine."

I do as he asks, and he moans in appreciation. He uses one hand to massage my inner thigh, working his way closer to my pussy, only to stop right before he reaches it. He shifts to the other thigh, teasing me in the exact same way. I hiss in frustration as he draws out the anticipation.

By the time he does that to the other leg, I'm ready to explode. He uses both hands to spread my legs farther apart, kissing and licking all around what would be my bikini line before he finally gives me what I'm aching for.

It's all I can do to stop myself from screaming his name when he runs his tongue from my pussy to my clit. His gaze holds mine the entire time.

He pulls his mouth away and says, "Fuck, this pussy is perfect, baby. And it's mine. Forever." His lips glisten with my arousal as he runs one finger around the edge of my pussy. My body writhes in response, completely consumed by his touch.

"Yesssss," I moan. "All yours. More. Please." I'm desperate now.

"Ahhh, my girl is greedy tonight. I think I need another drink before I demolish that pussy with my mouth, baby."

I prop myself up on my elbows to get a better look at him, seeing the heat and desire in his features. There's also mischief flashing in those crystal blue eyes as he stands back up and grabs the bottle of reposado off the counter.

He takes a sip right out of the bottle and passes it to me so I can do the same. When I give the bottle back to him, he gives me a smug smirk and then slowly pours some onto my chest. Because I'm sitting up a little, it spills down over my nipple..

I groan as his tongue swirls around it, licking up the tequila as he plays with me. He gives each breast ample attention and I feel I could explode at any moment. I'm so wet I'm surprised I don't slide off the damn counter.

"I don't remember tequila ever tasting this good." He motions for me to open my mouth so he can pour some of the liquor in. I swallow and wipe my mouth with the back of my hand. My skin is hot and tight, my body so tightly wound it's like a coil ready to spring.

He lowers himself back down to his knees, one hand

keeping my leg spread wide while the other holds the tequila. He's staring at my pussy like it's the eighth wonder of the world and pours a heavy serving of tequila all over it.

I gasp as the cool liquid hits such a sensitive part of my body. Before I know it, his mouth is on my pussy, lapping up the alcohol, and holy shit, I see stars. When he said he was going to demolish my pussy, he wasn't joking.

He's fucking feral for it, and he brings me to the edge in record time, pulling back right before I orgasm. I can't decide if I want to scream in pleasure or frustration, probably a combination of both. "I was wrong. This is definitely the best tequila I've ever tasted. Sorry to tease you, baby, but I'm not done eating yet."

And with that, he pours another serving of booze all over me, starting at my stomach this time and working his way back down to my pussy. He puts the bottle down, and the hand that was holding it reaches up to play with one of my breasts. His tongue moves side to side over my clit, and after every few swipes, he applies just a tiny amount of pressure. The kind that makes my head spin.

He moves the hand that was holding my thigh down to my opening and inserts two fingers, holding them still as he runs his tongue over me. He presses a soft line of kisses up and down my pussy a few more times before he goes back to that bundle of nerves.

I reach my hand down and comb it through his hair, holding his face to me. I'll die if he stops now, and he must feel that, because after a few more licks, I'm falling over the edge and claiming the most intense orgasm I've had since, well, this morning.

I scream his name as I ride out my orgasm, never wanting it to stop. My breath is deep and uneven as I come down from the high. Theo sits back on his heels and looks up at me.

"Damn, baby, the way you sound when you come undone is just about enough to make me explode. I'm going to fuck you so good, your pussy will be wet tomorrow just thinking about it." He kisses his way down my thigh before standing back up and taking another swig of tequila.

He pushes his sweatpants down and enters me with one thrust, all the way to the hilt. I gasp at how quickly and completely he fills me.

This is not the slow, leisurely kind of love-making we did last night. This is hard, untethered fucking, something only he's ever been able to give me, and I love every second of it.

It doesn't take him long to bring me to climax again as he pounds away, his hands holding my legs open. He pulls his cock out of me and finishes on my chest, using his hand to draw out streams of come.

"Give me that," I say when he's done, pointing to the bottle. He laughs as he passes it to me. Before I'm able to put it back down, he's kissing me. I can taste myself on his lips. When I pull back to take a breath, I look around and laugh. "We made a hell of a mess out here. Thank goodness I didn't have the El Tesoro on the counter. Would have been a hit to the wallet."

"Worth it, Sunshine," he says. He picks me up off the counter and, with my legs wrapped around his waist again, walks us both toward the bathroom.

We enter the shower and waste no time soaping each other up, rinsing off, and then falling into bed.

With Theo's body wrapped around me, holding me close to his, and Diego curled up by our feet, I eventually fall asleep, hoping another nightmare doesn't wake me up.

## THIRTY

*theo*

I FEEL helpless when Lyla wakes up again in the middle of the night. I've got a routine down now that it's the third night it's happened. I rub her back until the trembling stops and her breathing slows down, get her water, and then hold her while she falls back asleep.

Once I'm sure she's out, I let myself drift off, too. But tonight when she wakes up, she looks exhausted. There are dark circles under her eyes, and she yawns before she even gets out of bed.

"Stay in bed, baby. You could use a few more hours." To my surprise, she actually listens.

I'm on the couch reading when she wakes up a few hours later. Her eyes are bright and there's more energy in her movements as she fixes herself a cup of coffee. She heads for the patio and by the time I follow her outside, she's lounging with her notebook in her lap, Diego curled up next to her.

"Damn, he got comfy quick. Come on, Sunshine. Let's blow this popsicle stand for a little bit." She gives me a big smile. "Don't get too excited. I don't want us gallivanting around town and talking to people. We still need to lie low, but I figured we could take a ride up to 'Sconset and do the Bluff Walk."

Diego follows us to the door, and Lyla leans down to scratch his ears. "I know we owe you a beach trip, buddy. I promise we're not going there now."

The drive from Madaket to 'Sconset doesn't take us too long. We park and make our way to the hidden walking path that is a true gem on the island. It takes you along the coast, and while it seems strange to be walking this close, and sometimes through people's backyards, it's a public path that gives you insane views of the ocean and cliffs. Plus, you get to drool at some truly gorgeous houses along the way.

Lyla is a few steps ahead of me and stops to admire the view of the beach and ocean down below. The sky is finally blue, and the sun is out for the first time in days, but the ocean is still rough, with angry waves crashing into the beach.

She looks back at me, her hair blowing wildly in the wind and smiles. She looks so at peace being outside like this. Her cheeks have a healthy flush to them and there's no tension in her limbs. I pull out my phone to take a few pictures of her before walking closer to get a selfie of us together, ocean in the background.

"I'm assuming that the guy who attacked me is still tight-lipped? And the fed who is going to look into Clayton is still out of the office?"

"Correct and correct."

"It's killing you, isn't it? Being so far out of the loop?" she asks.

"Wild horses couldn't keep me away from you, Lyla. I feel infinitely better having you with me here. I wouldn't be allowed to talk to McDavid even if I was there. But this wait and see holding pattern we're in has me on edge." That's an understatement. I feel like I'm walking on a damn tightrope with no net beneath me. And it's windy as fuck.

We make it to the turn-around point, Sankaty Head Lighthouse, and sit down to soak in the sunshine before heading back. I pull her onto my lap and nestle her against me. These quiet moments with her are among my favorite. Feeling her heartbeat against my chest, the smell of her perfume that she wears daily, even when we're just at the cottage, the feel of her fingertips as she absentmindedly scratches the back of my neck. It all gives me a sense of peace that I haven't felt in years.

Eventually, we make our way to my truck and head home. Diego is waiting at the door for us, giving our legs a quick sniff to make sure we did not, in fact, lie to him and go to the beach.

I suggest we take advantage of the decent weather and eat on the patio, but when my phone rings and Lyla sees that it's Colin on the phone, she says, "I'm going to hop in the shower to clean off while you talk to him. Maybe he has an update or something."

I wait for her to head toward the bathroom before I answer, grabbing a bottle of red to open with dinner. "Anything new?" I ask Colin when I answer.

"Well, hello, Theo. I miss you, too," Colin says.

"Yeah, yeah. I know you're lost without me."

"But since you asked, there is an interesting development. We finally got the detailed phone records back for McDavid. He definitely had contact with someone shortly before both the incident at the Dusty Bird and the attack at the house."

There's a but coming. I can feel it. "The number he contacted was a burner?" I ask.

"Bingo. Took the wind right out of my sails when I saw that, but I guess we shouldn't be surprised."

"Clayton was on his phone shortly before both attacks," I remind him.

"Yeah, I know. But that could have been a coincidence. We really need something else to connect him to this."

I'm about to say something about him not having faith in my gut instinct, but I know that's just my frustration manifesting.

"I trust your gut, Theo. I really do. I just wish we had more to connect this guy to Clayton while we wait around for the feds to look into him."

"Nothing on McDavid's bank statements? And no secret accounts?" I ask.

"The feds couldn't find anything suspicious."

"Is that analyst who's going to be digging into Clayton going to dive into his financials, too? Because it needs to be more thorough than the background check he got when he was hired."

"Yeah, I think this is why we're waiting for this specific analyst. The agent said he owes him a favor, and since we don't have anything concrete to give them on Clayton, this is the agent cashing in his favor." Colin blows out a frustrated sigh. "Just hang in there, Theo. Hopefully, on Monday we can rule him in or out."

"See if they can look into his mom's accounts, too. She's the only family he has, and while he doesn't say much about her, I've always gotten the impression they were close. I don't know why I didn't think of that sooner. Shitheads like Marcus Hollman love to use people's weaknesses for their own benefit, and if Hollman has something on Clayton's mom, that would explain a lot," I say.

"This is starting to feel like a stretch," Colin says.

"I won't apologize for caring more about Lyla's safety than offending someone we work with."

"You're right. Shit, I didn't mean to make it seem like I care more about offending Clayton than figuring out if he's involved. I just... I guess I'm having a hard time with the idea that he could be a scumbag."

"Just talk to your dad. See if he can get them to look into the mom's finances, too. And if I'm wrong, you can say I told you so."

"That's a fucking deal. Is Lyla making you watch that stupid reality show she and Derek love?" he asks.

"Hah. Nope. I wouldn't dare step on Derek's toes when it comes to *Love is Blind*. It would negate all the progress we've made." We shoot the breeze for a few more minutes. Aside from my time in the military, we're not used to this much time apart, so Colin has plenty to say.

I'm about to hang up with him when Lyla walks out in pajamas, her hair wet from her shower. She motions that she wants to talk to him so II pass the phone over to her. I open a bottle of pinot noir and bring the wine and our sandwiches outside.

As promised, I fill her in on everything Colin and I talked about over dinner.

"I need you to elaborate more on what you think Clayton's connection is to all of this. I just can't imagine he could have pulled one over on all of you and been in bed with Hollman this entire time."

"I don't have anything other than the phone usage and my gut feeling. I know it sounds crazy."

"Why do you think they should look into his mom?" she asks.

"It's me grabbing at straws. If Clayton is clean, and there's nothing funny in his finances, maybe Hollman has something on someone he cares about. That's what those kinds of men do. They use the people you love against you."

"Kind of feels like something out of a crime show. Well, hopefully we'll get some answers." She makes it seem so simple, as if it's not a big deal that this man we all worked with could have anything to do with her being hurt.

By now, the sun is down, and there's a chill in the air. I tell her to head inside and pour some more wine. By the time I'm out of the shower, Lyla has our wine glasses refilled. She lit a few candles and is looking like the epitome of relaxed wrapped in a blanket with Diego laying in her lap.

I flop down next to her and take a sip of my drink. "What was your favorite thing about living in Vermont?" I ask her. She raises her eyebrows as if she's surprised by the question. "I guess I just want to know more about that chapter of your life."

"Hmm, the snow. We don't get enough of it here. Meeting Quinn. And there was this adorable little bookstore in walking distance from my house. It reminded me so much of One More Chapter. I spent an unhealthy amount of time there."

"You always did love a bookstore."

"This sounds cliché, but the fall foliage was stunning. I missed the beach. The smell of the ocean, and the sounds of the water, but those few weeks when the leaves turned... It was all the colors of the sun but on trees."

"Maybe we can go back there soon. Visit Quinn. You can take me to the bookstore. Show me what your life was like there."

She looks up at me and smiles. "I'd like that." I lean down to kiss her. "Oh! I have an idea! Let's make a bucket list of all the places we want to travel to."

She beams with excitement. It's so contagious I jump up to grab a notepad. For the next hour, we pass it back and forth, adding destinations to the list, debating others, justifying our reasons and crossing off ones we can't both get on board with.

"Jade Mountain just sounds bougie, Sunshine. Sell me on it."

"Babe, you have to google it. It's the most incredible

looking resort I've ever seen. The rooms are called sanctuaries, and they're all missing a wall, which sounds crazy, but it's because that open space gives you the most majestic view of the Pitons. Plus, the rooms have their own infinity pools. It's like heaven on earth." She talks with her hands and speaks a mile a minute.

"Sold," I say, and that elicits a laugh.

"Just trust me. You have to look it up."

Eventually, we make our way to the bedroom, falling into each other's arms and making love before falling asleep.

* * *

When I open my eyes, she's already awake. "No nightmares? Wait, are you spooning my cat?" I ask when I see her wrapped around his little body.

"Yeah, I guess I am," she says with a laugh. "No nightmare. This is going to sound bananas, Theo, but I swear this cat woke me up intentionally to keep me from having one."

"No shit?" I ask in disbelief.

"I woke up to this not-so-little furball all up in my personal space, purring so loud that I can't believe you didn't wake up, too. He gave me a nose boop and then snuggled me until I fell back to sleep. Maybe it was a random fluke, but it's like he knew to wake me up before I had the nightmare."

"Might be. Sounds like he's an evil genius. Guess we'll know for sure if he does it again tonight." I lean down to kiss her before I drag my ass into the bathroom. When I come back, I grab my phone. It's dead so I plug it in before crawling back into bed and pulling Lyla close to me.

The peace of the morning breaks when I turn my phone back on and it rings. I reach over to answer it. "What?" I grunt.

"Took you long enough. I've been calling you for like

twenty minutes. Your phone was off, and Lyla's just kept ringing. My dad is over here having a coronary thinking something
happened out there," Colin says.

"Sorry. It died and I just plugged it in. Lyla's must still be in
the kitchen." I look at the clock on the nightstand and see it's
after eight. "What's up?"

The cat leaves the room, no doubt expecting one of us to
follow and feed him breakfast. Lyla moves to pull the
comforter higher over her naked body. I yank it back down and
wag my finger at her, letting my eyes roam her perfect body.
She lies back down with a smile and a questioning look about
who's on the phone.

"Hollman is dead," Colin says.

I think my heart stops. I'm frozen in place, and I'm sure my
jaw is on the ground. I don't even know how much time
passes, but I vaguely hear Colin calling my name over the
phone. Lyla sits up more, and this time, I don't stop her from
pulling the blanket up over her body. "Theo, are you there?
Hello?"

"Are you sure?" I finally stammer out.

Even though he's been in jail awaiting his trial, he's still
been running his operation. Jail clearly didn't stop him from
trying to kill Lyla.

"Yup. My dad just got off the phone with the feds. He was
killed overnight. Someone shanked him in his cell." Again, I'm
at a loss for words. I'm filled with so much relief, I can barely
keep myself composed.

Lyla is on her knees now, her hands on my shoulders,
eyebrows raised while she gives me a look of curiosity.

"Holy shit," is all I can come up with.

"I know. It's over, dude. You guys can come home
anytime now," Colin says. "My dad is waiting for a callback
from the feds with more details, so I'll call you back when I

know more. We knew you guys would want to know right away."

"Thanks. I'm going to share the news with Lyla. Call me back when we know more." We say goodbye, and I toss the phone onto the bed.

"What is it, Theo?" Lyla asks, panic in her voice.

I pull her face to mine, one hand on either side, and say, "Hollman is dead."

"Wha... What? Dead? Like, no longer breathing?" she asks in disbelief.

"Yeah. Killed overnight in jail. It's over, baby," I kiss her and hug her tightly to me.

"It's really over," she says quietly, as if she doesn't truly believe the news. I nod and whisper in her ear that it is.

When she pulls back, she's crying, and I gently use my thumbs to wipe her tears away, kissing a few that escape down her cheeks. She sits back on her heels, holding the comforter to her chest as if she's still in complete disbelief. I give her a minute to absorb the news and lean back on the headboard.

"You okay, Sunshine?" I ask.

She sits close to me with her head on my shoulder, nodding. She's quiet for another minute before she finally talks.

"I'm not sorry he's dead. Does that make me a bad person?" she asks small.

"Fuck no, Lyla. And I can't stress that enough. Aside from the fact that the man tried to have you killed, he's a despicable human being who's responsible for the deaths of who knows how many people. The world is better off without him."

She nods.

"I'm just so relieved, Theo. I can finally breathe again and stop looking over my shoulder constantly. It's been months of unease and anxiety. It's like I've got a new lease on life," she says. It kills me that she's been so nervous and on edge for so long, especially since she was dealing with it on her own for the majority of that time. "So, we can go home now?" She sounds almost sad when she asks.

"Yeah, it sounds like we're in the clear."

"I'm a little sad knowing we're leaving this bubble we created out here," she says.

"So, we stay. We can stay until you're ready to go home, Sunshine."

"Don't you have to get back to work, though?"

"Work is the last thing on my mind. I have plenty of vacation time banked, so if you want to stay a few more days or a week or two, I can make it work. Whatever you want."

While I'm relieved beyond belief that the threat is gone, I'm not looking forward to going back to the real world, either. I'd happily stay on Nantucket as long as she wants. "Besides, we need some time out here to go into town and hit up all our favorite places now that we don't have to stay so hidden."

Lyla perks up immediately. "Okay, then. Let's stay a couple more days and then head home. Let's hit up Cisco Brewery today and relish in the fact that I no longer have a target on my back."

"Let's not get ahead of ourselves. I won't rest easy until we know for sure what, if any, role Clayton had in this." She waves me off like I'm being ridiculous. "Cisco it is."

## THIRTY-ONE

*Lyla*

WE CAPITALIZE on the sunny weather and ride bikes over to Cisco Brewers early in the afternoon. It's a brewery, winery and vodka distillery all on one property, and in the middle of the buildings that house separate bars for each offering, there are food trucks, picnic tables, and a stage for live music.

Now that the summer crowds are gone, the cornhole and horseshoes are back out for people to play with while they enjoy delicious beers, creative cocktails, and great food all while listening to music.

Basically, it's one of the most fun places on the island, and I'm so pumped to spend the day there.

As we bike, Theo says, "You've had that legal pad in your hands a lot the last few days."

"When I sit down and start drafting or plotting, I don't want to stop. I have to pull myself away from it to give my eyes a break. I haven't felt this excited about writing, or really anything work related, in a long time. I just feel really inspired and fired up, and I never want to miss jotting something down if it pops up in my head."

"That's awesome, Sunshine. I love seeing it again. I remember in high school if you didn't have a book in your hand, you had one of your leather journals."

I snap my head over to look at him. "You remember that?"

"I remember everything, Lyla. How many times do I have to tell you that? I love that you would randomly have a thought and immediately whip out that journal and write in it. It was as if your hand couldn't keep up with your mind."

"It feels like that again. I'm feeling inspired. And invigorated."

"Despite all the unknown stuff we're dealing with, you seem happy anytime you have that notepad in your hand."

"There are quite a few things that are making me happy these days, Theo." I give him a smile.

When we get to Cisco, we work our way down the vodka cocktail list, trying all of the ones that seem appealing to us. After so many months of anxiety and tension, it's nice to let my hair down and just *be*.

I don't miss the fact that Theo isn't quite as carefree as me. He's affectionate and playful, but I can see the worry lines in the corners of his eyes. Being out in such a public place has his protectiveness in overdrive, even with Hollman dead.

Some people might find it overbearing, but I actually love the fact that he gives any man who looks at me a dirty look. It makes me feel like I'm cocooned in safety. He's never not touching me in some way, which is partially due to his affectionate nature, but also a way of staking his claim.

We wait for our turn to play cornhole, sharing a small pizza while we sit next to each other at a picnic table. I lean over and kiss him before jumping up when our names are called. He slaps me in the ass in return.

We're playing against a couple of twenty-something dudes, and I can already tell Theo is not happy about it. After shaking hands, one of the guys wrings his out, as if Theo squeezed it a little too hard.

"Sorry about that. He's a bit overprotective," I say to our opponent with a laugh.

"Well, you're pretty hot so I get it. But I promise I'll be on my best behavior," he replies. He stays true to his word, and Theo only growls at him once or twice before we win the game.

We crush the next few matches until we're finally knocked off by a couple of senior citizens, which has us laughing our asses off. Those little ladies are spitfires, and they wipe the floor with us. Theo goes over to buy them another round of drinks while I chat with them before their next match.

"You've got yourself a good one, young lady," one of them says to me as he gives her a drink.

"Don't I know it," I say and smile at him. He gives me a wink and grabs my hand. We say goodbye to them and head over to one of the food trucks to get oysters. We grab one more cocktail and move closer to where the band plays.

I have enough of a buzz going that after we finish eating, I stand and attempt to pull Theo up to join me on the dance floor. He tries to resist, but I'm nothing if not persistent. "Come on, babe. You said it yourself that you can never tell me no."

He sighs and lets me pull him up, and I hold his hand and lead him to join the small crowd that's dancing. It's not a slow song, but he takes me in his arms like it is, his one hand dangerously close to my ass.

"This is the best you're getting from me, Sunshine," he says into my ear as we sway back and forth. He spins me around before pulling me back into his arms, and we dance for the rest of the song. I'm shocked when Theo doesn't try and escape the dance floor when the song is done.

He stays out there with me until the band finishes their set. They end with a slow song, which gives Theo an excuse to hold me close to him. He sings the words to "Kokomo" in my ear as the band plays. I laugh softly because I can't believe he knows the words.

"It's a classic, baby. Everyone knows the lyrics."

It gets close to last call, so I switch to water when Theo heads back up to the bar. "You going to be okay to bike home or should I call an uber?" Theo asks. The brewery shuttle isn't running so it's either walk or take our bikes back.

"I'll be fine to bike home. The path is wide enough for me to manage," I joke. He doesn't laugh, but instead gives me a worried expression. "I'm serious, Theo. I'm fine." *I think.* Thankfully, the road is pretty empty, and the ride home is uneventful.

We make our way back inside, and once the front door is shut and locked, Theo pushes me up against it, his hips pinning mine to the door. I drop my purse to the floor and wrap my arms around him.

"I've been wanting to get my hands on you all afternoon," he growls out as he kisses me, his tongue in my mouth before I can respond. I hook one leg up around his waist and feel his hard length against me. I moan in response.

"I've wanted to feel you inside of me for hours, Theo. You could have taken me in the bathroom. I had enough to drink where I would have been down for that," I say as his kisses move to my neck and down my collarbone.

"If there was a single stall option I would have done just that, baby." His hands move under my shirt and lace bralette, and the roughness of his hands on my nipples puts me in a tizzy. "Tell me, Lyla. Now that we're home... What do you want?"

"You, Theo. I want you," I say. He slides one hand down into my pants and hisses when he finds how wet I am.

"Oh, baby, I can feel how badly you want me. You're

soaking these panties. But I need you to be more specific." He moves his hands back to my waist, gripping me tighter as he kisses me breathless. "Tell me what you want, Lyla." He goes back to kissing my neck before continuing. "I've watched you come back into your own this week. Watched the fire return in those pretty eyes. The confidence. The fucking sass. You're taking your life back. Taking control again."

I'm not going to lie. I love that Theo is an alpha male, both in the bedroom and out. He's possessive in a way that isn't stifling. I love that he takes the lead when it comes to sex.

The man truly knows my body better than me, even after all the years apart. The idea of being in control is equal parts empowering and nerve-wracking for me, and he must sense my apprehension.

He grabs my chin and forces me to look him in the eyes. "Take control here, Lyla." I chew on my bottom lip before I reply.

"Get naked. I want your cock in my mouth first. Then I want you to bury it in my pussy while I ride you." My voice is low and husky. I almost don't recognize it.

Theo's eyes are dark with lust, and he licks his lips as he lets go of me to walk over to the couch. I lean back against the door and watch as he takes his clothes off, his eyes never leaving mine.

He starts with his shirt, reaching behind him to pull it over his head and then tossing it onto the floor. "God, you're hot." When he gives me a charming smirk, I realize I've said it out loud. I roll my eyes at him. At myself.

But really, he *is* fucking hot. He has a sculpted jawline and days-old scruff on his face. His arms are muscular, his shoulders broad, and his abs are defined. He has a body built by physical activity and hard work. That V that leads below his waist is covered in a smattering of dark hair that I want to trace with my tongue.

His tattoos only add to his appeal. He moves with confidence as he unzips his shorts and shoves them down, leaving him standing there in his boxer briefs, his massive dick barely contained.

When he finally pushes his boxers down and grabs his cock in his big bear paw hand, I'm pretty sure I lick my lips. He gives it a few tugs while he looks at me, waiting for me to tell him what to do next. His eyes are that dark midnight blue, but smoldering like they're on fire.

"I'm desperate for you to fuck my mouth, Theo."

"Then get on your knees, baby. You're running things tonight." His voice is deep and gravely, and I can't wait to make this man moan.

Still in my clothes, I drop down to my knees. I kiss his inner thigh, working my way closer to his enormous cock. I lick my lips and look up at him before taking the tip of it in my mouth. His eyes roll to the back of his head, and his moan is loud and guttural. I swear I could get high just from the sounds this man makes.

I swirl my tongue around the head of his cock while I slowly work my hand up and down his shaft. I spit on his dick, working it up and down him before removing my hand from the equation and taking him deep in my mouth.

"Fuck, I love when you do that. When you make it as wet as I know that pussy is."

I alternate my pace to keep him guessing, taking him all the way into my mouth so that I can feel him hit the back of my throat. He grunts as he begins to move his hips back and forth, giving me what I want and fucking my mouth. He brings one hand to the back of my head and gently grips my hair, holding me in place while he moves.

I use one hand to cup his balls and give them a gentle squeeze before I start massaging them. "Fuck, Lyla. Yesssss. Goddamn, what a time to be alive."

I love being on my knees for this man. Hearing him moan in ecstasy. Feeling him lose control. His thighs tighten, and his hands hold my head in place as he fucks my mouth. It's fucking exhilarating having this much control over his pleasure, to know it's my mouth that's bringing him to the precipice.

I stop sucking and pull back for a breath before I lick up and down his shaft, slowly, languidly, as if we have all the time in the world. All the while, I keep one hand on his balls, the other gripping his firm ass.

"Goddamn, pretty girl. You suck my cock so well. This mouth of yours is fucking magical."

I smile as I take him back in my mouth again, sucking harder as his cock somehow feels even harder. My eyes water from the size of him, but I don't stop. Even when he tells me he wants to come inside of my pussy and not my mouth, I don't relent. Instead, I pick up the pace.

"Lyla, I know I said you're in charge tonight, but I don't want to come in your mouth. Please," he says with a raspy voice. With a final swirl of my tongue around the head of his cock, I let him go and stand up.

I nod my chin toward the couch and he sits down, his legs spread wide, his length still rock solid and glistening from my saliva and his precum. I walk over so that I'm standing in front of him, positioned between his legs.

I pull off my sweater and let it drop to the floor, followed by my shirt. I unbutton my shorts and slowly lower the zipper, pushing them down and kicking them out from under me.

I stand there in my matching bra and thong, a sheer red that makes me feel sexy as hell. He hasn't touched me yet, but already, my body hums with anticipation.

I'm already so close that it doesn't take me long to straddle him. His hands immediately go to my ass, gripping my cheeks and squeezing. His dick is long and hard, and I can't stop myself from grinding on him a few times, making my clit throb with need.

Heat pools in me as he pulls me closer to him, burying his face in my tits, just like I wanted. He moves one hand away from my ass and fists my hair, softly pulling so that I'm forced to look up. "God, Theo, I want you so badly."

"Your pussy is dripping for me, baby. I can feel it on my cock already," he says before he starts kissing my breasts, moving from one to the other, giving my nipples the attention he knows I crave.

He licks, sucks, and gently bites each through the thin mesh of my bra. All the while, I grind into him, knowing if I don't stop, there's no doubt I'll come all over him before he's even inside of me.

His hand hovers near the clasp on my bra, and with a breathy voice, I tell him to take it off. "I was hoping you'd say that, baby." He unclasps it and pulls back just enough to take it off me, tossing it to the side before his mouth goes back to my tits.

After a few minutes of him playing, I grab his face and bring my mouth to his, kissing him deeply. Both of his hands are back on my ass, squeezing hard and hovering between that delicious line of pleasure and pain.

I may start the kiss, but Theo takes over and ravages my mouth, his tongue in complete control of mine. He can't help himself, and I let him.

I know what else I want from him, something I know he's been holding off on doing since I was attacked—probably because he's afraid I'm not ready. I'd usually be too shy to ask for it, but he makes me feel like such a goddess with the way he worships me.

I pull away from the kiss and move my lips to his ear. "Spank me, Theo. The way you always used to." He leans his head back so he can look at me, asking me if I'm sure with his eyes. "Please. I've never let anyone else touch me that way."

His eyes somehow get darker with desire, telling me he knows exactly what I want from him. He all but growls as he grabs me by the back of my neck and pulls me to him, his other hand winding around my body and delivering a stinging smack to my ass that makes my pussy even wetter.

"Oh god, yes," I moan, and he smacks again. I arch into him and shudder from the pleasure.

"Fuck, I've missed doing that," he grunts. He moves his hand to my pussy and groans when he feels me. "I see you've missed it, too."

I murmur in agreement as he kisses down my throat to the spot where my collarbone meets my neck.

He stops there and sucks lightly before saying, "You're goddamn right no other man has touched you the way I do. This pussy is the only one I've ever had. It's mine. This ass is mine. It always has been, even when we were apart." I nod my head to confirm what he's saying. "That's a good girl," he says as he uses his hand to rip my thong off my body.

"Hey! You just ruined this set!" I say.

"I'll replace them, baby," he says as he brings the now broken thong up to his face, groaning in pleasure when he smells it.

His cock is so hard, and I am more than ready for him to be inside of me, so I prop myself up on my knees and reach my hand down to guide him into me, slowly lowering myself back down over him a little at a time.

"Yes, baby. I want you to feel every inch of me."

And I do. Every delicious inch, vein, and pulse of his dick.

"You feel so fucking good, Theo," I manage to get out. He slaps my ass again, and I arch into him. I start to slowly rock my body, feeling every inch of him as I move.

He reaches his hand down and circles my clit with his finger a few times before pulling it back and wrapping it around my body to my ass.

With his finger slick from my wetness, he slowly circles it around the hole that no other man has ever been allowed to touch. He slowly works the tip of his finger into my ass, and I have to stop moving for a second to let my body adjust.

"You like that, baby?" he asks as he grabs my face with his other hand and brings my mouth to his. I moan out something that sounds like a yes as I start to slowly rock my hips over him again. He keeps his finger still, allowing me to do the work as I move my hips back and forth.

Between his huge cock and his finger in my ass, my body is so full I feel like I could explode. "That's a good girl. Letting me fill you everywhere," he says, his breath heavy. "I thought you looked good with my dick in your mouth, but this, me filling you everywhere while those tits bounce in my face... You're a fucking work of art, baby."

The hand that holds my face moves down to my ass cheek, and he squeezes hard while burying his face in my tits. When I'm riding him like this, my clit hits just right and in a way that only adds to the intensity of what we're doing.

Every nerve in my body is alive and raw, desperate heat consuming me. As much as I want to come, I don't want this to end, so I slow down.

I switch to moving my hips in a figure-eight pattern, and we both groan in ecstasy at the sensation. I know I'm not going to last much longer and can feel Theo's dick get harder, a sure sign that he's close to losing it. I know he's dying to grab my hip and move me faster on top of him, but he won't do it when he wants me to be in control.

Theo is the consummate gentleman, but my god, he can fuck like a savage. Watching him struggle to maintain self-control only turns me on. His jaw is clenched, and the vein in his neck is more pronounced as he wrestles with his desire, thrusting his hips up and hitting me deeper.

My vision gets fuzzy, and I'm hit with a rush of euphoria as my orgasm hits. Within seconds, I feel the warmth of Theo's cum as he releases inside of me.

He slows the pace of my hips and stretches out his orgasm. It's pure fucking ecstasy, and we stay like that for awhile, both of us trying to catch our breath.

"Holy shit, Lyla," Theo finally says as I come back to planet earth. He grabs my face with both hands and kisses me. "That was fucking unreal." I wrap my arms around his neck and let my tongue explore his mouth. I know we're both a mess from the sweat at come, but I don't want to move.

I break the kiss so I can look him in the eyes and say, "I love you." He smiles and tells me to say it again. "I love you, Theo."

"Promise me you'll never stop. Promise me you'll say it everyday. I need to hear it, Lyla," he whispers. The sound of his voice, and the pleading look in his eyes, remind me that I'm not the only one with a heart on the line.

"I promise. On my life, Theo."

"That's my line, baby." He hugs me tightly and uses his strong legs and abs to stand up with me still straddling him. He walks us down the hallway and into the bathroom, only putting me down when he starts the water.

*theo*

"THIS CAT HAS SEEN some things the past week. I'm almost embarrassed to look him in the eye," Lyla says to me as she sits at the counter, drinking a cup of coffee, her pen to paper. Diego is sitting on the stool next to her, and she has music playing softly on her phone.

"Hah. Ain't that the truth."

"We still need to book ferry tickets for tomorrow," she says, a tinge of sadness in her voice.

"I own this house, Sunshine. We can come back anytime you want."

"I know, I know. Let me look up the times." I pour myself another cup of coffee while she opens her laptop. We decide on an early afternoon ferry, and she buys the tickets. "What's the plan for our last day?"

"I'm thinking we hit the beach since it's probably the last decent beach day we'll get this year, and then I have dinner reservations for somewhere special tonight." She looks at me with raised eyebrows. "You'll see, but it's in town, so if you want to head in early we can walk around before we eat."

"Sounds perfect."

I walk around the island so that I'm behind her, putting my hands on the counter and effectively locking her in place. I nuzzle her neck and ask, "What are you working on?"

She leans back into me. "Some developmental stuff for my main female and male characters."

I kiss her neck and say, "I'll pack some towels and snacks."

"We owe this guy a trip to the beach," she reminds me, using her thumb to point to Diego.

"Indeed, we do. Let's do 40th Pole again. The water will be calm." I kiss her cheek and stand up straight.

My mind wanders to what we'll need for a few hours at the beach. I've been on edge since I woke up this morning, unable to stop myself from thinking about what the analyst might find on Clayton. What it might mean for Lyla's safety. I look over at her, deep in thought as she writes and bites her lip. She scribbles frantically, as if the ideas might disappear if she's not quick enough.

The idea that she could still be in danger haunts me. The thought of losing her damn near brings me to my knees, especially after living without her for so long. But the idea of running, like I did last time, doesn't take hold of me. I'll never run from her, from us, again. If it was up to me, we'd never spend another night apart.

I'm relieved as hell that Marcus Hollman is dead, but my gut is telling me this isn't over yet. It feels too easy, and nothing is ever this simple when it comes to shitbags like him. I'm about to send Colin a text when I see Lyla stand up and stretch.

"I'm going to get my bathing suit on, then I'm ready to rock when you are," she says as she walks to the bedroom. I make a mental note to text Colin when we get to the beach instead.

We're out the door, Diego included, twenty minutes later. I have no idea what bathing suit Lyla is tempting me with today.

I only hope it's warm enough at the beach that she'll take her coverup off.

It's a quick ride to 40th Pole, and when we drive onto the sand we see it relatively empty.

Once we park, I set up the chairs, and Lyla plops the cat down on the blanket.

"Just leave his leash on. It makes him easier to catch if he starts wandering," I say. I'm already sitting down when she takes off her dress. My mouth immediately starts watering.

Her bikini is navy with white stripes, and she's showing way more skin than she did the last time we went to the beach. Her perky tits are on display, barely covered by the scraps of fabric that tie behind her neck and back. Her ass, firm and round, looks like a peach I could bite into.

The bruises on her torso are mostly gone, but even their minimal presence is enough to distract me from the way she looks in that skimpy suit and clench my teeth in anger. I count down from ten to calm myself and focus on the other parts of her body, the parts that aren't black and blue.

My dick hardens just from looking at her. I tear my eyes away to see if anyone else is checking her out. The possessive caveman in me wants to tell her to put her clothing back on so no other man can get a look at the way her tits look in that top.

I bite my tongue though, because if I ever said it she'd likely go prancing down the beach drawing attention to herself just to spite me.

When she turns around to put her towel on the chair, I get a better look at her ass. "Jesus, Lyla. You're going to be the death of me," I grunt, rubbing my chin as I stare at her. She turns and gives me a slow smile.

"You don't like it?" she asks innocently.

"I more than like it. My dick is aching for you. I just don't like other men seeing you in it," I say with clenched teeth.

"I didn't wear it for anyone else; I wore it for you. And I highly doubt anyone else will notice me in it," she says matter-of-factly as she sits down and fiddles with the speaker.

I see a group of guys who look like they're in their twenties a little ways down. They've already noticed how hot my girl looks. I grumble about how wrong she is, pulling her chair closer to me.

I grab my phone to text Colin about what's been on my mind all morning.

**Me: What's going on with Hollman's crew? Anyone assert themself as the new head honcho?**

**Colin: Good morning, Theo. I'm doing great, thanks for asking.**

**Me: Jesus, I forgot how much coddling you need.**

**Me: Good morning, buddy. How the hell are ya?**

**Colin: I'm fine. Thanks for asking. To answer your other question, looks like his second in command is taking a stab at the gig. Ryan Hughes. A few years younger than Hollman was. Not a blood relative.**

**Me: I've heard that name before. Never cared about keeping his image squeaky clean like Hollman, so this should be interesting.**

**Colin: I reached out to a few guys I know in Boston. They didn't know shit about Clayton, but I'm hoping they have some dirt on this guy. I don't see why he'd be after Lyla. That was Hollman's beef, but you never know with these shitbags.**

**Me: How's Clayton been acting?**

**Colin: He seems a little more talkative lately, more relaxed, but I'm trying not to look into that too much. Keeping an eye on him. Derek and I are going to meet him and Drew tonight. See if he loosens up at all with a few drinks.**

**Me: Keep a leash on your brother.**

**Colin: Noted. When you guys coming home?**

**Me: Tomo. We'll be at Sunday dinner.**

**Colin: See you then.**

**Me: Later.**

I toss my phone onto the blanket and blow out a sigh of frustration. Diego gives me a look of disgust for having the nerve to distract him from the bird he's stalking.

"What's wrong?" Lyla asks, concern evident in her voice.

"Nothing. Everything. New guy in charge of Hollman's crew is a piece of shit."

"Were you expecting a swell, law-abiding citizen to take charge of his criminal organization?" she asks with a slight chuckle.

"I was kind of hoping it would all go away. That no one would take his place and the rest of his guys would fall off the face of the earth."

"And I hope my first book is a bestseller, and Netflix snatches up the movie rights. But then I come back to planet Earth and realize I'm being unrealistic."

I reach for her face and pull her to me, bringing her lips to mine. "Your sarcasm is noted and will be dealt with later," I tell her before I kiss her.

"I'm going to hold you to that, babe," she replies. She leans back in her chair and turns her face up toward the sun. With her arms over her head, she's the picture of relaxation. After a few minutes of quiet contentment, she turns to me. "You haven't asked if I've dated or been with anyone over the past six years."

"Nope. Don't want to know."

"It almost did me in asking you about your past. I was petrified of the answer but I had to know."

"And I respect your curiosity. I also knew my answer wouldn't be a kick in the stomach for you. Sunshine, you are stunning. And intelligent as hell. You're a catch, and I'm not naive enough to think you haven't been with anyone else. But I can't think about it. The idea of another man's hands on you, touching you, kissing you, in your bed... It makes me want to put my fist through a wall. And drywall is a bitch to repair. So, no, I don't want to know."

"Fair enough. I respect that. I just wanted to make sure you didn't want to have a conversation about it."

"I'm all about moving forward, baby." I say.

The next few hours fly by, and before I know it, we're packing up and heading home. Our dinner reservation isn't until six, but I know Lyla wants to walk around town for a little bit before we eat.

I'm in the bedroom getting dressed when I hear her shout from the bathroom. "Babe! I put something on the bed that I thought might be fun for dinner. Take a look."

I walk from the closet over to the bed and see a small box. When I pick it up and find the words *secret panty vibrator*, my cock immediately wakes up. With the box in hand, I stick my head in the bathroom where she's putting on mascara.

"You naughty, naughty girl," I say playfully.

She looks at me, a slight blush on her cheeks and shrugs her shoulders. "It's kind of self-serving, but I thought it might be a fun way to spice up dinner."

"I'm going to be hard the entire night, knowing you have this in your panties," I say as I scurry back to our bedroom to open it up. I wait for Lyla to finish getting ready, sitting on the bed with my ankles crossed, watching her hem and haw over what to wear.

She chooses a black lace bra with matching panties that have me salivating. I'd be content watching her all night, but she finally decides on a short navy dress that shows off her killer legs. Lyla walks over and stands in front of me.

She reaches for me, taking my chin in her hands. She bites her lip as she looks at me. I know that whatever she says is going to have me wishing I could have my way with her before we walk out the door.

"Will you put it in?" She gives me a slow smile. "On your knees?"

*Fuck me.* My voice is husky when I say, "Baby, I will worship you anytime, anywhere."

I sink down to my knees in front of her and slowly push her dress up over her hips. She runs her hand through my hair as I kiss her stomach and down to her panties before dipping my hand in to feel her. I moan in appreciation of how wet she already is.

I want to rip her clothes off and fuck her on the floor right now, but somehow I resist. It takes a second to get the vibrator secured in the right position, but once it is, I stand, fixing her dress before I pull her in for a kiss.

"I hope you took the time to figure out how the remote works before you put it in there, or I'm going to be in for a really interesting night," she says. I laugh in response because I absolutely did read the manual while she was finishing her makeup, and I'm very well-versed in how it works.

* * *

Downtown Nantucket is like something out of a magazine. The streets are cobblestone, and there is a huge variety of stores, from souvenir shops to high-end clothing and everything in between. We pop in and out of stores along Main Street and the side streets.

We stop in a gallery of a local island photographer and

drool over some of his amazing photos. Lyla makes conversation with the man, asking questions about what type of lens he used for certain shots.

They swap stories about favorite locations for shooting sunsets on the island. I make a mental note of the ones that Lyla really likes and think about where we can hang them back at the house. After, we get lost in Nantucket Bookworks for almost an hour before we meet at the front of the store.

Lyla holds up a couple of books—a new political thriller and an autobiography—and says, "Thought you might like these." She puts them on the counter with a few she picked out for herself.

I slap down my card before she can fish her wallet out of her bag and sneak a kiss on her cheek. "Can't wait to read them."

From there, we head to dinner. The Pearl has been a popular restaurant on the island for decades, but was recently bought by a new group of investors. They completely redid the interior and revamped the menus.

I've been anxious to try it since it reopened but have been waiting for a reason and a person, mainly the one I'm with, to share the experience with.

We're shown to our table, and once we're seated and handed menus, I reach for the tiny remote that's in my pocket, pressing the button to turn the vibrator on at its lowest setting. Lyla immediately looks up at me and gives me a mischievous grin before reaching for the drinks menu.

"I'm definitely going to need a cocktail. If I don't relax, I'm going to be dragging you in the bathroom and having my way with you," she says.

The waitress comes over to go over the specials and take our drink order. Once she walks away, I turn it up a notch. Lyla's eyes widen, but I give her an innocent smile.

I'll let her stay on that intensity for a little bit while we wait for our drinks. We talk about the menu, debating on what to order. When the waitress drops them off, we order an appetizer but ask for more time to decide on the rest. When Lyla reaches for her cocktail, I ask her to wait a second.

"Thank you for giving me, for giving us, another chance. You're my everything, Lyla. The person I love most in this world. Having you back in my life makes me feel complete. I didn't just fall for you all those years ago. I dove in headfirst, and I never looked back. Even when we weren't together, I was always yours. You own me, baby, every part of me. I promise to cherish you and keep you safe. I want you forever."

"Forever, Theo," she says as reaches across the table to squeeze my arm. "I love you so much," she whispers.

"Forever it is, Sunshine." After a quick cheers, I lean across the table to give her a kiss before sitting back in my chair. I wait until she takes another sip of her cocktail before turning up the vibrator again. She gives a little yelp before looking at me, slightly panicked, and then asks if I think anyone else can hear it. I laugh and say, "No way. There's enough hustle and bustle and conversation going on that no one hears a thing."

Our appetizer is dropped off, and when the waitress stops back at our table, we order our entrees and another round of drinks. I turn the vibrator up a little more and notice that Lyla is looking a little flushed. "You good, baby?" I ask innocently.

I stretch my legs out under the table, letting them rest on either side of hers. I'm dying to touch her, to feel the soft skin of her thighs, but I know that would be wildly inappropriate and would only give me a raging hard-on. I settle for reaching across the table and caressing her forearm. She still hasn't said a word, but there's lust in her eyes. She's biting her lip in an effort to control her emotions.

She's turned on as hell, and holy fuck, is it hot. I lean

toward her and quietly, *tauntingly*, say, "You gonna be able to come quietly, Sunshine?" Her lack of response makes me think she's not so sure. "You want to come now or after dinner?"

"Now," she whispers, her voice shaky. I reach into my pocket and grab the remote, pressing the button that switches to a different vibration pattern and turn it up again. Her lips are in a tight line and she tips her head back, her eyes closed. She squeezes her legs together tighter. "Oh my god, Theo," she says quietly as she shifts in her seat. I don't need to turn it up. She's close.

I quickly take my eyes off her to look around the restaurant, making sure nothing is amiss and no one is throwing us any suspicious glances. I'm thankful we're tucked into a corner table with my back against the wall so I can look around. It helps Lyla is facing me. It means no one else will see her expression when she comes.

"My cock is so hard right now, Lyla. Just from watching you. Let go, baby," I say to her in a quiet, gruff voice. It pushes her tense body over the edge, and she does her best to stifle a moan as her eyes roll to the back of her head. She shifts in her seat, quietly riding out her orgasm. "You're so fucking naughty, Lyla. Coming right here in the middle of dinner service." She looks me in the eyes as she takes a few deep breaths before reaching for her cocktail and draining the rest of the glass.

"I think I need another," she finally says.

"Orgasm or cocktail?" I ask with a smirk.

"Cocktail for now, but I'll take another orgasm later."

I tell her that can be arranged. She waits a few more minutes before excusing herself to the restroom. I notice a waiter checking her out as she walks away, and I give him a death stare when he glances at me. He lowers his head in apology and moves along.

She comes back to the table, and we fall into conversation

while we wait for our dinner. She asks about my earlier conversation with Colin, and I let her read the messages.

"I can't imagine this new head honcho will give a shit about little old me, Theo."

"We can't rule it out. Not yet. Not until we hear about Clayton. Your brother said he's been more talkative the past couple of days. That's suspicious to me," I say.

"You're scared." It's a statement, not a question.

"You know that I am." There's no point in denying it.

"I'm scared, too. And not just because of the nightmares and the unknown." She brings her eyes to mine, and I see a twinge of doubt in them. "I'm scared this will cause you to run again..."

"Never," I say, cutting her off.

"I think I can handle anything else that's thrown at me, Theo. But not that."

"If I have to reassure you every day, I will. I'll remind you what I said on the beach. I'm dealing with my biggest fear right now, and I'm not running. I'll do whatever it takes to keep you safe, no matter the risks. Nothing life throws at us will ever drive me away. No fear, no threats, *nothing*. I will never run again, unless it's toward you."

She nods.

"I know it's my own fault that you have these doubts."

"I don't want them, Theo. I don't want to doubt you or us because I know that you love me. But there's still a tiny part of me that can't let that fear go."

"I know. All I can do is prove it to you, and I will. If you let me, I'll prove it to you every single day for the rest of our lives. Because I'm the luckiest, Lyla. I'm the luckiest guy on earth to have somehow convinced you to give me another chance. I'll never throw that away."

Lyla reaches across the table to grab my forearm and gives

it a squeeze just as our food arrives. From start to finish, it feels like such a special meal, which is exactly what I wanted. Take her somewhere special so we could celebrate being together again.

We opt out of dessert, and instead, head over to The Juice Bar for ice cream before taking the long way back to the truck, enjoying our waffle cones as we walk hand in hand.

"I'm going to miss my little nightmare gatekeeper when we get back to Sandpiper," Lyla says as she licks her ice cream. I have to adjust my pants and will my dick to calm down. She's turning me on without even trying, without even realizing. "I finally feel well-rested again, thanks to that evil genius."

Before I can even stop myself, I blurt out, "Well, Diego and I would love to continue this cohabitation thing when we get back to the Cape."

She stops dead in her tracks, and I panic over coming on too strong. "Are you being serious?" she asks.

"Hell yes, I'm being serious, Lyla." And I am. I might have said it impulsively, but I'd be lying if I said I haven't been thinking about it every single day since the first morning we woke up together here, despite the fact that I slept on the floor. "That first morning on the island, I knew I never wanted another night alone or another morning when you weren't in bed next to me. I knew it that night at the hospital, too."

"Well, what if you get called out for a case and have to pull another all-nighter? Therefore forcing me to go to sleep and wake up without you?" She asks it with a smile, which makes me think she's really considering it.

"Well, then I'll have to be okay with knowing you're in our bed, keeping it warm while you wait for me. I promise I'll always make it up to you when I do get home," I say.

"This feels wildly insane. How about I just stay at your place for a little before we make it official?"

"It's spontaneous as hell, Sunshine, but nothing ever felt so right." She smiles in agreement. "But we can keep it unofficial until you're ready."

She bites her lip and smiles. "Okay."

"Yeah?" I ask, unable to keep the excitement out of my voice.

"Yeah." I wrap my arms around her and lift her off the ground.

"Love you, Sunshine."

"I love you, too. And thank you, Theo, for a beautiful night. And for the orgasm."

"Anytime, baby," I reply with a laugh. "Let's go home." I mean that in every sense of the word. The house on this island is *ours*. It was empty without her, just like my life. But it's not anymore, and I plan to hang onto that forever.

## THIRTY-THREE

*Lyla*

THERE ARE VERY few things better than waking up with Theo Morgan's hands all over my naked body. They're commanding and comforting, calloused and gentle, all at the same time.

It doesn't matter where on my body they are, his touch gives me a sense of peace and stillness while also managing to light me up at the same time.

It's still dark out when he kisses his way down my neck and says in a husky voice that's still full of sleep, "Want to go watch the sunrise?" When I feel his hard length against my back, I'm tempted to say no. "I'll ravish you when we get back, if that's what's making it hard to decide."

"It's like you can read my mind," I say, my eyes still closed as I wiggle my ass into his groin.

"Well, if you keep doing that we're not going to get out of this bed so make the final call, Sunshine." I move my ass again, and his grip around me tightens. One of his hands lightly traces its way down my stomach and between my legs. He groans the second he feels how wet I am. "Goddamn, baby. You woke up ready to play."

"So did you," I say as his dick pokes my back.

"I can tell this won't take long," he says in a gravelly voice as his fingers work their way between my folds. I arch into him, and the arm that's around my chest tightens, his free hand going to one of my breasts as he squeezes and kneads it.

I moan as he works a finger into my pussy, using the palm of his hand to rub my clit. "Oh my god, babe," I manage to get out as he twists my nipple between his thumb and finger.

I start to rock my body as the pleasure builds, but he pulls me closer to him, holding me snug against him and throwing a leg over me to keep me close.

"Fuck, baby, this pussy is pure heaven. So tight. So hot. I fucking love it," he says before he starts sucking on my shoulder. I fucking love when he does this—when he claims me. "Tell me who's pussy this is, Lyla," he says, licking my neck.

"Yours," I reply as he adds another finger and works them faster, curling them inside of me. I gasp over how good it feels.

"Mine. Forever," he says gruffly.

"Forever. It's always been yours," I manage to get out between moans.

"You're goddamn right, Sunshine. Forever," he says, but I can also hear the desire in his voice. He goes back to sucking on my neck. The minute I feel his mouth, my orgasm rips through me.

"Oh my god, babe," I say as I groan in pleasure, Theo milking every last drop out of me. My breath is heavy as I ride it out, and once I come back down to earth, he moves his arms so that he has them both wrapped around me, holding me closely to him. He gently kisses my shoulder before I attempt to turn around in his arms.

"Nope. Sunrise. Then we come back to bed," he says.

We get up, throw on sweats, grab the cat, and are out the door in five minutes. The beach is chilly, and I relish being cradled in his arms while we sit on our blanket, watching as the first light of the day breaks over the horizon, casting a beautiful, warm glow.

My brothers and I all find comfort in being outside. Colin has always found peace in the woods, and for Derek, it's always been the water. For me, my solace has always come from the sun. The sunrise and sunset have always given me a sense of tranquility and grounded me, no matter where I am.

Whether I'm at a high or a low point in life, the sunrise always offers the promise of a new day. The sunset always serves as a reminder that I've made it through another one, and this is the sky's way of celebrating that.

Watching the sun come up with Theo evokes a feeling of tranquility and stillness that I haven't felt in a long time, and my body melts into Theo's as that sense of calmness washes over me. As the golden and red hues spread out over the sky, Theo says into my ear, "It's like I can feel the tension in your body dissipate, Lyla."

"Between the solace the sun always gives me and the steadiness I get from you, I feel like I can let my guard down here."

"Makes me wonder what chills you out more—the sunrise or an orgasm."

"Guess you'll have to do a comparison when we get home."

"Deal," he says.

With Diego sitting next to us, we watch the sun rise completely above the water, looking like a ball of fire and reflecting on the water. The orange, red, and golden orb spreads its colors throughout the entire sky, making it look like it's on fire in the most spectacular way.

We stop for donuts on the way home and fall into bed, Theo determined to see if an orgasm relaxes me more than the stunning sunrise we just watched. Two orgasms later, we're both thoroughly sated and sweaty.

"My legs are like jello," I say, and he laughs.

"Yup, that definitely means you're more relaxed now than you were on that beach."

The morning passes all too quickly, and before I know it, we're heading back to town to catch our ferry home. My dad sends a text to let me know he and my mom will be at the dock waiting for us.

As sad as I am to leave Nantucket, and the level of comfort I felt being there, I'm excited to see my family and get back to some semblance of a routine.

I spot my parents as we disembark, and my mom runs up to me, throwing her arms around me and pulling me close. "I've missed you, sweetie," she says.

"I missed you guys! I'm glad it's all over and we can finally move on." Theo mumbles something about not being sure about that. "Guys, Hollman is dead."

My dad pulls me into his arms to hug me and says, "We'll talk about this in the car, kiddo. You look great."

"I feel really good. No headaches for a few days now."

My mom hugs Theo. "Thanks for keeping her safe, honey. And for loving her the way you do. I told you honesty was the key," she says with a wink.

"In case you were wondering where Colin got his love of saying 'I told you so,' look no further than my mom," I say with a laugh.

Once we're in my parents SUV, my dad asks, "Am I dropping you off at your place, Theo, or are you coming back to the house?"

"Back to the house, Dad." I answer for him before jumping back into the topic of Marcus Hollman. "I get that you guys want to make sure Clayton isn't involved in anything, but with Hollman dead, I think we can all relax and go back to business as usual, no?"

"I'd appreciate a few more days of vigilance, just until we hear back from that analyst," my dad says.

"Why is it that you guys couldn't do this digging on your own at Sandpiper PD?" I ask.

"Because we don't have any evidence of probable cause to get a subpoena to pull his financials or phone records," Theo says.

"And the feds do?"

"No. But they have better analysts. Come on, Sunshine. You've watched enough *Criminal Minds* to know that Penelope Garcia can sniff out nefarious information from behind her computer screen," Theo says.

"The analyst who is doing us this favor is doing it unofficially. The feds in charge of the Hollman case trust him to do the digging quietly since it's off the books."

"Ahh, I get it now. That's why we're waiting on this guy. Got it," I say, finally piecing it together. "A few more days of vigilance, Dad." He looks at me through the rearview mirror and smiles at me.

When we pull up to the house, I see both of my brothers' trucks in the driveway. I jump out of the car as soon as it's in park, rushing into the house to greet them. Colin gets to me first and scoops me into his arms for a hug.

"So glad to see you, Ly," he says.

I turn to Derek and he holds me at arms length, as if checking for injuries. Once he's satisfied that I'm in one piece he throws an arm around my shoulder and gives me a squeeze. "We're so far behind on *Love is Blind*. It's about time you guys came home."

I smile at him and say "I've missed you too, Derek. Are you good?"

"Yeah, just really glad you're okay."

I look over to see Colin embracing Theo as if he's been gone for months.

"Aww, it's okay, buddy. I'm here now," Theo says as he pats his back.

"Not a moment too soon, either. Work is boring as fuck without you. No offense, Dad," Colin says.

Derek walks over to Theo and, to my surprise, pulls him in for a man hug.

"I knew I'd win you over eventually," Theo says.

"Asshole," Derek mutters.

"You kids hungry?" my dad asks, already taking out his pancake supplies. I bend down to let Diego out of his carrier, and he goes around begging for attention before retreating to a quiet spot for a nap.

The kitchen bustles with noise and movement as my parents make breakfast. The boys and I sit around the table and catch up, with Theo pulling my chair as close to his as possible and letting his arm rest behind me. He's never not touching me in some capacity. As if he's gone so long without it, he can't bear to miss out on the contact now.

As my dad sets down a big platter of food, I say, "I have an announcement to make." All eyes turn toward me. "I know this may come as a surprise to you guys, but..." I take a dramatic pause and look around at everyone before continuing. "Colin believes in soulmates."

Colin gasps.

Theo and Derek burst out into laughter while Colin, red in the face, opens his mouth to reply before closing it again. He looks from me to Theo and then shakes his fist at the man next to me.

"You asshole! That was a private conversation. You weren't supposed to share it with anyone!" he yells at Theo, which only serves to make us all laugh harder. My mom bounces in her seat, clapping her hands in delight.

"Oh, Colin! I'm so glad to hear this. Gives me hope that one day you'll stop sleeping your way around Cape Cod and eventually find a nice girl and give us some grandchildren," she says through her laughter.

Derek pretends to cough and mutters, "Pussy." My dad reaches over and smacks him in the back of his head, causing Colin to finally chuckle over the entire situation.

"Why don't you ever complain about Derek not being wifed up yet?" Colin asks before shoveling a fork full of pancakes into his mouth.

"Because Derek doesn't sleep his way around Cape Cod, sweetie. And before you open your mouth, if he is, I haven't heard about it, and I don't want to," she says as Derek sits there, a smug smile on his face

"In my defense, you never told me that was confidential information," Theo finally says after he catches his breath.

"I thought it went without saying, Theo. That's the kind of information that can really ruin my reputation. I don't need it getting out." He does the whole I'm watching you thing with his fingers, pointing to his eyes and then to each person at the table, causing us all to erupt in laughter again.

"In all seriousness, I do have something to say. I'm going to stay with Theo for now. Nothing official, but it just feels right," I say before taking a sip of coffee.

My dad is quiet as he takes in the news. His brows pinch together as he silently eats his breakfast. My mom, on the other hand, has a smile so big it stretches from ear to ear. Colin takes out his wallet and counts out a hundred bucks, passing it over to Derek with a pout.

"Did you just settle a bet?" I ask.

"Yup," Derek says with satisfaction as he stuffs the money in his pocket, smirking at Colin. "Told you, bro. Don't be a sore loser." Colin gives him the finger before turning his attention back to his pancakes.

"Sorry to spring this on you guys. I know it seems fast, but I assure you, it's not an impulsive decision. You know it's all I've ever wanted, and I promise you I'll take good care of her," Theo says as he squeezes my shoulder.

"Well, I think it's great. Lyla, we'll still have our girls' dinners. And book club!" my mom says.

My dad finally speaks. "Sweetheart, you went through a seriously traumatic event in this house just a few weeks ago. I just need to ask, are you rushing to move out because you're afraid or uncomfortable being in this house?"

"No, Dad. I promise. It just feels like the right step to take. I'm not afraid to be in this house. This is our family home. It's where we grew up. I won't let that piece of shit take away every happy memory I've made in this house," I say with conviction. "I do appreciate that you guys did some rearranging in the living room, though. My mind didn't go right to the attack when I walked in earlier."

"Okay, kiddo. As long as you're sure," he says as he nods in satisfaction.

"I'm beyond sure, Dad." I smile at him before reaching over and squeezing Theo's leg. "The bonus is that I don't have to lose my appetite when you grab Mom's butt before you leave for work in the morning."

My brothers fake gag.

"You sleeping here tonight or at Theo's?" Mom asks.

"I actually haven't thought that far ahead. Babe?" I defer to Theo.

"Whatever you want, Sunshine."

"You're back to work tomorrow right?" He nods. "Okay, I'll pack up a few things, and we can head home."

He leans over and brushes a kiss across my forehead. "I like hearing you call it home," he says with a smile.

"Oh dear god, I don't know if I can handle this," Derek mutters under his breath.

"Speaking of work. What's Clayton's vibe been like?" Theo asks.

"I mean, he's never been a super chatty dude, and I don't want to look into things too much, but I do feel like he's been a little more chipper since Hollman was whacked," Colin says. "But maybe you've gotten in my head about him."

Derek jumps in. "I thought he was more talkative than usual when we were out on Wednesday."

"Derek, you are the least unbiased person on the fucking planet," Colin says. He's not wrong.

"I'm not going to deny that. But this time around that might work in our favor. I don't know him as well as you guys. It's easier for me to say if he's acting differently because I can notice a change versus just wanting to see it because there's no other lead. His behavior was definitely odd at the Dusty Bird," Derek says. "Dad, what do you think?"

"I hate to feed into Theo's theory before we have any more to go on, but I actually agree with you two. Always respectful at work—that's never been an issue—but he has definitely been more friendly the past week," my dad says.

"How so?" I ask.

"He makes a point to pop his head in my office to say hello. Brought a box of donuts one morning. Asked if I wanted anything for lunch when he was going out to grab something for himself one day. He's definitely been making much more of an effort to interact with me this past week. Asked me twice how you were doing and when Theo was coming back to work."

"He asked me a couple of times, too. And repeatedly asked me how Lyla was doing," Colin said. "I can see him asking once if she's doing okay, but he never really showed much interest in her before. Rubbed me the wrong way when he brought her up."

"I have a bad feeling about this," Theo says.

"I told you, I should have been tailing him. See what the fucker has really been up to," Derek says, shaking his head.

"And I told you that was a terrible idea," Theo replies. Colin voices his agreement out loud.

"Derek, if he is dirty the last thing we need is someone tipping him off that we're suspicious. And if he's not dirty, the last thing we need is him accusing you of harassment. This week, boys. This week we'll know what's what," my dad says before changing the subject. "Is the plan to get married?"

"Yes, sir. I'd marry her tomorrow if she'd have me," Theo says, and my heart swells in my chest. My dad nods with satisfaction.

"I love you like a son, Theo. You know this. But I'd be remiss if I didn't say that you better take care of her. You break her heart again, you won't live to see another day." Dad's dead serious when he says this.

Theo looks my dad in the eyes when he replies. "Understood, Chief. She's all that matters to me. I failed her once; it won't happen again." His tone is serious, his words deliberate.

"We still get Wednesday nights at the Dusty Bird together. Lyla can't take that from me," Colin says. I start to laugh but immediately try to stifle it when I see that he's completely serious.

After we eat, we send the boys outside to relax while my

mom and I chat and clean up. "Thinking about the conversation we had on the phone last week. I'm glad you have faith in him, Lyla. I don't think it's misplaced. That man worships you, looks at you like you hung the moon. He won't ever let you down again."

"I'm still scared, Mom. If I'm being honest, it terrifies the shit out of me that he could leave. But my feelings for him, the pull I feel toward him, I guess it just outweighs those fears."

"You deserve all the happiness in the world, Lyla. You both do." She gives me a smile.

"Any good town gossip since I've been gone?" I ask. She dives into telling me about the latest specials at the coffee shop, the drama between the two flower shops in town, and informs me that city hall finally approved fixing some potholes.

"I'm going to go switch the laundry, and then I can help you pack some things if you'd like," she says as Theo walks in from the patio. He stands behind me, caging me in as I finish washing the coffee pot. He playfully kisses my neck as Colin walks in.

"You guys... We're going to have a serious talk about boundaries around me. I can't spend the rest of my life dealing with you two groping each other and whispering sweet nothings."

Just to piss him off, I turn around and wrap my soapy hands around Theo's neck, pulling him closer.

"I'm outta here. Theo, call me later when you find your balls." Theo and I both burst into laughter. We put Colin out of his misery and let each other go.

"I'm going to pack a few bags with my mom, and then we can head back to your house if that sounds good."

"Our house, Sunshine. It's *our* house." The smile he gives me almost takes my breath away. It's genuine and reaches his eyes, which are a beautiful light blue. I nod in response. An hour later, we head to Theo's house, my Jeep packed with a few duffle bags and Diego on my lap.

"I should warn you, Lyla. This house is not nearly as up-to-date as the one on Nantucket," he says, sounding nervous.

"Theo, I've been inside of your house a million times. Why are you nervous to bring me there now?"

"I poured everything into "Sunshine," which hasn't left much for this place. And truthfully, this house doesn't mean as much to me. Don't get me wrong; it's clean and functional, but it's not overflowing with homey vibes, that's for sure." he says.

"Good. Because that means we can make it into a home together."

"Love you, baby," he says as he reaches for my hand. He squeezes it and then holds on to it for the rest of the drive. We pull up to the curb, and from the outside, I can see it's gotten a slight facelift.

The siding is a darker blue than it used to be and he replaced the old front door with a wooden one that matches the garage doors. The lawn is well manicured and the flowerbeds are full of hydrangea bushes.

Once the car is in park, Theo reaches over and grabs Diego. He places the cat on the ground and then walks around to open my door. He pulls me towards the front door, the cat right behind us.

"Alright, babe, it's been years since I've been here, and I have no idea how you have it set up. Do you still sleep in your old bedroom?" I ask right before he scoops me into his arms and carries me across the threshold of the front door.

"Hah. Figured since I owned the place, it was time for me to take the master. I ripped up the carpet and repainted the bedroom so that it didn't feel like I was still living in my dad's house. Otherwise, it's a blank canvas that your brother would probably love to get his hands on."

Being here with him, in this house we'll work together to make into a home, fills me with gratitude and so much affection for this man that I can't help but say, "I am so fucking excited to live with you, babe."

We spend the next hour reorganizing the closet and dressers in our bedroom to make room for the stuff I brought over. We take a break and go outside to the backyard.

"Ooooooh! You didn't mention a hot tub, Theo!" I say as I wiggle my eyebrows suggestively. .

"You have no idea how many times I've fucked my hand to thoughts of you in it," he says, and I feel the heat rise between my legs.

"Well... I can't wait to get fucked in it then. And there's no better time than the present," I say as I look around the yard, appreciating how private it is. There's a high wooden fence that's also lined with pine trees, effectively blocking the yard from any prying eyes.

"As much as I'd love to, I can't trust that the chemicals are balanced or that there's no algae." I sigh dramatically and he continues. "Doesn't mean I can't bend you over that couch in there and fuck you quick and hard before we go back to get more of your stuff, though."

"Yes, please," I say, leading him back into the house. Once he shuts the door, I turn to him and start stripping out of my clothes.

Theo checks that the front door is locked before stalking over to me. His eyes devour mine as he rips his shirt over his head and drops it. I'm so turned on that when I reach down I can already feel how wet I am. I lean over the couch, pushing my ass toward him and say, "Quick and hard, Theo, like you just said." I groan as he reaches around and brings a hand to my pussy. He tangles his other hand in my hair and gently pulls it back, giving himself access to my neck.

"Already so wet for me, baby," he says as he sucks my neck. I can feel his cock, silky smooth, and rock hard against my ass.

"Always, Theo. I'm always so fucking wet for you," I say in a breathy voice. He uses his feet to gently spread my legs a little wider and pulls my ass to his crotch, rubbing his shaft between my ass cheeks before lining it up to the entrance to my pussy. I moan loudly and reach an arm behind my head so I can wrap it around his neck.

"This pussy is ready for me. So ready for my cock to destroy it," he grunts as he rubs his hard length on me.

"Fuck me, Theo. Please," I beg.

"You got it, baby." He enters me with one thrust, going so deep we both gasp. "This is how I know this pussy is mine. You take me so fucking perfectly, Lyla."

He pulls out slowly and slams into me again and again and again. I moan every time he thrusts, his dick pounding me so deep I think I'll still feel it there even after he pulls out. He grips my hip with one hand and continues, picking up more speed.

I moan his name, and he growls in response, his finger circling my clit. It only takes about ten seconds of that before I'm coming all over him and screaming his name. He comes right after, squeezing my ass as he does, his thrusts slowing as he empties himself into me.

He kisses his way up my spine and asks, "Quick and hard enough for you, baby?"

"I'd say so," I say with a soft laugh, still trying to catch my breath. He pulls out of me, his cock glistening with both of our orgasms, and walks over to where he dropped his shirt on the floor. He cleans me off before using it to wipe himself down.

He leaves me for a second, presumably to get a clean shirt,

and I throw myself onto the couch, still naked and trying to recover.

"Now that's a view I can get used to, Sunshine," he says as he comes back in and finds me sprawled out. We finish getting dressed and make a grocery list, deciding a trip to the store is priority number one. I'll go back to my parents' house tomorrow to get more of my things.

When we return, Theo sorts through the mail on his counter and hands a package to me. I look at him, puzzled as to how I already have mail coming here. He just smiles.

I look down and see that it's from Cosabella, my favorite lingerie company. I tear into the package and hold up a dark blue lace bra. "Are you kidding me right now?" I ask in disbelief.

"Hey, I owed you panties," he says with a shrug.

"Yeah, one pair. This is like five-hundred dollars worth of bras and panties," I say as I continue to root through the package.

"Should be some more nighttime apparel in there, too. Couldn't help but think of how hot you'd look in it," he says.

"When did you do this? And how?" I ask as I open the next item, holding up a tiny lace thong.

"This crazy thing called the internet. I looked in the drawer of what you had and found it online. Got a little sidetracked with the website. They have some sexy shit on there, but there are at least two thongs to replace the one I ripped."

"You're ridiculous, but I love it. Thank you, babe."

"I swear I didn't go on a shopping spree to butter you up, but...do you still want to share those letters with me?" he asks, hope in his voice. "You don't have to. If you don't feel ready or if you just don't want to—"

"I know I don't. And I'm not sure I'll ever really want to, but you deserve to read them. I'll get them from my parents' house tomorrow. Just promise you won't read them in front of me."

"I promise."

We order a pizza for dinner and then relax, watching a Bruins preseason game before heading to bed. As we take turns in the bathroom, I'm struck by how easy and natural living with him is. How at home I immediately feel. And I realize it wouldn't matter where I was, just being with Theo is enough.

## THIRTY-FOUR

*Lyla*

FOR THE FIRST time since we've become inseparable, I'm awake before Theo, and I plan to take full advantage of that. The man knows no limits when it comes to taking care of me so when I wake up to his morning wood poking me in the back, I decide to immediately give him some pleasure of his own. Plus, hearing him moaning my name turns me on.

He's lying on his back with one hand over his head. The other was holding me close to him, but now that I've vacated that spot, he has it spread across his abdomen. I gently pulled the covers down and take a minute to enjoy the specimen in front of me.

His hair always looks like it's in need of a trim, even more so now. He has days-old scruff that only makes him sexier and adds to the appeal of his head between my legs.

I take a long look at the tattoo he has on his shoulder that runs down his bicep and upper arm. The one that is so similar to mine, it still blows my mind. It's intricate and simple at the same time. I gently brush it with kisses before leaning back again.

My eyes work their way down his powerful chest and to his

defined abs until they land on his cock, which is already awake and standing at attention for me. I smile to myself as I lean down and gently wrap my hand around it, giving it a few tugs before taking him in my mouth.

He groans and whispers, "Jesus, baby." Now that I know he's awake,

I suck him harder, but slowly, so I can really savor him. I take as much of him as I can, feeling his enormous shaft hit the back of my throat, and because I'm addicted to his moans, I do that a few more times before I come up for air and look at him.

"Morning, babe," I say as I work my hand up and down the full length of his cock again.

"Hmm, what did I do to deserve this wake up call, Sunshine?" he asks as he reaches forward to get his hands on my tits for a squeeze.

"I've been wanting to do this for days, but you're always up before me, and I've been sleeping like a rock. Just relax while I have my fun." I take him in my mouth again, working my hand at the same pace like he loves.

His precum mixes with my salvia as I work my hand and mouth together. Theo breathes heavily, and a string of expletives flies from his mouth. He moves his hand up to my head, running it through my hair before gently guiding me.

I keep one hand gripping his quad and move the other one to his balls, massaging them as I work my tongue around the head of his dick.

He moans and thrusts his hips up. I do that a few more times before running my tongue slowly up and down his shaft. With his hand controlling my head, I alternate between bobbing quickly and working my way languidly up and down, sucking hard as I do.

He hardens even more, letting me know he's close. I work

faster, teasing the head of his cock in a way that I know will make him come.

"Holy shit, Lyla," he grunts as he gets closer to coming. The pressure between my own legs builds, but I resist the urge to let one of my hands wander down to my clit for relief. This is about him, and while I know he would love to watch me touch myself, I want his orgasm to be the focus.

Like he can read my mind, he says, "Play with that pussy while you suck me off."

"Uh uh. This morning is all about you," I say before putting his cock back in my mouth.

"And you don't think me watching you play with yourself is something I'd enjoy immensely?" he asks, breathing heavily.

Ignoring the temptation to do what he suggests. I suck hard and work my mouth up and down while I grip him firmly. "Yessss, baby. I'm going to come in a second..."

I know he's telling me to give me warning in case I want to stop, but there's no way I'm doing that. I grip his quad tighter while I move my head up and down until he explodes in my mouth.

"Fuuuuuuck," he grunts as he spills into me. I take every last drop of him into my mouth and swallow it down like a fucking champ. He grabs my arms and pulls me off his cock and up to his chest where he kisses me with reckless abandon, not caring where my mouth just was. "That was a damn fine way to be woken up, Lyla," he says as he rolls me to my back. Before he can climb on top of me, I stop him.

"Good to know I've still got it," I say with a smirk.

"Fuck, I don't want to get out bed now," he groans.

"The sooner you go, the sooner you come back. Remind me later that I want to get back to running tomorrow," I say as I stretch my arms over my head and wrap them around Theo.

"Go back to sleep, Sunshine. There's no reason for you to get up with me."

"Yes, there is. It's your first day back to work, and I need to see you off," I say.

He kisses his way down my neck to my chest, but then his phone rings. We both groan with displeasure at the interruption.

"It's your brother," he mumbles, and I grab the phone out of his hand.

"Theo's answering service. Theo's busy right now, but how can I help you?" I answer in an obnoxiously cheerful voice as Theo goes back to kissing my chest.

"No. No, no, no. We are not doing this. I don't want to know what he's busy doing, just put *my* best friend on the phone," Colin says. I laugh and pass the phone over.

"What's up, bro?" Theo says as he leans back on his heels. "Yeah, I kind of forgot about that. I was going to make eggs. Later." He tosses his phone on the bed and leans down to kiss me. "I told your brother I'd make him breakfast since he has to pick me up, anyway."

"Do you two clowns carpool every day?" I ask as we get out of bed and throw sweats on.

"No. Only when we're short cars. I left mine at the station while we were gone."

"He's having a hard time sharing you, isn't he?" I ask with a laugh as we make our way to the kitchen.

"He might have a heart attack if I ever bail on a guy's night. Just keep that in mind when making plans for us."

"Got it. Wednesday nights are your date night with Colin. Check. That actually works out perfectly because that's the night I'm going to do book club at One More Chapter."

I start the coffee pot while Theo sets to work making breakfast. I stare at him while he adds at least three spoonfuls of sugar to his mug, the disgust probably all over my face. He looks at me and smiles. "What?"

"I just... I know you like your coffee absurdly sweet, but watching you actually heap spoonfuls of sugar, I can't believe your teeth haven't fallen out."

"This coming from the woman who would consider Haribo gummy bears their own food group," he says with raised eyebrows.

I roll my eyes and laugh because he's got me there. Twenty minutes later Colin knocks on the door, and we sit down for breakfast.

"How's the writing going, Lyla?" My brother asks in between bites. "You going to investigate another drug kingpin to take down? Not sure I can handle the stress of it, if I'm being honest."

"I have one last freelance article to send off, and then I'm officially caught up on all of those jobs. I'm going to try my hand at writing a novel next."

He raises his eyebrows. "No shit?" he asks. "What kind of book?"

"I haven't gotten far into things yet, mainly just some outlining and character development. At first, I was thinking I'd go with a twisty thriller, but I realized I needed to add more happiness to the story, so it's tracking more along the lines of a romantic suspense."

"You're writing a porn book, aren't you?" he asks, and I choke on my coffee.

"It'll be more sophisticated than that, Col. I promise."

"I can't read your book if it's porn, Lyla. That would be too weird," he says matter-of-factly.

"Let me write the book first, then we can figure out if you can handle reading it."

"Deal," he agrees.

Colin and I clean up breakfast while Theo goes to get dressed and pack a gym bag. When he comes back out, he pulls me into his arms to kiss me goodbye.

"You'll see her in like eight hours, bro," Colin says as he walks out the door to wait in the car.

"Keep in touch with me throughout the day. Alarm on when you're home, okay?"

"Yes, babe. I'm going to my parents' and then coming back here. Don't worry about me."

"I always worry about you, baby." He kisses me, his tongue dancing with mine, before he pulls away, leaving me wanting more.

* * *

I shoot Derek a quick text, making plans to have lunch with him this afternoon. Then I text Quinn to set up a Facetime date.

**Me: You around for a Facetime date later?**

**Quinn: Yes! I'm actually off today for an appointment. Give me five minutes.**

**Me: Sounds good. Back in Sandpiper Cover and lots to catch you up on.**

**Quinn: Can't wait. Talk soon.**

My phone lights up with Quinn calling, and I quickly answer. Her long chestnut hair is up in a messy bun, and she's got a chunky turtleneck sweater on, her brown eyes rimmed with red. I immediately ask her if she's okay.

"I'm fine! Was just arguing with Justin earlier but it's all good," she replies, forcing a smile I know is fake.

"You don't look like it's all good, QB. What's going on?" I ask.

She finally gives me more of an answer. "I'm just exhausted

from the fighting. I can't do anything right for this man. Somehow, I can do exactly what he asks, but it still ends up pissing him off. I know he's stressed, but I'm tired of him taking it out on me." It's the most she's ever said about her issues with Justin.

"I'm getting really fucking tired of this man making you feel like shit all the time, Quinn. You need to put some boundaries in place and stand up for yourself. Or leave his miserable, controlling ass. I'm worried about you," I say.

"That's the thing... I'm actually off today because I made an appointment with a therapist. I thought it would be helpful to talk things out with someone who doesn't have a dog in the fight. I hate blowing a sick day this early in the school year, but I was able to get in much quicker than anticipated."

"That's great, QB. I know therapy can be scary, but once you find the right one, it can change your life. I'm really proud of you for taking that step."

"Thanks, Ly. Now, tell me what's going on with you. Where are you? I don't recognize that room."

"Damn, you're good," I say with a chuckle. "I'm actually at Theo's." Her jaw drops. "I didn't officially move in, but he asked me if I wanted to. I mean, I guess I technically did since I don't have any plans to leave."

I feel a pang of guilt in my chest being this happy when it's obvious my best friend is dealing with her serious relationship issues.

"Holy shit! I'm so happy for you, boo. How did this even happen?" she asks.

"Well, he finally opened up about why he left, and while it still hurts to think about, I've learned that it wasn't something I did wrong. It was how he was dealing with his own emotional traumas from past events."

She nods.

"I was still really torn about opening my heart to him again. The idea that something could trigger him to run away again... Well, it shakes me to the fucking core. I get queasy just thinking about it. But something my mom said, about having more faith in him than fear, stuck with me. It's just... It's just always been him, QB. I was angry at him for so long, and bitter and resentful, but I never wanted anyone else. Being with him again, I can't explain it. I just feel alive again. Like he brought all of the color back into my world."

"I can see it in your body language, Lyla. You look refreshed. It's not a look I've ever seen on you. You're glowing."

"That's probably from all the sex," I laugh.

She hesitates before wistfully asking, "He makes you feel safe?"

"Beyond safe and protected."

"You deserve it, Lyla."

"So do you, Quinn. Don't ever forget that. I'm afraid, though. I feel like life is so good right now, despite the recent events, that the rug is going to get pulled out from under me."

"That's understandable, but I think it's a far-fetched fear, Lyla. Just enjoy where you are now. Don't go borrowing trouble." She asks about the Hollman case and if they ruled Clayton out, so I fill her in on all of that. I tell her how I've been writing, and like Theo, she's full of encouragement.

"I want to be a beta reader! Or is there someone who reads even sooner? Is there such a thing as an alpha reader? I'm going to google it because I want the job."

"I actually have no idea. I'm fucking clueless when it comes to writing a novel. I've just been thinking about the story and running with it, figuring I can do the rest later. Perhaps I should reach out to a few people I know in the field for some guidance."

I make a mental note to send some emails this week. We

talk for a few more minutes when Diego saunters into the room. I pick him up and show him off on camera, and I swear he hams it up. "Promise you'll come see me soon. The next long weekend you have? Maybe Thanksgiving?! If things are rocky with Justin, tell him you'll make your own plans."

She promises to consider it, and we hang up.

\* \* \*

I still have plenty of time before I'm supposed to meet Derek for lunch, so I send my mom a text that I'm coming over. She has a cup of coffee waiting for me when I walk in the door.

"What brings you by so early?" she asks.

"I wanted to get a few more things, and since I'm already up, I figured I'd get moving so I wasn't tempted to crawl back into bed with the cat and go back to sleep."

"That was smart. You settling in over there?"

"I am! It actually feels really natural to be there, which reassures me that staying there is the right decision."

Once we're done with our coffee, I head back into my bedroom to pack a few more things in the empty bags I brought from Theo's house—*my* house.

I dump my bathing suits and the rest of my workout clothes in them before stuffing the last one with shoes. I make a couple trips out to my Jeep before going back into my room.

I look around, at the collages on the wall, the pictures that chronicled my teenage years and early twenties, and for the first time in years, I smile. Those pictures, that include Theo or Olivia, used to be such a source of heartbreak. The pain I'd get in my heart and gut when I looked at them felt like a sucker punch. But now, I see the joy in those pictures.

I've learned that it's still full of promise. Even when it goes off track, you can find your way back. The path might be different than you expected, than you envisioned. It might be full of rocky roads and heartbreak, but there's beauty in that divergence.

I head over to my closet and dig out the box of letters that feel like literal skeletons in my closet. My chest feels like an elephant is sitting on it just from holding the box, and it becomes clear to me that they have more power over me than I ever noticed.

Maybe it's because they take me back to such a dark place in my life. Maybe it's because I felt so hopeless when I wrote them, and the fear of ever going back to that place cuts me to the quick. Maybe it's because by giving them to Theo, I'm letting him see such a vulnerable side of myself that I've never shared with anyone.

Whatever those feelings are, I sit in them for another minute before I pick up the last duffle bag and say goodbye to my mom.

"Where are you off to now?" she asks as she walks me to the door.

"I think I'm going to pop over to One More Chapter to touch base with Kristin about the book club I'm starting. I've kind of dropped the ball on it after everything happened, so I want to make sure she's still okay with it. Then I'm supposed to meet Derek for lunch."

"Tell them both I said hello. I'll talk to you later." She gives me a hug, and I head out to my car.

\* \* \*

I'm able to find a parking spot not too far from the bookstore, and I grab my purse before getting out. I close the door and immediately feel a chill rush over me. I look over my shoulder to see if anything is amiss.

*Chill out, Lyla. Hollman is dead. No one is following you. Get out of your head,* I say to myself as I take a few deep breaths.

The bell dings as I walk into One More Chapter and, for a second, I freeze. I remember seeing Scotty McDavid in here shortly before my attack.. My breath races.

"Lyla, honey, are you okay?" Kristin asks as she comes out from behind the register.

It takes me a few beats before I can reply. "Yes. Sorry. I just... It's the first time I've been in here since that man attacked me. Knowing I ran into him here before it happened has me shook up."

"Oh, dear. I'm so sorry." She takes my arm and leads me to one of the leather reading chairs. "Let me get you some water," she says once she sits me down.

"I'm so embarrassed, Kristin. I'm sorry," I say as she passes me a bottle.

"Nonsense. I can't believe what happened to you. And that piece of garbage was here, following you around, before he attacked you. Thank god he's sitting in jail. I hope they throw away the key," she says, and I give her a small smile.

"I came to talk to you about the book club. I got a little sidetracked after the incident, but now that I'm back in town, I'm going to work on getting it set up. I was hoping to do the first meeting next week? To drum up interest, I can bring snacks, announce the book, that sort of thing."

"Sure, dear. Whatever you want. Just let me know the title in advance so that I can order enough copies. Are you sure you're okay?" she asks.

"I am. Thank you—for taking care of me and for letting me start the book club."

"Of course!" The bell dings, alerting her to a new customer, and she rushes off to greet them.

Once my breathing slows and my heart stops racing, I

stand up to peruse the aisles. My TBR pile is never-ending, but I can't stop myself from picking up a couple more titles, as well as a book on writing with emotion that might be helpful as I work on my manuscript. I pay before heading back to my car.

I hear my phone ding with a text from Derek.

**Derek:I have to bail on lunch. Crisis at the site that I need to deal with so we don't get off track on the timeline.**

**Me: Everything okay?**

**Derek: Yeah, it will be. Raincheck for *Love is Blind* night instead?**

**Me: Wednesday night? Or do you want to go to Dusty Bird with the boys?**

**Derek: *LIB* night. I'll bring pizza.**

**Me: I'll make margs.**

He gives my last message a thumbs-up, and I head home. I spend the rest of my day being productive as hell. I unpack my clothes, somehow managing to squeeze them all in without having to kick Theo out of the closet.

I marinade chicken for dinner, and I finish the last freelance article on my plate, giving it one last read through before sending it over to the editor. I fire off a few emails to some contacts I have in the publishing world, putting feelers out about my new venture and asking for guidance.

When Theo gets home, I'm in the kitchen working on a salad, the box of letters sitting on the table.

"Hey, Sunshine," he says as a smile spreads over his face. "I'm really loving this view."

"Me in the kitchen?"

He laughs. "No, baby. You and the kitchen aren't on the best of terms. You here when I get home, looking beautiful and smiling."

"Well, I marinated chicken for you to throw on the grill so get that going, and we can sit down and catch up on our days."

Before he does anything else, he takes my face in his hands and plants a huge kiss on my lips.

"Those your letters?" he asks, nodding his chin toward the box.

"Yup. The ones on pink paper are the ones I wrote. They're numbered. Sorry in advance for how much of a bitch I was in the beginning."

"No apologies, Lyla. Thank you for sharing them with me. I promise I won't read them in front of you."

"Thanks," I say, giving him a small smile.

We eat dinner, and I ask him about his day. "You play nice with Clayton today?"

"Ugh, yes. Smug little shit." I don't miss the way his shoulders tense up or how his left hand clenches into a fist at the mention of his colleague.

"I'm going to assume you would have called me with any pertinent news, but I thought that analyst was supposed to look into him."

There's a bite to his voice when he says, "He wasn't in the office today. Your dad got his number from the agent in charge and reached out. He assured your dad he will be in the office tomorrow and will touch base with him in the morning."

"Okay, well one more day doesn't make a difference at this point." I internally weigh whether or not I want to say anything about what happened when I was in town but decide against it.

"Hot tub ready yet?" I ask.

"I checked the levels when I was outside earlier. Should be good to go by tomorrow."

"Yessss!" I squeal, already thinking about which bathing suit I'm going to wear.

* * *

I'm startled awake by a nightmare, the first in quite a few days. When I look at the clock, I see that it's just after 3 a.m.

"You okay, baby?" Theo asks, his eyes alert despite the fact that it's the middle of the night.

"I had a nightmare again," I whisper as I hold my hand to my chest, willing my heartbeat to slow down.

"Same one?" he asks as he rubs my back in soothing circles.

I shake my head and look at him. "No. This one was different. It was my parents' house, and Derek didn't get there in time." I'm so shaken up, I can't stop the tears that spring to my eyes.

Theo pulls me into his arms and holds me tight. "You're okay, Lyla. Look at me," he pulls back, holding my face with his hands. "It was a dream. You're safe."

I nod, gripping his hands with my own. "I'm okay. It was just a nightmare," I softly repeat. I'm scared to fall back asleep, petrified that the nightmare will happen again. He leans against the headboard and continues to hold me. I don't know how long it takes, but I eventually doze off.

## THIRTY-FIVE

*theo*

AS MUCH AS I love living with Lyla, it's hard as hell leaving her in the morning. The only silver lining is that the analyst should be in the office today.

When I get to the station, I spend a chunk of my morning getting caught up on a few reports that have been hanging over my head. I mill around Chief's door, waiting for him to tell me to come in because he has news, but it's not until after lunch that he finally walks up to my desk and tells me we're going to get coffee.

Colin follows us out of the office, and we walk the couple of blocks to Morning Current. I can tell from his posture alone that Lyla's dad is not happy. Without any conversation, we order our coffees and take them back outside.

"I wanted you to be wrong, Theo. Because if you weren't, it would mean that we have a fox in our hen house. A fox *I* hired." *Fuck.* He blows out an angry sigh. "I spoke with the analyst. We'll call him Smith. His immediate search showed nothing suspicious in Clayton's finances. He said he was clean. Too clean. So he dug a little deeper. Our boy is living in a house here and driving a car that his salary can't cover. Couple that

346

with the fact that he owns an apartment back in Boston that his mother lives in. His mother who doesn't work or contribute in any way financially. Smith is convinced he has money hidden somewhere because there's no way he would be able to swing these things if he didn't."

"Christ. I didn't want to believe it, but this is not good," Colin says.

"According to the analyst, there's no family money. It's just him and his mother. No trust fund, no rich dead grandparents. Nothing."

"Which means he's got another source of income that is likely not legal," I say, anger building in me.

"That's what Smith thinks. He's a hound on the scent now. All but hung up on me after saying something about this motherfucker being up to something, and he's going to drink espresso until he figures out what it is." I'm relieved we have this guy on board.

"This means Lyla could still be in danger." It's Colin who says what all three of us are thinking. "Should you guys go back to Nantucket?"

"I'd hate to uproot her again, but it might not be a bad idea. She had a terrible nightmare last night, and this new information isn't going to help."

"Let's stay put for now," Chief says, and I can see the wheels turning. "As far as Clayton knows, she's still living at my house. I'll casually reiterate that in conversation here and there so he doesn't know any better. Hollman is the one who wanted her dead. With him gone, I don't know why she would still be in danger. But we're not taking chances."

"So what do we do? Just keep tabs on Clayton?" Colin asks.

"Stick to him, Colin. You've known him the longest. You can play up that Theo is spending all his time with your sister now, so it's only natural you'd need someone to pal around with. I'm going to work something out so we have someone keeping an eye on him when he's off duty," Chief says, and Colin nods in agreement.

"Who do we trust enough to ask to do surveillance on one of our own?" I ask.

"Some of my golf buddies who retired from the force. I trust them with my life, so I trust them enough to enlist them in this."

"I have a bad feeling about this," Colin says. "I don't like it. I don't like playing nice with a guy who could be dirty as fuck."

"None of us like this, Colin. I want to beat the everliving fuck out of that snot-nosed shit. I'm sure Theo feels the same, but we have to see it through. If we can get confirmation that he's dirty, we can take him down. Hopefully, Smith will get back to me sooner rather than later, and we can put this shit to bed before anything else happens. Until then, everyone plays nice." He looks Colin in the eyes before turning and looking at me. "I mean it, Theo. We don't want him to know we're on to him. And if you're not at work, you're attached to Lyla's hip."

My head moves in quiet agreement.

"Okay, let's head back," Chief says. We start walking and he asks, "What's this about nightmares?"

"They started in Nantucket but only lasted a few nights. Then last night she was up again, and this one scared her even more. She's able to fall asleep once she calms down, but she's absolutely terrified when she wakes up."

"What are they about? What happened at the house?" Colin asks.

"The first few were about the incident at the Dusty Bird. Last night was about the night at your parents'. All she said was Derek didn't get there in time, and I didn't push her. My heart damn near broke at how petrified she was. I could see it in her eyes, and she was shaking uncontrollably. Held on to me like a lifeline."

We get back to the station and go about the rest of our days. The other set of detectives get called for a case, putting Colin and me at the top of the rotation which stresses me out. I rationalize that if I'm called out for a case it'll keep me busy and Lyla can stay with her parents or Derek can crash at our house.

Chief doesn't hear back from Smith for the rest of the day, which also grates on my nerves. When my shift ends, I pack up my things, grab my laptop, and stick my head in his office to say goodbye before walking out with Colin.

"You heading home?" he asks.

"Yeah, I was going to stop at the liquor store, but I just want to get back. Thinking I'll scoop Lyla up, and we'll run a few errands."

"Sounds good. Call me if you need anything. I'm going to lie low tonight, but I figure I'll see if Clayton and Drew want to grab some beers tomorrow night. Keep up normal appearances." I nod and tell him that's a good plan before parting ways.

I have one nonnegotiable stop to make on my way home to Lyla. I park a block away just in case I run into anyone I know. Lord knows small towns like to talk, so I rush to my appointment at Sandpiper Jewelers. The owners are long-time residents who are known for being steel traps when it comes to townies shopping there.

One of the owners, Dana, sees me as I walk in and waves me over.

"Oh, honey, I was hoping this day would come eventually. Please tell me it's for Lyla," she says as she gives me a hug.

"I wouldn't buy a ring for anyone else," I say with a smile, returning her embrace. "Thanks for fitting me in. I need to be quick."

"Of course. Let's start with this case over here. Any idea as to what shape you want for the stone?" she asks as she rubs her hands together.

"Yellow stone, round or oval. On a rose gold band. Thin and sparkly."

She nods, as if impressed. "A man who knows what he wants. I like it. Diamond or sapphire?"

"Sapphire. She never wanted a diamond."

"Size?"

"She won't want anything ostentatious. Two carats, tops."

She laughs. "Okay, I don't have anything in the shop right now, but that's easy to get from my dealer. Let's look at settings. I have a few that would fit the bill."

She shows me a few, the third option being exactly what I envision on Lyla's finger. I hold it up for her.

"That's the one I thought you'd pick, but I wanted to give you options. I'm pretty sure I have her ring size on file in the system from years ago, but I'll let you know if I need it. I'll text you when the stone comes in. I'll want you to approve it before we set it."

"Great. How long do you think?" I ask.

"After all these years, now you're in a rush?"

"I have to lock her down before she changes her mind," I joke with a laugh. Really, I'm just so fucking excited to be taking this next step that I want the ring yesterday.

"I'll text you after I talk to my gem gal. Now, get outta here before anyone else spots you."

"Thanks, Dana!" I call as I turn to leave, rushing to my car so I can get home to my girl.

* * *

I walk through the door in a hurry, excited to be home. I yell out, "Honey, I'm home!". She's not in the kitchen and seconds that feel like minutes tick by with no response. In fact, the house is eerily quiet, and I immediately panic, running my hands through my hair as I toss my keys on the counter.

I rush through the kitchens and family room, making my way down the hallway, my footsteps heavy and my breathing erratic. When I find her in the office with music playing, dancing in her seat, a bag of gummy bears nearby as she writes I breathe out a sigh of relief.

"Hey, babe!" She turns and gives me a big smile, one that reaches her eyes. I breathe a sigh of relief before I walk over, lean down, and kiss her.

"Come on. Let's go get ice cream and tequila."

"Two of my favorite things!" She's in such a good mood I feel bad knowing I'm going to burst her bubble with what we've learned so far.

We hit the liquor store for some wine and a bottle of Cazcanes reposado before heading to Scoops for ice cream.

We drive the two minutes from the ice cream shop to the beach, but since it's a bit windy, we decide to stay in the car to eat. "Ice cream for dinner? By the water? I feel like you're about to drop a bomb on me, and this is your way of softening the blow," she says as she digs into her sundae.

I fill her in on everything we learned about Clayton. She nods, stoically taking it all in.

"So what do we do, Theo? I don't want to run away from this. If he's dirty, maybe it's better if I'm here, and he comes after me again." The idea of that has the bile rising in my throat.

"Under no circumstances would him coming after you be a good option, Lyla. What I want to do is run away to Nantucket and stay in that protective bubble we were in, but your dad wants us to hold off. He has some retired friends who he's going to task with keeping an eye on Clayton when he's off shift. We're really hoping that Smith comes back with something that confirms he's dirty so we can take him down as quickly as possible."

"It just doesn't make sense, though. Hollman is dead. The guy who took his spot in their organization is probably happy he's gone. You'd think he'd be sending me flowers, thanking me for orchestrating Hollman's demise. Why would Clayton, or anyone else, be after me?" she asks.

"Not sure, Sunshine. These guys don't follow a moral code of conduct here. Sometimes there's no rhyme or reason for what they do. But I promise you, we won't let anything happen to you. Look at me, Lyla," she turns attention from her sundae to me. "We are not going to let anything happen to you. Colin, your dad, Derek, me... We'll do whatever it takes to keep you safe. I promise. On my life."

She nods and goes back to her ice cream. I hate that she's still potentially in the crossfire of something we don't even know about. I hate that she keeps having nightmares. I feel completely helpless, and the last time I was in this position, I broke both of our hearts. That's not an option this time around.

I change the subject in an effort to turn her mood back around. "Did you have a productive day?" I ask.

"Moderately so. I finally started writing today, and I got a few thousand words down which made me feel accomplished. I still have no idea what the fuck I'm doing when it comes to this part of the writing industry, but I love the story-telling aspect, and I love writing creatively again."

"That's wonderful, Sunshine. I can't wait to read what you've been working on." I notice she's biting her lip so I call her out on it. "What else is on your mind."

"I'm not sure if it's crossed your mind, but if you're at all worried about me contributing to the bills I have plenty of money saved. I can pay my share of things. I can always take on freelance jobs if I need to subsidize my income while I work on my novel." She talks quickly, like she's nervous.

I hold a hand up. "Lyla, slow down. The deal my dad gave me on this house... The mortgage is basically nothing. Just worry about writing what you love. I'm not worried about finances or income. You shouldn't be, either."

"I'm not a freeloader, Theo," she says.

"I know you're not. You can contribute whatever you want, but I don't want you to divert your focus away from working on your manuscript because you're afraid that you're not paying enough of the bills. We'll make it work, okay?"

"Okay. Thank you for being so supportive."

I give her a smile. "Always, baby."

It starts raining on our way home, dashing all of my plans to soak in the hot tub. When we get back, I take a look around the yard to make sure nothing looks out of place before heading inside. I feed the cat and make sure the alarm is on for the night.

The outdated bathroom doesn't allow for both of us to fit in there together, so I tell Lyla to go first. I hop in when she's done.

When I walk into our bedroom, she's lying on top of the covers wearing one of the pieces of lingerie I bought for her. The black number that's sheer, sexy as fuck, and leaves nothing up to the imagination. I stop dead in my tracks.

My body and hair are still wet from my shower, and the towel around my waist just barely hangs on. Lyla looks at me like I'm her next meal. The fire in her eyes makes my dick rise to attention. She licks her lips as she stares at me.

"Don't move a muscle, Sunshine. I'm going to grab some

champagne." I rush to the kitchen and back, pop the cork on a bottle of bubbles, and pour us each a glass. Lyla sits up and kneels closer to the edge of the bed to take hers. I climb in after her.

"Goddamn, Lyla. I don't even know where to start tonight. You're smoking hot in this. I'm really good at picking out lingerie."

We get lost in each other, mouths and hands roaming all over each others' bodies, taking breaks to sip champagne and refilling our glasses as we go.

I lay her down on the bed and hold myself over her, sucking her shoulder hard enough that I know it'll leave a mark. "I can't keep my hands off of you," I mutter as I paw at her tits through the flimsy nightgown. "Change of plans, baby." Lyla props herself up on her elbows, looking love drunk and one thousand percent fuckable.

"I want you to ride my face," I say and lie down on my back, waiting for her to climb over me. She positions her pussy right over my mouth and grabs onto the headboard.

I grab her ass cheeks and pull her to mouth, groaning the second I taste her.

"Theo," Lyla moans as I lap at her.

"Move, Lyla. Ride my face," I command before diving back in. I slap her ass, and it only makes her wetter. "I could eat this pussy every day, and it still wouldn't be enough."

Lyla gets louder as she rocks her hips, slowly at first but picking up in pace as I get lost in her pussy. When I gently suck on her clit, she lets a string of expletives fly.

"Fuck, fuck, fuck, Theo," she chants.

"Yes, babe. Your tongue is magical," she mutters.

"Not yet, baby. I've gone too many years without eating this pussy, and I'm not done yet." I slow my pace to keep her on edge and circle my tongue around her clit.

Every time I think she's about to come, I pull back and swirl my tongue over her. Her arousal coats my face, and I relish in it.

"Ride me harder, Lyla," I demand as I press my tongue to her clit and gently suck. I use my hands to wiggle her ass back and forth. It doesn't take long for Lyla to come all over my face.

"Theo, Theo, Theo," she chants as she rocks. I drink up every last drop of her.

"You might be my favorite dessert, baby. Let me have it every night, and I'll be one happy man," I say as I kiss her inner thigh. She scoots down my body, and I sit up, holding her so she doesn't fly off of me. "I want to get behind you," I say. She gets on all fours, her ass up in the air and I can't resist giving it a slap.

I slowly push my cock into her, watching it disappear before I pull it out and sink it in again and again, my hands gripping her hips. Eventually, I pick up my pace, slamming into her over and over, her pussy squeezing me like a vise.

"Fuck, Theo, you feel so good.".

I tip my head back as I pump into her. "That's because this pussy was made for me, Lyla. Now, let me play with what's mine."

Lyla's moans and the grip of her tight, wet pussy has me on the verge of coming. I reach a hand around and roll her clit between my fingers. A few more thrusts and she screams my name again as she comes.

My orgasm rips through me right after, and it's so intense it has me seeing spots. Eventually, my movements slow until they stop altogether. I slowly pull my cock out, our come dripping over the bedspread. I flop down and pull her next to me. We lie there, tangled in each other as we come down from the high.

"I read your first few letters today," I finally say once I can talk again. She tenses in my arms. "Relax, Sunshine. I mean, I can fuck the tension out of you if you give me enough time but don't get worked up over it."

"They get nicer, I swear," she says as she tightens her grip on me.

"I'm looking forward to that because you really ripped me a new one in those first few. Very colorful language."

"You need to get through the first dozen at least."

"Thanks for sharing them with me. It's a kick in the balls, seeing a first-hand account of how much I hurt you, but I need to read them. I need to know the depths of your anger and hurt." I lean down and kiss her before we roll out of bed to use the bathroom and clean up.

By the time I walk back in, Lyla is lying on her side, Diego curled up by her face. I pull her close to me and throw my arm over her waist.

"We running tomorrow?" I murmur into her hair.

"Yeah. It's been awhile, so let's just start with three miles. Wake me up when we need to go."

"Night, Sunshine," I whisper as she drifts off, hoping like hell she isn't going to be woken up by another nightmare.

## THIRTY-SIX

*Lyla*

.

MY FURRY EVIL genius is back on the job. It's not a terrifying dream that has me stirring in the middle of the night. Instead, Diego purrs loudly on my chest until I acknowledge him. I roll into Theo's arms after and fall back asleep. I wake well-rested when Theo's alarm goes off.

"Ugh, I don't want to get out of bed. You're so warm," I gripe as I snuggle deeper into Theo's arms.

"I'd be just as happy to get some cardio done in bed as opposed to going for a run, but you said you wanted to get back into a routine." He nuzzles my hair.

When I scoot my ass closer to his groin I can feel his cock waking up. I feel the thick shaft hardening against me and know that if I don't roll out of his arms right now, we're definitely not going to go for a run. "Damn it, you're right." I let out a dramatic sigh. "Okay, I'm going." I roll out of his arms and grab the workout clothes I left on top of the dresser.

By the time I get out of the bathroom, Theo is already dressed and staring intently at his phone. Without saying anything, he walks back to the gun safe that's on his nightstand, unlocks it, and grabs his firearm.

"What's wrong?" I ask.

"The motion detectors went off a few times overnight. Just stay inside while I do a loop around the perimeter."

My head snaps in his direction. I'm immediately on edge. I think about the strange feeling I had in town the other day—the one that had me near a full-blown panic attack at One More Chapter. The same feeling I stuffed down and convinced myself was just fallout from being attacked.

I follow him down the hallway, and he quickly turns the alarm off. I lock the door behind him as instructed. My hands are clenched so tight my knuckles turn white. Time feels like it stands still until I hear a few knocks on the door.

"It's me, baby. Open up."

I let out the breath I didn't even realize I was holding and rush to the door. "You're freaking me out a little here, babe."

"Sorry. It was the sensors on the side of the house that were triggered. I didn't see anything on the cameras. It was probably just an animal."

"I didn't hear any alert on your phone."

"Yeah, I usually keep them silenced for those cameras because animals run through at night. I always check them in the morning to make sure nothing popped up. You still want to go?"

A part of me wants to say no. Wants to crawl back in bed, hide under the covers, and pretend I wasn't silently panicking over someone lurking around the house. But I know it's a slippery slope when it comes to shying away from the things that scare me.

I know that Theo won't let anything happen to me when we're out, so I push the nerves away that bubble up in me and tell him I want to go.

I leave my earbuds at home, and we head out, Theo letting me set the pace. Because it's been a few weeks, I go slow to ease back into it. This allows for us to have conversation as we run. Theo is hyper vigilant as we go, his eyes alert and constantly on the move as if someone could jump out at any time.

"If you're sure it was an animal, why does it look like you're watching a tennis match with the way your eyes are all over the place?" I ask.

"Can't be too careful."

"Does that camera get triggered often?"

"Not really," he replies.

"Well, like you said, it was likely just an animal. Or a little animal family. I know you're on edge with the whole Clayton thing, but I think it was just coincidental that the alerts went off a handful of times."

"I don't believe in coincidences, Sunshine. You know that."

I do know that. Theo has always been a cut and dry kind of guy. He's never had that 'everything happens for a reason' mentality, so it does shake me a little bit that he's so on guard.

Thankfully, our run is uneventful, and we're back home in half an hour. Theo hops in the shower while I make breakfast, and before I know it, he's kissing me goodbye and heading out the door. I lock it, turn on the alarm, and take my laptop over to the kitchen table. I pour myself another cup of coffee and hunker down to get some writing done.

* * *

When Theo comes home, he has a brown paper bag in his hands and a smile on his face. He pulls me out of the chair I'm working in and wraps his arms around me. "Missed you, baby."

"Missed you, too. Kind of got used to being attached at the hip."

When he releases me, he offers the paper bag, and I throw a curious gaze his way. I pull out a thousand-piece puzzle and immediately look up at him, a huge grin on my face.

"Figured it's been awhile since we've done one of these together," he says with a sheepish smile.

"My gosh, how many puzzles do you think we've done?" I ask as I check out the picture on the box. It depicts a bookstore with dozens of cats scattered throughout, sleeping on any available surface they can find.

"At least a hundred."

I hold it to my chest and look at him. "This is really thoughtful of you. Thank you, babe. Where can we work on it?"

"I bought one of those puzzle boards a while ago but never got around to using it. We can slide it under the couch when we're not working on it, which will keep wandering paws from walking all over it and ruining our hard progress."

"Can we start it now? Derek's coming over later for *Love is Blind* since it's guys night."

"I'm not going to go," he says.

"Oh no. I will literally never hear the end of it from Colin if you miss a Wednesday night out."

He shakes his head. "Tough. With the motion camera going off overnight, and still not hearing back from the analyst about what he's been able to find, I don't want to leave you."

"Derek will be here before you leave, so I won't be alone at all. He'll be insulted if you don't trust him to keep me safe. Would be a huge step backward in this whole friendship thing you guys are working on. Plus, I'm sure Clayton will be there. You can sniff around and see if he says anything suspicious."

"It's hard enough keeping myself from punching him in the face at the station. I'm not sure I can stomach pretending to be boys with him in a social setting."

"So there's really been nothing at all from Smith yet? Not even a little teaser?" I ask.

"He texted your dad and said he had to tackle a few official things and then would get back to it, so hopefully tomorrow."

Theo's phone rings and he answers, putting Colin on speakerphone.

"Don't even think about bailing on me, Theo," Colin says, diving right in. "You promised me Wednesday nights!"

"Theo, just go," I say. "You know he won't drop it until you agree, and I can't handle his pissing and moaning."

"I'd hardly call holding my best friend to his word pissing and moaning," Colin says.

"Seriously, babe. It's fine. Derek would much prefer watching *Love is Blind with* me rather than pretending to play nice with Clayton."

"As if Derek can play nice. His resting bitch face says what his mouth doesn't," Colin says, and I laugh at the accuracy of the statement.

"Everything went to shit last time I left you to go to the Dusty Bird, Lyla," Theo says. Even Colin doesn't argue with this point.

"But this time is different. We don't even know that there's a threat out there. In fact, it's doubtful that there is. And again, Derek will be here before you leave, so I won't be alone at all."

"Yeah, he said he'd pick me up after he grabbed pizza so it's all good. Plus, it'll be good to keep things normal with Clayton. If he gets a buzz going and spills something, you're going to want to be there."

Theo blows out a deep breath. "Fine. But only because Derek will be here the whole time. Colin, we'll see you guys in a few hours." He disconnects the call. "How do you want to sort the puzzle?"

I scoff at him and say, "As if it's not sacrilegious to start any way other than separating the border pieces first."

He digs out the puzzle board, and we decide to work on it on the floor in the family room. Music plays in the background, Diego snoozes nearby, and we sip on wine and I munch on some gummy bears as we sort.

I relish in these little moments of quiet intimacy. Working on a puzzle, the time we've spent reading on the couch together, sipping coffee in bed, always having Haribo gummy bears at my disposal. Romantic gestures are nice and all, but it's these small moments that I've yearned for over the last half dozen years.

$$* * *$$

By the time my brothers show up, we've made a decent dent in the border, and Theo shoves the board under the couch. Derek sets the pizza on the coffee table and the six-pack of Cisco Brewery's Pumple Drumkin beer in the fridge before grabbing one for himself. The boys talk for a few before Theo gives me a hug and kiss goodbye.

When he shoves his tongue in my mouth, Colin says, "Ew, gross. I'll wait in the car." Theo laughs when he pulls away, telling me to arm the alarm when he leaves, adding that the hot tub is ready and uncovered for when he gets home, which has me squeezing my legs in anticipation.

We dig into our pizza, and Derek turns on our favorite reality show. "These two are terrible. They deserve each other," he says through a mouthful of pizza.

"The absolute worst," I say. I pour myself another glass of wine and get him a beer before digging into another slice.

"If this show does a season in Boston, I'm totally signing Colin up for it," Derek says, and I double over laughing.

There are so many things I adore about both of my brothers. I don't just love them because we're related. I genuinely like them because they're fantastic guys. Colin is the carefree, playful one—always quick with a joke and a total flirt. Derek is introspective and broody.

Both of them would give you the shirt off their backs, and I know that when they're ready, they'll both make incredible husbands and fathers. I'm staring at him, smiling at the thought of it when he does a double take and looks at me.

"What?" he asks.

I shrug my shoulders and take a sip of my wine. "Nothing. Just thinking about all three of us having kids one day and how fun it will be to watch them all grow up together." He stares at me like I've lost my mind. "What? Don't you want a family?"

He sits back and thinks about it. "Yeah. I do. I don't want to be alone the rest of my life. It's just hard to find someone here. The tourists look for a good time. It's not like the movie *Summer Catch* where the summer girl falls in love with the townie, and they live happily ever after."

"I'm sure there are plenty of local girls who'd be happy to shack up with you. You're a catch, Derek."

"It's getting harder and harder to find someone that Colin hasn't already slept with," he says with a laugh, but it doesn't reach his eyes. It feels forced.

"Well, don't settle for anyone who's less than amazing. Because that's what you deserve. And also because I won't allow my future children to have a bitch for an aunt."

"Sometimes I worry that I missed my chance," he says, his voice quiet, the words heavy.

I look at him in disbelief. "Missed your chance? What do you mean? Was there someone who got away?"

I can't recall the last time Derek had a serious relationship. He's much more reserved than Colin, but I know he's had plenty of company in the form of beautiful women over the years. While my mom might have herself convinced that he doesn't hook up with a lot of women, I know better.

He's quiet for a solid minute before he answers. "I think I should have made different choices a long time ago, Lyla. And if I did, maybe I wouldn't be so lonely."

It hurts my heart to hear the sadness in his voice. There are a million questions running through my head. *What choices? Who is she? Can we fix it now?* But I don't want to pry because if Colin is an open book, Derek is a steel trap.

"I thought you liked your solitude. I didn't realize you felt that way. I'm sorry I haven't paid more attention," I say softly.

"I do like my time alone. Don't get it twisted. But sometimes the endless disconnect with the women in my bed starts to feel too cold, too detached."

"Maybe it's time to let go of the regret you feel about those past choices, Derek. And focus on making decisions based on the here and now."

"Maybe," he says as he pounds the rest of his beer. "Let's do a shot. I need to shake off this emotional conversation part of the evening and get back to the trashy reality show. Besides, Colin is driving me home, so I want to take advantage of having a designated driver."

I would love to get deeper into it, learn more about whoever it is that haunts him, but this is his way of ending the conversation, and I have to respect that. Despite our close relationship, this is the most he's ever opened up about love life.

Without waiting for my response, he hops up from the couch and goes rooting through the liquor cabinet, coming back with a couple of glasses and the bottle of Cazcanes we just got.

"Theo would say that reposado is meant to be sipped, not thrown back," I say as he pours.

He looks around and says with a smirk, "Well, I don't see Theo around right now, so let's live a little."

He suckers me into two shots before I tell him I'm done. It's not long until I have a healthy buzz going on. So does Derek.

I hear the garage door open and turn to him. "Thanks for hanging with me tonight. I had fun."

"You're one of the most important people in the world to me, Ly. You don't have to thank me for hanging out with you. Same time next week?" he asks. I confirm with a nod. I get up to put the dishes in the sink.

The boys come barreling in through the door. "Hey, Sunshine," Theo says as he comes up behind me at the sink, wrapping his arms around me and nuzzling my neck.

"Guys, please! I can't do this PDA for the rest of my life," Colin says.

"When you find your soulmate you'll understand, Colin," Derek says, which causes all of us to laugh. "You guys behave yourselves with that shithead tonight?"

"It wasn't easy, but having Drew there helped keep tension from rising," Colin says.

"The fact that Colin only had one beer kept him in check, too," Theo adds. "Man, I want to punch that guy every time I look at him."

"That's mature," I say.

"Fuck being mature. He had a hand in what happened to you. I'm sure of it. And when your name came out of his mouth tonight, the urge to throttle him and throw him through the window was all-consuming. He makes my skin crawl. Thank god Colin was there to answer for me."

"Wait... Why is he bringing me up?" I ask.

"He was asking how you were. What you've been up to. Shit like that. I don't like it. He still thinks you live at your parents' house, FYI."

"Oooookay. Why? After everything that happened, and with you being gone for weeks, it's not surprising he would bring me up."

"Just don't want him knowing where you are," Theo replies.

Derek taps his fist on the coffee table and stands up. "Come on, bro. Let's get out of here before he kisses her again."

When I look at Theo, I notice he's also got a slight buzz going. He gives me a mischievous smile before asking, "Want to get naked in the hot tub?"

I don't answer him. I grab the tequila and pour each of us a glass before stripping in the kitchen, letting my clothes fall to the floor. Theo's eyes turn a dark blue, filled with desire and want. With an extra sway to my hips, I grab my glass and head out the door that leads to the patio.

## THIRTY-SEVEN

*theo*

SLEEP ESCAPES ME. Sex, especially heart-pounding makes-you-weak-in-the-knees fucking, is usually the best appetizer for a good night's sleep.

But even after the hour Lyla and I spent in the hot tub, with me getting her off time and time again before finally letting myself come, I still can't turn my brain off. I'm coiled like a snake and impending doom hangs over me.

It's after two when I get out of bed, moving slowly so I don't disturb Lyla. I quietly make my way to the kitchen and chug a glass of water. I grab a couple letters out of the box Lyla gave to me and prepare myself for the onslaught of emotions that come whenever I read them.

Theo,

Do you remember the first time you told me you loved me? Madaket Beach. We biked there from your grandparents' cottage and watched the sunset. And it was probably the most amazing sunset we'd ever seen. It was pure magic. The sun looked like it was literally melting into the water, setting the sky on fire in every shade of red, orange, and yellow you could imagine.

As I sat between your legs, with your arms wrapped around me, I remember thinking that if I had to pick one word to describe the view it would have been passionate. Because the sky looked like it exploded into a fiery ball of passion as it went down. And you whispered in my ear that you loved me. That you always would. It was the first time you ever said the words "on my life."

God, I remember it like it was yesterday. I close my eyes, and I can still see the sky on fire. Still hear the waves. Still smell you—that beachy woodsy scent you wore. Still hear your voice when you said that phrase. When did you stop? When did you decide that was an empty promise? That "on my life" was a hollow vow? Did you know that breaking it would crush me? Would change the way I thought about myself?About love? About the future? When did you stop loving me, Theo?

Lyla

I lean my head back against the couch and close my eyes. *Fuck me.* Her words are like a knife to my heart. Like a punch to the stomach. Like a kick in the balls. I deserve all three of them. For hurting her, for walking away, for making her doubt herself.

I know I have a lifetime to right these wrongs, but it still feels like I'll never be able to do or say enough to fix the hurt I caused. I decide not to torture myself with another and put them back in the box.

It's as I'm climbing back into bed that I see Diego in action. I watch in disbelief as he slowly climbs onto Lyla's chest and lies down, his face mere inches from hers. His purring sounds like a little motorboat, but it's not aggressively loud.

It doesn't take long for Lyla to stir, her eyes barely opening as a small smile graces her face. She whispers, "Thanks, buddy," before turning onto her side and throwing her arm across my chest. Diego curls up on her other side, still purring as he cuddles close.

I hold her and kiss her head, softly saying, "Never, Sunshine. I never stopped loving you." I don't know how long it takes, but eventually I fall into a fitful sleep.

* * *

I'm fucking exhausted when I wake up. I feel like I'm hungover but not from booze. From the overwhelming guilt that consumes me after reading Lyla's letter. I wake up before her and watch her sleep, savoring her warmth, her naked body wrapped up in mine. She has one arm resting on my chest, the other nestled under her chin. Her hair is splayed out on the pillow. She's a picture of tranquility.

I turn off my alarm before it goes off and slip out of bed. I'm sitting at the table drinking my coffee, scrolling Etsy for a gift I have in mind for her, when Lyla pads into the kitchen wearing one of my worn shirts and a pair of fuzzy socks.

"You didn't wake me up," she says, her voice sleepy.

"You looked so peaceful I thought you could use the extra sleep. I would have said goodbye, don't worry."

She pours herself a cup of coffee and sits next to me, putting her feet in my lap.

"You look exhausted, babe. Did you not sleep?" she asks.

"Not well," I admit, and she gives me a sympathetic look.

"Anything I can do?"

"Nope. Just promise me you'll be careful today."

"I promise. I actually don't plan on going anywhere. Want to get some writing done and figured I'd use the garage gym to get a workout in."

I nod, feeling relief that at least I'll know where she'll be all day. I still can't shake off the knot of fear in my stomach.

She walks me to the door when I leave, and I take her face in my hands, deepening a kiss I have no business starting. When she pulls back, I growl out, "Not enough." I pick her up, my hands gripping her ass, and turn so that her back is against the door. I kiss her like it's the last time I'm going to see her. The thought scares the shit out of me. "I regret starting this. I do not have time to fuck you this morning," I say when I finally put her down.

"Well, you can think about that all day then. Or maybe you can come home for a lunch quickie," she says with a wink.

"Yeah... It'll be really fun explaining that to my partner, who's your brother," I reply with a laugh. I give her one more peck before saying, "Let me know if you go anywhere. Doors stay locked. Don't stop by the station at all. As much as I'd love to see you, I don't want you around Clayton."

"Deal," she says, giving my ass a playful slap as I leave. I sit in my car for another minute or two before backing up, trying to shake the dread that threatens my sanity.

## THIRTY-EIGHT

*Lyla*

MY DAY IS a mix of productivity and slug-like behavior. I throw in a load of laundry before settling down at the kitchen table where I light a fall-scented candle and open my laptop. I bounce between my notes and my laptop, a pencil between my lips so I can easily scribble down thoughts as they come to me. I have a playlist of instrumental cover songs going at a low volume to keep me focused, and when I look at the clock, three hours have gone by.

I stand up to stretch, grabbing another cup of coffee when my phone rings. I roll my eyes and smile, assuming it's Theo checking in on me again, but I'm pleasantly surprised to see that it's my mom.

"Hey, Mom! What's up?"

"Hey, sweetie. I'm about to walk into the coffee shop. Want anything? I'll stop by."

"I think I met my coffee quota for today, but I'd love a green tea latte with almond milk. Thanks!"

"See you soon."

Twenty minutes later, she's ringing the bell, arms filled with our drinks from the Morning Current and a small box of donuts from the Glazed Gull. My mouth immediately starts watering. I let her in and wait for the inevitable text from Theo to make sure everything is copacetic, even though I'm certain he'll check the doorbell camera.

"What's all of this?" my mom asks, pointing to my computer and the notes I have scattered all over the place.

"Well, I decided to take the leap from freelance to fiction. I'm working on my first manuscript."

"Lyla! That's amazing, honey. Tell me all about it!"

"It's a romantic suspense story leaning heavily on the second chance trope. Feel like I have some good insight there." I open the donut box and immediately grab my favorite item on the menu—a cinnamon sugar donut that has a scoop of apple pie filling and caramel drizzle on top.

"Hah, you sure do. I can't wait to hear more about it as you continue to work on it. How are things here? You have a lightness to you that I haven't seen in a long time."

I smile because I know what she's saying is true. "Well, I think I'm finally where I'm supposed to be. I'm excited about what I'm writing. And I made an appointment with my therapist for later this week to deal with the residual nightmares and anxiety I've been having since the attack."

She nods, liking everything I'm telling her. "I'm glad to hear you reached out to her."

"She's been such a mainstay in my life for years now, but it's been a few months since I've had an appointment with her. I got lazy once I moved back, and honestly, just didn't want to face the gauntlet of emotions I was wrestling with since being in Theo's orbit again. It's time, though. The only way I'm going to move past what happened is by going through it again with her."

"Proud of you for taking control over your mental health. I

know it isn't always easy." She reaches over and gives my shoulder a squeeze.

My mom stays for another half hour as we finish our drinks and devour the scones and muffins she brought. Once she leaves, I plop down on the couch and mindlessly flip through channels until I find something to watch while I fold laundry.

Once the laundry is away and the kitchen is clean, I rummage through the fridge to find something to make for dinner, only to discover it's slim pickings, and I need to grocery shop tomorrow.

Theo texts me to tell me he should be leaving the station shortly. I ask him what he's craving and his response is simple —*you*. I smile and ponder the idea of being naked in the hot tub when he gets home from work.

I work on a list for the food store, and then, since I have some time before Theo gets home, I head out to the garage to squeeze in a quick workout.

I usually like getting them done early, but I needed to capitalize on the creative juices when they were flowing earlier. I open the garage door to get some air flow and start.

I'm no workout expert, but I know what works for my body —a solid mix of running, pilates with my mom, and strength training. I always stick to the basics when it comes to lifting, keeping my weights light since I'm just getting back into it.

I hear a car pulling up and assume it's Theo, so I finish the set of shoulder presses I'm working on.

When I hear, "Hey Lyla!" in a voice that is not Theo's, I nearly jump out of my skin. When I turn around, I come face-to-face with Clayton. He's wearing casual clothes, holding two pizzas and a twelve-pack of beer.

"Clayton, what are you doing here?" I ask. I've never been alone with him before, barely know him, actually. My spidey senses go on high alert immediately.

## THIRTY-NINE

*theo*

THE MINUTE I walk out my front door and hear Lyla lock it behind me, the floor drops out from under me. As someone who's been kept alive from instinct alone, I almost want to call out sick and spend the day watching Lyla like a hawk.

My shitty night sleep doesn't help matters. But I know she'd never let me, and I want to be at the station when we hear from the FBI analyst.

It's early and the roads are empty, allowing me to make it to the station in about ten minutes. I beat Colin, which is no surprise, but Chief Sullivan is already in his office.

I dump my gym bag at my desk and walk over to knock on his open door. He looks up at me from his desk. When he sits back and grabs his coffee, I take it as my invitation to come in. I plop down in one of the chairs.

"You don't even need to say it, Theo. I'm not happy, either. Once the clock hits eight, I'm going to give him a call."

I nod as I try to collect my thoughts. "I had such a bad feeling when I walked out the door today, Chief. I can't put my finger on it, but now I'm wondering if it's warranted or if it's just my head fucking with me." I lean forward, resting my elbows on my knees.

"I trust your gut over most other things, kid. It's because of you that we're still digging into him. Hang in there a little while longer. What's Lyla have planned for the day?" he asks.

"She's staying home. Writing and doing some house work."

"You two seem like you've settled into living together well."

When I look up at him, he's smiling. "Best thing I've ever done, sir." I return his smile. "I'm going to get some work done."

I'm almost to the door when he says, "Stay away from him today, Theo. You're wound tight, and it's not going to take much for you to snap. Without turning around, I nod my head in silent agreement as I leave.

The desks Colin and I use are in the middle of the room, facing each other. There are three other pairs of desks set up the exact same way in the open space.

Colin's just walking in the door when I sit down. He drops a brown bag next to a stack of papers I've been working on organizing before sitting down at his own desk.

"I stopped for bagel sandwiches on the way in," he says. "Figured you'd be stressing out and could use one."

"Thanks, dude," I reply, immediately opening the bacon, egg, and cheese sandwich. I wolf it down at warp speed.

"Damn, my sister not feeding you at home?" he asks.

"Actually, I've been cooking breakfast all week," I say between bites, and he rolls his eyes. "Maybe I've just been working up an appetite with all the late nights we've been having."

"Motherfucker. You are not allowed to talk about my sister

like that," he says pointing a finger at me. "In my head, you guys haven't even made it past first base." I cackle at that.

"You took it there, bro. How do you know we're not just staying up late working on puzzles?"

"You baited me! If you had a sister I was sleeping with, you would feel the same way," he says.

"You're just so easy to rile up."

"Asshole. Next time I won't get you a sandwich." He flips me the bird and picks up his coffee.

When Clayton walks in a little while later, it's like all the air is sucked out of the room. "Act normal, Theo," Colin mutters under his breath.

"Morning, boys. I didn't get a chance to workout this morning. You want to hit the gym at some point?" Clayton asks.

The fact that he can act completely normal around us, when I'm so convinced he's dirty, has me wanting to climb over my desk and deck him.

Colin answers for the both of us. "Yeah, if we're around when you want to do it, we're in but don't wait on us."

"Sounds good." He gives a nod before walking into the kitchen.

We spend the next few hours being productive as hell, which feels like an accomplishment in and of itself, considering my inability to focus.

I've checked on Lyla more times than usual, and she's already made a couple of comments about that. She sends me a selfie of her with Diego curled up in her lap. Her hair is up in a messy bun, a few loose pieces framing her face. She looks completely relaxed. I smile as I read her response.

**Lyla: All good here, Babe. The guard cat is sleeping on the job, though.**

**Me: What are you thinking for dinner?**

**Lyla: I'm going to cook takeout for dinner.**

I laugh out loud at that response.

**Me: Sounds good. You look hot.**

**Lyla: I'm a mess.**

**Me: I love messy. The messier the better.**

**Lyla: Let's see how messy we can get tonight.**

**Me: Fuck, Sunshine. I don't particularly want to walk around the station with a hardon.**

And if I don't end this conversation that's exactly what will happen.

**Me: Love you. See you soon.**

It's creeping up on four o'clock when Chief Sullivan bellows from his office, "Morgan! Sullivan! Get in here, now!" His tone has me jumping out of my seat and all but sprinting across the room.

Colin has the wherewithal to comment, "Jeez, what did we do now?"

"Shut the door," Chief says, his voice serious. He motions for us to come closer to the desk. "Smith, I have you on speaker now. Go ahead."

"This guy is as dirty as the day is long. I was in the field all day yesterday and this morning, so my apologies for the delay. It took me a while to figure it out, longer than I'd like to admit, but he has his shit buried deep."

*Motherfucking piece of shit.* Sometimes being right sucks.

Smith continues. "He's got money in a couple offshore accounts. And when I say money, I mean lots of it. Not sure how we didn't catch it earlier, but he's related to Hollman."

My body breaks into a sweat as my pulse quickens. My heart is pounding so loud I can feel it reverberate through my entire body. Any second I'm going to start seeing spots. I look at Chief and his face is white, like he can't believe what he's hearing.

I know he's kicking himself for missing this when background checks were done to hire Clayton. Smith continues to talk, but I can't tell you what he's saying. All I can think about is Lyla, the fact that she's alone in our house, and how that piece of human garbage is directly involved in everything that happened to her over the past month.

## FORTY

*Lyla*

"THEO DIDN'T TELL YOU?" Clayton asks as he slowly walks closer to me, like a panther stalking his prey. I resist the urge to back away from him. I don't want to show my cards—the cards that say I'm scared shitless—too early. I shake my head to say no. "Well, this is awkward. He invited us over for pizza and beer tonight. Figured he'd give you a break from cooking."

I don't cook. Anyone who knows me knows that. There isn't a snowball's chance in hell that Theo invited this man to dinner at our house tonight.

"Oh. No, he didn't mention it to me. Let me just call him real quick to confirm," I say, doing my best to keep my voice steady.

"No need to call. I'm here with the goods, so that's pretty good confirmation. Theo told me to grab the pies from Sal's. Probably should have gotten some wings, too," Clayton says.

Theo hates Sal's. He has since we were younger. He thinks the sauce is bland, and the crust is too thin. He would rather eat cardboard.

"Well, let me at least find out what time he's going to be

home. Wouldn't want you waiting for nothing in case he's still tied up at work," I offer as I casually look for my phone.

"Lyla... Let's just go inside. We can wait for him there, yeah?"

I weigh out my options, thinking of throwing a dumbbell at him and then running or knocking the pizza boxes out of his hand. I could book it out of the garage.

But when he gets all up in my personal space, I realize I might be completely out of options. I try my best to play it cool, but inside, my heart beats a million times a minute.

"Sure. We can head inside. I'm glad you got two pies because I told Derek he could mooch dinner off of us tonight, too. That guy can put back a lot of pizza. He should be here any second." I say it light-heartedly as I slowly walk toward the door to the house.

I try to buy time by pausing and saying I want to grab my water bottle, but Clayton is so close to me that there's no room for me to move. He keeps walking which effectively forces me to open the door and enter the house.

The door from the garage opens into the kitchen, and I stop there and hold out my hands, offering to take the pizza boxes. He ignores my offer and places them on the counter. Neither of us says a word. Instead, we stare at each other for what feels like eternity, sizing each other up.

Eventually, I just nod at him, not in a way of surrendering to whatever it is he plans to do, but more so to show him that I get it now. I know why he's here. Theo's gut was spot on, as usual.

I teeter between being scared out of my wits and being beyond pissed off that this piece of shit asshole has been involved the entire time. Here he is—a wolf in sheep's clothing, forcing me into a corner in my own home.

And he doesn't even have good taste in pizza.

"Why? Hollman is dead." I finally ask.

He puts the case of beer on the counter and opens it. He cracks a can and offers it to me, but I shake my head no. I want to kick myself for rejecting it because I could have thrown it at his head and made a run for it. He reaches behind his back and pulls out a gun, placing it on the counter in front of him.

"He was my cousin. Did you know that?" he asks before taking a sip. I tell him no. "So much for being an investigative journalist."

The fact that this dickbag just insulted me tips the scales toward being pissed off rather than scared.

"I never said I was, asshole."

"That smart mouth of yours is going to get you into more trouble, Lyla."

"Seems like I've already gotten myself into quite a pickle, Clayton," I snap back. "So why don't you get to the point. Hollman is dead, and I offer zero condolences for your loss."

"While I'd love to go into more detail, it's only a matter of time before your pain in the ass boyfriend shows up. With Marcus dead, Ryan Hughes took over. Seemed like the natural progression of things—"

Because I can't help myself, I interrupt him.

"And why would Hughes give a shit about me? He should be thanking me for paving the way for him to be promoted."

"Oh, he sends his gratitude. But this is a dirty business. Lots of snakes in the grass. Hughes doesn't really love the idea of keeping those who were closest to Marcus around. Doesn't trust their loyalty. I fall into that category." He takes a long pull of his beer. "So, I made him an offer."

"I'm going to assume that offer has something to do with why you're in my house with a gun pointed at me."

"Ah, not just a pretty face, Lyla. But yes, you're correct. I'm not interested in losing the streams of income I have from this organization, so to prove my loyalty, I told him I'd get rid of you once and for all."

I nod in understanding and will myself not to cry. The realization that this is happening, that he's here to kill me, sinks in. If I can get the gun away from him, I might have a fighting chance. If I try to run and he catches me, I'm fucked. "I can see your mind working there, doll. There's no way out of this."

"Was this why you came to Sandpiper Cove?" I ask, trying to stall, to keep him talking.

"Nope. But you can only imagine how thrilled Marcus was at this happy coincidence. Your father, your brother... They've always been good to me. I feel bad I have to do this but it is what it is."

I bite my lip as I take in all of this new information. The fact that this man can talk so casually about taking my life is eerie as fuck.

"So what's the plan? Shoot me and scurry on off like the rat you are?" I ask.

He takes a few steps closer, making it less likely for me to snatch the gun. "Well, as much as I'd like to stick it to your boyfriend and have my way with you first, I don't think I can risk it. That's what fucked it up for Scottie McDavid. He couldn't resist the chance to get his hands on you, and I admit, I've thought about it." He's so close his chest touches me. "Thought about getting my hands on that body." He leans forward and brings his mouth to my ear. "See how tight that cunt is. Your boyfriend has been so fucking happy every morning when he comes into work. You must be a damn rockstar in bed, Lyla." He steps back a little and takes another sip of beer. "But alas, there's no time."

"Well... I guess you better get to it then," I say. I put my hands on my hips in an effort to hide the fact that they're shaking.

I don't know why I'm goading this man, but the reality is, I need to make a move because this is fucking torture.

Do I want to die? Hell no. The impact this would have on my parents, on my brothers, crushes me. The impact it would have on Theo nearly brings me to my knees. I always wondered if that whole "life flashes before your eyes right before you die" thing was real. I can confirm it is.

Because as I stand here, trying to think of what my next move is, I see everything I'm going to miss with Theo—getting married, writing our vows, our first dance, having babies, seeing him as a dad, vacations, hard moments, laughter, concerts, sunrises and sunsets, publishing a novel, coffee in bed, Nantucket, stargazing, watching our grandkids romp around the beach, the big things, the little things. I could go on and on, but I have to stop myself because I don't want to cry.

I won't show this man my fear, and I won't go down without a fight.

*theo*

"WHERE THE FUCK IS, CLAYTON?" I ask, not caring that I'm interrupting Smith. Colin goes to the door and opens it, rushing to the locker room and asking everyone if they've seen him. No one has.

I hear Drew say something like he saw him walk out a little while ago, but he didn't say goodbye, so he's not sure if he was leaving for good or to go somewhere else. Colin disappears, going outside to check the parking lot.

When he sprints back into the office, he says, "His patrol car is here, but no one has seen him."

I look at Chief and shake my head. Chief's face is hard, his eyes angry as he says, "Smith, we've gotta go. We don't have eyes on him. I know you have more to tell us, and I want to hear it all, but right now—"

Smith interrupts him. "Get to your daughter. I'll send you everything I have, and I'm going to talk to the lead on the Hollman case to fill them in. We'll talk more after you know she's safe." He hangs up, and we all make our way to the door.

"Every available officer needs to be on their way to Morgan's house STAT. No lights or sirens." He shouts out my address twice. "Do not communicate via radio—cell phones only. Keep it off the channels. Clayton is considered armed and dangerous. My daughter is the priority."

The small station flips into a frenzy, and we're out the door in seconds. I sprint to my car with Colin hot on my trail.

"I'll drive!" he says, and I toss him my keys. Once we're in the car, I call Lyla but she doesn't answer. I send her a text and call her again. Colin fishes his phone out of his pocket and passes it to me. "Try her from mine. Just in case."

I try again and nothing.

"Fuck!" I yell, throwing his phone at the dashboard. "She's a fucking sitting duck, and this time, Derek isn't on his way to save her." I grind my teeth together, not stopping until I feel a shot of pain go through my jaw.

"She's going to be fine. We'll deal with this. Now check your emotions and lock in." Colin is calm with his words, but the panic in his voice betrays him.

I pull my gun out of my holster and make sure it's loaded and return it, keeping the holster unsnapped for easy access once we pull up. The next two miles feel like we're treading through quicksand until we finally pull onto my street.

He slams on the brakes when he gets to my driveway and throws the car in park. Clayton's personal car is parked in front of my house, and the garage door is open. We're both out of our seats like bats out of hell.

My heart feels like it's going to beat out of my chest. The fact that I have no idea what we're about to walk into scares the shit out of me. We unholster our guns as we head toward the garage. Lyla's water bottle and phone are on the floor by the gym equipment. We make our way to the door that leads into the kitchen.

To my surprise, it's unlocked, and I enter slowly, Colin

right behind me. The kitchen is quiet, but when I get to the family room, I stop dead in my tracks.

Time stands still and my life, our future, flashes before my eyes when I see Clayton and Lyla. He has one arm wrapped around her neck, using her body to block his. She's silent but tears spill from her eyes. Clayton's other hand holds a gun to her head.

## FORTY-TWO

*Lyla*

"I THINK I will take that beer, Clayton," I say, pointing to the case on the counter.

He reaches over and pulls one from the box, cracking the top and passing it over to me without his eyes ever leaving mine. I take a small sip and lick my lips before winding up and launching the can at him with as much force as I can muster.

The second it leaves my hand, I turn to sprint toward the front door. The only perk of him being so close to me is that I don't miss. I don't know where I hit him, but based on the fact that he calls me a bitch, it's safe to assume I make contact.

I'm halfway through the family room when he fires off two rounds, one that's so close to my ear I can feel it fly by. I freeze. I'm too far from the front door to make it... There's no way he'll miss again, not with me this close.

Considering he's a cop, I'm shocked he missed me the first two times. Makes me think it's intentional, and he's just toying with me.

I turn so that we're facing each other again. I throw my hands up and ask, "How do you want to do this, Clayton? I'd rather not go down without a fight, but if your plan is to toy with me because you want to tell Theo you tortured me before you killed me, I won't give you the satisfaction."

"I hadn't really thought about doing that, but it might be fun to tell Theo how you screamed and pleaded for your life before I finally put you out of your misery," he says. I'm pretty certain he's actually considering it.

*Jesus, how did no one pick up on the fact that this guy is a full-blown sociopath?*

"Fuck you," I spit out. His shirt is wet from a few drops of beer, and I can see a small knick on his eyebrow from where the can hit him. It's bleeding but not enough to be an actual distraction.

He starts losing his patience with me. I can tell by the way he stomps over to where I'm standing. I suppose the fact that he grabs me by the throat and calls me a bitch is also a pretty good indicator. I slap at his hands but it does little to help me.

He pushes me up against the wall, hand still on my throat, when I change my strategy and start kicking. I try to make contact with his groin, knowing it will give me the best chance of him letting go. He growls and slaps me across the face.

I'm getting a little fucking tired of these assholes putting their hands on me, and it lights a fire inside me. I give up slapping and grabbing at his hands and instead flatten my own hand and jab him in the throat as hard as I can.

He gags and his visceral reaction is to let go of my throat to grab his own. He drops his gun, and the second he does, I kick him in the balls as hard as I can. I gasp in relief and try to push past him so I can get my ass to the front door, to freedom.

He's still coughing but grabs me by the hair before I'm out of reach. He yanks me back to him, this time my back to his front. I yelp in pain as tears spring to my eyes. His movements are rough and he has no problem manhandling me as he squats down to pick up his firearm.

"You fucking bitch. I felt bad before but now I can't wait to put a bullet in your fucking head," he hisses, spitting as he talks.

It's at that moment the garage door opens. Clayton clearly hears it as well because he tightens the grip he has around me and holds the gun to the side of my head, the cold metal kissing my temple. I can't stop the tears that come.

I know it's Theo. I can feel it in my bones. This is my worst nightmare, because not only is this guy about to kill me, he's going to make Theo watch.

I don't say a word, and I don't attempt to stop my silent sobs. I want to close my eyes, but I'm afraid if I do, I'll never see Theo again.

*theo*

I SLOWLY MOVE into the family room with Colin right behind me. I scan the space, quickly taking stock of the situation. We don't even have to communicate about how we need to handle this scenario. It comes from years of training and the trust and faith in a partner who's like a brother. I know he'll take the lead with dialogue and the rest will be up to me.

I take a few deep breaths to steady myself and focus on the task at hand. I swallow back the fear that rises like bile in my throat.

What we're dealing with in the present moment makes her attack a few weeks ago seem like child's play, and that's something I never imagined saying.

Maybe it's because the threat was already neutralized by the time I got there, whereas this time there's a very real chance I could lose her right in front of my eyes. Chills run down my spine, and I start to spiral. The fear whips around me, threatening to choke me, sucking all of the air out of the room.

This is the worst fucking time for me to toe the line of having a panic attack, but the fact that I'm facing the possibility of losing Lyla all while having a fucking front row seat shakes me to the core. I'm having a hard time regaining focus as every possible way this scenario could go wrong runs through my mind— Clayton shooting her, Clayton snapping her neck, Lyla getting hit by a bullet from my gun because Clayton uses her as a shield.

I want to kill this man with my bare fucking hands. But I tuck that anger away, and my face becomes a mask of indifference. I make eye contact with Lyla and give her a barely perceptible nod.

"Took you long enough to figure it out. Not very impressive detective work, boys," Clayton says. His voice, his entire demeanor, is different from the Clayton we've known. There's an edge of nastiness to him, an arrogance, because he knows he has the upper hand.

"In Theo's defense, he's been saying it for a while now," Colin says.

Clayton scoffs in disgust. "Bet you're wishing you guys never came back from Nantucket, eh, Theo? She's feisty as fuck, man, and this body... Bet you're going to miss it when I'm done here."

My hands tighten around my gun, my knuckles surely white from my grip, but I don't outwardly react. Seeing this piece of shit with his hands on her, a gun to her head, has me seeing red.

I keep still as I swallow down my anger and fight to keep that rage in check. In an attempt to keep focused on his actions more than his words, I chew on the side of my cheek. Eventually I'm met with the tangy, metallic taste of blood.

I hear more cars pulling up to the house, doors slamming shut and shouts coming from outside. Without lowering his weapon or looking down, Colin reaches into his pocket for his phone and tells Siri to call his dad before bringing it up to his ear.

"Yeah, they're here. You can see the current situation from the front window. Nope, you guys should all stay outside. Don't think that will help at all. That's not a bad idea, though." He hangs up without saying goodbye. "So what's the plan, Clayton? You know if you shoot her, you're dead. There's no way you're walking out of here alive, so how about you take a minute to think about how you want to handle this."

The reality of his situation, the fact that he's surrounded by cops and there's no real way out for him, must finally dawn on him. There's a crack in his facade of confidence.

His eyes narrow and his lips are in a straight line as he ponders his options. When he digs his gun deeper into the side of Lyla's head. She squirms in discomfort.

The key to getting out of this with Lyla in one piece is making sure she keeps as still as possible, so I make quick, pleading eye contact with her the second she moves in hopes she picks up on the fact that her movements cause a shift in my concentration.

The woman turns into a statue, no matter how much he moves his gun, so I know she understands. Colin continues to distract him with conversation, slowly moving closer to Clayton as they talk. This action has Clayton slightly shift his stance.

"This is why you came to Sandpiper?" Colin asks, casual and cool.

"Your sister asked the same thing, but the answer is no. I needed to get out of the city and always wanted to try my hand at coastal living. Just a happy accident that I ended up working for the very man whose daughter caused so much trouble for my cousin," Clayton says.

"Ahh, yes, your cousin Marcus. Such a pillar of the community. Sorry for your loss. Heard he cried like a baby when he got shanked," Colin says.

"You know... I was feeling bad about having to do this since you and your dad were always cool to me. I even said it to Lyla earlier. Tell him, Lyla." He jerks her body, his way of encouraging her to speak.

"He said it," she confirms, her voice shaking.

"See? But now I'm glad you'll get to see it happen, you arrogant asshole. With these close quarters, her blood will be all over you."

He doesn't loosen his grip on her, but Clayton does shift again, moving Lyla slightly off-center. It's wild to me that, even as a cop, Clayton doesn't realize he's falling into the trap of distraction.

"And then I'll send your heart back to your mother in a fucking box," Colin spits, losing his own composure for just a split second. He takes a breath before he switches gears to ask Clayton about Scottie McDavid.

This questioning manages to confirm that Clayton was indeed the one feeding McDavid information about Lyla and her whereabouts. While Clayton brags about his brilliance, he opens himself up to my line of fire.

This kind of scenario requires you to think quickly and act even faster. I have to gauge when to take the shot. The goal is to get him in a position that will give me the cleanest shot, but it has to be done without him noticing.

Between my military and cop training, I've fired thousands of rounds, but this will be the most important shot I've ever taken in my life. It's not just Clayton's life that hangs in the balance here; it's Lyla's and, by default, mine as well.

It's now or never.

## FORTY-FOUR

*Lyla*

CLAYTON IS A SUPREMELY arrogant cockgoblin who can't stop talking about himself. He clearly has an overinflated sense of self-worth and is not nearly as smart as he thinks he is.

As he rambles about how dumb everyone is for not realizing they were working with the enemy, he shifts the way he's holding me.

I'm no longer directly in front of him, but off to his side, which leaves him more vulnerable.

After a few more minutes of talking, Colin takes another step closer to us. Theo still hasn't moved a muscle, his feet firmly planted and gun still raised.

He doesn't want me to move. I could tell when his eyes flashed to mine earlier that he was trying to tell me how important it was. So, despite the fact that my body is literally trembling from fear, I try to stay as still as humanly possible.

I focus on the conversation that unfolds. If I let my mind wander back to all of the things I'm afraid I'll miss out on if this asshole puts a bullet in my head, I can't promise I'd be able to stand here like a statue. I can't let my thoughts splinter.

Despite the fear that threatens to take over my body, I will myself to stay rooted where I am.

Colin keeps him talking, taking one more small step toward us, lowering his gun slightly to appear as less of a threat. I'm not sure how much more of this purgatory I can handle.

Turns out I don't have to wait much longer, because about ten seconds later, Theo fires, executing a perfect headshot. A spray of blood hits me. It's so loud my ears ring, and the next twenty seconds are a bit of a shit show.

There's lots of swearing. The hand that was holding the gun to my head falls away, Clayton falling backward. In an instant, Colin is next to me all but shoving me out of the way.

I collapse to my knees and bury my head in my hands, sobbing. I don't know if it's from relief, from fear, from the erupting chaos, or from the fact that there's a dead body mere feet from me and the man's blood is on my skin. The smell alone is going to haunt my dreams.

Colin takes a step back once Theo is at my side, his arms wrapped around me so tightly I can barely breathe. I look up and see the front door swing open.

My father comes barreling in, officers behind him and entering through the garage door. It's like deja vu—me being a crumpled mess on the floor of a living room as cops pour in with their guns drawn.

Without saying a word, Theo stands up and takes me in his arms, moving me into the kitchen. We sit on the floor, and he holds me as I fall apart. With my head on his chest, I can feel the erratic beat of his heart.

Despite the soothing circles he rubs on my back and the soft voice he uses as he says, "It's over, baby," in my ear over and over again, this experience has shaken him to the core as well.

"Don't run," I desperately plead through my tears, grabbing his face with my hands. "I can see the fear in your eyes, Theo. And I can feel your heart racing. Don't run." I see a flash of hurt in his eyes, but it quickly passes.

"Never, Lyla. Only toward you." I throw my arms around his neck, holding on to him for dear life.

After a few minutes, my heart no longer feels like it's pounding out of my chest. My tears subside, and my body stops trembling. His hands go to my shoulders and he takes a good look at me, checking for any bruises or marks.

"Your ear, baby," he says as his fingers brush the top of it. With everything that happened, I completely forget about the sting that came over me when Clayton fired that first bullet. Judging from the way involuntarily winced at Theo's light touch, I'd say the bullet definitely nicked me.

"It doesn't even hurt. I thought I'd never see you again, Theo. And then I thought your last image of me would be him killing me in front of your eyes."

As if he knows it's the only way to stop me from talking, he leans forward and kisses me. His lips brush against mine, once, twice, three times. When I don't pull away he runs his tongue along my lips, as if asking me to open.

He takes his time as he explores my mouth. When I groan into him, he moves a hand to the back of my head. That slow, lazy kiss quickly turns into one that packs a lot of heat and a sense of urgency. As if we both just remembered what could have happened. His tongue moves in and out of my mouth as we battle for control over the kiss. It's not until we hear a cough from behind us that we break apart.

He touches my forehead with his. "We're going to get through this, Lyla. And we're going to have everything we ever wished for. You and me," he says before pulling me back in for a hug.

My dad comes into the kitchen and breathes a sigh of relief. He squats down next to us, and all but yanks me out of Theo's arms so that he can hug me himself.

"You okay, kiddo?" he asks, his voice shaky. I nod and tell him the blood isn't mine as he continues to embrace me. When he finally pulls back, I ask him to help me up. I'm uninjured aside from my ear but nervous my legs will be like jelly.

When we stand up, my dad pulls me in for another hug. "I don't know how we're going to explain this to your mother," he says with a sigh.

"Maybe we can just not tell her?" I recognize that it's a weak attempt at humor and it does nothing to calm the nerves that rip though my body.

"I'm so sorry, Lyla. This whole time he was tied in with Hollman. I don't know how he got by our background checks, but I intend to figure it out. I can't believe I hired that piece of shit," my dad says, his eyes darkening as his tone gets lower.

Before I can respond, someone calls his name from the family room, and he tells me he'll be back. Theo suggests we go outside and leads me to the back door when something dawns on me.

"Diego! Where is he?" I panic.

Theo tells me that he's sure he's just hiding from the commotion.

"Theo, he fired two shots before you got here. What if one of them hit him?! Please! I won't move a muscle until you come back."

I push him back into the family room, and he makes his way through the crowded room toward the hallway that leads to our room. Colin comes over to me while I wait and hugs me.

"You're in one piece?" he asks, leaning back to give me a once-over. I nod, and when I look in his eyes, I see they're watering. "I need a fucking drink, Lyla." He gives me a kiss on the top of my head and then goes back to the officers.

Seconds crawl by while I wait for Theo to come back out, but eventually, he makes his way back into the family room with a shell-shocked Diego.

When they reach me, I breathe a sigh of relief and grab him out of Theo's arms, holding him close to me so I can feel his purrs. Theo guides us through the kitchen and out the back door. We sit on the patio couch without saying a word. I hold Diego, Theo holds me, and I don't even realize I start crying again. This time not out of fear but relief, until Theo wipes away the tears.

*theo*

IF I COULD BRING Clayton back to life for the sole purpose of getting to kill him again, I'd do it. Especially when I see the nick on her ear which was most definitely the result of a bullet graze.

I don't consider myself to be a blood-thirsty person, but when it comes to the woman I love, I guess I am.

As I hold her trembling body in my arms, I will myself to calm down. My heart feels like it's going to beat out of my chest. I close my eyes while I attempt to slow down my breathing, but it just makes things worse.

Even though I feel the weight of Lyla in my arms, with my eyes shut, all I see is Clayton with a gun to her head. I see her looking at me, those eyes begging me to save her life. I heard her voice shaking when he made her answer a question.

I can't unsee these things and I have no idea how to deal with it. I understand now why Derek was having nightmares after he walked in on her being attacked. I foresee a lot of sleepless nights in my future.

We're sitting on the patio when Chief Sullivan comes outside to let us know we need to be interviewed about what happened. It would be a conflict of interest for him to interview any of us, so he mentions that Deputy Chief Gallagher is on his way to speak with Colin, Lyla, and myself.

Chief says he'll sit in on the interview with Lyla and reassures her that it's just a formality. I nod in understanding. I'm not worried about myself or Colin. It was a clean shot, and we handled the situation perfectly, especially considering our connection to the victim. I just hate that Lyla will have to relive the entire scenario again.

Lori comes tearing through the gate and into the backyard, her eyes frantic until they find Lyla. She rushes over to where we sit on the couch.

"Lyla, you're okay? Oh my god. Are you okay? The blood?!" she asks as she wipes tears from her face.

"I'm good, Mom. The blood isn't mine."

Lori squats down and throws her arms around both of us.

"Oh, thank god. When your dad called he barely said anything, just to get over here. He said you were fine, but I needed to see for myself." Lori stands tall again, yanking me up by the hand to pull me into another hug. "You're okay, too?" She looks me up and down, searching for harm.

"Yup. We're all in one piece. Here, take my seat."

Lori sits down next to her daughter and wraps an arm around her before zeroing in on the wound on Lyla's ear.

Chief sticks his head out the back door and motions for me to join him. As we go into the family room, I see that Deputy Chief Gallagher has arrived and is assessing the scene before mentioning to Colin that he'd like to speak with him. I tell them to head down the hallway to the office and use that space.

It only takes about twenty minutes before they're back in the room, and he's motioning for me to join him. I ask him for one second, just so I can stick my head back outside to check on Lyla.

Logically, I know she's fine. Clayton is dead, the house is swarming with cops, and she has her parents and Colin with her, but the idea of her being out of my sight makes my stomach churn. Coming so close to losing her has me on edge, but I know I need to get this interview over with.

It takes about a half an hour to go through all of the questions, and at the end, Deputy Chief Gallagher assures me that we're all good. He stands up with me, commends me for a job well-done, and shakes my hand before telling me that he's glad we're all okay. He follows me through the house and outside so he can speak with Lyla next.

Derek arrives while I'm in the office. When he sees me, he immediately comes over to give me a hug. Not a bro hug either, but a real one.

Chief tells us to go hang out in the front yard while Lyla talks to Gallagher, stressing that we are to stay out of everyone's way and not set foot in the house while they work on the crime scene.

I squat down in front of Lyla, taking her face in my hands to ask if she's okay. She nods yes. "I'll be right out front. I'm going to send the medic back to look at your ear."

Derek, Colin, and I walk through the gate to get to the front of the house. As promised, I head right over to the medic and send him to the yard, letting him know it's just a graze and likely doesn't need stitches.

"Guys... What the actual fuck?" Derek asks as we stand around. Colin and I fill him in on everything—what we found out from the analyst, what happened when we got to the house, what we learned from Colin's conversation with Clayton. "Thank god for your expert shot, Theo."

"And my excellent conversation skills," Colin says. I look at Colin and blow out a breath.

"I'll never admit to saying this, but you were picture-perfect in there, bro. I thought we were going to lose him when you threatened to send his mother his heart in a box, but you reined it back in. Textbook execution," I say to him. And because I'm overcome with emotion, I reach out and grab his shoulder, pulling him in for a hug.

"Scariest moments of my life," he says, completely serious now. "But I'll never forget your praise. 'You were *picture-perfect.*' Going to get it put on a mug for everyone at the station."

I call him an asshole and slap his back. I know he's not bullshitting me, and there will, without a doubt, be a box of mugs with my words on them at work in the very near future.

Lori pops her head through the gate to say they're all done and we rejoin Lyla, her parents, and Deputy Chief Gallagher in the back. Unable to keep myself from touching her for another second, I scoop Lyla up and sit on the couch with her in my lap.

"This was a clean shoot, sir," Deputy Chief Gallagher says to Lyla's dad. "Not that I doubted these guys for a second, but better safe than sorry when it comes to covering our asses since he was one of our own. You boys earned yourself a week or so of administrative leave while paperwork is being processed. You'll need to come in to read it over and sign it, obviously. Lyla, I'm so sorry you went through this. We're going to get things wrapped up here as quickly as possible, but I'd recommend you find somewhere else to stay tonight."

I figured he'd say that. While I'd love nothing more than to hop on the last ferry of the day and get us over to Nantucket, I know it'll give everyone a piece of mind if we stay with Lyla's parents instead.

"Sleepover party at the Sullivan house tonight. That works for you, Sunshine?" I ask. She nods in agreement. "I'll come back tomorrow and get everything cleaned up, and we'll go from there."

Her brothers say they'll meet me in the morning to help out. Because I'm sure the family room is still a bloody mess, I tell Lyla to stay put, that I'll go pack us a bag, and then we can head over. It's all Chief can do to get Lori to leave her side, but he convinces her that we'll be right behind her.

* * *

An hour later we're at Lyla's parents house. We're showered and in cozy clothes, sitting on the back patio with a fire going in the Solo Stove. Lyla is curled up next to me while Diego stalks a fly in the yard.

"I ordered Mexican food from Taco Cat. Derek is going to pick it up on his way over," Lori says, stepping onto the patio to join us.

"Did you get nachos?" Lyla asks. They've always been the way to her heart.

"Of course, with extra jalapeños, too. I know the drill," Lori replies.

We have an easy conversation while we wait for Derek to arrive with the food. Lyla looks exhausted but refreshed. I still haven't heard about what happened before Colin and I got to the house this afternoon, but I don't want to bring it up when she's finally calmed down. I know she went over everything with Gallagher, and she'll tell me when she's ready to talk about it, but I'm dying to know.

Derek arrives with the food and we move into the kitchen to eat. The mood is relaxed, like the tension has finally started to dissipate. Colin raises his beer to make a toast. "Cheers to Lyla being okay. To that piece of shit being dead. And to Theo, who said, and I quote, that I was picture-perfect today."

This elicits laughter from all of us.

Eventually, the boys leave and Lyla's parents head to bed. I follow Lyla into her bedroom, and she closes the door behind me. "Gonna be weird sleeping in clothes," she says.

"Hah, yeah. But under your parents' roof there's no other option."

Once we're both in bed, I roll to my side so that we're facing each other and pull her close to me, letting my leg fall on top of hers. With one arm above our heads and the other wrapped around her, I rub her back. "Fuck, Lyla. I've never been so scared," I finally say with a raspy voice. Her eyes fill with tears.

"I knew it the second he showed up at the house... He was there to hurt me. I tried to stall for as long as I could, hoping and praying you would get home in time."

I close my eyes and will myself not to think about what could have happened if Colin and I got there even just a minute or two later.

She keeps talking. "I chucked a beer can at his head and tried to run. That's when he fired the two shots, but I think he did that just to fuck with me. He could have easily hit me... I think he just wanted to prolong the torment a little bit. When he got close enough, I tried to kick and scratch wherever I could, hoping to do damage. Then you guys got there. Theo, I thought he was going to kill me in front of you. I was saying goodbye to you in my head over and over again, thinking about all of the things we would miss out on."

"I'm proud of you, Lyla. You were strong as hell throughout the whole ordeal. I'm in awe of how resilient you are."

I didn't think we could get any closer, but she gently pulls at the necklace I have around my neck and burrows deeper into my arms.

"I'm sorry you had to kill someone for me," she says softly.

"I'm not. I don't mean to sound cavalier when I say that, but I'm not, Lyla. I only wish I could have done it before he held a gun to your head," I say, trying not to get worked up again.

"Did you know? Is that why you and Colin came?"

I tell her about the phone call with Smith, what he found out, and how he pieced things together. How we all bolted from the station, keeping things off the airway in case Clayton had his radio on him. She listens to everything quietly, nodding her head a few times as I explain.

"And you and Colin are both in the clear, right? No charges or anything?" she asks with concern in her voice.

"All clear, baby. You heard the deputy chief. Smith had more intel to give us, but he warned us to get to you first, that he'd fill us in on the rest later. I'm sure it'll further prove Clayton's ties to Hollman's organization. Your dad will speak with him tomorrow, bring the feds up to speed with what happened today, see if they can take down anyone else with the information. But you don't need to worry about any of that."

"When I asked him why he said it was because the new guy wanted to get rid of the guys closest to Hollman. That he offered to kill me to prove he could be loyal to the new boss," she says.

"That sounds par for the course with these scumbags. It's over, Lyla. Try and get some sleep and we can talk more tomorrow. I don't want you going to bed with this shit in your head."

She leans up to kiss me and tells me she loves me.

"Love you, too, baby. So much."

Her exhaustion must finally catch up with her because eventually the hand that holds my chain becomes lax.

I play with her hair, going over the entire scene in my head. I'm afraid to close my eyes, afraid of the nightmares that will most definitely come.

## FORTY-SIX

*theo*

I HAVE a fitful night's sleep, trying not to toss and turn because I don't want to disturb Lyla. She sleeps like a rock, but I don't get more than a couple hours throughout the entire night.

As predicted, every time I close my eyes, I'm greeted with terrible visions of what could have gone wrong. I give up on sleep for good sometime after six and just soak in the sound of her rhythmic breathing while she sleeps next to me.

Despite being wide awake, I stay in bed until Lyla wakes up a little after eight. We throw on clothes and make our way into the kitchen, where her mom is making oatmeal.

"I'm going to head to the house. Your brothers are going to meet me there so we can assess the damage and get it cleaned up," I say. Lyla makes a cup of coffee for herself and then pours some in a travel mug for me.

"Okay. I'll just hang here with my mom, if that's okay. Not sure I'm ready to go into the house yet."

"There's no rush or time frame you need to conform to, Sunshine. When you're ready, I'll take you home. Love you" I lean down and kiss her before leaving.

Colin and Derek pull in behind me at my place. When we go in, I see that it's not terrible, but we have our work cut out for us. The task list includes clean the blood stains from Clayton's head shot, patch the holes from the two rounds he got off, eventually paint those spots once the spackle dries, and thoroughly clean the family room and kitchen since there were so many people coming and going.

Derek will likely have the holes patched before Colin and I even get started. While we break for lunch, I tell the guys I need to duck out for a few errands.

"What could be more important than making sure the house is up to snuff for my sister to come back home to?" Derek asks.

"Well, if you must know, Derek, the stone I picked out for Lyla's engagement ring came in yesterday, and the jeweler wants me to approve it before she puts it in the setting," I reply, giving him a sheepish smile.

Colin jumps up out of his chair and reaches over to give me a one-armed hug. "Fuck yeah, bro! I'm fucking amped. Does she have any idea? When are you going to propose? Did you ask my dad yet?" We stare at him. "What? I'm excited for you two crazy kids. Give me a break. I love love."

Derek calls him a pussy under his breath.

"She doesn't have a clue so don't say a thing. Not sure but if we head back to Nantucket, I want to do it there. Stopping at the station to see your dad is my second errand. That cover all your questions?" I ask Colin. He nods in satisfaction. "Loose lips sink ships, Colin," I warn.

"Get out of here, bro. We'll finish getting the house in order and wait until you get back." Derek says, reaching over to shake my hand. I bid the guys farewell and head out.

It doesn't take long to get to the jewelry store. Dana sent me a few pictures of the stone options she got in, and I already know which one I'm choosing. She insisted I come see it in person before she moved ahead, though. She puts the options on display in front of me, and I immediately zero in on the oval one.

"This is the one," I say, holding the yellow sapphire up.

A yellow stone for the woman who has always been the brightest light in my life. I have no idea what I'm looking at in terms of gemstone specifics, but it shimmers and sparkles under the fluorescent lighting.

"It's going to be exquisite in the setting you picked, Theo." She takes the stone from me and holds it up to the rose-gold setting.

"It's perfect. How quickly can you get it set?"

"I can have it done by tomorrow morning, first thing. That work?"

"Yup. Shoot me a text when it's ready, and I'll grab it." If Lyla wants to head out to Nantucket for a few days, I want to be able to bring it with me.

My next stop is the police station, and I say quick hellos to everyone as I walk to Chief Sullivan's office. He's surprised to see me, but I tell him everything is okay before he opens his mouth to ask. I close the door and sit down.

"What's up, son? I've been going back and forth with the feds all day. Figured I'd give you the update when I got home from work."

"Can I marry Lyla?" I blurt out. I'm such a fucking idiot. I practiced an entire speech on my way here, but it all flies out the window. He gets the biggest smile on his face and stands up.

"It's about damn time, Theo. I have watched you love that girl since you were kids. There is no one—*no one*—on this planet I trust more than you to keep her safe and give her the life she deserves." He walks around his desk, and I reach my hand out to shake his. He knocks it out of the way and grabs me by the shoulder, pulling me in for a hug.

"Thank you, sir. She's the love of my life, and I'll never let a thing happen to her."

"I know that, Theo. Can I tell Lori?"

"Can she keep it a secret?" I ask and he laughs.

"That's a good question. She *can* keep a secret, but I'm not sure she can play it cool in front of Lyla. I fear she won't be able to contain her excitement. When are you planning to do it?" he asks.

"I just came from the jeweler. The ring will be ready tomorrow. Since I'm off next week, I figured we'd head out to Nantucket at some point. I'll do it out there."

"I'll keep it close to the vest until you guys leave for Nantucket."

"Fair enough. The boys already know. I'm outta here. Thank you, sir! See you back at your place later." I race home where the boys are on the patio drinking beers. I duck back into the kitchen to grab one for myself.

"Mission a success?" Derek asks when I join them.

"Yup. Picking the ring up in the morning. Your dad said he's glad to finally have a son who isn't such a pain in the ass, and he's not telling your mom until after we leave for Nantucket," I say before taking a sip of my beer. Colin throws his bottle cap at me. "The house looks great, thanks for finishing the job."

I'm filled with gratitude for these guys who have been like brothers to me for as long as I can remember. I just hope Lyla can stomach being in this house again after what happened, but if she can't, I'd throw it on the market tomorrow. I shoot her a text and let her know I'll be heading back to her shortly.

I vaguely listen to the boys bust each other's balls about god knows what. My mind is elsewhere. I'm thinking of proposal ideas and checking the weather forecast for the next few days on Nantucket. We're getting later into fall, which means the weather will start getting dicier, but I can still plan something special.

All I know is I can't wait to propose to this woman. I hope she doesn't want a long engagement because if it was up to me, we'd go to the courthouse.

Don't get me wrong, I'll gladly profess my love to her in front of the people we love most in the world. I'll shout it from any rooftop, but I just want to do it as soon as possible.

When you live without the person you love most in this world for as long as I've lived without Lyla—and when you almost lose her twice in the matter of a month—it really puts things into perspective.

She's always been the sun my world has revolved around, and I can't wait to make her mine for good.

# FORTY-SEVEN
## Lyla

WALKING BACK into Theo's house, our house, feels surreal. It's clean as a whistle, no blood stains or holes in the wall. You'd never be able to tell what happened here yesterday. But I know what happened, and I'm afraid I won't be able to forget it.

"You okay?" Theo asks. He's standing behind me, his arms wrapped around my waist, chin resting on my shoulder.

"I don't know. You guys did a great job with everything. Can't tell anything happened. But I can't unsee it when I close my eyes."

"Lyla, it's unrealistic to think you'd come skipping in here and not be triggered by what you went through."

"What if I can't get over it?"

"Say the word Lyla, and I'll sell this place. You won't ever have to step foot in this house again if you don't want to."

I turn my head back at him. "You'd do that for me?" I ask, my heart fluttering, feeling like the Grinch when his heart grows three times in size. The man's steadfast devotion to me knows no bounds, and it never fails to make me feel warm and fuzzy.

"Without a second thought. Don't you get it, Lyla? There's nothing I wouldn't do for you. No stone I wouldn't turn. I'd burn the world down for you, so I think I can handle selling a house if that's what you wanted. You don't have to decide right now. We can stay at your parents' again tonight and head out to Nantucket tomorrow or the day after. You heard our boss. Colin and I are on administrative leave next week while they do the after-action paperwork. Hell, we can go on a real vacation if you want."

For a second, I contemplate his offer. Theo and me in bathing suits all day on a beach somewhere tropical with cocktails and vacation sex. The perks do sound kind of glorious. But Nantucket has always been my happy place, especially after the weeks we just spent out there. Even though the beach weather is long gone, another week of relaxation, good food, and lots of sex sounds just as fabulous.

"A vacation is tempting, but if it's okay with you, I think I'd rather just go to your place on Nantucket."

He turns me in his arms and says, "Our place, Lyla. Like this house, Sunshine Cottage is *ours*."

"Theo, it's been in your family for years. I don't have any claim on it."

"You're my family, Lyla. What's mine is yours, always." He leans down and softly brushes his lips against mine.

"Okay, then can we just go to our place in Nantucket?" I ask, and he smiles and nods.

"Yup. We can head out anytime you want this weekend," he says. I think about it for a minute and ask if Sunday sounds good to him. "Works for me."

"You're sure you don't mind staying with my parents' again? I don't think I'm ready to come back here yet. I have my appointment with my therapist tomorrow, and I want to talk things out with her."

"Whatever you want, Lyla."

"I want to be okay in this house again. I don't want to let Clayton ruin all of the things I've been picturing here."

"What kind of things have you been picturing, Sunshine?" he asks, his voice playful.

"Giving it the facelift it deserves. Lots of sex. Laughter. Holidays and birthdays. Bringing babies home to raise. Watching our grandkids run around the backyard."

"You think about that stuff?" he asks.

"Of course I do. It was all I could think about when Clayton had that gun to my head."

"We're going to have it all, baby. And if you want to have it in this house, that's what we'll do. But if you decide you can't, we'll find a house that we can do all of those things in and more. It'll still be just as special."

"I want to grow old in this house, Theo. With you."

\* \* \*

The next morning, my dad asks me to tag along to get coffee and bagels, so I kiss Theo goodbye and head out with him. We're waiting in line at Hot Bagels when he asks, "You excited to get back out to Nantucket?"

"I am. I could use the peace and serenity that island brings me."

"How did you feel going back into the house yesterday?"

I grimace. "So-so. The house looks as good as new but being there again..." I close my eyes and try to shake the thoughts away. "It was harder than I expected. I want so badly to be able to move past it. I don't want to be taken back to those moments every time I walk through the door."

"What if you decide you can't stay there?" he asks.

"Theo said he'd put the house on the market ASAP if that's what I wanted," I say.

"Good man. Well, don't be too hard on yourself, kiddo. You need to give yourself time to heal from what happened. I know you'll do that with your therapist, and we're here to support you, too."

"Thanks, Dad."

We enjoy our breakfast at one of the outside tables, interrupted a few times by people my dad knows who stop to say hi or have heard through the grapevine what happened to me. Small-town living for you—everyone knows everything, and I can't say I hate it. My dad suckers me into running a few more errands before he stops to grab my mom a bouquet of flowers prior to heading home.

"You guys are couple goals, Dad. Thanks for showing me to never settle."

He reaches over and musses my hair as we drive home.

My parents drop us off at the ferry later that afternoon. I pack heavier than necessary so I can leave some stuff at the cottage. We unload our suitcases with the handlers, grab Diego's carrier, and board the ship. Theo pulls a paperback from his bag to read while I relax and look out the window for the ride, popping my favorite candy in my mouth as we go.

An hour later, we're exiting the ferry, and I already feel more at ease. It's cool and foggy, and I breathe in the Nantucket air. We grab our bags from the luggage carts and seek out Theo's truck that Lou was nice enough to drop off for us.

This time we do our own grocery shopping, stopping for

provisions on the way home. The rain starts just as we pull into our driveway. We rush Diego and our bags inside.

Just like when we were here a few weeks ago, it rains the first few days we're on the island. We spend our time bingeing Netflix, working on a puzzle, and fucking on every surface in the house.

A few days later, we finally wake up to blue skies and sunshine. We take advantage of the weather and go for a long walk. As we're making our way back up the driveway, Theo glances down at and then says, "The forecast doesn't show much wind at the beach on this side of the island. Want to pack a lunch and hit Madaket? Might be our last opportunity this fall to do it?"

"That sounds great. I'm in. Should we pick up from Millie's?" Theo gives that suggestion a thumbs-up.

"Sounds good. Let me know what you want and I'll call it in and get a cooler packed," he says as he looks down at his phone again.

"Everything okay?" I ask.

"Yeah, just your brother driving me crazy with work stuff."

That immediately makes me nervous. "You guys are on leave all week, what could he possibly want? It's not about the Clayton thing is it?" I ask in panic.

"No. It has nothing to do with Clayton, I promise. Something completely unrelated." We're out the door about half an hour later, armed with a portable speaker, beach blanket, and cooler, Diego on his leash.

After a quick stop at Millie's, we pull into a spot by the beach and head down. Save for a few fishermen and a couple of people with their dogs, we're the only ones here. We get set up and comfortable on the blanket, and I set about putting on music while Theo sorts our lunch.

"Penny for your thoughts, babe?" I ask as we dig in. "You've been quiet today."

He looks at me and gives me a smile, the panty-dropping one that reaches his eyes. "Just enjoying being out here with you, Sunshine. I was thinking, if you decide you don't want to stay in the house, we can leave Sandpiper. Move out here full-time. We'll still be close to your family."

My jaw drops. "What? Theo, we can't do that. You have a job, a career that you love, in Sandpiper."

"I can't imagine it would be hard to get a job out here if they're hiring an officer. I have experience and ties to the community. Either way, I'd figure something out. My priority is us, you, and ensuring that you're comfortable and feel safe in our home. Everything else will fall into place once we have that."

Tears well up in my eyes, but I wipe them away so I can see Theo more clearly.

"I'm not ready to let go of everything I envisioned for us in your house back home. I love this island, you know that. And I love that you have this home we can always come to, but I want to try and build that life in Sandpiper Cove."

He nods and leans forward to give me a quick kiss. Diego, who has been lurking nearby waiting for a handout, wanders off the blanket and watches a few seagulls farther down the beach.

"Can you grab him before he goes too far? I'll watch the food for dive-bombers," he says, glancing up at the birds in the sky.

I stand up to chase Diego down, grabbing his leash before scooping him into my arms. When I turn back around to walk back to the blanket, Theo is down on one knee. I immediately gasp and reach one hand up to cover my mouth. I slowly walk back toward the blanket, brimming with excitement.

"Babe, what are you doing?" I ask with an unsteady voice.

He holds his hand out for the cat, and I pass him over. Theo puts Diego back on the ground and ties his leash to the cooler so he can't take off.

"Lyla, I have loved you for as long as I can remember. I love your wit and your intelligence. I love your kindness and the fact that you always see the good in everyone and everything. I love your resilience and how you never give up...on anything or anyone. I love your laugh. It's the best sound in the world, and it lights up the room. I love the fact that you make everyone around you feel important and seen. You are the best part of my life, Lyla. The best part of every single day. I will never stop counting my lucky stars that you love me back." He stops to compose himself, and I take that opportunity to wipe the tears that leak out of the corners of his eyes. I ignore the ones that run down my cheeks. "Whew. Hang on baby. Let me get through this. Our love is one for the ages, baby. It's pure. It's fierce and all-consuming. You make me want to be a better man, a man worthy of you. You're the sun, and I want to spend the rest of my life revolving around you. I want every moment with you. The big ones, the little ones, the hard ones, the heart-breaking ones, the funny ones, the complicated ones... All of them, with you. I want to spend the rest of my life taking care of you, protecting you, making sure you know how much I love you every single day. On my life, Lyla, I will make all of your dreams come true. Baby, I could sit here and talk until I'm blue in the face about all of the reasons I love you and how your love sets my soul on fire. And I'm happy to do that... Hell, I'll do it for the rest of our lives. Will you marry me?"

I nod my head for the last half of his speech, but somehow, I finally find my voice and say, "Yes." Softly, at first, and then I repeat myself. "Yes! Yes, I will marry you, Theo."

He jumps to his feet and sweeps me into his arms, hugging

me tightly and swinging me around. I throw my arms around him, feeling like no matter how close we are, it's still not close enough. When he stops moving, I wrap my legs around his waist, and he pulls his head back to kiss me.

"I love you so fucking much, baby. On my life, Lyla, I promise I will only run toward you or with you," he says as he kisses me deeply, his tongue roaming my mouth and dancing with mine.

I don't want this moment to end, but eventually, he pulls back enough so that he can place the box with my ring closer to my face. "Now, do you want to see your ring?" he asks before he kisses me again.

The last thing I want to do is let go of him, but I'm really excited to see what he picked out for me, so I unwrap myself from his body and take a step back. He sinks back down to his knee and Diego walks up and plops down next to him. "I want to hear you say yes again," he says with a sheepish smile.

"Well, then you better ask me again."

"Lyla Sullivan, will you marry me?" he asks with a huge smile.

"You make me happy to be alive, Theo. The emptiness I felt over the last few years, no matter how many people are around, dissipates the minute you're in my vicinity. You bet your ass I'll marry you," I say, matching his smile with a big one of my own.

He slides the ring onto my finger and stands back up, pulling me in for another hug. I steal a glance at my hand as I wrap my arms around him again and use my other hand to cover the gasp that escapes my mouth when I see the large stone that sparkles endlessly is yellow. We haven't talked about it in years, but he still remembered I never wanted a traditional diamond. "Theo, it's beautiful."

He pulls back and looks nervous when he asks, "Are you sure? If you don't like it we can take it back."

"I love it, babe. Almost as much as I love you. It's absolutely stunning." I mean that with every fiber of my being. It's the most beautiful ring I've ever seen in my life, and I can't believe how perfect it is.

"It's a yellow sapphire—a sunny stone for the sunshine of my life," he says.

"I love it so much, Theo. Thank you." I cannot wait to spend my life with this man.

We sit back on the blanket, me between his legs, and relax, watching the waves ebb and flow and enjoying the moment. "While I know you'd love to stay for the sunset, we have to be at Galley Beach by six for our reservation," he says. My eyes light up, and I turn to look at him.

"Really?! You thought of everything, babe. This is the best day ever."

We finish our drinks, pack up our stuff and head back to Theo's truck. When we get home, Theo unlocks the door and ushers me in first.

I gasp when I look around and see that there are flowers everywhere, on every possible surface. Roses, wild flowers, hydrangeas, orchids. You name it, they're somewhere in this house. "This is amazing. How did you do this?" I ask in disbelief.

"I've got skills, baby." I look at him with a raised eyebrow. "Okay, Lou and Holly helped me out while we were at the beach. Come on, let's take a soak in the tub before we need to get ready for dinner."

He leads me down the hallway and into the bathroom, where there are flowers placed on the shelves by the tub. The lights are dim, and Theo quickly lights candles and pops the champagne that soaks in an ice bucket.

We strip and climb into the tub facing each other. I ask him a million questions about how he planned everything and how he picked out the ring. I can't stop staring at the beautiful gemstone sparkling on my finger.

His eyes never leave my face as he massages my calves, answering every single part of my inquisition. His hands wander up my legs, and eventually, he pulls me onto his lap, silencing my questions with his mouth.

With his hands on my ass, I lift myself slightly. I reach down and grab his cock, angling it just right so I can feel him at my opening. I slowly lower myself, feeling every inch, every ridge, including the vein that runs down him. His cock is like a steel rod in me, but soft like velvet, and he fills me to the hilt.

I wrap my arms around him as I start to rock my hips. He pulls back from kissing me and leans his head back so he can look me in the eyes. His hands grip me as I move, and with the way my clit rubs against him, and how deep inside he is, I know he won't need to use his finger to get me across the finish line.

We make love while the music plays and candles burn and the smell of all the fresh flowers surrounds us. No words are exchanged. We're completely lost in each other, in this moment. It's unhurried and tender, like we're savoring each other. Like we have all the time in the world, which it feels like we finally do. It's been such a long road getting here. So much heartbreak and loneliness. So many years of feeling incomplete and broken. And now that we're in this moment, neither of us want to rush it. Neither of us will ever take it for granted.

\* \* \*

Our Uber is set to arrive in ten minutes, and I quickly put the finishing touches on my makeup and give myself a final once-over in the mirror. Theo comes up behind me and wraps his arms around me, nuzzling my neck. "You look stunning, wife," he says.

I smile and say, "Ahh, I can't wait to be your wife."

"I'll go to the courthouse tomorrow, baby," he says. I laugh but I'm seriously contemplating it. "I'm kidding. Well, not kidding, but no pressure. You deserve the wedding of your dreams." I can feel his dick getting hard against my back. "I need to leave the bedroom before I get us into trouble. Your ass in that dress is next-level." I smile, glad that he appreciates the long-sleeved, low back navy mini dress I have on with a pair of nude wedges.

"No undies. And I'm not wearing a bra, either," I say with a wicked smile. He groans and adjusts his cock before quickly exiting the room.

\* \* \*

Galley Beach is a restaurant that boasts some of the best sunset views on the island. The food is outstanding, and they have a kick-ass cocktail list. Theo checks us in at the hostess stand and places his hand on my lower back as we follow her through the dining room and to the beach. I squeal in sheer delight when I see my parents, Colin, and Derek are waiting for us at a large round table. I turn to Theo, who mouths, "Surprise!" For what feels like the millionth time today, I've got tears in my eyes. "Thank you," I mouth back.

My family stands up, and my mom plows through my dad to get to me, enveloping me in a hug and bouncing up and down. "The ring! I want to see the ring!" she all but shouts. She takes my hand to get a closer look, gasping, "It's beautiful. Theo! It's beautiful." She hugs me again before moving on to dote on Theo.

My dad wraps me in a hug and says, "Congrats, Sweetie. We couldn't be happier."

"Thanks, Daddy," I say softly.

It's a huge hug fest, with Colin and Derek pushing each other out of the way to hug me first, but eventually, we finally make our way to our seats.

Theo pulls my chair out for me, and when he sits down, he pulls me closer to his side and leaves his arm wrapped around me, playing with a strand of my hair. The waitress delivers a bottle of champagne and pours us all a glass. My father gives a simple but beautiful toast just before the sun sets.

We all clink glasses and settle in to watch the sunset. It's quick, but heart-stoppingly beautiful, the sky ablaze with color as if it's on fire. Once the sun dips below the horizon, the navy sky attempts to overtake the last of the day's light.

Dinner is out of this world, and the drinks are flowing as we laugh and tell stories. As we're enjoying dessert and a final round of drinks Theo leans close to me and says into my ear, "I can't wait to fuck you when we get home."

He sits back and rejoins the conversation, his finger lightly tracing up and down my bare spine. I squeeze my legs together in anticipation of what's to come.

When the check is dropped off, my dad and Theo fight over it, with Colin pretending to offer as well. Eventually, my dad tears the bill out of Theo's hands and scurries off to find the waitress before Theo can.

"We're going to head to the Chicken Box for some drinks, you wanna come?" Colin asks. We decline the offer, as do my parents.

"Just promise me you'll be back at the hotel by a decent hour, boys. Our boat is at 9 a.m.," my mom says. I must have a surprised look on my face because she turns to me and asks, "You didn't think we would be imposing on you two tonight, did you?" I shrug my shoulders because that's what I assumed. "Heck no. We got a couple of rooms in town."

We all say goodbye before parting ways in our Ubers.

"Thank you, Theo, for arranging this. It was so special to be able to celebrate with them. This has been the best day of my life."

He leans over and kisses me quickly before pulling me to his side. "Night's not over yet, Sunshine," he says with a wink. We make casual conversation with the driver, and he offers us congratulations and a knowing smile when he drops us off at home.

When we walk in the front door, we're once again greeted by the aroma of all of the beautiful flowers. Once the door is locked, I drop my purse on the floor and throw my arms around Theo's neck.

He leans down and scoops me up, tossing me over his shoulder. I squeal as he slaps my ass and stalks toward our bedroom, setting me down on my feet once we get there.

He's on his knees, taking my shoes off one at a time, my skin on fire from his light, feathery touch. He stands back up and feels around my dress before grunting, "Where the hell does this thing come off?"

I laugh and show him the side zipper. He pulls it down and slowly removes my dress, letting it fall to the floor. I'm standing there naked except for my black lace thong. His hands go right to my chest.

"I've been thinking about these luscious tits all night, baby."

I try to unbutton his shirt, but when he starts tugging at my nipples, I have a hard time concentrating. Eventually, I get through all the buttons and push it down his arms, letting it join my dress on the floor. I feel the loss of his warm hands when he reaches behind his neck to pull his shirt off. I start with his belt buckle next.

Apparently, I take too long because he pushes my hands aside and takes care of it himself, yanking his jeans down and stepping out of his shoes.

He picks me up and tosses me onto the bed before dropping to his knees and pulling me to the edge of the bed by my ankles. Without a single word, he dives into my pussy, using his fingers, his tongue, and his lips to drive me fucking wild. The scruff on his face only adds to the pleasure. My hips buck, and I'm so close to coming before he pulls back, sitting on his heels and licking his lips.

"God, this pussy is perfection, baby. You taste so fucking good."

"Then go back to eating it, Theo, and make me come," I say, practically begging. He does what I ask, licking his way up my inner thigh until he reaches my center.

He leisurely drags his tongue from my pussy to my clit then does the same thing up my other thigh. I grind my hips, and my body is so close to the edge I feel like I'm going to combust.

With his mouth on my clit, I reach down and hold him there, running my hands through his hair as I move my hips. He groans as he licks and nibbles, and when he sucks on my clit again, my orgasm rips through me. I scream his name as I ride it out with his face still buried in my pussy.

When he finally sits back, his lips and his scruff are glistening from me. I try to catch my breath. I scoot farther back on the bed, and Theo climbs on top of me, his forearms on either side of my head. I can taste my orgasm on his tongue as he kisses me hard. "I can't wait to be your husband, baby," he says before kissing me again.

"Then fuck me like you mean it, Theo."

I don't want slow lovemaking tonight. We had that earlier in the tub. Tonight is feverish and animalistic, with heavy breathing and moaning the only noises in the room. He leans back and slowly pushes his cock into me. I groan in pleasure when he starts to play with my tits again, something he knows I can never get enough of.

He leans back so that he's resting on his knees more and spreads my legs wider. "Bend your knees, baby," he commands. When I do, he places his hands on my knees to keep my legs wide and starts grinding his pelvis in slow circles. I tip my head back, letting out a guttural sound I'm certain I've never made before.

"Oh my god, Theo. Yesssss."

Holy shit, this is heaven. Eventually, he transitions to thrusting his hips back and forth, starting slowly and then picking up speed. He reaches one hand down to my clit and begins circling it with this thumb.

A few seconds of that and I'm literally screaming his name in ecstasy as I come. He keeps thrusting as I ride out my orgasm, and then he reaches his own climax, grunting as he comes inside of me. Once he's done, he leans down and rests his forehead on mine.

"Damn, wife. It just keeps getting better with you."

I laugh as he kisses me before he pulls out and lies down next to me. Eventually, we both recover and hit the bathroom to clean up and brush our teeth. We fall back into bed, a tangled mess of limbs as we hold each other. I have this man for the rest of my life, and I still feel like it won't be enough.

"Thank you for loving me the way you do. And for fucking me the way you do," I say, my head on his chest, and my hand playing with the chain he wears.

"Forever, baby."

He leans down and kisses me and for the first time in weeks, Theo falls asleep before me. I relax as I listen to his breath and feel his chest move up and down under my head. Strong and steady... That's what he's always been for me. Diego makes his way into bed and curls up at our feet.

Even though I know he can't hear me, I reiterate what he said before he fell asleep. "Forever, baby." I definitely fall asleep with a smile on my face, feeling the happiest I've ever been.

I wake up the next morning in Theo's arms with the sunshine streaming in through our bedroom window. It dawns on me that it's the first time in over a week that Diego hasn't needed to interrupt my sleep, nor do I have a nightmare.

For the first time since Liv died, I'm completely at peace, and I know it has everything to do with the man who put a ring on my finger, the man who's still holding me, even in his sleep.

The man who promised to love me forever.

On his life.

# *epilogue*

Lyla

I LOOK DOWN at my flowers, a bouquet of white roses—Olivia's favorite—hydrangeas, and orchids and take a few deep breaths. As we make our way towards Madaket beach, Theo's and my favorite Nantucket beach, I soak in the beauty of my surroundings. Of the stunning house we rented for the celebration. The backyard is beautifully landscaped—the grass lush and the flowers vibrant.

"You ready, kiddo?" my dad asks, squeezing my arm. I smile and grip his arm tighter as we walk through the yard. Eventually we reach the short path that will take us directly onto the sand where the ceremony will take place.

As we get closer to the aisle, I take a glance at the people who are seated down near the water. We decided to keep the guest list small, with just around thirty people in attendance.

Aside from our parents and my brothers, Quinn is here—sans Justin, thank goodness—along with Drew, a few guys

428

from the station, some family members, Lou and Holly, and Olivia's parents.

When we finally reach the aisle, my dad pauses and says, "I love you, Lyla. And you look stunning." He opens his mouth to say more but then shuts it again. He looks like he's fighting to keep his emotions in check.

"Love you, too, Dad. Thank you for teaching me to have such high standards."

He nods and starts walking again.

I don't pay attention to the simple, yet beautiful flowers that line the aisle. Instead, my eyes are on the man standing under an arch made of driftwood and accented with the same flowers I'm holding. Theo made the arch, and we plan to use it in the backyard at our house after the wedding.

Theo, looking devastatingly handsome in his khaki suit doesn't even try to fight back his tears as I walk to him. I'm just as emotional as him, and it's only because of my dad's grip on my arm that I don't break into an all out sprint to get to him.

Once we reach the altar, Theo shakes my dad's hand and immediately pulls me into his arms for a hug. "I missed you today, Sunshine," he whispers in my ear before letting me go and using the tissue Colin passes him to wipe his eyes.

The ceremony, written by Theo and me, is heartfelt and moving—a true celebration of our love and the obstacles we overcame to get here. The same beach where Theo first told me he loved me when we were just teenagers and where we got engaged, not to mention countless other memories made in between those two events.

Finally, after years together, followed by heartbreaking years apart, I relish in the fact that we'll never be apart again.

We both wipe away tears as we slip rings onto each other's fingers and say our vows. Vows we wrote for each other but didn't share with the other until this very moment. At one point, I place my hand on Theo's chest while he reads his, briefly thinking about the tattoo he recently got. "On my life" right over his heart.

Despite the laughs interspersed throughout them, like when I promise to never use the grill, and Theo promises to always start with the border pieces when we do a puzzle, there's not a dry eye on the beach. There's something to be said about the man you love having a hard time keeping it together while he pledges to love, protect, and cherish you for the rest of your lives.

When the officiant finally pronounces us husband and wife, Theo pulls me close to him, holds onto my face with his hands, and kisses me. It's tender and dynamic at the same time, as if a promise of what's to come tonight. It goes on for far longer than is probably appropriate, but we're so lost in this moment, in each other, that we don't even notice.

I grip his arms and moan into his mouth, getting weak in the knees as I wish this moment would never end. Eventually, the officiant clears his throat, and we hear laughter from our guests. He gives me one more peck on the lips and lets my face go, grabbing my hand as we walk back up the aisle.

We stay on the beach to take pictures with everyone before sending them up to the backyard to enjoy cocktails and hors d'oeuvres. After a few pictures with Diego, who is behaving like a perfect gentleman, we make our way up to the lawn to celebrate with our favorite people.

As much as I would have loved to have the reception on the beach itself, our event coordinator convinced us the grassy lawn would be the better option. She arranged for a huge dance floor with a bar set up in one corner.

We opted for one long table so that we could all sit together as a family. Since the forecast was perfect, we chose not to get a tent. It would only get in the way of the perfect ocean view. She strung fairy lights up all over the yard to add to the romantic vibe.

We take the dance floor for our first dance as husband and wife to "The Luckiest" by Ben Folds, which has always been our song. Theo holds me as close as humanly possible and sings along to the lyrics in my ear. We have surf and turf, and the wine and cocktails flow, including our signature drink—a spicy margarita, of course.

My dad's toast makes me cry, my brothers' toast makes me laugh, and Quinn's toast does a little bit of both. Colin and Quinn, who have been spending lots of time in very close proximity to each other the entire weekend, once again seem inseparable. He takes every opportunity he can to refill her drink or chat her up. When I remind him that her relationship is very up in the air, he rolls his eyes and tells me he knows that, and he's just being nice before scurrying back off to her side.

Once dinner is over, the DJ kicks the music up a notch. For a small group, our dance floor is packed. He does a great job of mixing oldies and current hits and throws in a healthy dose of slow songs here and there. When he starts playing "She Likes It," Theo pulls me back into his arms.

"This is kind of a scandalous song to be playing, babe," I say as he nuzzles my neck, his hands migrating down to my ass.

"I figured your dad and brothers have had enough to drink by now that they won't notice the lyrics or me groping you on the dance floor." I laugh when he lowers his hands and squeezes my ass before he pulls me closer to him, his length hardening between us. "You know I can't resist this ass, baby. Have I told you how amazing you look tonight?"

"Only a few dozen times, but it never hurts to say it again," I say.

I chose a form-fitting V-neck lace gown with a low back.

The fabric hugs all the right places. It's timeless and elegant, and I feel sexy as hell in it. Seeing as though Theo can't keep his eyes off of me, especially my ass, I feel confident I made the right choice.

His grip tightens as he leans down, his lips brushing against my ear. His voice is husky, dripping with want when he says, "Absolutely mouthwateringly brings-me-to-my-knees stunning in this dress, baby. I can't wait for it to be in a pile on the floor of our room later." His rough voice, the way he holds me close, the grip on my ass—it all has me weak in the knees and raring to go at the same time.

All of a sudden, I hear laughter, and when I look to see who it is, I find Quinn dancing in Colin's arms, wiping tears away from her eyes from laughing so hard. "Oh boy," I say. "That could get messy."

Theo looks over to see what catches my eye.

"Sunshine, I have a feeling that's about to get very messy. But tonight, it's all about us, and I'm hard as fuck thinking about how messy *we're* going to be getting later when I finally get to plow into my wife's sweet pussy."

He pulls my face to his and kisses me, softly and sweetly, before wrapping his arms around me again as the song ends. Giving me a mischievous look, he says, "Waited forever to dance with you at our wedding, Lyla. And I can't wait to get naked and celebrate all night long, and every night after for the rest of our lives."

# what's next?

Colin and Quinn's story is coming in 2026! Read on for a (raw, unedited) sneak peak and follow me on Instagram at @genevievepaulauthor for updates!

"So what's up with the boyfriend?" There's no way he doesn't feel the way I tense up in his arms when he asks that question and I can almost feel the happiness draining out of me when I start to think about Justin.

"It's complicated," I finally respond, looking him in the eyes.

He gives me a smile and says, "Is that what your Facebook status says?" It's like he realized it's a sticky situation and is giving me an out if I want it. A small laugh sneaks out of me before I decide to be honest.

"I don't even have Facebook. But I guess if I did, that would be the status. Things have been going downhill for a while. We fought, I told him I wanted space, and here we are. I know I want to end things with him for good, but it's not something I want to deal with while I'm out here. Now I'm just taking your sister's advice—letting my hair down and having fun." His blue eyes pierce mine as he studies me. I feel the intensity of his stare all the way down to my toes.

"I'm not going to try and get you into bed tonight, in case you were wondering," he says.

*Ouch,* I can't help but think.

"That's good because I wasn't planning on jumping into bed with you either," I snap back. The song is still playing but Colin stops moving, still holding onto me tightly.

"Don't misunderstand me. It's not because I'm not attracted to you. I am. You're fucking gorgeous. I hope you're single the next time I see you. Not because I want to fuck you into oblivion. I do. I don't even want to get into all the things I want to do to you because I'll end up with a bigger hard-on than I currently have. But because I think you're dynamic," he says. It takes me a second to get my bearings and formulate a response.

"Into oblivion, huh?" I say and I know I'm blushing. I feel the heat pool in my core as my body tingles at the idea of this man fucking me into oblivion.

"Into the next fucking galaxy, Wildflower," he says before he pulls me closer and starts dancing again. I swear the air crackles between us. It's electric. I let him hold me close for the rest of the song while I absorb what he just said and think about how happy and carefree I've been tonight.

I've laughed more the past two days than I have the past two years and it makes me realize how unhappy I've been; how much my relationship has sucked the joy out of me. I want to feel more happiness and appreciation for the things that make life fun. I want to feel like I can be myself and laugh until I cry. I want to surround myself with people who bring those things out in me.

Once that realization finally hits me, I bring my eyes back up to look at Colin and find myself getting lost in his blues. It's dangerous how quickly that happens. His gaze is piercing, like he sees things in me that I don't show to anyone else. Despite being surrounded by people, it feels like we're in our own world.

He cracks another joke, I assume to break up the sexual tension that is between us. It works because he once again has me laughing out loud–this time at Derek's expense.

Because we're so lost in our little bubble, I don't even notice him until I hear him. In an instant, the laughter and joy are snuffed right out of me and my stomach drops into my shoes.

"Can I cut in? Seeing as though you've got your arms around my girlfriend?" I audibly gasp when I finally realize that Justin is standing next to us. He has a smile on his face but it feels forced and I can tell by the anger reflecting in his dark eyes that he's less than thrilled to see me dancing with another man.

# *let's connect*

Follow me on Instagram.
@genevievepaulauthor

Visit my website.
https://www.authorgenevievepaul.com/

## *acknowledgments*

To you, the reader—Time is the most precious commodity, and the fact that you spent yours reading this book means more than I can begin to put into words. Being an author is something I've dreamed about my entire life. Thank you for taking a chance on this book–on me.

To my editor, Sara Tallary—Saying that you have the patience of a saint would be the understatement of the year–maybe even the century. "Thank you" doesn't begin to convey my gratitude, but I'll say it anyway. Thank you for your patience, your expertise, and your creativity. You've been an incredible mentor as I've navigated the writing and publishing process. Sorry to say that you're now stuck with me.

To my proofreader, Sue—Your feedback was truly invaluable. Sorry for not giving you more of a heads-up about the spicy scenes... I just wanted to keep you on your toes. I appreciate you so much, and I'll be sure to keep your notebook in a safe spot for the next one.

I have the best hype girls in every facet of my life. My Dusty Birds—my biggest cheerleaders who keep me sane. Kristin— The best work wifey a girl could hope for. Thank you for your constant encouragement and for always believing in me. Dana —My go-to alpha-reader. You've seen this manuscript at its worst and still loved me. Thank you for all of your help and feedback. Christina—Thank you for being so invested in my journey and for always offering your support. Jen and Taylor—Your willingness to stop what you were doing and read whatever I sent means the world to me. I'm so grateful for your insight and support. Mary—Always thankful to have you in my corner. Jen—From the day I first told you about this adventure, you have never failed to check in on my progress every single time we talked. Thank you for being one of my loudest cheerleaders. Jenna and Katie—Ooooof. I cringe thinking of the draft you guys had to read. Thank you for your endless support and encouragement through it all.

Nancy—I'm endlessly grateful for the strategies, habits, and confidence you have given me.

My family—Don't say I didn't warn you to stop reading at the end of Chapter 23 and skip straight to the Epilogue. Thank you for your enthusiasm and encouragement. Love you guys so much.

My son—Besides the playlist, this is the only part you're allowed to read. "I believe in you." That's what you wrote on my white board when I was only a few chapters into the first draft. It's still there. Those four words are what kept me going on the days I wanted to throw in the towel and delete the whole document. I hope I inspire you to never give up on your dreams. And I promise–you can help with the playlist on the next one. Love you mostest, kid.

My husband— It was easy to create a dreamy MMC because I'm married to one. There is so much in Theo that is inherently you (except the ink, which I'll never stop asking for). Thank you for loving me the way you do—for taking such good care of us, for being my biggest cheerleader and my safe place to land. You have always been the calm to my storm and there is no one on the planet I'd rather be doing life with. I am the luckiest. I love you.

## about the author

Genevieve Paul writes romantic suspense filled with swoon-worthy heroes, strong (and stubborn) heroines, off-the-charts chemistry, and tension that will keep you reading way past your bedtime. When she's not writing, she's thinking about the current–and next few–works in progress, reading, listening to music and spending time with the people she loves most— likely with a cup of coffee or a spicy margarita in hand (depending on the time of day). While she dreams of Massachusetts beaches, Genevieve lives at the Jersey Shore with her husband, son and spoiled tabby cat. She's always up for a good true crime podcast, a bag of Haribo gummy bears, and a sunset.